BADLANDS™

STEVEN GRANT   VINCE GIARRANO

BADLANDS™

STEVEN GRANT   VINCE GIARRANO

Steven Grant	*Writer*
Vince Giarrano	*Artist*
Clem Robins	*Letterer*
Vince Giarrano	*Cover Art*
Steve Buccelato	*Cover color*
Barbara Kesel	*Series editor*
Kij Johnson	*Collection editor*
Brian Gogolin	*Collection designer*
With an introduction by Frank Miller	

DARK · HORSE · COMICS

This book is for Linda, who told me to.

— SG

A RED FIST PRODUCTION

Published by Dark Horse Comics, Inc.
10956 SE Main Street
Milwaukie, OR 97222

ISBN: 1-878574-53-1
First edition: May 1993
10 9 8 7 6 5 4 3 2 1
Printed in Canada.

INTRODUCTION BY FRANK MILLER

If you catch one of us who makes comic books when he's in a bad mood, he might sound a bit like a cross between Aretha Franklin and Rodney Dangerfield.

We don't get no respect.

Comic books have never been a well-regarded field. To say the least. No matter how many times we try to call our stuff "graphic novels" or "sequential art," comic books is the name that we're stuck with. And it sounds pretty stupid.

Comic books. To most people, the name still represents not a way of telling a story, but a particular kind of story, and a particularly low level of quality. Comic books are perceived as trashy little pamphlets featuring trashy little power fantasies for trashy little minds.

If a reviewer wants to call a movie overstated and under-thought, he calls it a "comic-book movie."

Our reputation is in the toilet.

But maybe it's better that way.

It's amazing what you can get away with when almost nobody is watching.

While it is rather sad that my field has wallowed in self-contempt for better than fifty years, we have enjoyed, especially recently, a level of creative freedom not available in other visual media. Bold work, ranging from the lousy to the brilliant to the pretentious to the offensive to the utterly silly, has seen print. Most of it has been bad work, but what medium is that not true of? And when comic books are good, they offer virtues that cannot be found anywhere else.

We don't get no respect. And that's fine by me.

I regard the desire for respectability to be a dangerous thing. In the comic-book field, this desire has mostly been one to seize the opportunity to exploit Hollywood's newfound interest in comic books. To become, in fact, much more like Hollywood.

But watch what you wish for.

Take a look at what brought us to Hollywood's attention in the first place. It is precisely the personal, energetic, even peculiar results of talent working freely that have made the moviemakers take notice. Trashy as we often are, juvenile as our works may be, we're having an absolute ball. And it shows.

Not that movies aren't fun to make. It's just that very few good screenplays ever make it all the way to the theatres, and of those that do, only a tiny, tiny fraction even resemble the idea that got everybody excited to begin with.

Movies cost millions of dollars, even tens of millions, to produce. This understandably and inevitably imposes a climate of pressure and even fear upon the producers, writers, directors, and executives involved. Add to the production costs those of publicity and distribution, and a movie that cost fifty million bucks to make (FIFTY MILLION BUCKS!) must go on to make three times that at the box office — or it's a flop. For this reason, in most cases, a screenwriter's original script is subjected to the scrutiny of dozens of very nervous people whose jobs may well be on the line. Rewrites follow rewrites, and, unless there is a singular intellect forcing his or her vision through the long, costly, jittery process of making a movie, the final product will be compromised, if not turned into a pile of junk.

Of course, good movies do get made. Even great ones. But from the beginning of the process to the end, movie-making is an exercise in tenacity. And many good ideas are usually lost along the way, especially those that are the most quirky, personal, and potentially objectionable to critics, focus groups, and whatever idiots happen to wander into a screening or whisper to a terrified producer's ear.

By way of contrast, a comic book can be produced for a few thousand bucks, and in a relatively short amount time. You write it, you draw it, and it's out there. And if a few thousand people buy it, nobody loses his or her shirt.

True, the comic-book field has its own standards as to what is commercial or not. And they're pretty screwy standards. You're not as likely to sell in the millions with a book like *Badlands* as you are with the latest teenage superhero group. But the point here is that *Badlands* was published, without compromise or apology, and is now collected in a permanent edition. It never suffered through a "development meeting." It never faced "standards and practices" or "ratings" or any of the other current euphemisms for self-censorship.

I'd venture to say its author was never once told it should be more "balanced," "up," or "feel-good." Or that its characters should be more "reliable."

It is what it is. What it was intended to be.

And it is one damn fine comic book. And that's a good thing to see.

To hell with respect. Freedom's better.

—**FM**

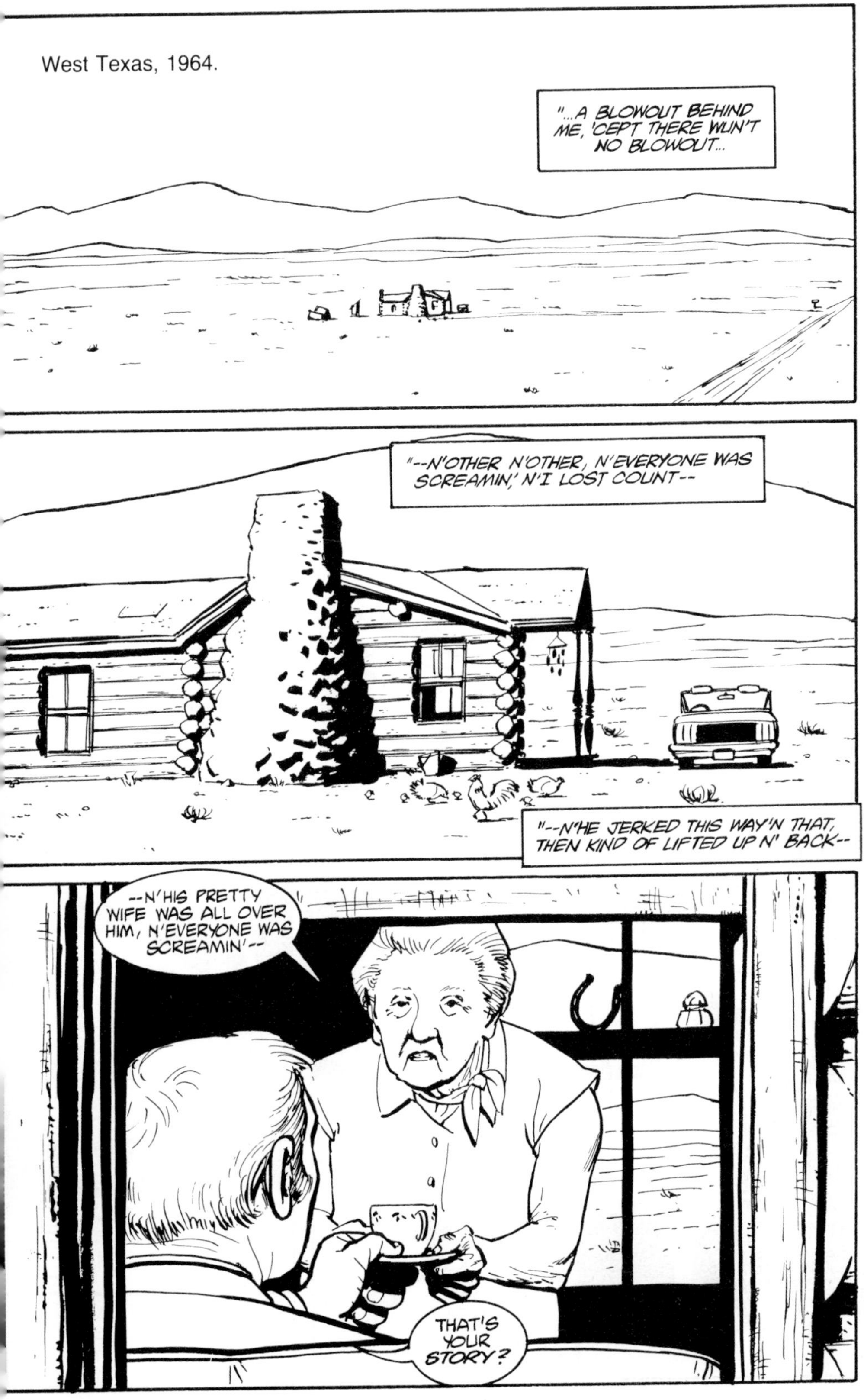
West Texas, 1964.
"...A BLOWOUT BEHIND ME, 'CEPT THERE WUN'T NO BLOWOUT...
"--N'OTHER N'OTHER, N'EVERYONE WAS SCREAMIN,' N'I LOST COUNT--
"--N'HE JERKED THIS WAY'N THAT, THEN KIND OF LIFTED UP N' BACK--
--N'HIS PRETTY WIFE WAS ALL OVER HIM, N'EVERYONE WAS SCREAMIN'--
THAT'S YOUR STORY?

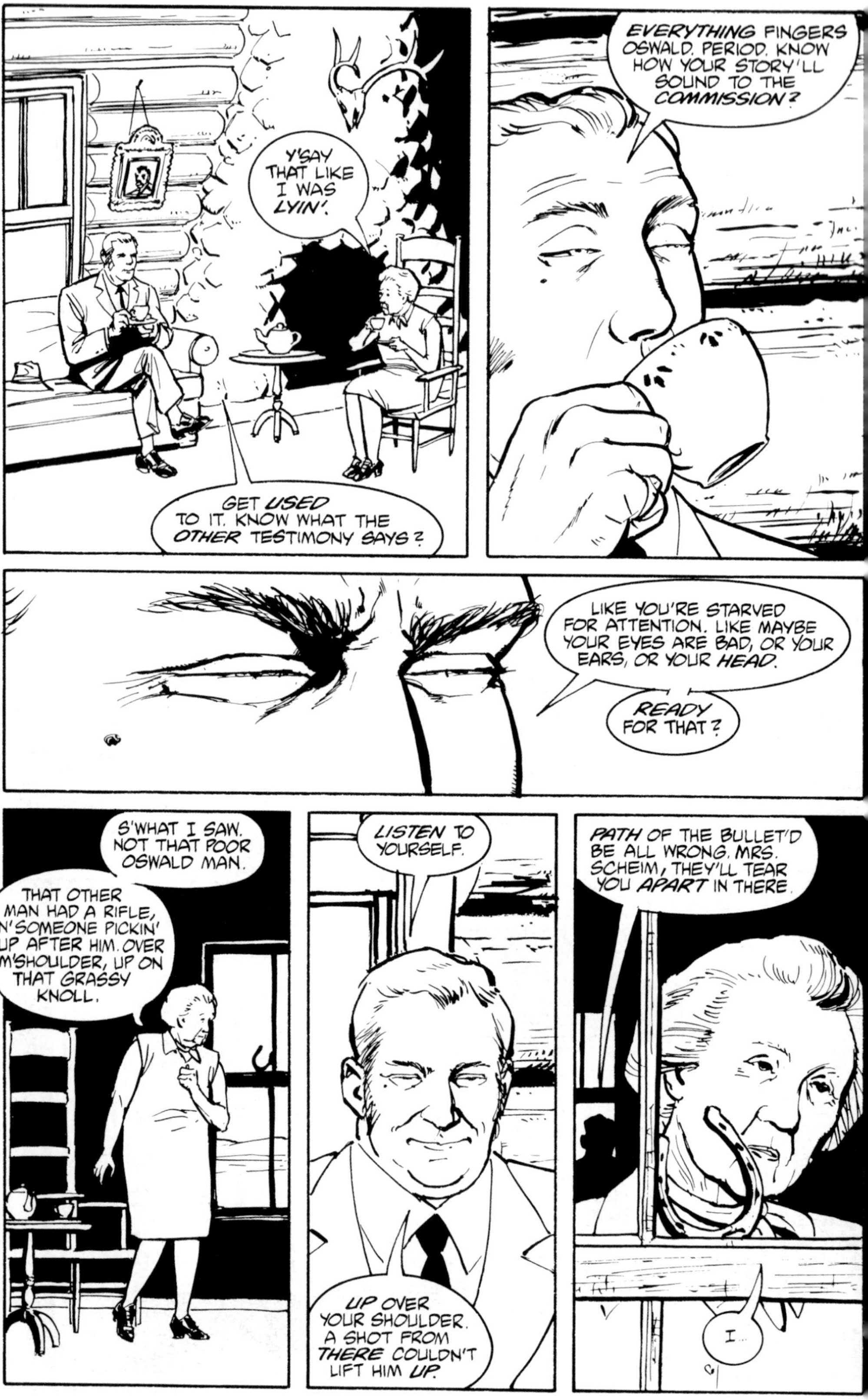
Y'SAY THAT LIKE I WAS LYIN'.
GET USED TO IT. KNOW WHAT THE OTHER TESTIMONY SAYS?
EVERYTHING FINGERS OSWALD. PERIOD. KNOW HOW YOUR STORY'LL SOUND TO THE COMMISSION?
LIKE YOU'RE STARVED FOR ATTENTION. LIKE MAYBE YOUR EYES ARE BAD, OR YOUR EARS, OR YOUR HEAD.
READY FOR THAT?
S'WHAT I SAW. NOT THAT POOR OSWALD MAN.
THAT OTHER MAN HAD A RIFLE, N'SOMEONE PICKIN' UP AFTER HIM. OVER M'SHOULDER, UP ON THAT GRASSY KNOLL.
LISTEN TO YOURSELF.
UP OVER YOUR SHOULDER. A SHOT FROM THERE COULDN'T LIFT HIM UP.
PATH OF THE BULLET'D BE ALL WRONG, MRS. SCHEIM, THEY'LL TEAR YOU APART IN THERE.
I...

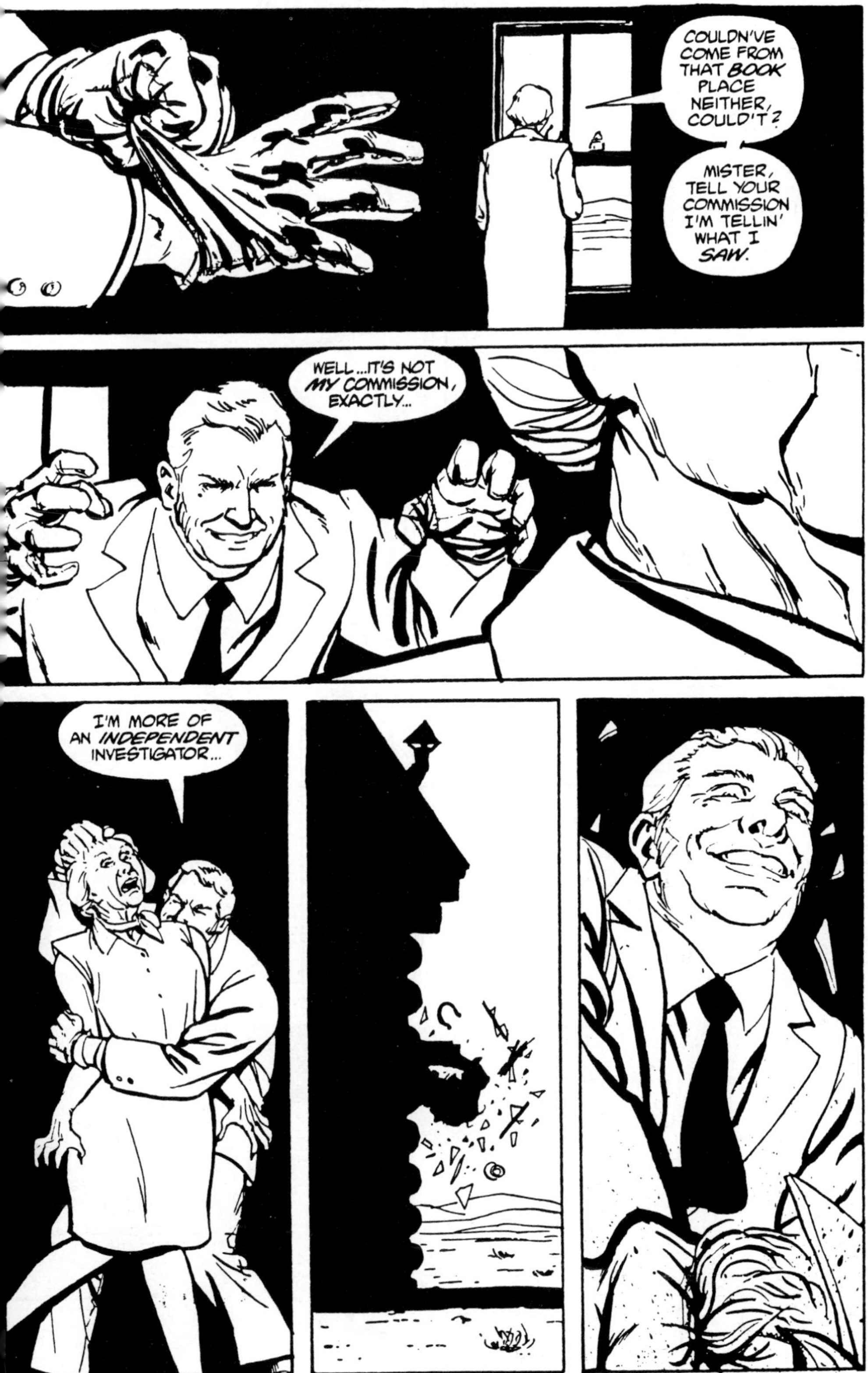
COULDN'VE COME FROM THAT BOOK PLACE NEITHER, COULD'T?
MISTER, TELL YOUR COMMISSION I'M TELLIN' WHAT I SAW.
WELL...IT'S NOT MY COMMISSION, EXACTLY...
I'M MORE OF AN INDEPENDENT INVESTIGATOR...

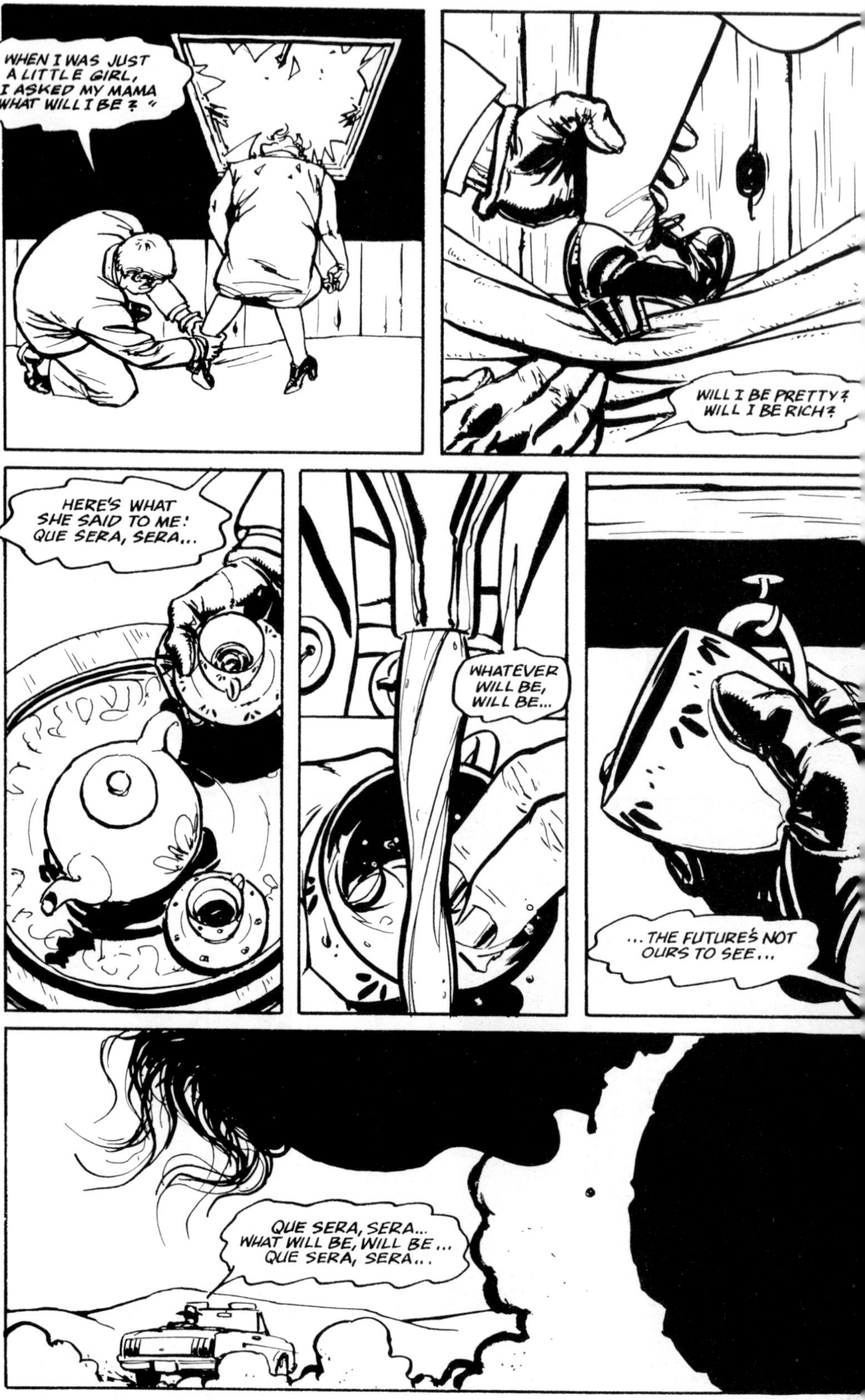
WHEN I WAS JUST A LITTLE GIRL, I ASKED MY MAMA "WHAT WILL I BE?"
WILL I BE PRETTY? WILL I BE RICH?
HERE'S WHAT SHE SAID TO ME: QUE SERA, SERA...
WHATEVER WILL BE, WILL BE...
...THE FUTURE'S NOT OURS TO SEE...
QUE SERA, SERA... WHAT WILL BE, WILL BE... QUE SERA, SERA...

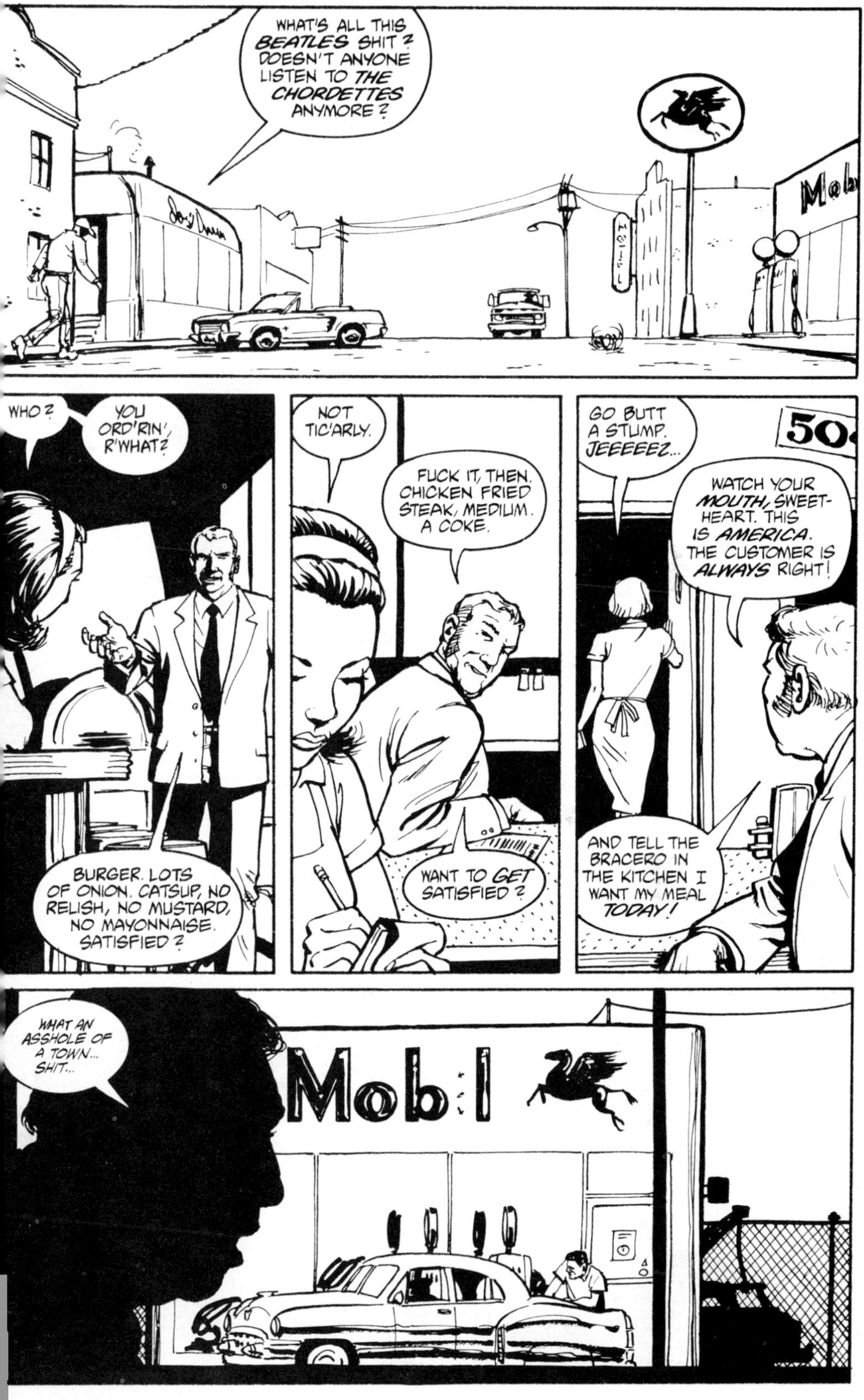
WHAT'S ALL THIS BEATLES SHIT? DOESN'T ANYONE LISTEN TO THE CHORDETTES ANYMORE?
WHO?
YOU ORD'RIN', R'WHAT?
BURGER. LOTS OF ONION. CATSUP, NO RELISH, NO MUSTARD, NO MAYONNAISE. SATISFIED?
NOT TIC'ARLY.
FUCK IT, THEN. CHICKEN FRIED STEAK, MEDIUM. A COKE.
WANT TO GET SATISFIED?
GO BUTT A STUMP. JEEEEEZ...
50
WATCH YOUR MOUTH, SWEET-HEART. THIS IS AMERICA. THE CUSTOMER IS ALWAYS RIGHT!
AND TELL THE BRACERO IN THE KITCHEN I WANT MY MEAL TODAY!
WHAT AN ASSHOLE OF A TOWN... SHIT...
Mob l

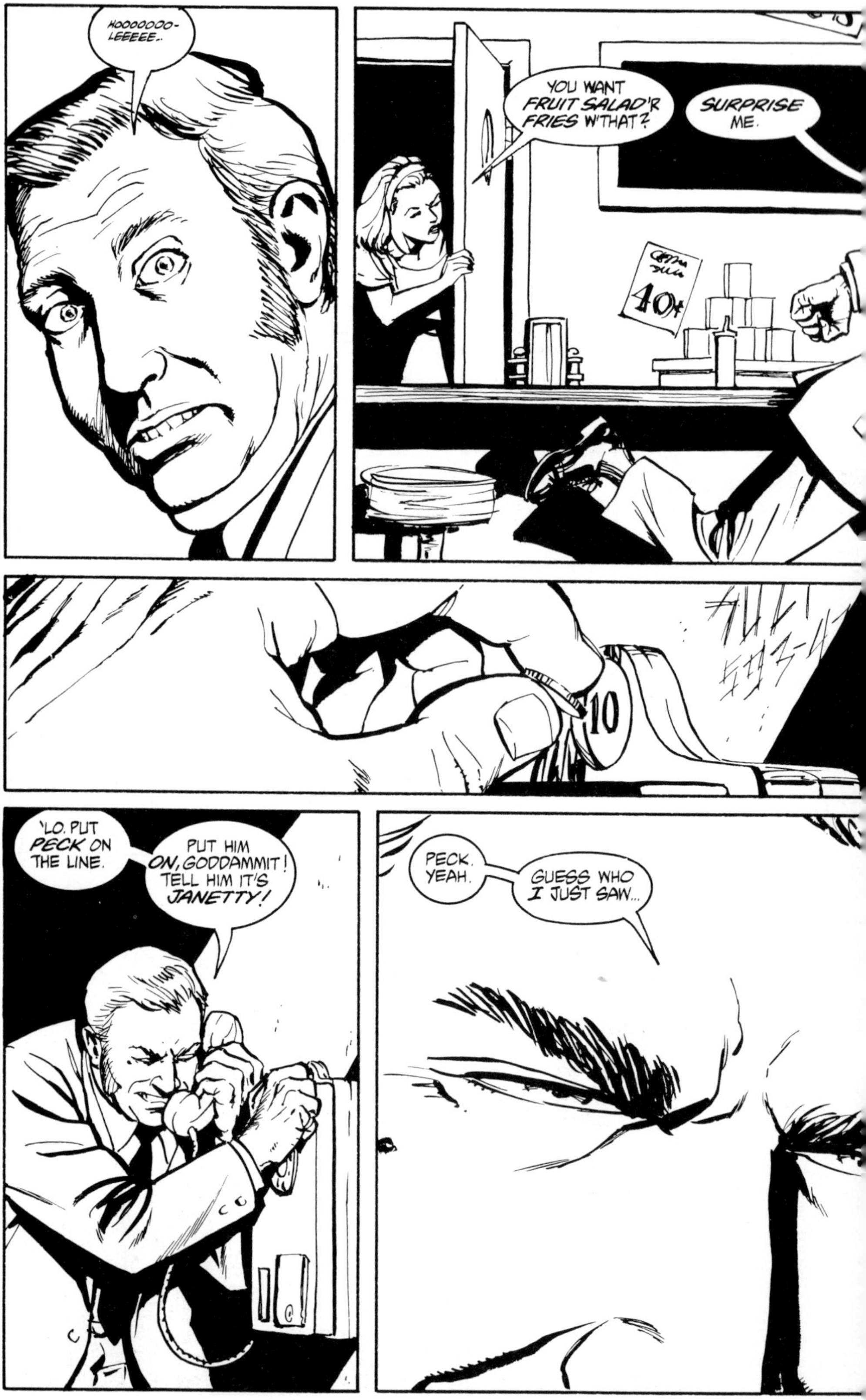
HOOOOOOO-
LEEEEE..
YOU WANT FRUIT SALAD'R FRIES W'THAT?
SURPRISE ME.
40¢
10
'LO. PUT PECK ON THE LINE.
PUT HIM ON, GODDAMMIT! TELL HIM IT'S JANETTY!
PECK. YEAH.
GUESS WHO I JUST SAW...

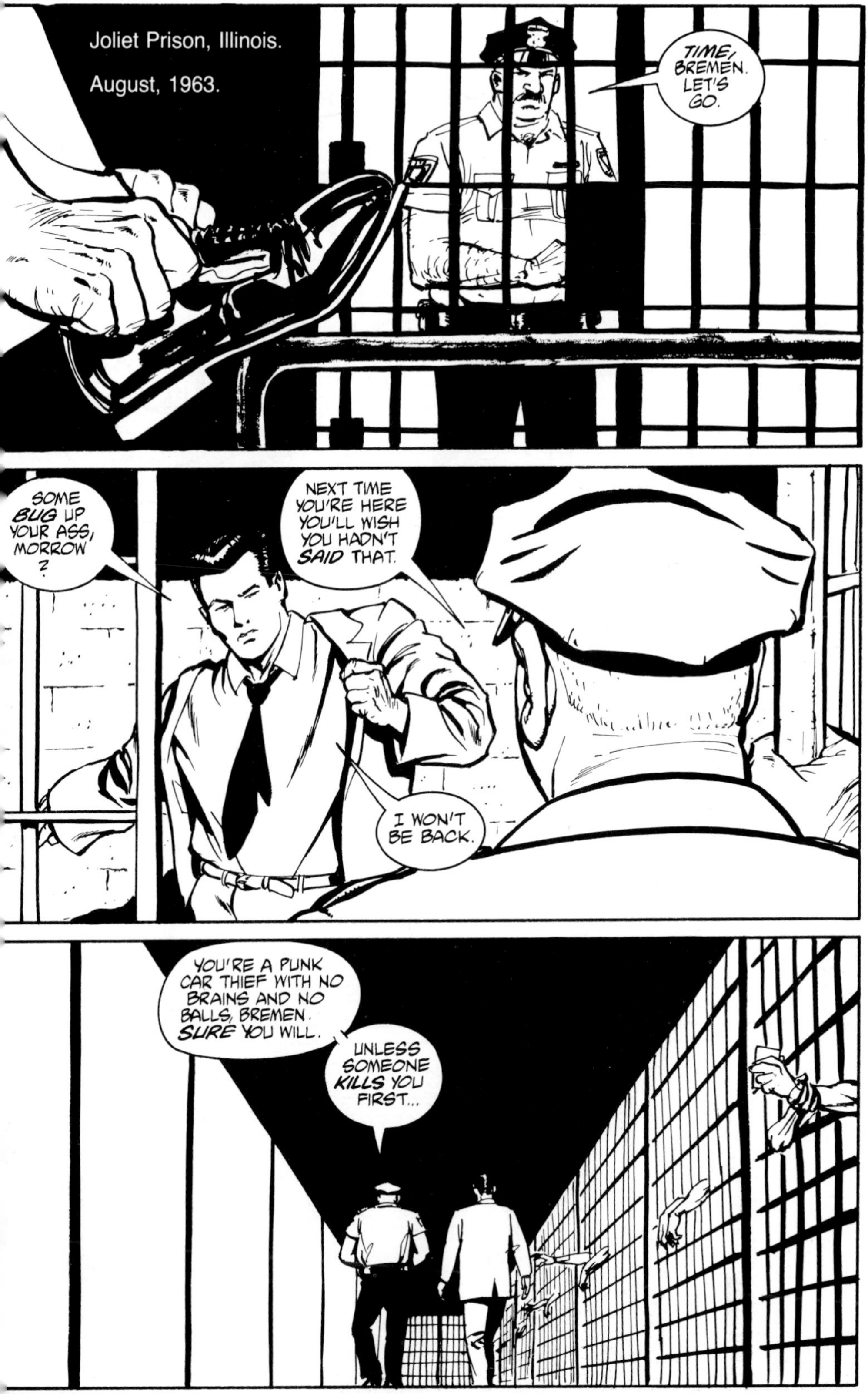
Joliet Prison, Illinois.
August, 1963.
TIME, BREMEN. LET'S GO.
SOME BUG UP YOUR ASS, MORROW ?
NEXT TIME YOU'RE HERE YOU'LL WISH YOU HADN'T SAID THAT.
I WON'T BE BACK.
YOU'RE A PUNK CAR THIEF WITH NO BRAINS AND NO BALLS, BREMEN. SURE YOU WILL.
UNLESS SOMEONE KILLS YOU FIRST...

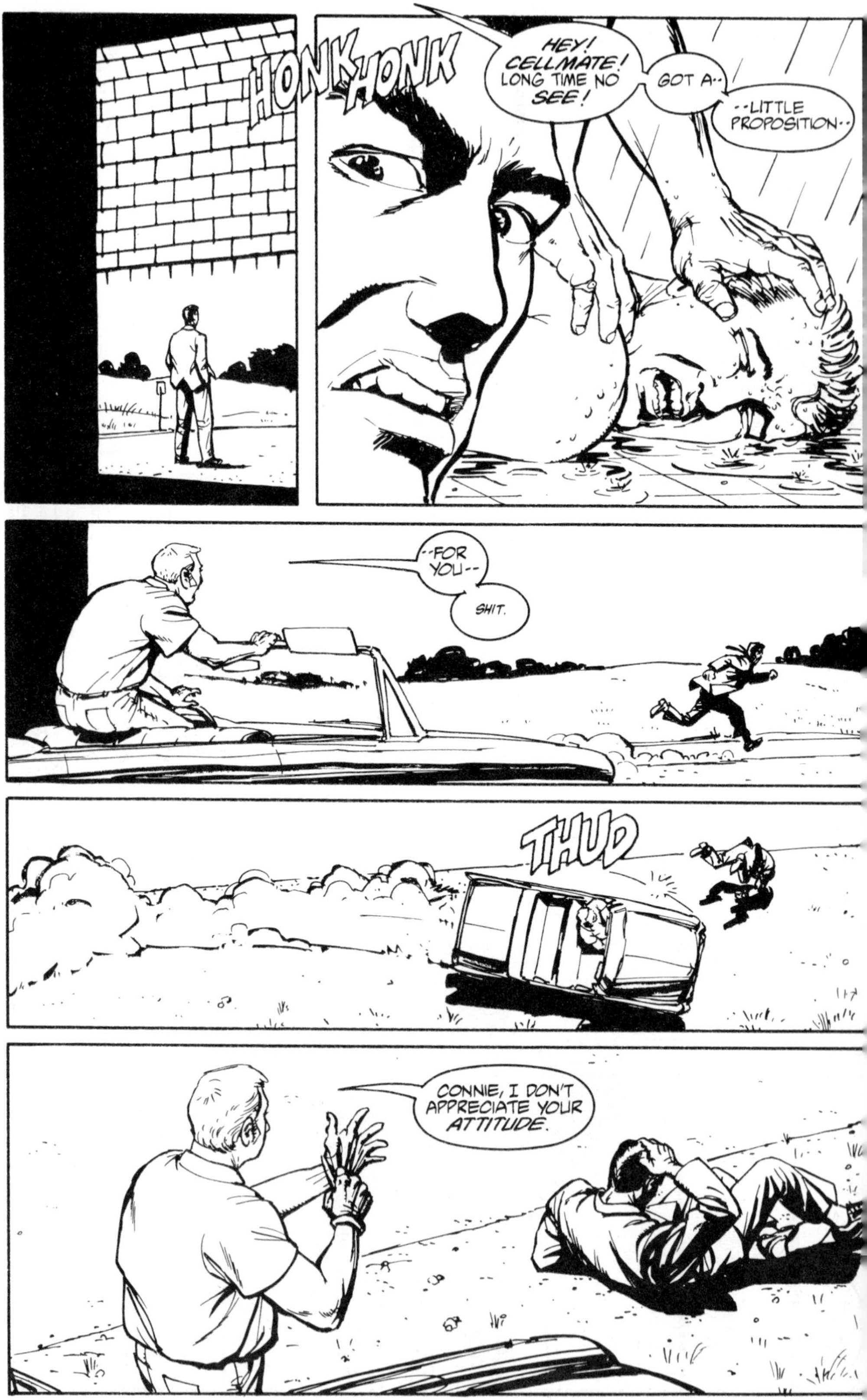
HONK HONK
HEY! CELLMATE! LONG TIME NO SEE!
GOT A--
--LITTLE PROPOSITION--
--FOR YOU--
SHIT.
THUD
CONNIE, I DON'T APPRECIATE YOUR ATTITUDE.

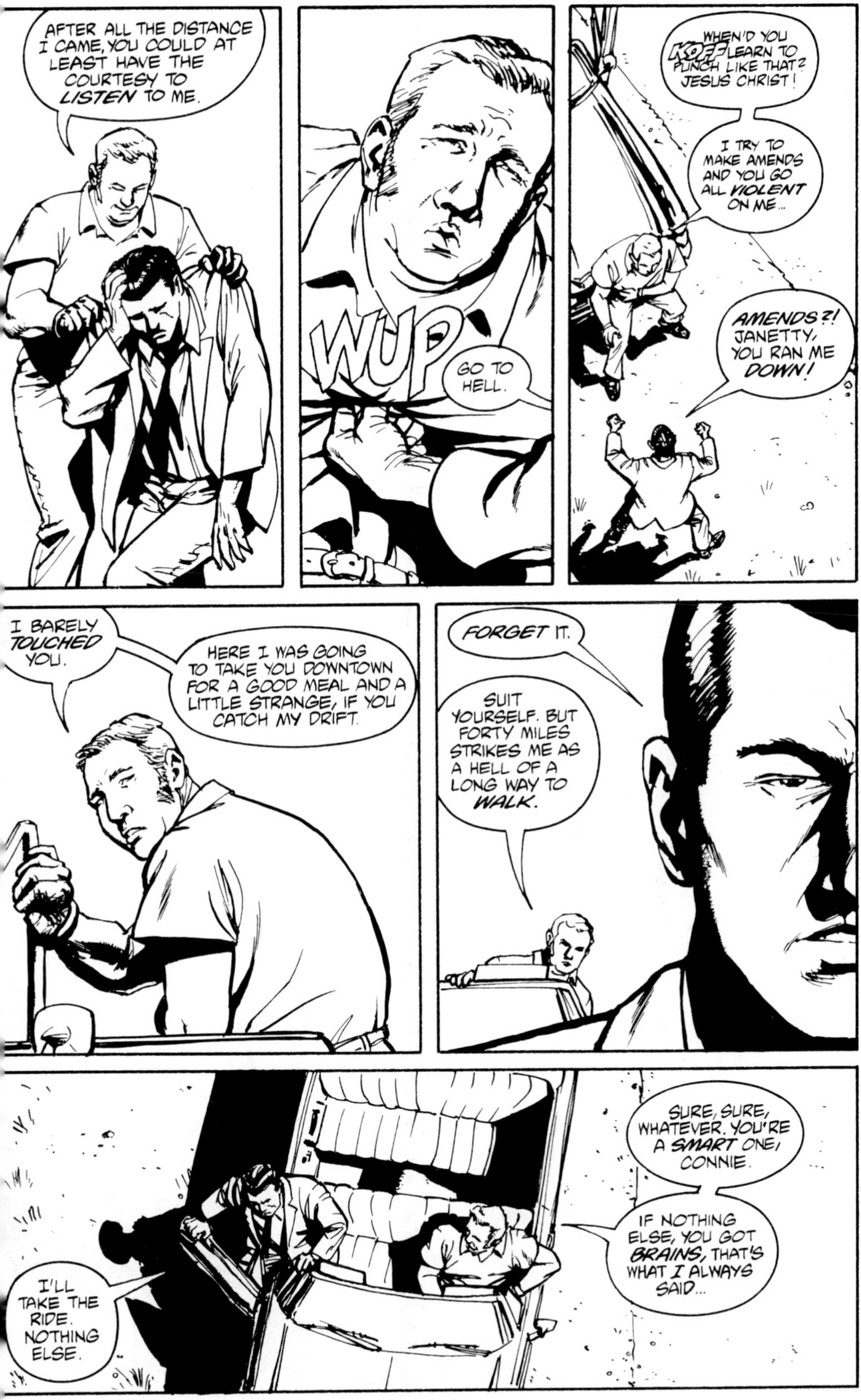
AFTER ALL THE DISTANCE I CAME, YOU COULD AT LEAST HAVE THE COURTESY TO LISTEN TO ME.
WUP
GO TO HELL.
WHEN'D YOU KOFF LEARN TO PUNCH LIKE THAT? JESUS CHRIST!
I TRY TO MAKE AMENDS AND YOU GO ALL VIOLENT ON ME...
AMENDS?! JANETTY, YOU RAN ME DOWN!
I BARELY TOUCHED YOU.
HERE I WAS GOING TO TAKE YOU DOWNTOWN FOR A GOOD MEAL AND A LITTLE STRANGE, IF YOU CATCH MY DRIFT.
FORGET IT.
SUIT YOURSELF. BUT FORTY MILES STRIKES ME AS A HELL OF A LONG WAY TO WALK.
I'LL TAKE THE RIDE. NOTHING ELSE.
SURE, SURE, WHATEVER. YOU'RE A SMART ONE, CONNIE.
IF NOTHING ELSE, YOU GOT BRAINS, THAT'S WHAT I ALWAYS SAID...

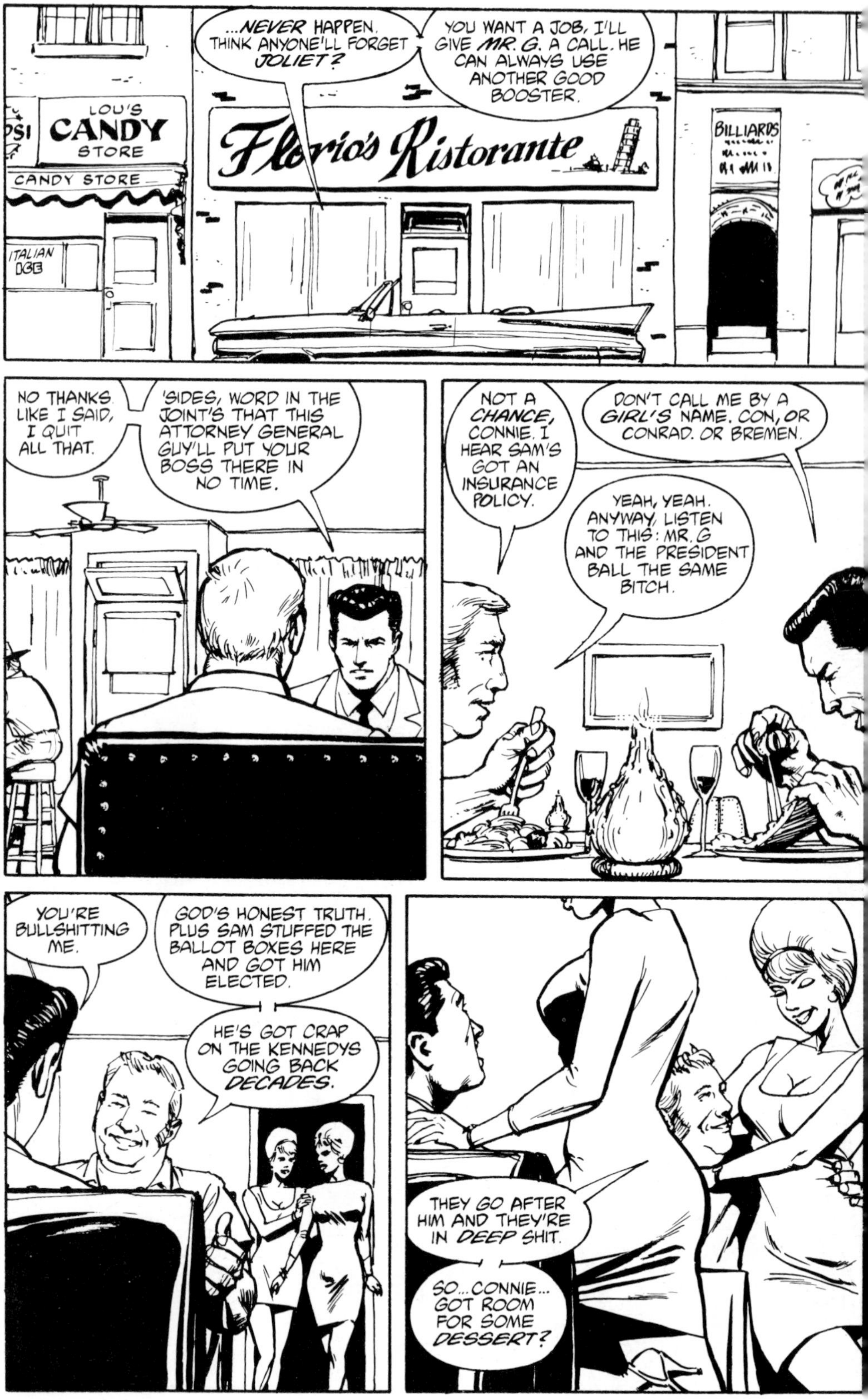
...NEVER HAPPEN. THINK ANYONE'LL FORGET JOLIET?
YOU WANT A JOB, I'LL GIVE MR. G. A CALL. HE CAN ALWAYS USE ANOTHER GOOD BOOSTER.
LOU'S CANDY STORE
CANDY STORE
ITALIAN ICE
Florio's Ristorante
BILLIARDS
NO THANKS. LIKE I SAID, I QUIT ALL THAT.
'SIDES, WORD IN THE JOINT'S THAT THIS ATTORNEY GENERAL GUY'LL PUT YOUR BOSS THERE IN NO TIME.
NOT A CHANCE, CONNIE. I HEAR SAM'S GOT AN INSURANCE POLICY.
DON'T CALL ME BY A GIRL'S NAME. CON, OR CONRAD. OR BREMEN.
YEAH, YEAH. ANYWAY, LISTEN TO THIS: MR. G AND THE PRESIDENT BALL THE SAME BITCH.
YOU'RE BULLSHITTING ME.
GOD'S HONEST TRUTH. PLUS SAM STUFFED THE BALLOT BOXES HERE AND GOT HIM ELECTED.
HE'S GOT CRAP ON THE KENNEDYS GOING BACK DECADES.
THEY GO AFTER HIM AND THEY'RE IN DEEP SHIT.
SO...CONNIE... GOT ROOM FOR SOME DESSERT?

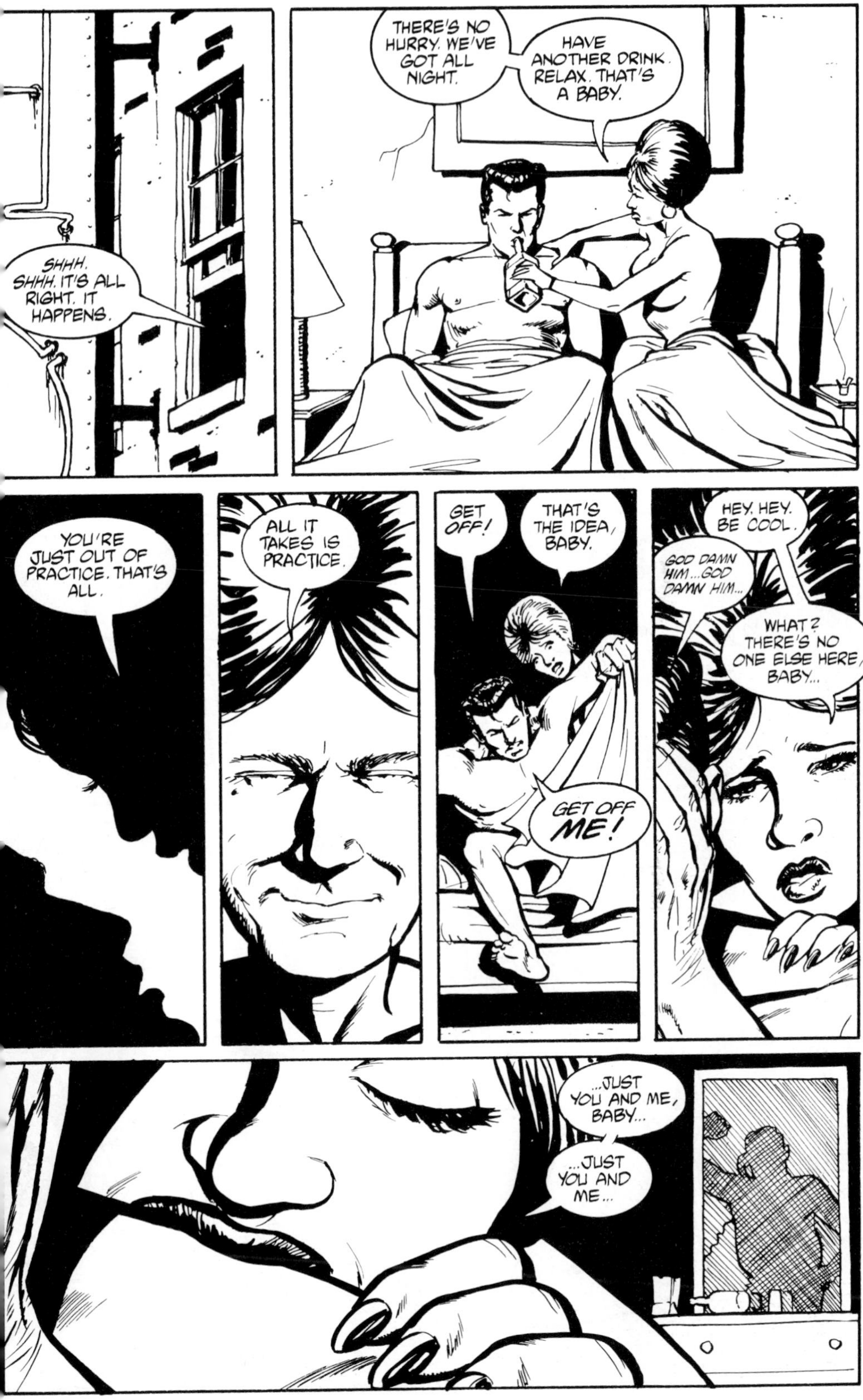
SHHH.
SHHH. IT'S ALL RIGHT. IT HAPPENS.
THERE'S NO HURRY. WE'VE GOT ALL NIGHT.
HAVE ANOTHER DRINK. RELAX. THAT'S A BABY.
YOU'RE JUST OUT OF PRACTICE. THAT'S ALL.
ALL IT TAKES IS PRACTICE.
GET OFF!
THAT'S THE IDEA, BABY.
GET OFF ME!
HEY, HEY. BE COOL.
GOD DAMN HIM...GOD DAMN HIM...
WHAT? THERE'S NO ONE ELSE HERE, BABY...
...JUST YOU AND ME, BABY...
...JUST YOU AND ME...

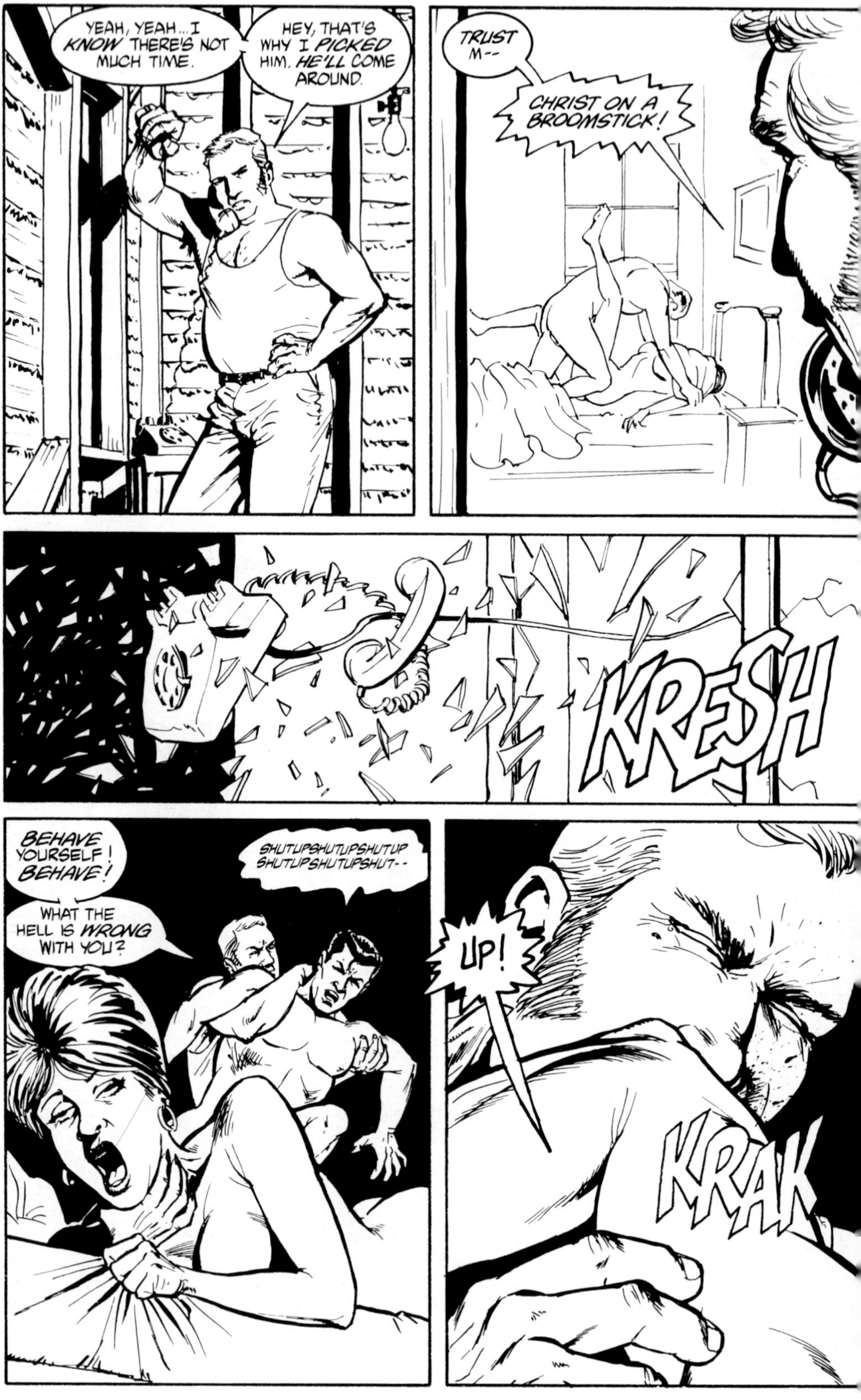
YEAH, YEAH... I KNOW THERE'S NOT MUCH TIME.
HEY, THAT'S WHY I PICKED HIM. HE'LL COME AROUND.
TRUST M--
CHRIST ON A BROOMSTICK!
KRESH
BEHAVE YOURSELF! BEHAVE!
WHAT THE HELL IS WRONG WITH YOU?
SHUTUPSHUTUPSHUTUP SHUTUPSHUTUPSHUT--
UP!
KRAK

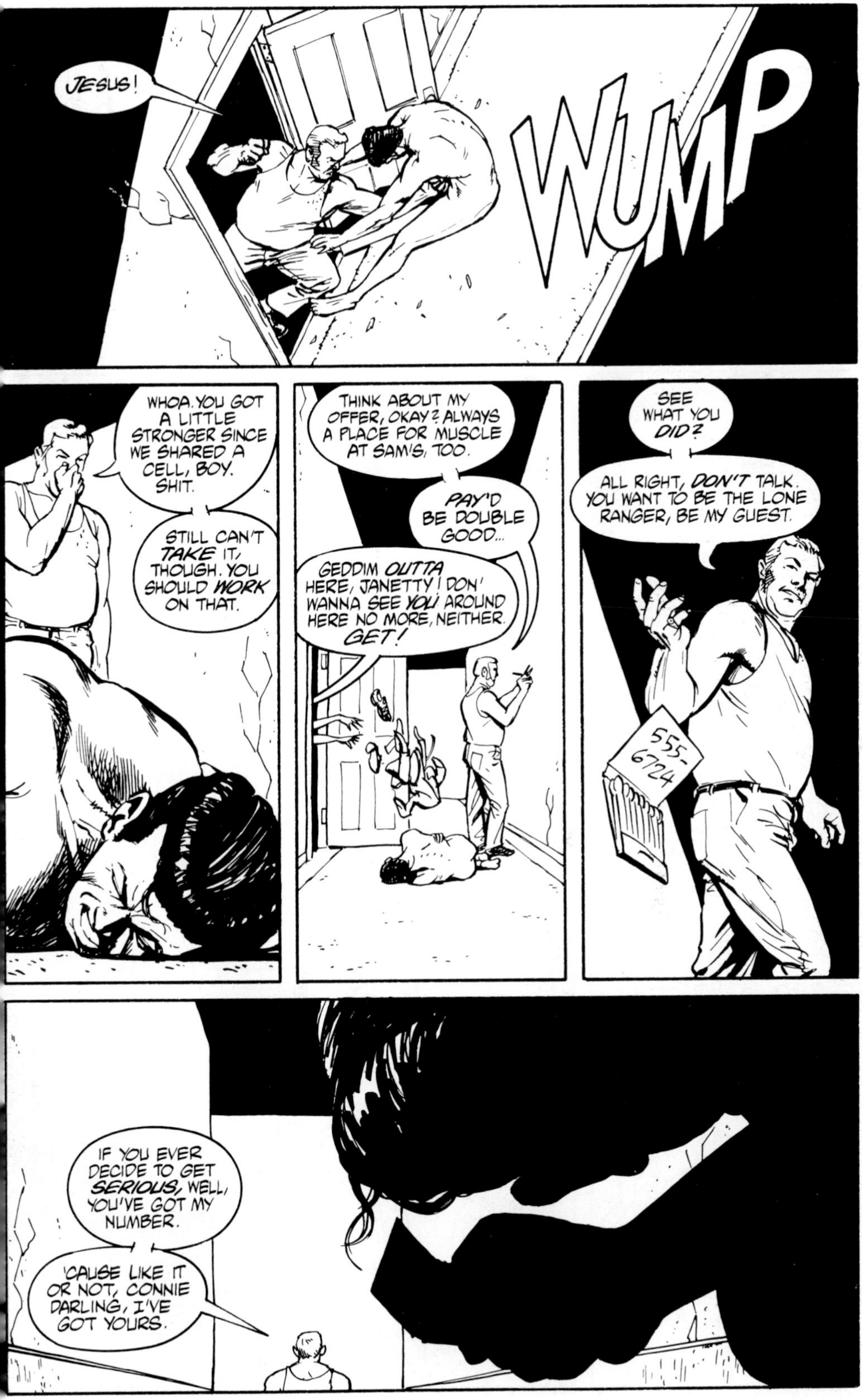
JESUS!
WUMP
WHOA. YOU GOT A LITTLE STRONGER SINCE WE SHARED A CELL, BOY. SHIT.
STILL CAN'T TAKE IT, THOUGH. YOU SHOULD WORK ON THAT.
THINK ABOUT MY OFFER, OKAY? ALWAYS A PLACE FOR MUSCLE AT SAM'S, TOO.
PAY'D BE DOUBLE GOOD...
GEDDIM OUTTA HERE, JANETTY! DON' WANNA SEE YOU AROUND HERE NO MORE, NEITHER. GET!
SEE WHAT YOU DID?
ALL RIGHT, DON'T TALK. YOU WANT TO BE THE LONE RANGER, BE MY GUEST.
555-6724
IF YOU EVER DECIDE TO GET SERIOUS, WELL, YOU'VE GOT MY NUMBER.
'CAUSE LIKE IT OR NOT, CONNIE DARLING, I'VE GOT YOURS.

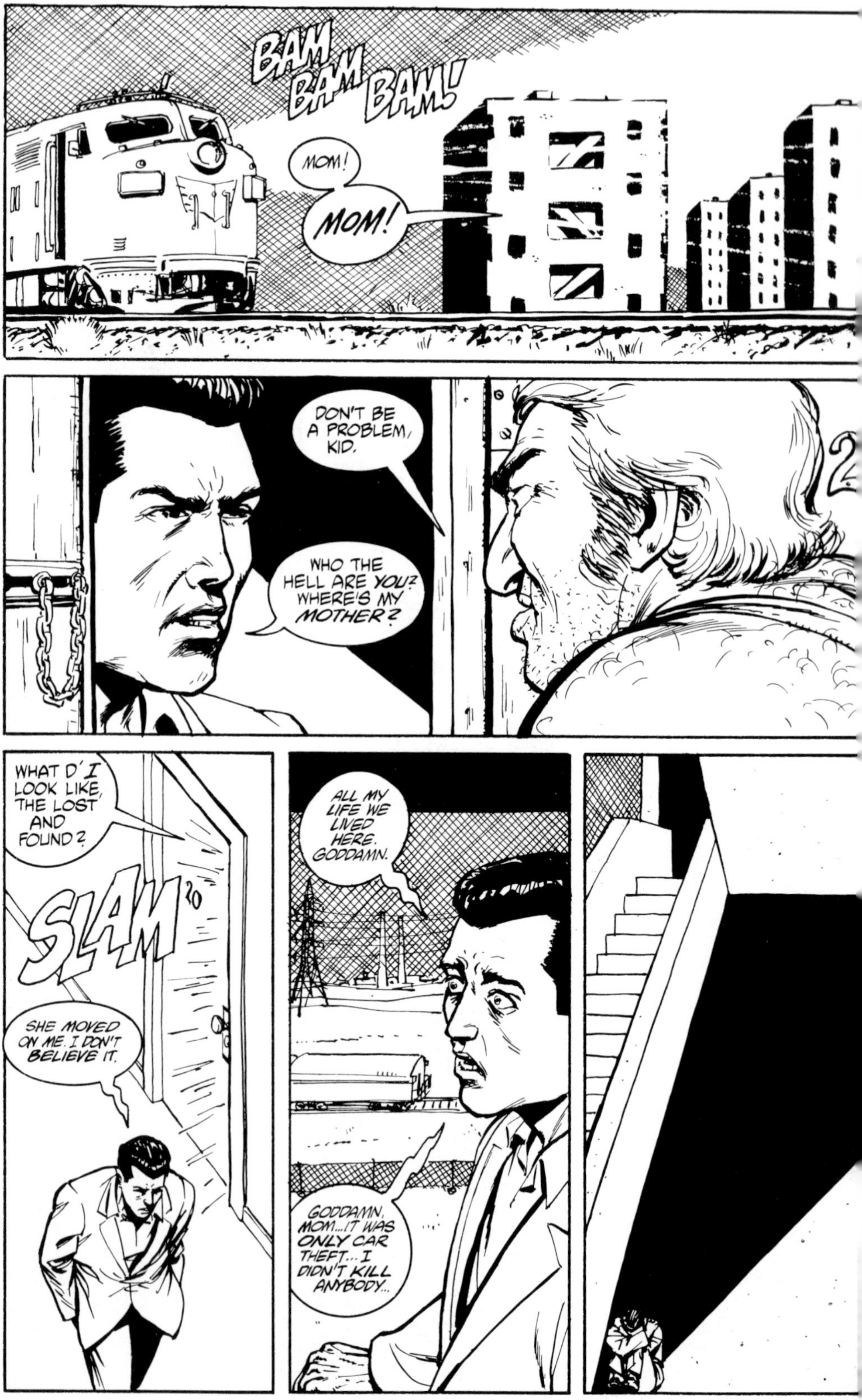
BAM BAM BAM!
MOM!
MOM!
DON'T BE A PROBLEM, KID.
WHO THE HELL ARE YOU? WHERE'S MY MOTHER?
WHAT D' I LOOK LIKE, THE LOST AND FOUND?
SLAM
SHE MOVED ON ME. I DON'T BELIEVE IT.
ALL MY LIFE WE LIVED HERE. GODDAMN.
GODDAMN, MOM... IT WAS ONLY CAR THEFT... I DIDN'T KILL ANYBODY...

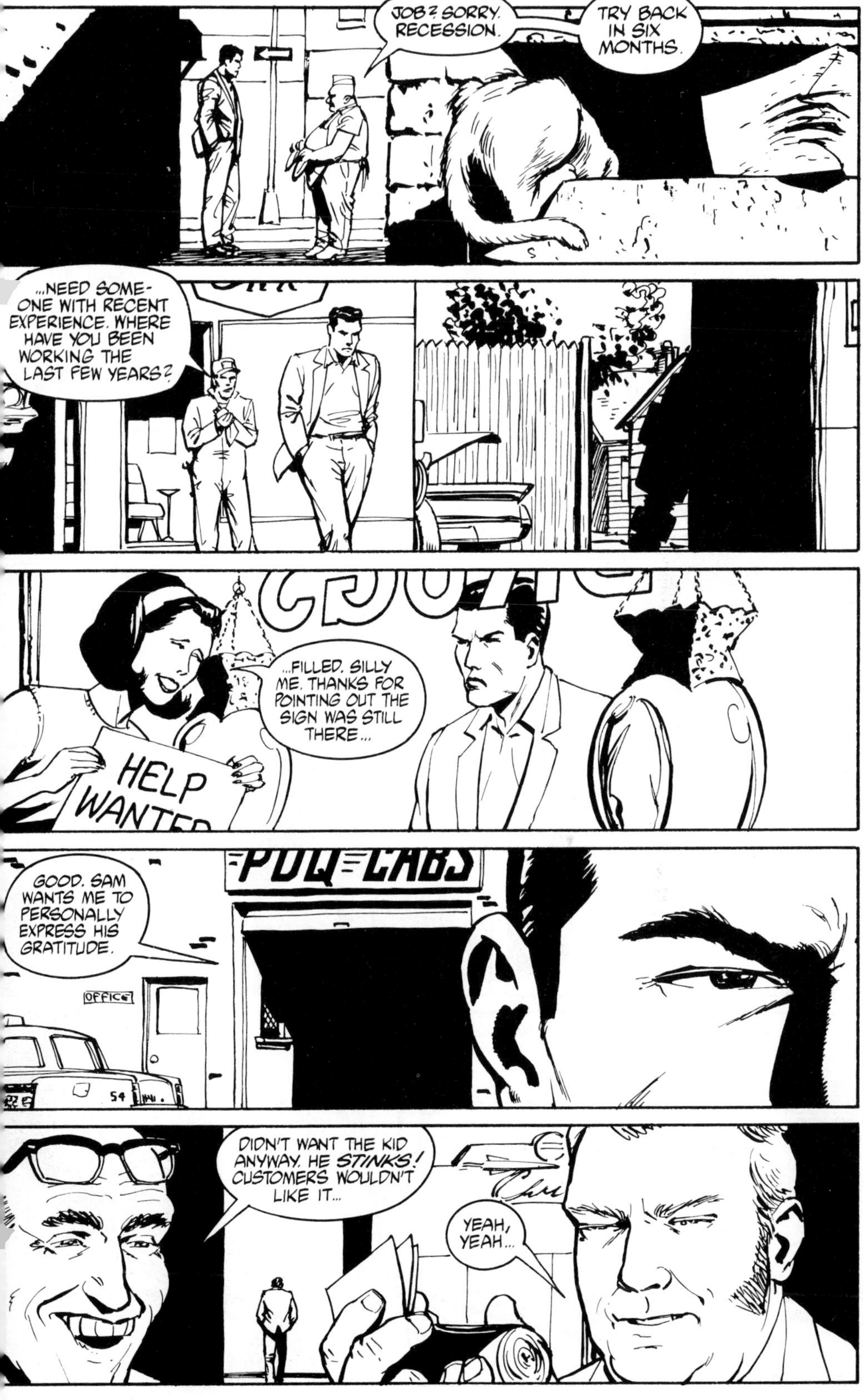
JOB? SORRY. RECESSION.
TRY BACK IN SIX MONTHS.
...NEED SOME-ONE WITH RECENT EXPERIENCE. WHERE HAVE YOU BEEN WORKING THE LAST FEW YEARS?
...FILLED. SILLY ME. THANKS FOR POINTING OUT THE SIGN WAS STILL THERE...
HELP
PDQ CABS
GOOD. SAM WANTS ME TO PERSONALLY EXPRESS HIS GRATITUDE.
OFFICE
DIDN'T WANT THE KID ANYWAY. HE *STINKS!* CUSTOMERS WOULDN'T LIKE IT...
YEAH, YEAH...

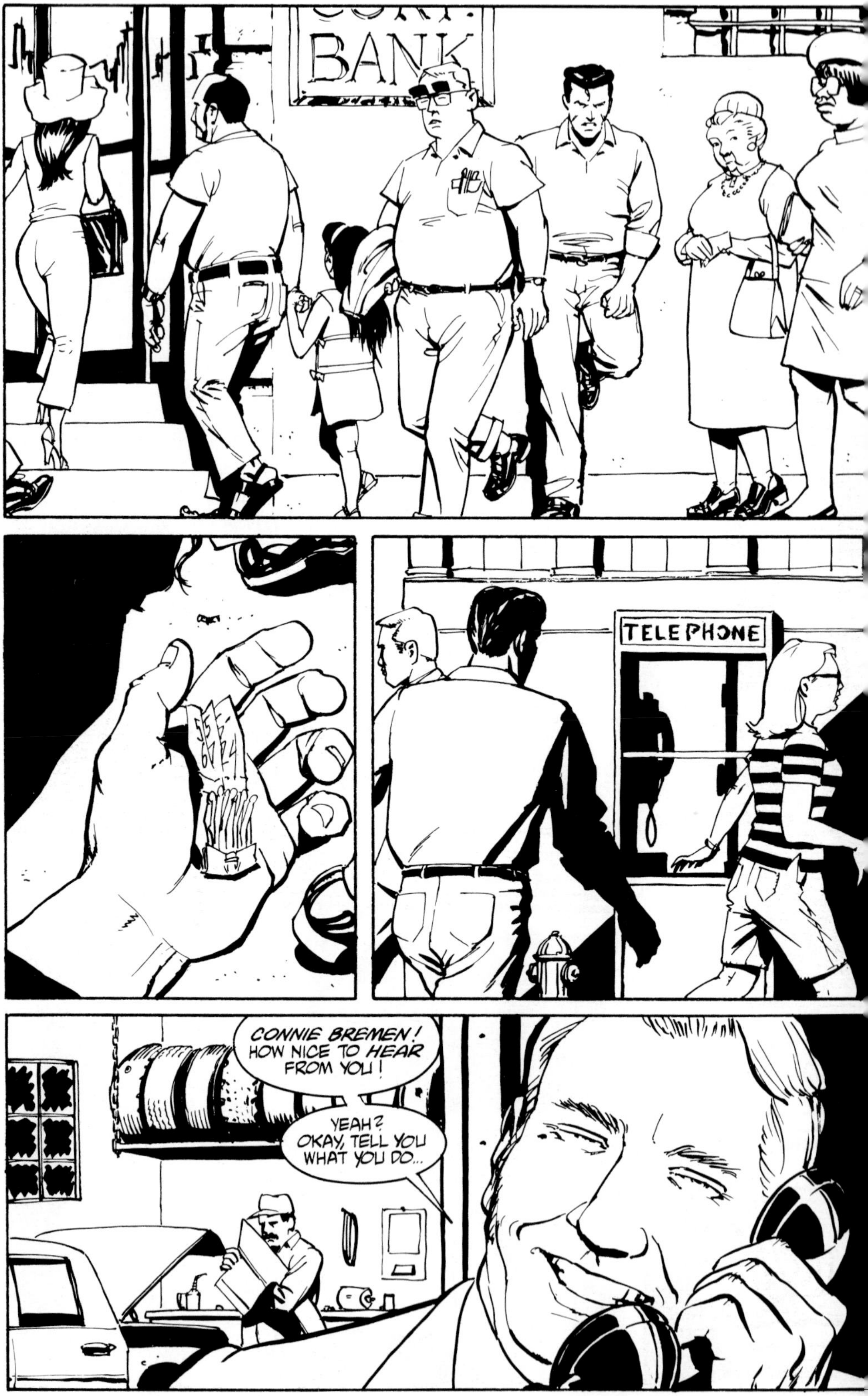
BANK
TELEPHONE
CONNIE BREMEN! HOW NICE TO HEAR FROM YOU!
YEAH? OKAY, TELL YOU WHAT YOU DO...

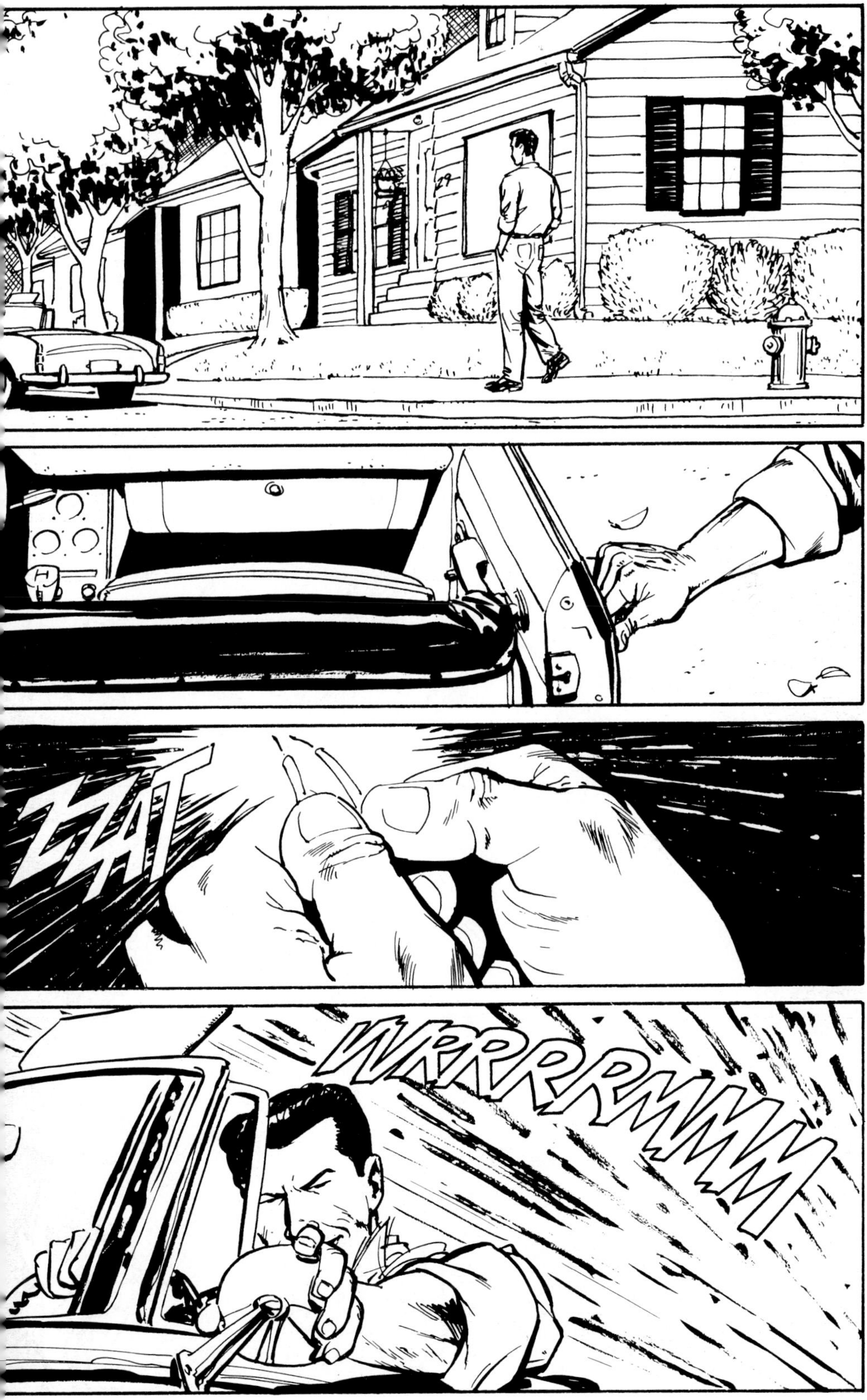
29
ZZAT
WRRRRMMMM

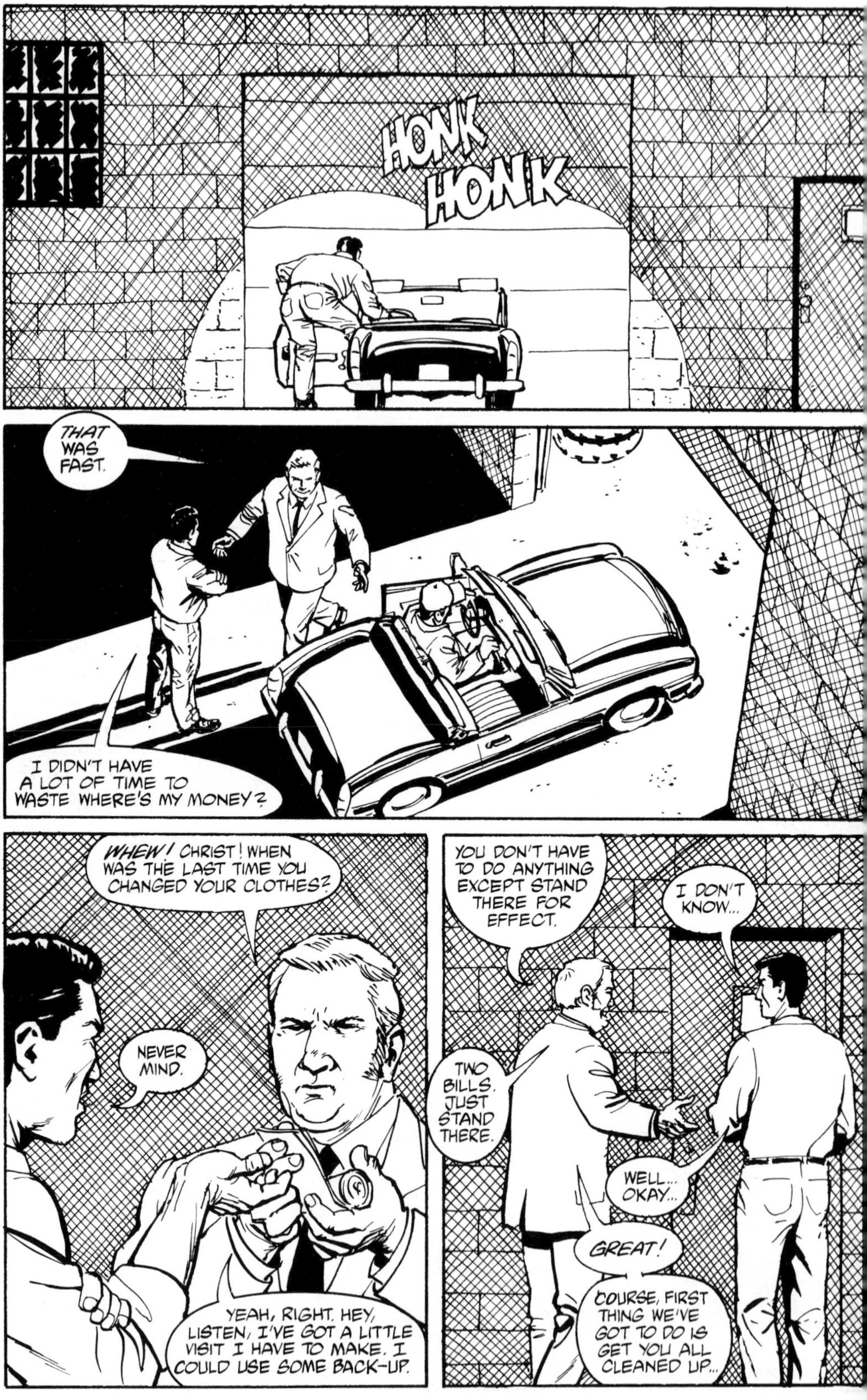
HONK HONK
THAT WAS FAST.
I DIDN'T HAVE A LOT OF TIME TO WASTE WHERE'S MY MONEY?
WHEW! CHRIST! WHEN WAS THE LAST TIME YOU CHANGED YOUR CLOTHES?
NEVER MIND.
YEAH, RIGHT. HEY, LISTEN, I'VE GOT A LITTLE VISIT I HAVE TO MAKE. I COULD USE SOME BACK-UP.
YOU DON'T HAVE TO DO ANYTHING EXCEPT STAND THERE FOR EFFECT.
I DON'T KNOW...
TWO BILLS. JUST STAND THERE.
WELL... OKAY...
GREAT!
COURSE, FIRST THING WE'VE GOT TO DO IS GET YOU ALL CLEANED UP...

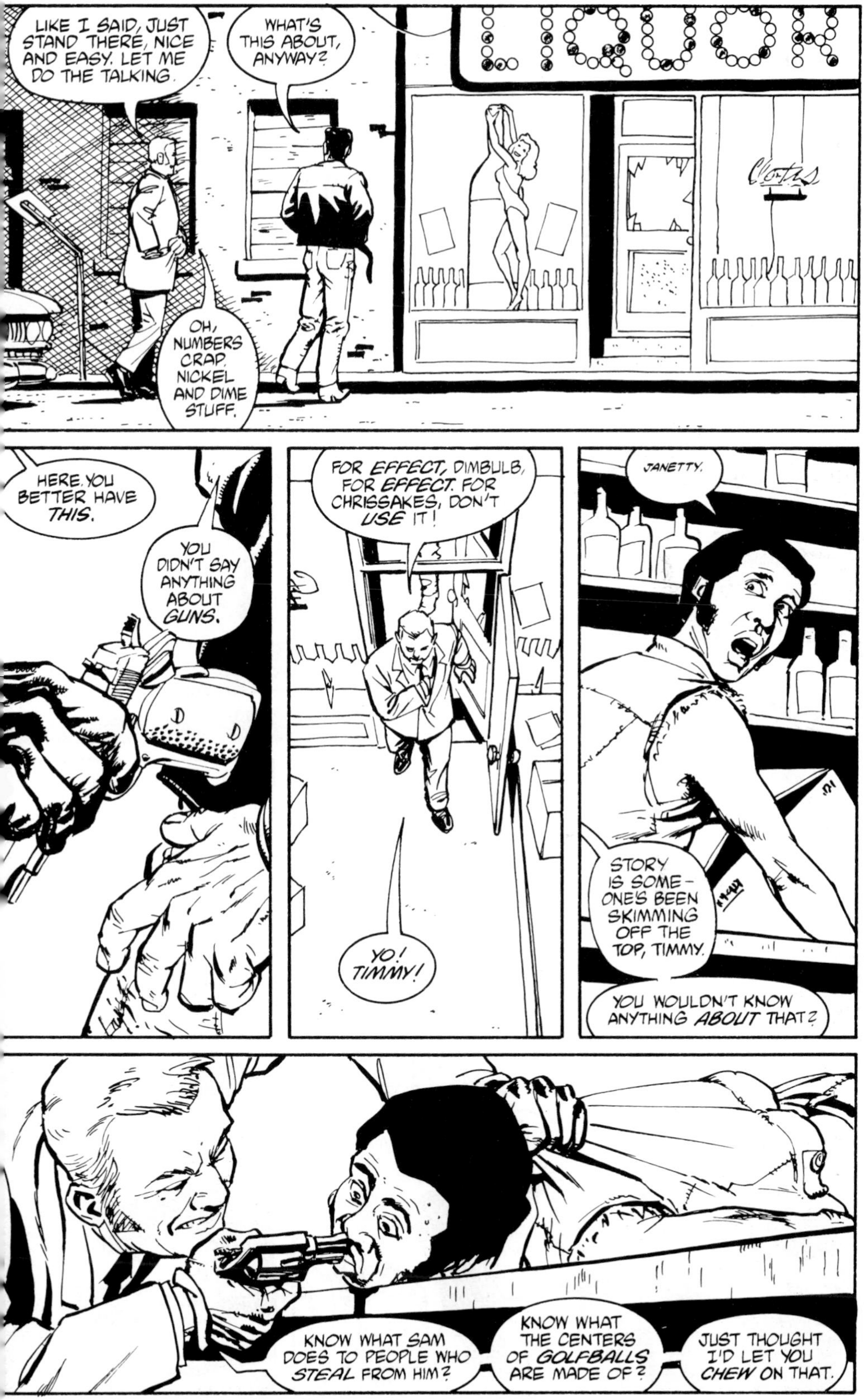
LIKE I SAID, JUST STAND THERE, NICE AND EASY. LET ME DO THE TALKING.
WHAT'S THIS ABOUT, ANYWAY?
OH, NUMBERS CRAP. NICKEL AND DIME STUFF.
LIQUOR
HERE. YOU BETTER HAVE THIS.
YOU DIDN'T SAY ANYTHING ABOUT GUNS.
FOR EFFECT, DIMBULB, FOR EFFECT. FOR CHRISSAKES, DON'T USE IT!
YO! TIMMY!
JANETTY.
STORY IS SOME-ONE'S BEEN SKIMMING OFF THE TOP, TIMMY.
YOU WOULDN'T KNOW ANYTHING ABOUT THAT?
KNOW WHAT SAM DOES TO PEOPLE WHO STEAL FROM HIM?
KNOW WHAT THE CENTERS OF GOLFBALLS ARE MADE OF?
JUST THOUGHT I'D LET YOU CHEW ON THAT.

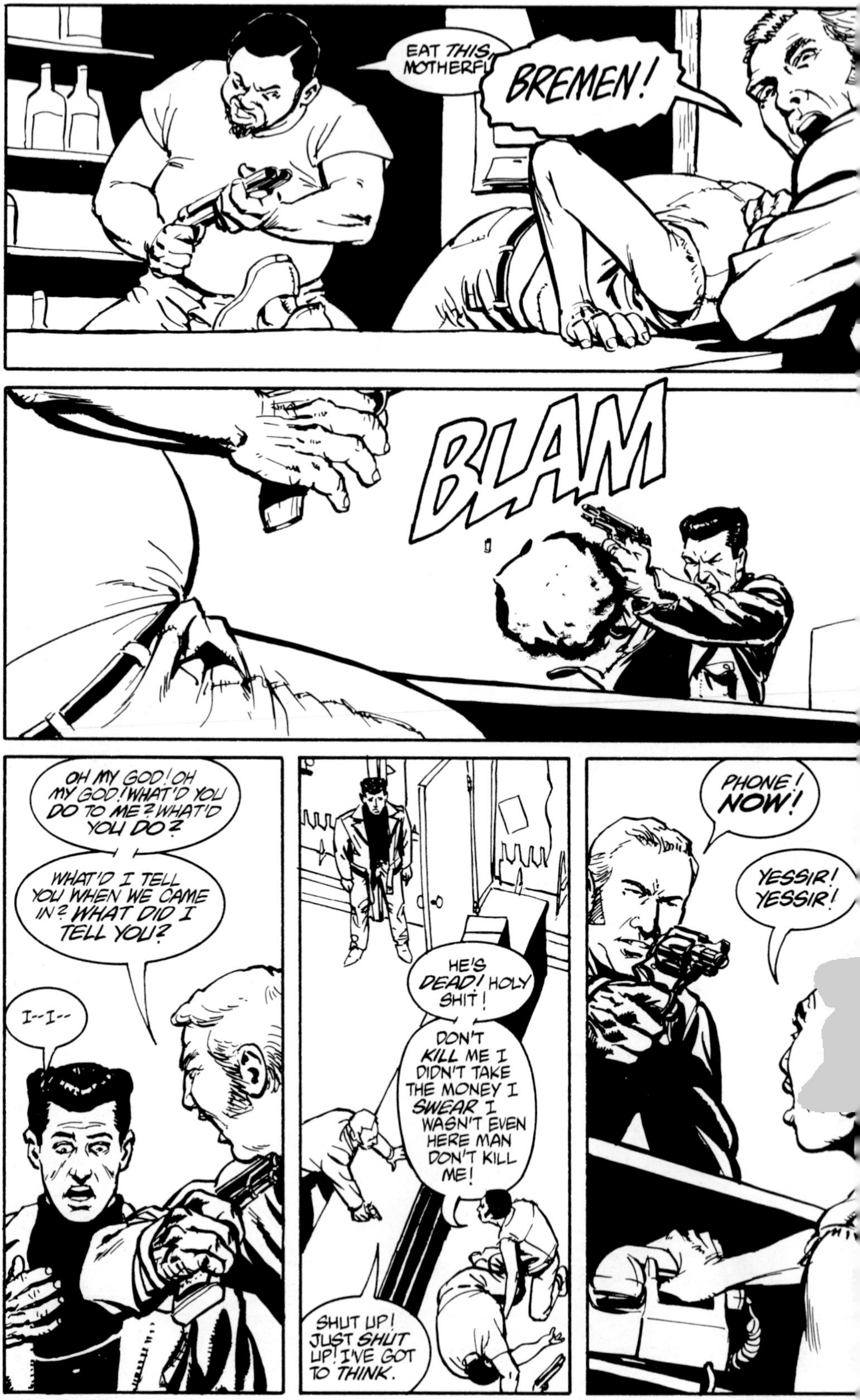
EAT THIS, MOTHERF
BREMEN!
BLAM
OH MY GOD! OH MY GOD! WHAT'D YOU DO TO ME? WHAT'D YOU DO?
WHAT'D I TELL YOU WHEN WE CAME IN? WHAT DID I TELL YOU?
I--I--
HE'S DEAD! HOLY SHIT!
DON'T KILL ME I DIDN'T TAKE THE MONEY I SWEAR I WASN'T EVEN HERE MAN DON'T KILL ME!
SHUT UP! JUST SHUT UP! I'VE GOT TO THINK.
PHONE! NOW!
YESSIR! YESSIR!

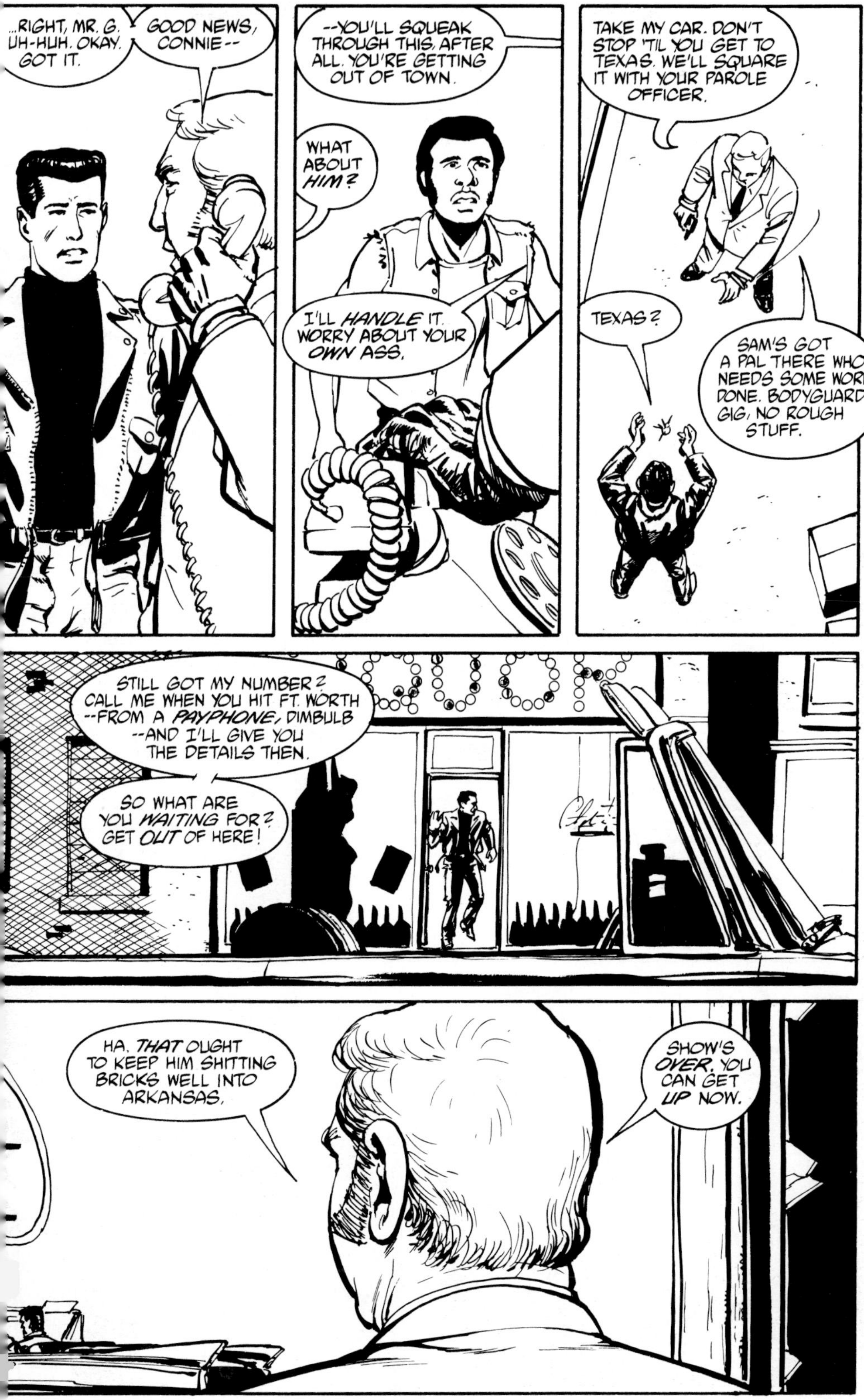
...RIGHT, MR. G. UH-HUH. OKAY. GOT IT.
GOOD NEWS, CONNIE--
--YOU'LL SQUEAK THROUGH THIS, AFTER ALL. YOU'RE GETTING OUT OF TOWN.
WHAT ABOUT *HIM*?
I'LL *HANDLE* IT. WORRY ABOUT YOUR *OWN* ASS.
TAKE MY CAR. DON'T STOP 'TIL YOU GET TO TEXAS. WE'LL SQUARE IT WITH YOUR PAROLE OFFICER.
TEXAS?
SAM'S GOT A PAL THERE WHO NEEDS SOME WORK DONE. BODYGUARD GIG, NO ROUGH STUFF.
STILL GOT MY NUMBER? CALL ME WHEN YOU HIT FT. WORTH --FROM A *PAYPHONE*, DIMBULB --AND I'LL GIVE YOU THE DETAILS THEN.
SO WHAT ARE YOU *WAITING* FOR? GET *OUT* OF HERE!
HA. *THAT* OUGHT TO KEEP HIM SHITTING BRICKS WELL INTO ARKANSAS.
SHOW'S *OVER*. YOU CAN GET *UP* NOW.

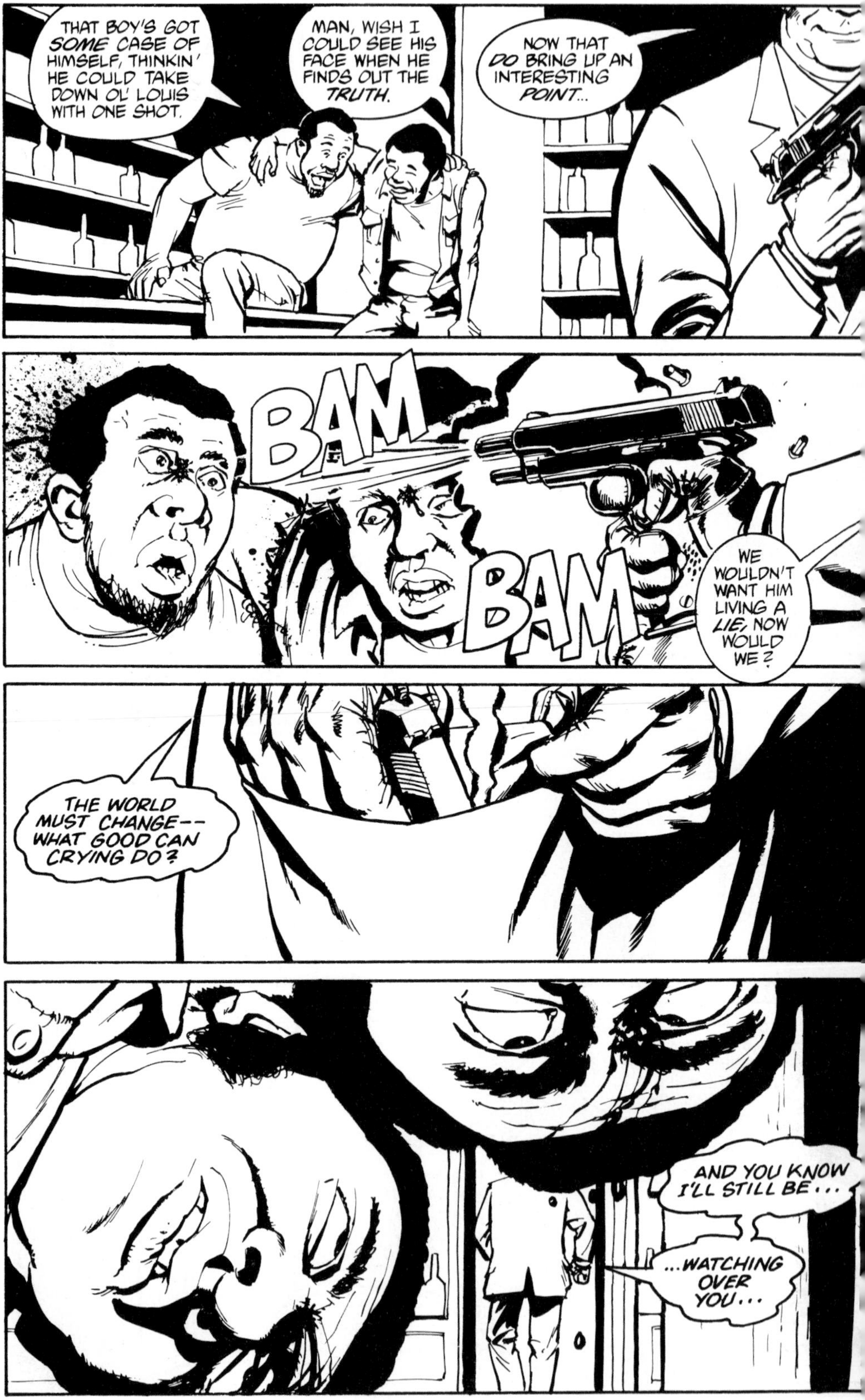
THAT BOY'S GOT SOME CASE OF HIMSELF, THINKIN' HE COULD TAKE DOWN OL' LOUIS WITH ONE SHOT.
MAN, WISH I COULD SEE HIS FACE WHEN HE FINDS OUT THE TRUTH.
NOW THAT DO BRING UP AN INTERESTING POINT...
BAM
BAM
WE WOULDN'T WANT HIM LIVING A LIE, NOW WOULD WE?
THE WORLD MUST CHANGE-- WHAT GOOD CAN CRYING DO?
AND YOU KNOW I'LL STILL BE...
...WATCHING OVER YOU...

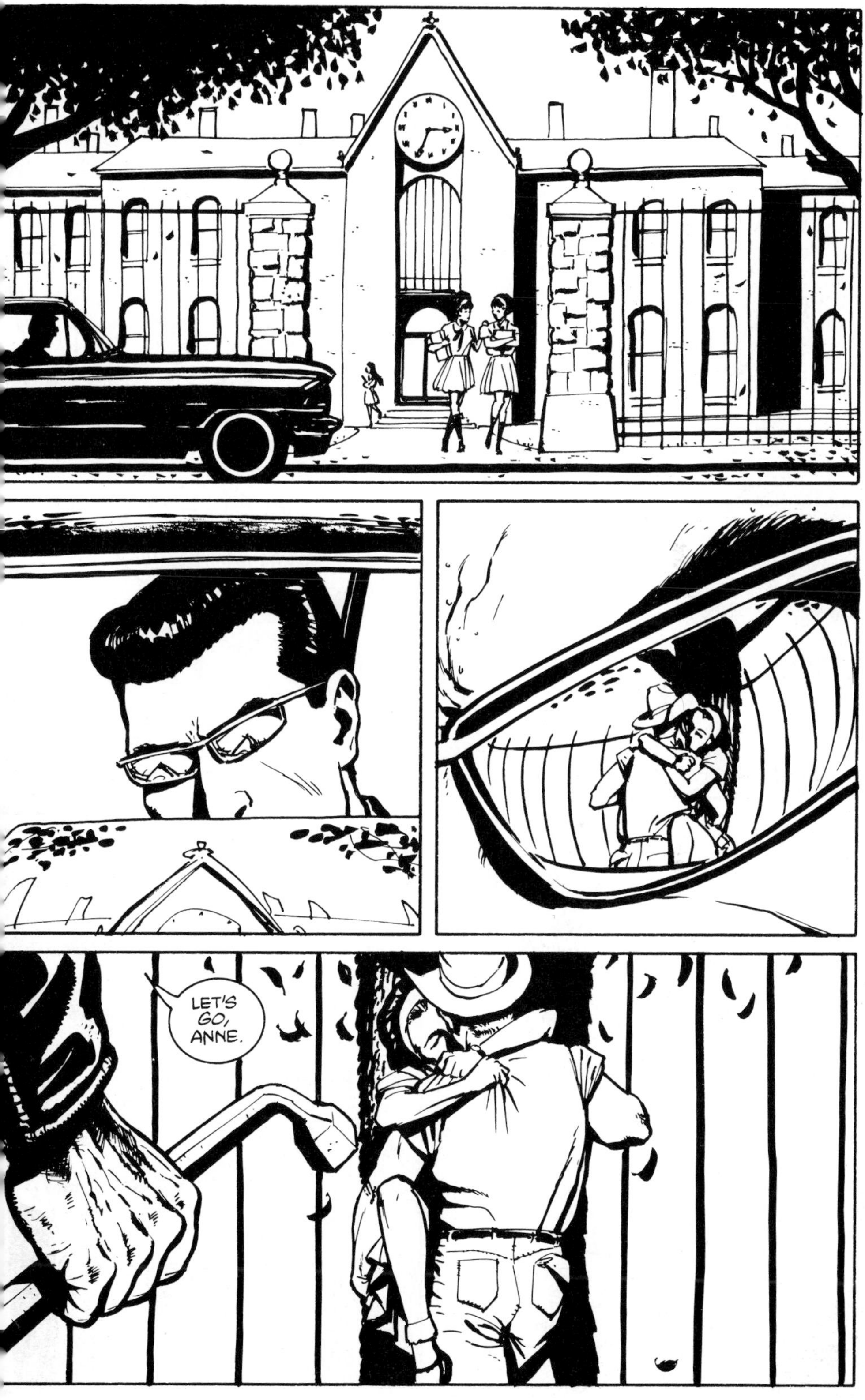
LET'S GO, ANNE.

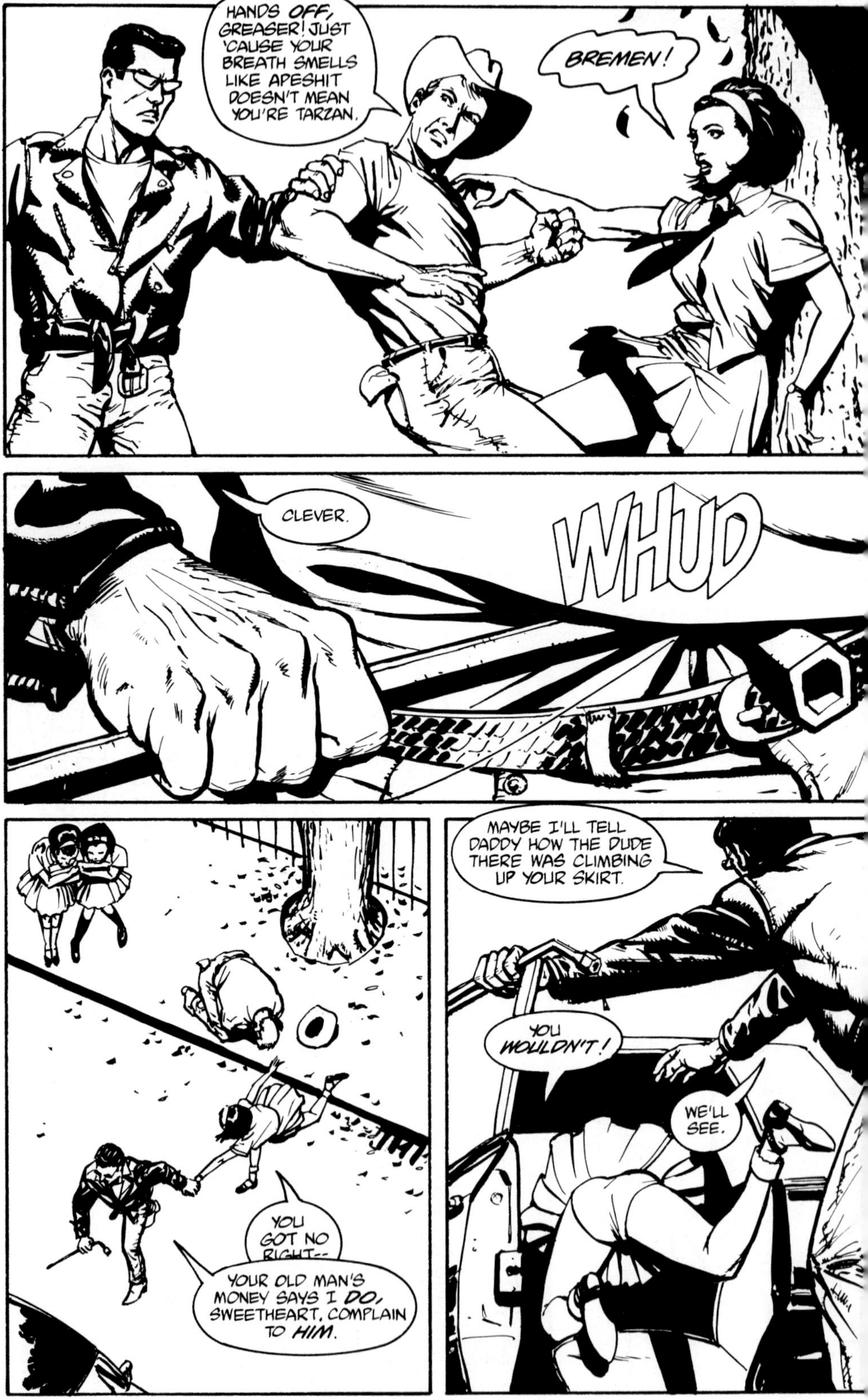
HANDS OFF, GREASER! JUST 'CAUSE YOUR BREATH SMELLS LIKE APESHIT DOESN'T MEAN YOU'RE TARZAN.
BREMEN!
CLEVER.
WHUD
YOU GOT NO RIGHT--
YOUR OLD MAN'S MONEY SAYS I DO, SWEETHEART. COMPLAIN TO HIM.
MAYBE I'LL TELL DADDY HOW THE DUDE THERE WAS CLIMBING UP YOUR SKIRT.
YOU WOULDN'T!
WE'LL SEE.

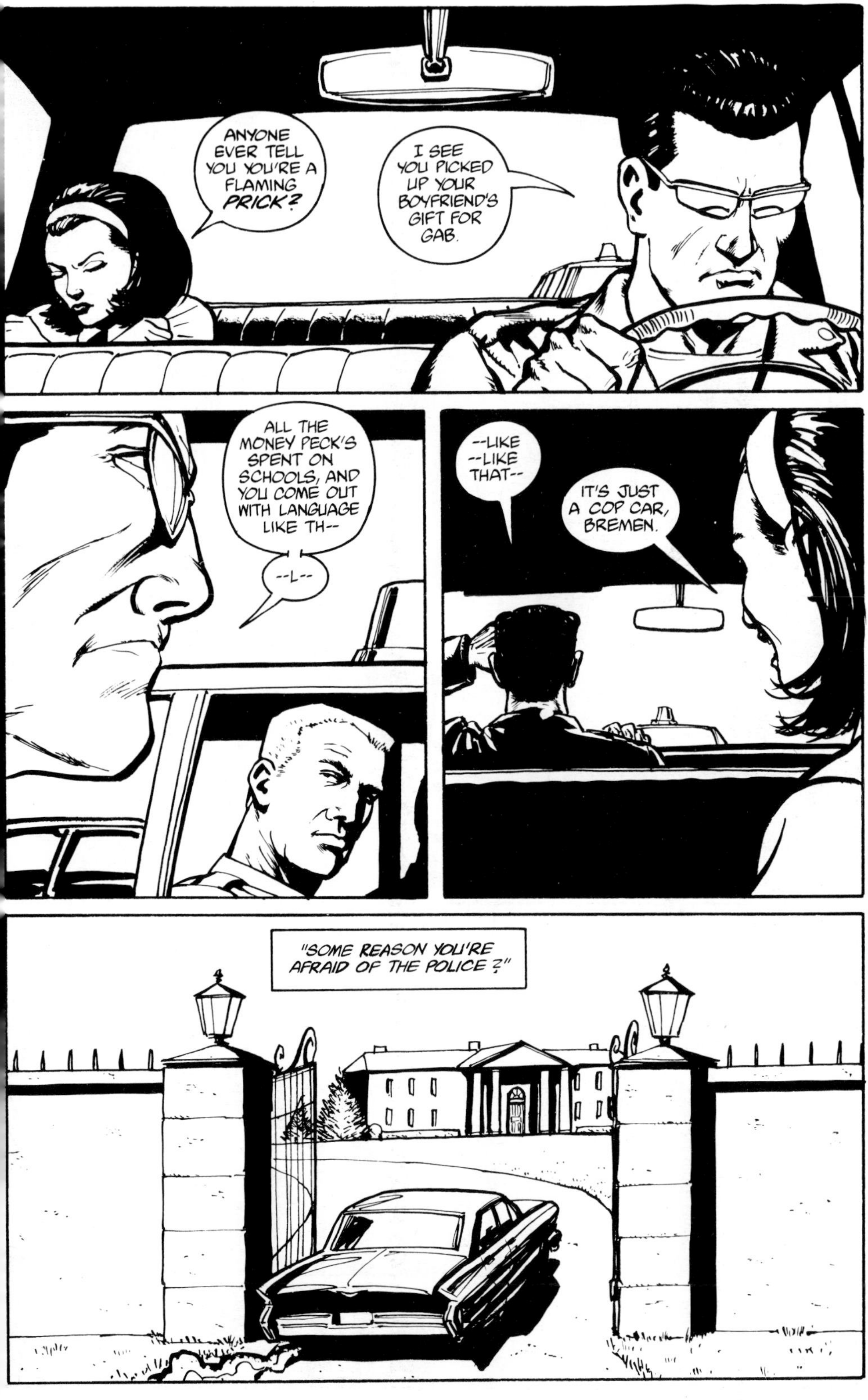
ANYONE EVER TELL YOU YOU'RE A FLAMING PRICK?
I SEE YOU PICKED UP YOUR BOYFRIEND'S GIFT FOR GAB.
ALL THE MONEY PECK'S SPENT ON SCHOOLS, AND YOU COME OUT WITH LANGUAGE LIKE TH--
--L--
--LIKE --LIKE THAT--
IT'S JUST A COP CAR, BREMEN.
"SOME REASON YOU'RE AFRAID OF THE POLICE?"

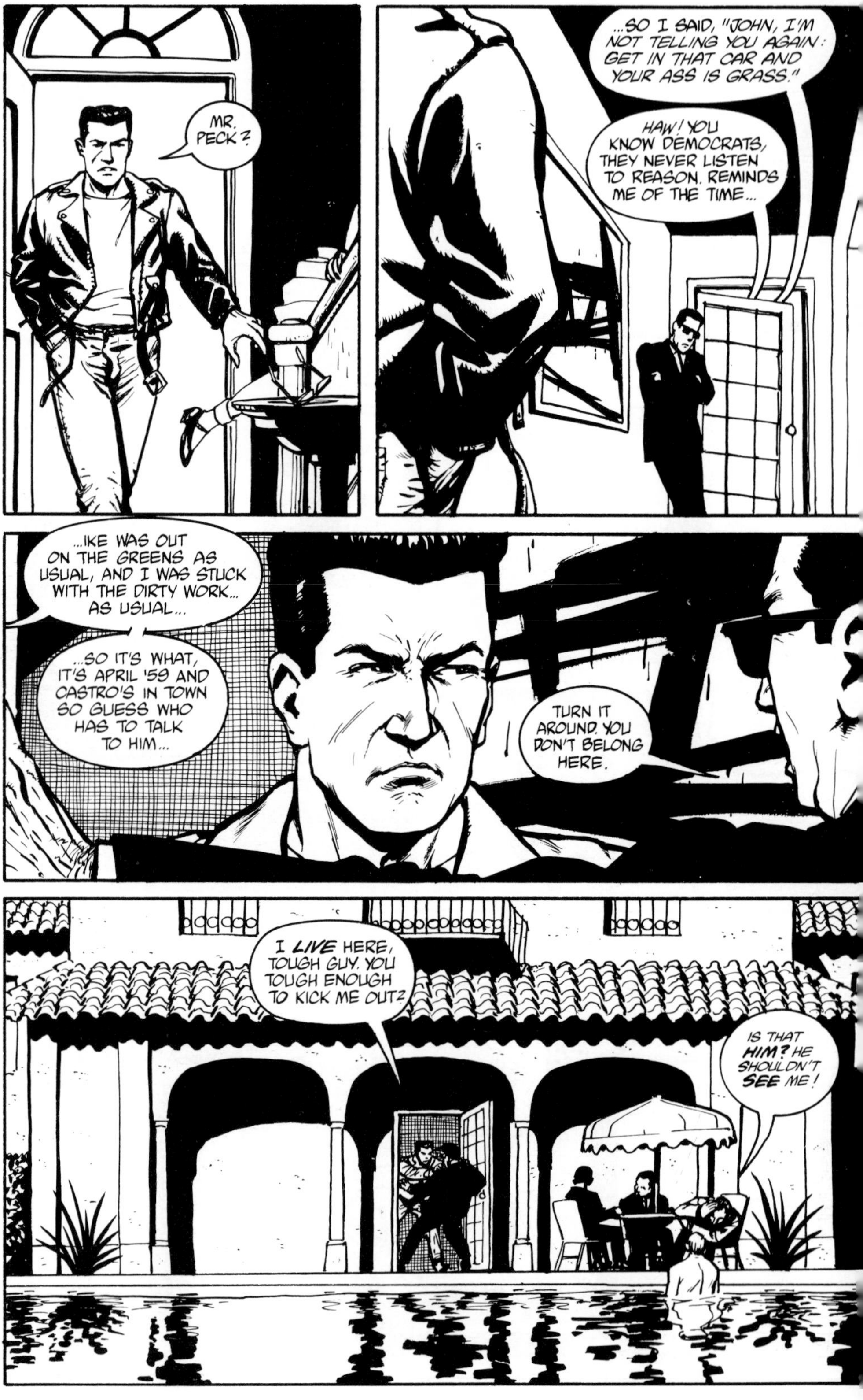
MR. PECK?
...SO I SAID, "JOHN, I'M NOT TELLING YOU AGAIN: GET IN THAT CAR AND YOUR ASS IS GRASS."
HAW! YOU KNOW DEMOCRATS, THEY NEVER LISTEN TO REASON. REMINDS ME OF THE TIME...
...IKE WAS OUT ON THE GREENS AS USUAL, AND I WAS STUCK WITH THE DIRTY WORK... AS USUAL...
...SO IT'S WHAT, IT'S APRIL '59 AND CASTRO'S IN TOWN SO GUESS WHO HAS TO TALK TO HIM...
TURN IT AROUND. YOU DON'T BELONG HERE.
I LIVE HERE, TOUGH GUY. YOU TOUGH ENOUGH TO KICK ME OUT?
IS THAT HIM? HE SHOULDN'T SEE ME!

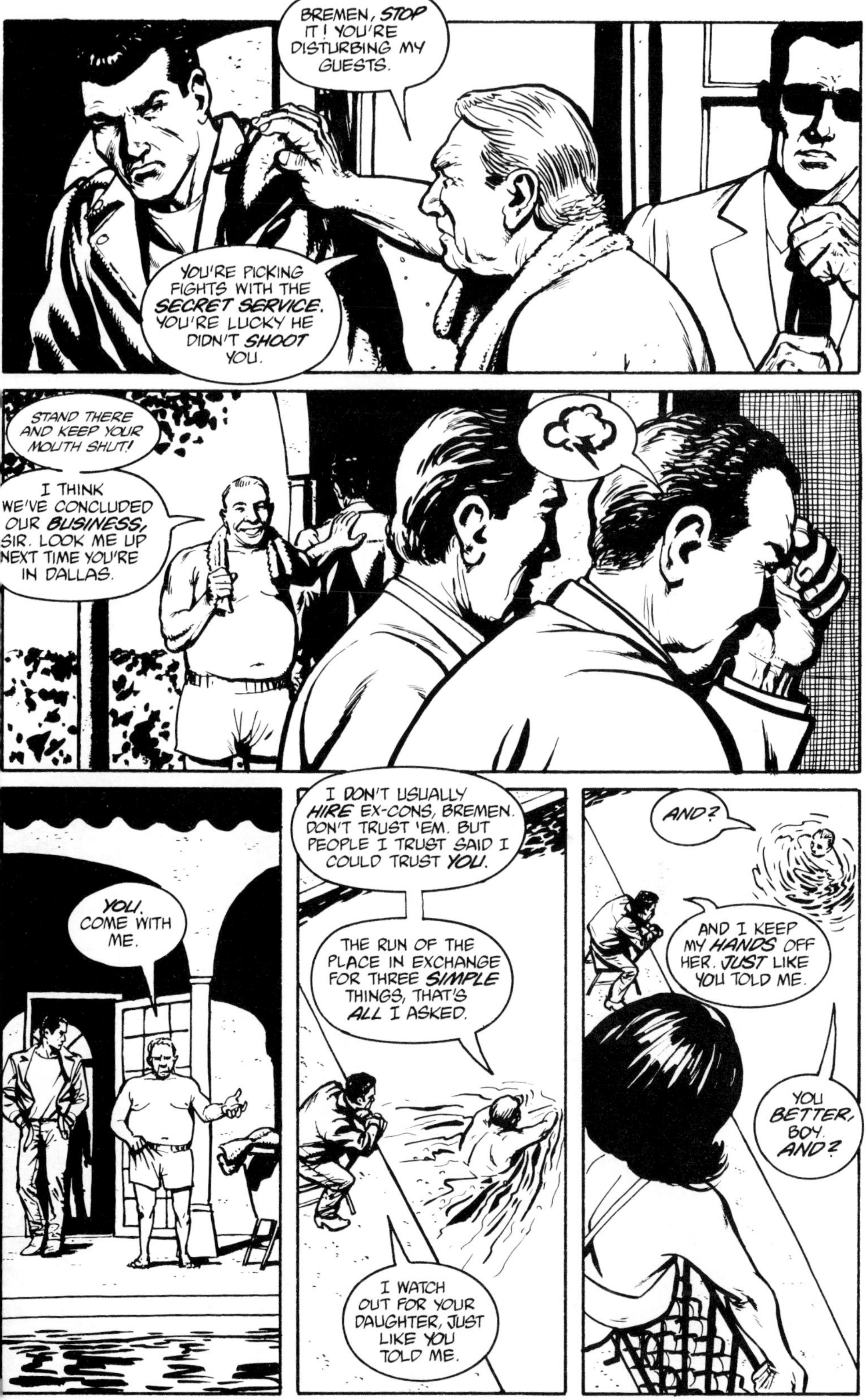
BREMEN, STOP IT! YOU'RE DISTURBING MY GUESTS.
YOU'RE PICKING FIGHTS WITH THE SECRET SERVICE. YOU'RE LUCKY HE DIDN'T SHOOT YOU.
STAND THERE AND KEEP YOUR MOUTH SHUT!
I THINK WE'VE CONCLUDED OUR BUSINESS, SIR. LOOK ME UP NEXT TIME YOU'RE IN DALLAS.
YOU. COME WITH ME.
I DON'T USUALLY HIRE EX-CONS, BREMEN. DON'T TRUST 'EM. BUT PEOPLE I TRUST SAID I COULD TRUST YOU.
THE RUN OF THE PLACE IN EXCHANGE FOR THREE SIMPLE THINGS, THAT'S ALL I ASKED.
I WATCH OUT FOR YOUR DAUGHTER, JUST LIKE YOU TOLD ME.
AND?
AND I KEEP MY HANDS OFF HER. JUST LIKE YOU TOLD ME.
YOU BETTER, BOY. AND?

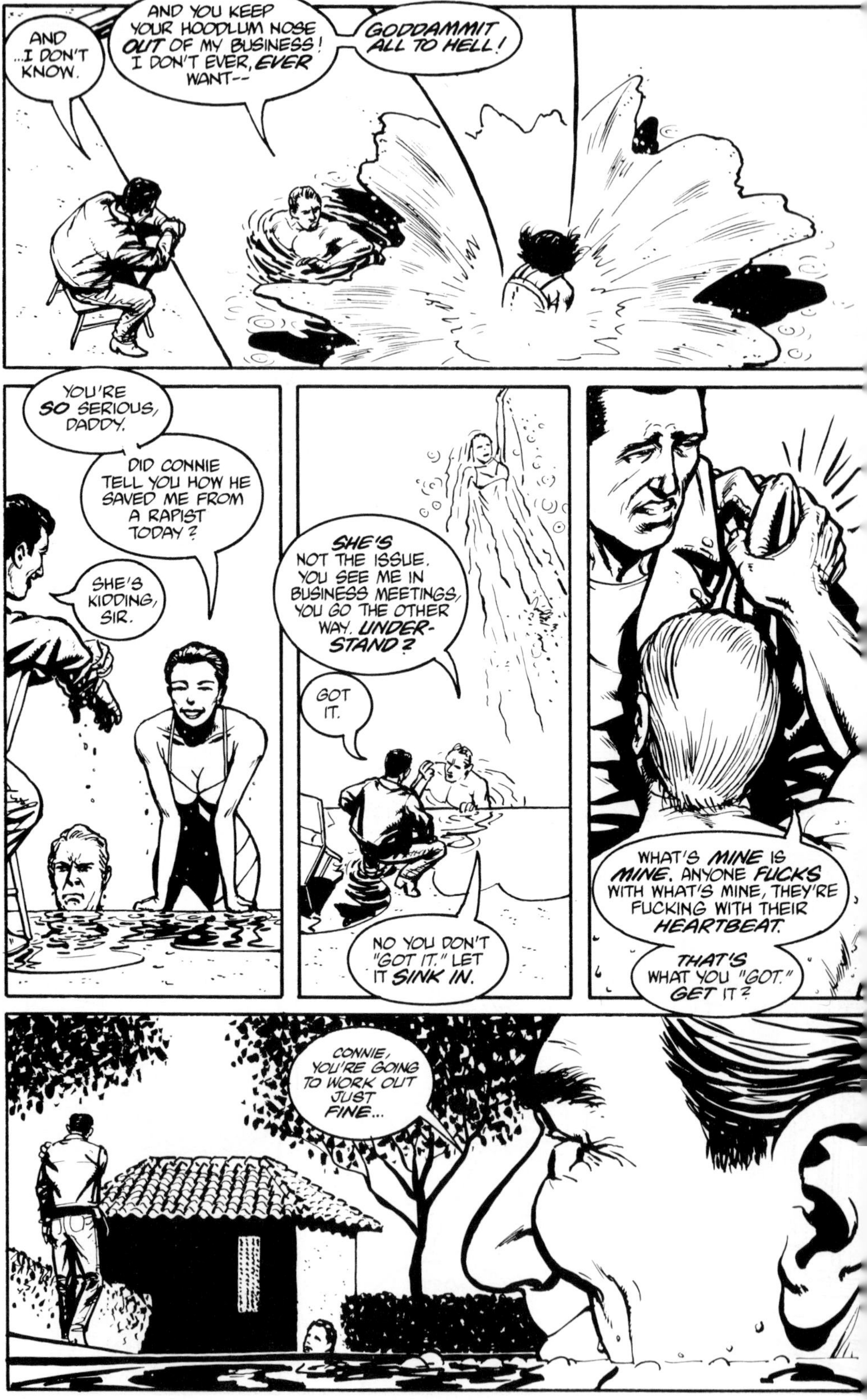
AND ...I DON'T KNOW.
AND YOU KEEP YOUR HOODLUM NOSE OUT OF MY BUSINESS! I DON'T EVER, EVER WANT--
GODDAMMIT ALL TO HELL!
YOU'RE SO SERIOUS, DADDY.
DID CONNIE TELL YOU HOW HE SAVED ME FROM A RAPIST TODAY?
SHE'S KIDDING, SIR.
SHE'S NOT THE ISSUE. YOU SEE ME IN BUSINESS MEETINGS, YOU GO THE OTHER WAY. UNDERSTAND?
GOT IT.
NO YOU DON'T "GOT IT." LET IT SINK IN.
WHAT'S MINE IS MINE. ANYONE FUCKS WITH WHAT'S MINE, THEY'RE FUCKING WITH THEIR HEARTBEAT.
THAT'S WHAT YOU "GOT." GET IT?
CONNIE, YOU'RE GOING TO WORK OUT JUST FINE...

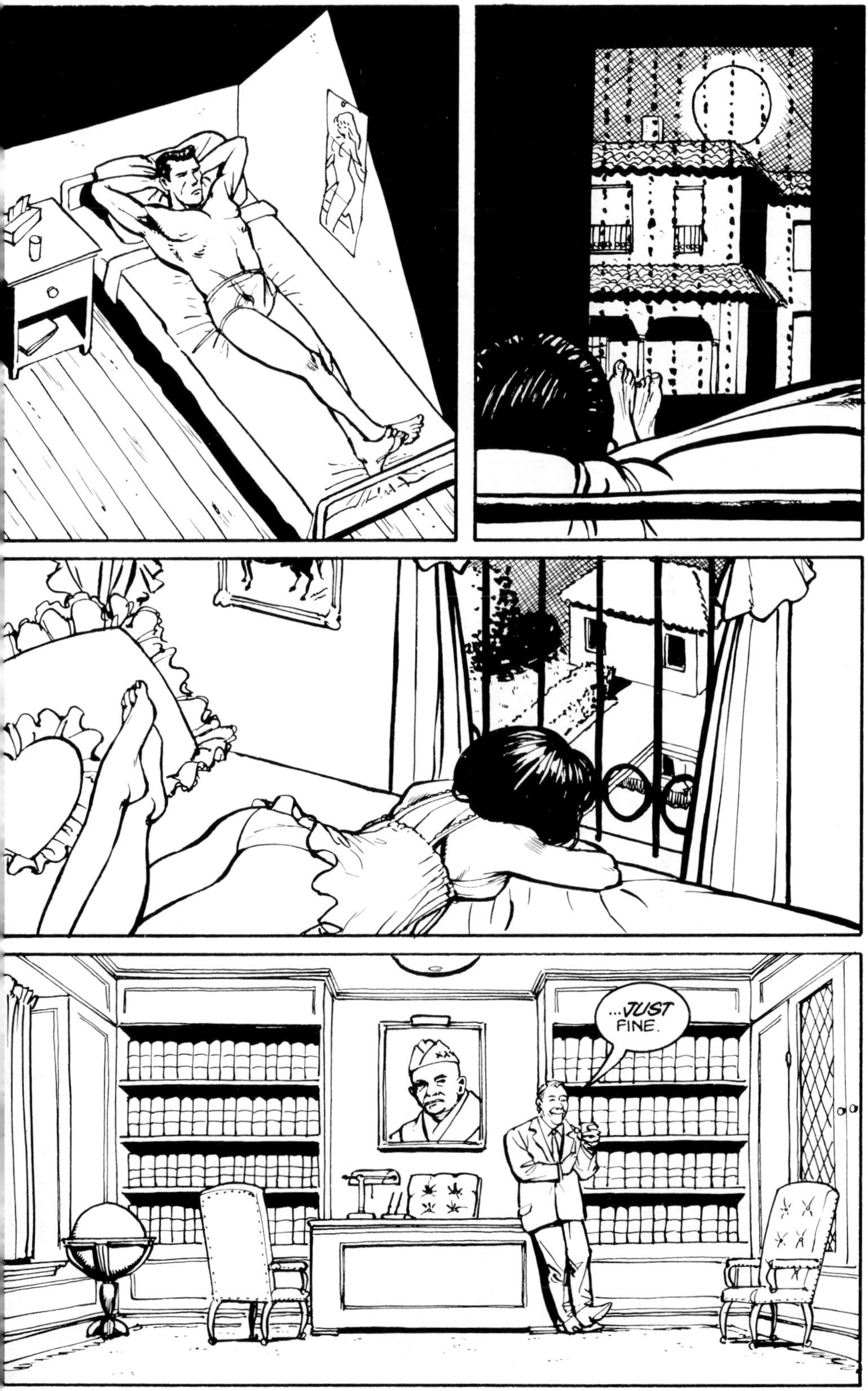
...JUST FINE.

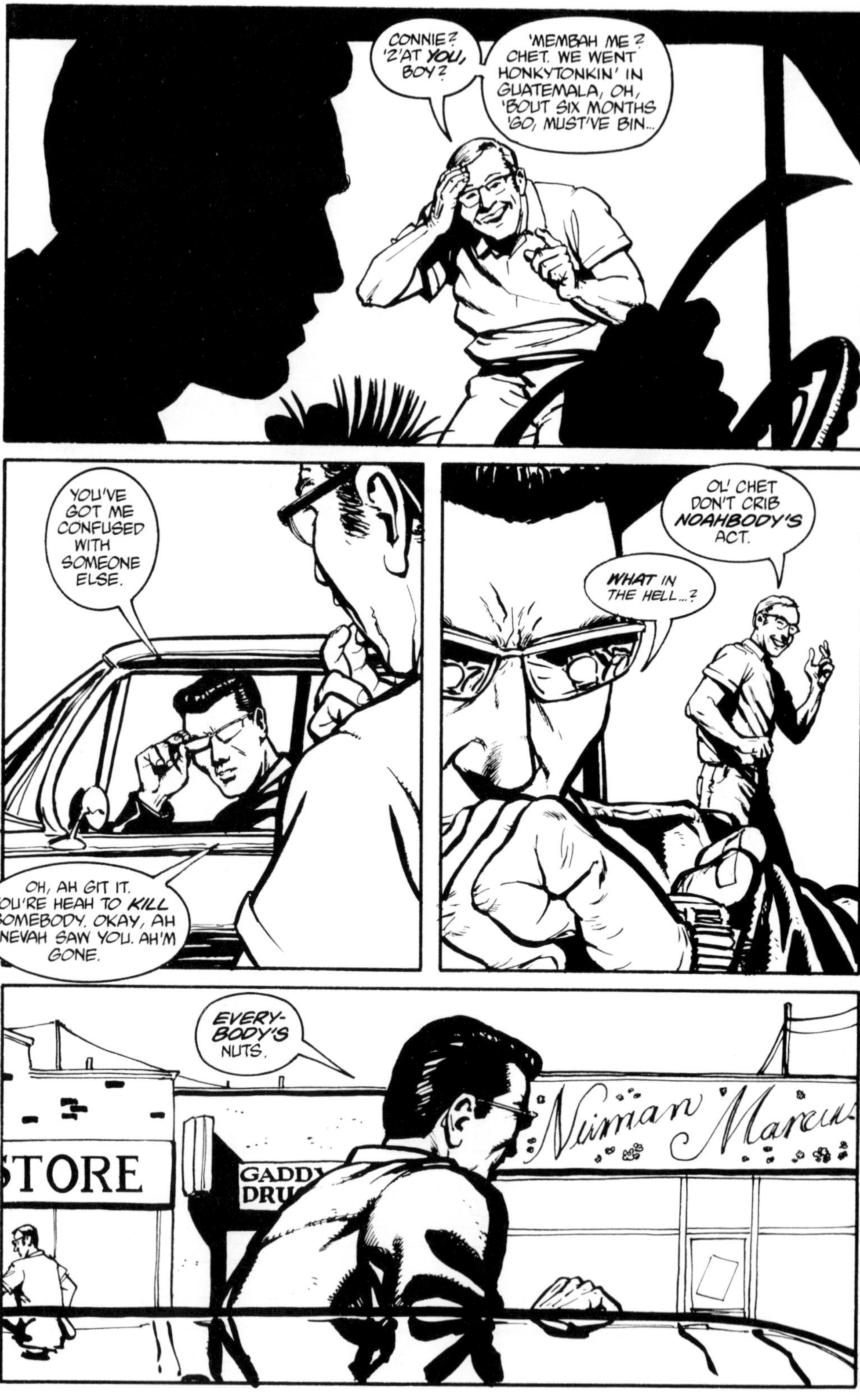
CONNIE? 'Z'AT YOU, BOY?
'MEMBAH ME? CHET. WE WENT HONKYTONKIN' IN GUATEMALA, OH, 'BOUT SIX MONTHS 'GO, MUST'VE BIN...
YOU'VE GOT ME CONFUSED WITH SOMEONE ELSE.
OH, AH GIT IT. YOU'RE HEAH TO KILL SOMEBODY. OKAY, AH NEVAH SAW YOU. AH'M GONE.
OL' CHET DON'T CRIB NOAHBODY'S ACT.
WHAT IN THE HELL...?
EVERY-BODY'S NUTS.
STORE
GADDY DRU
Niman Marcu

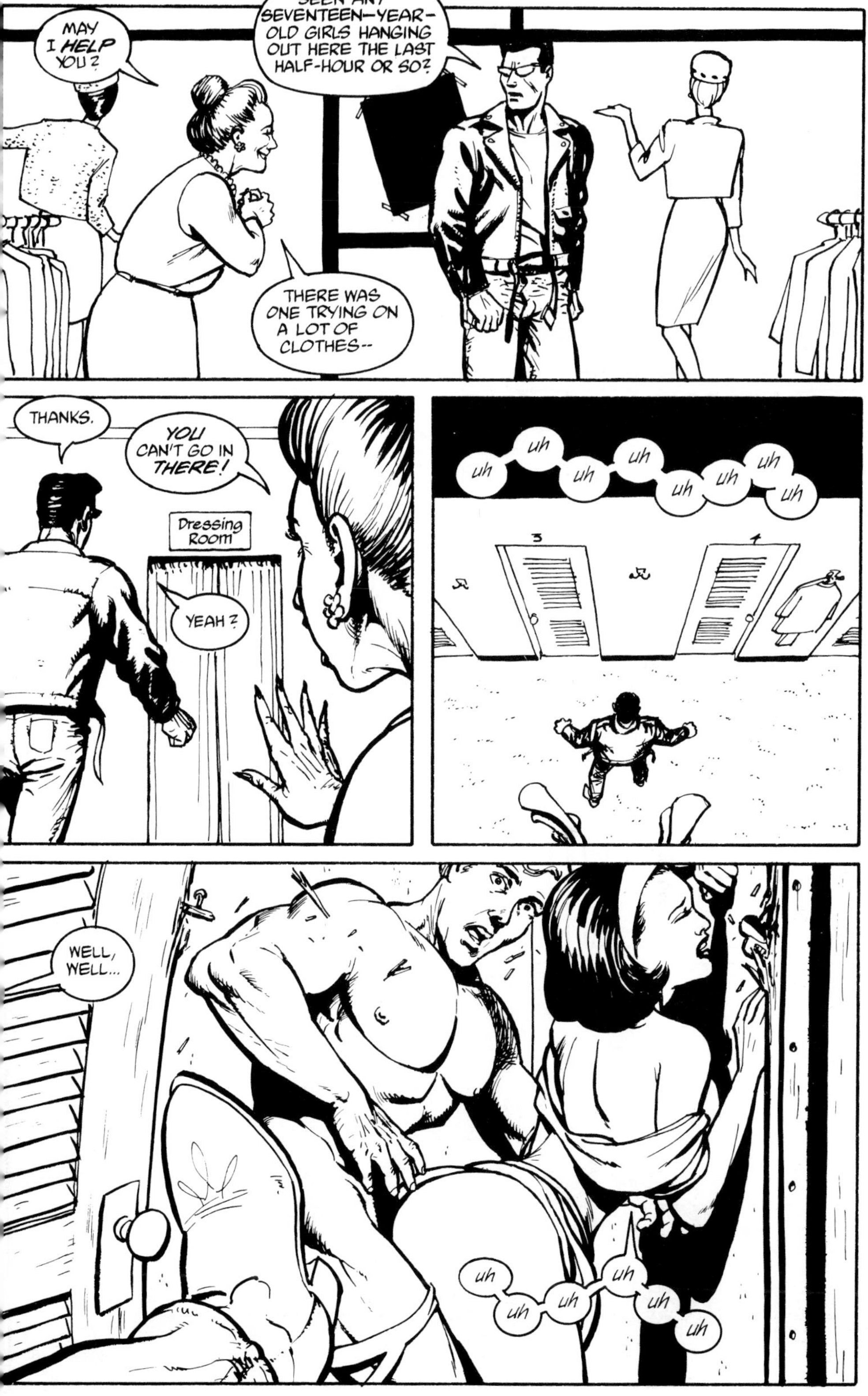
MAY I HELP YOU?
SEEN ANY SEVENTEEN-YEAR-OLD GIRLS HANGING OUT HERE THE LAST HALF-HOUR OR SO?
THERE WAS ONE TRYING ON A LOT OF CLOTHES--
THANKS.
YOU CAN'T GO IN THERE!
Dressing Room
YEAH?
uh uh uh uh uh uh uh uh
3
4
WELL, WELL...
uh uh uh uh uh uh

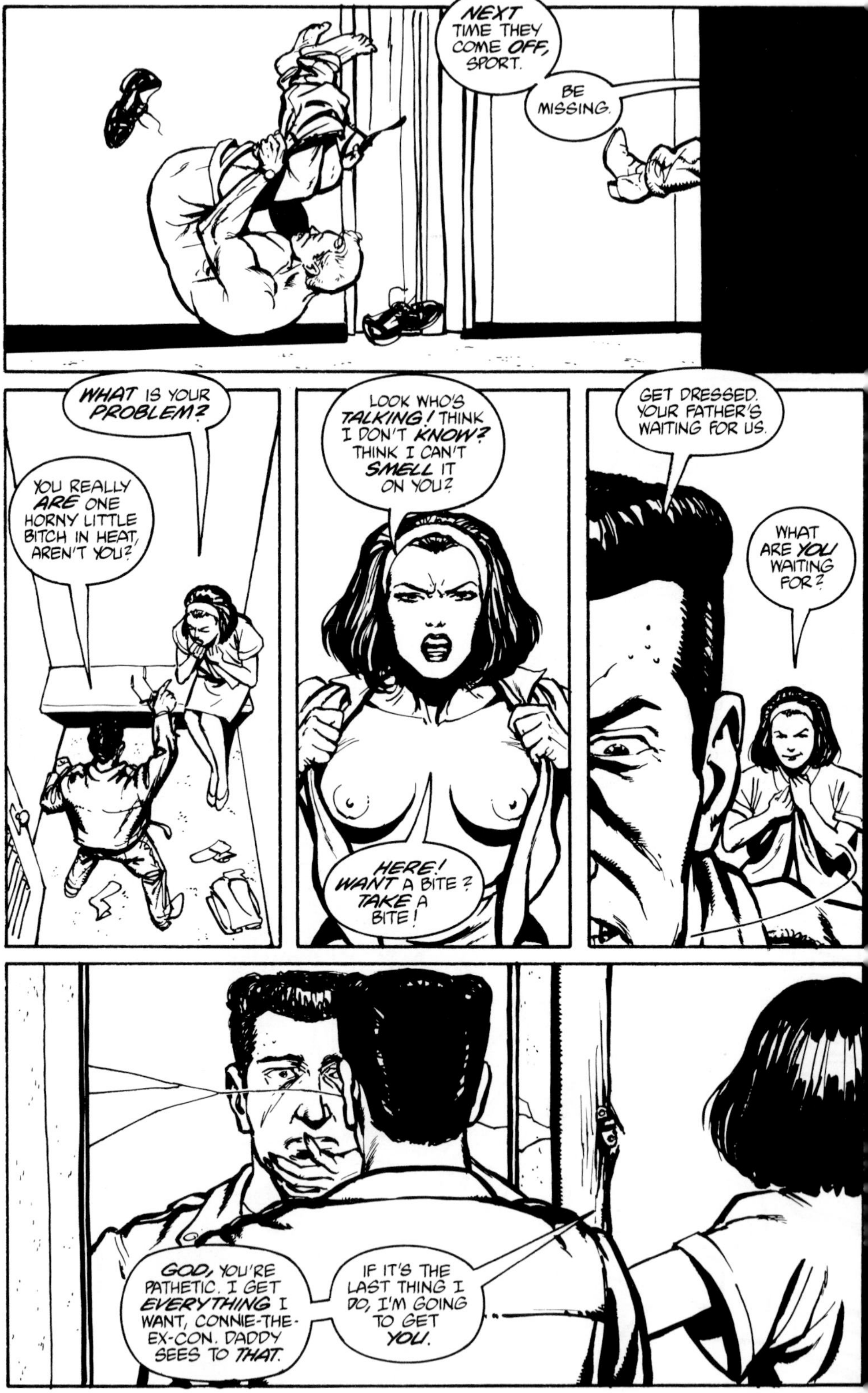
NEXT TIME THEY COME OFF, SPORT.
BE MISSING.
WHAT IS YOUR PROBLEM?
YOU REALLY ARE ONE HORNY LITTLE BITCH IN HEAT, AREN'T YOU?
LOOK WHO'S TALKING! THINK I DON'T KNOW? THINK I CAN'T SMELL IT ON YOU?
HERE! WANT A BITE? TAKE A BITE!
GET DRESSED. YOUR FATHER'S WAITING FOR US.
WHAT ARE YOU WAITING FOR?
GOD, YOU'RE PATHETIC. I GET EVERYTHING I WANT, CONNIE-THE-EX-CON. DADDY SEES TO THAT.
IF IT'S THE LAST THING I DO, I'M GOING TO GET YOU.

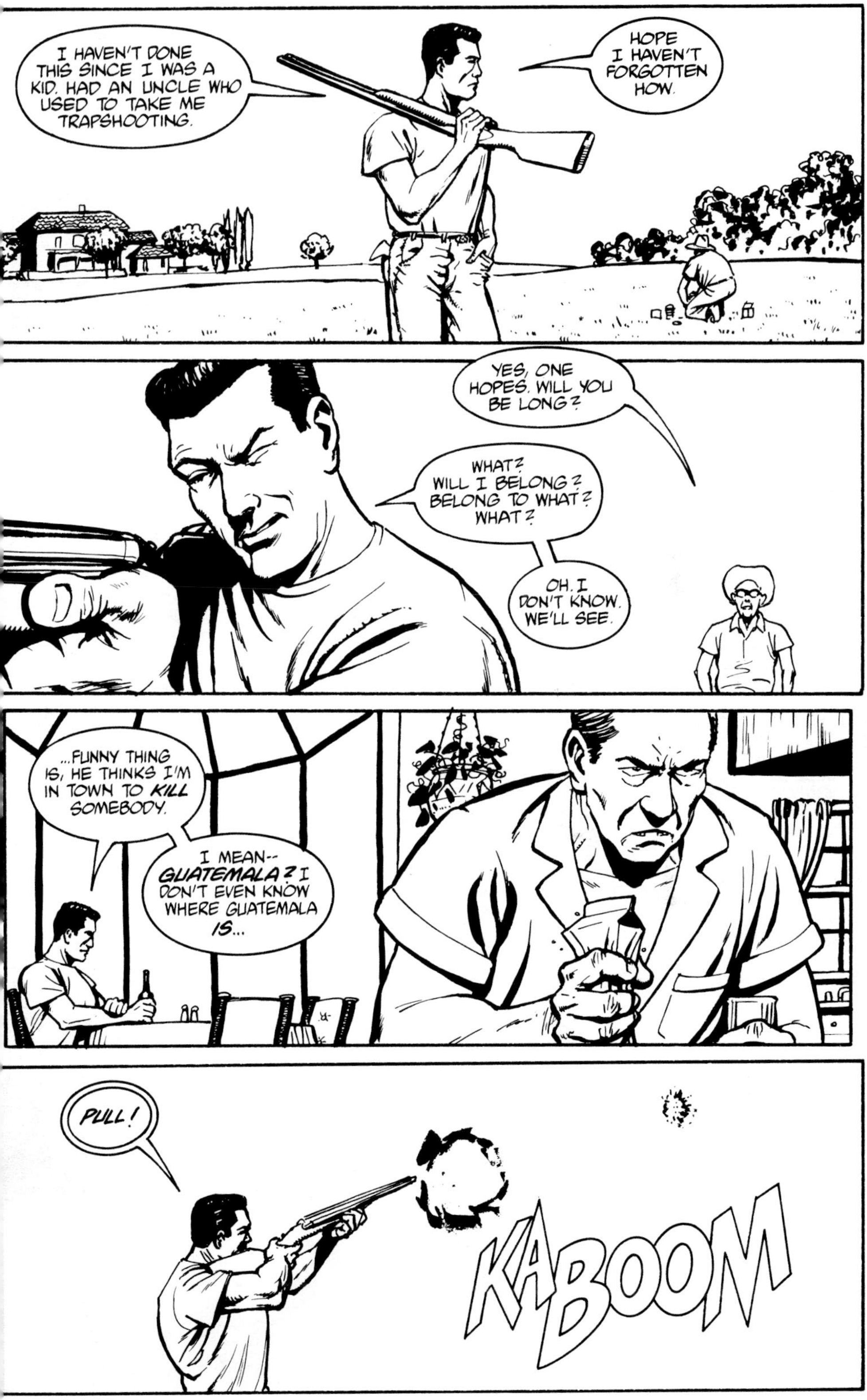
I HAVEN'T DONE THIS SINCE I WAS A KID. HAD AN UNCLE WHO USED TO TAKE ME TRAPSHOOTING.
HOPE I HAVEN'T FORGOTTEN HOW.
YES, ONE HOPES. WILL YOU BE LONG?
WHAT? WILL I BELONG? BELONG TO WHAT? WHAT?
OH. I DON'T KNOW. WE'LL SEE.
...FUNNY THING IS, HE THINKS I'M IN TOWN TO *KILL* SOMEBODY.
I MEAN-- *GUATEMALA?* I DON'T EVEN KNOW WHERE GUATEMALA *IS*...
PULL!
KABOOM

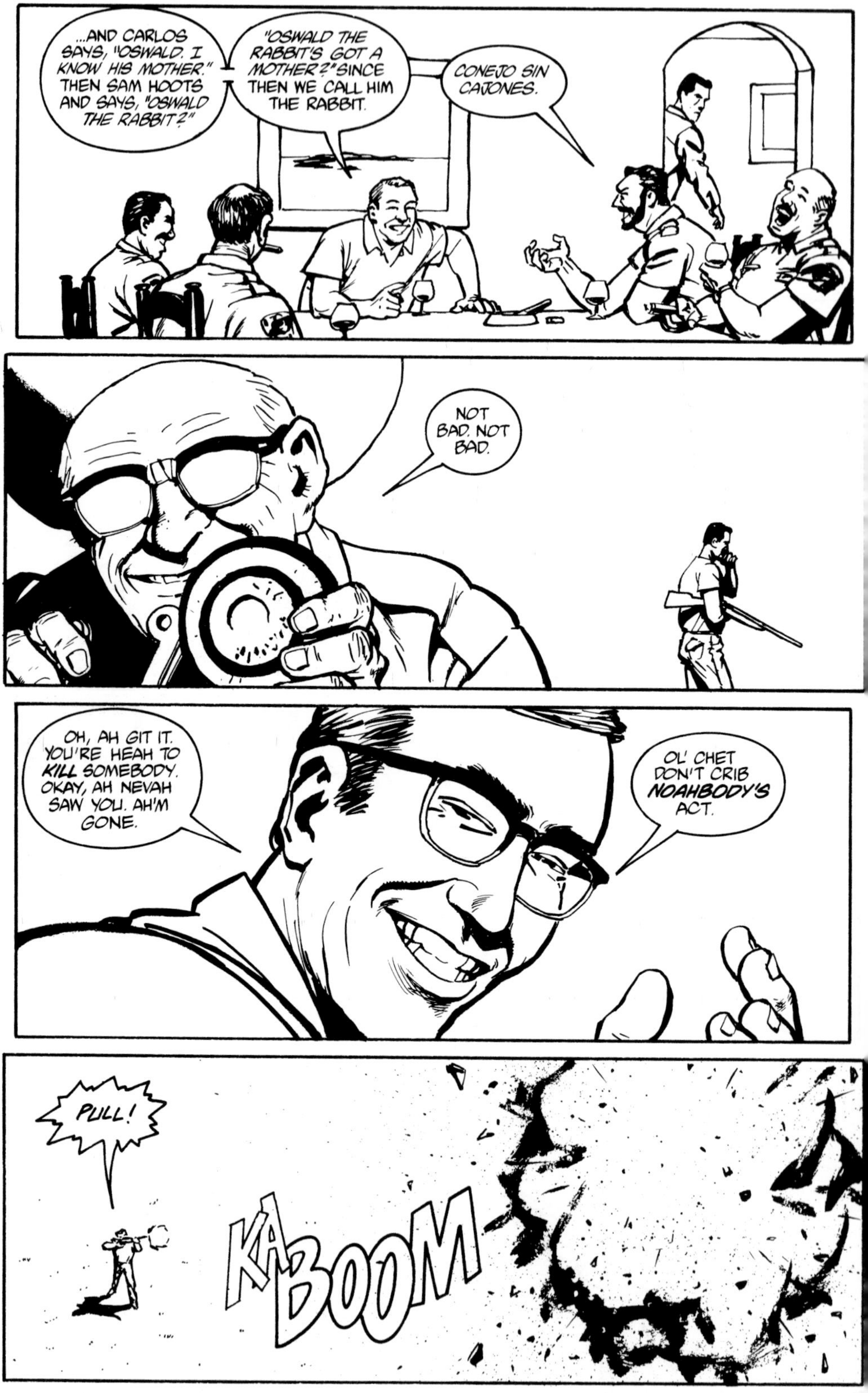
...AND CARLOS SAYS, "OSWALD. I KNOW HIS MOTHER." THEN SAM HOOTS AND SAYS, "OSWALD THE RABBIT?"
"OSWALD THE RABBIT'S GOT A MOTHER?" SINCE THEN WE CALL HIM THE RABBIT.
CONEJO SIN CAJONES.
NOT BAD. NOT BAD.
OH, AH GIT IT. YOU'RE HEAH TO **KILL** SOMEBODY. OKAY, AH NEVAH SAW YOU. AH'M GONE.
OL' CHET DON'T CRIB **NOAHBODY'S** ACT.
PULL!
KA BOOM

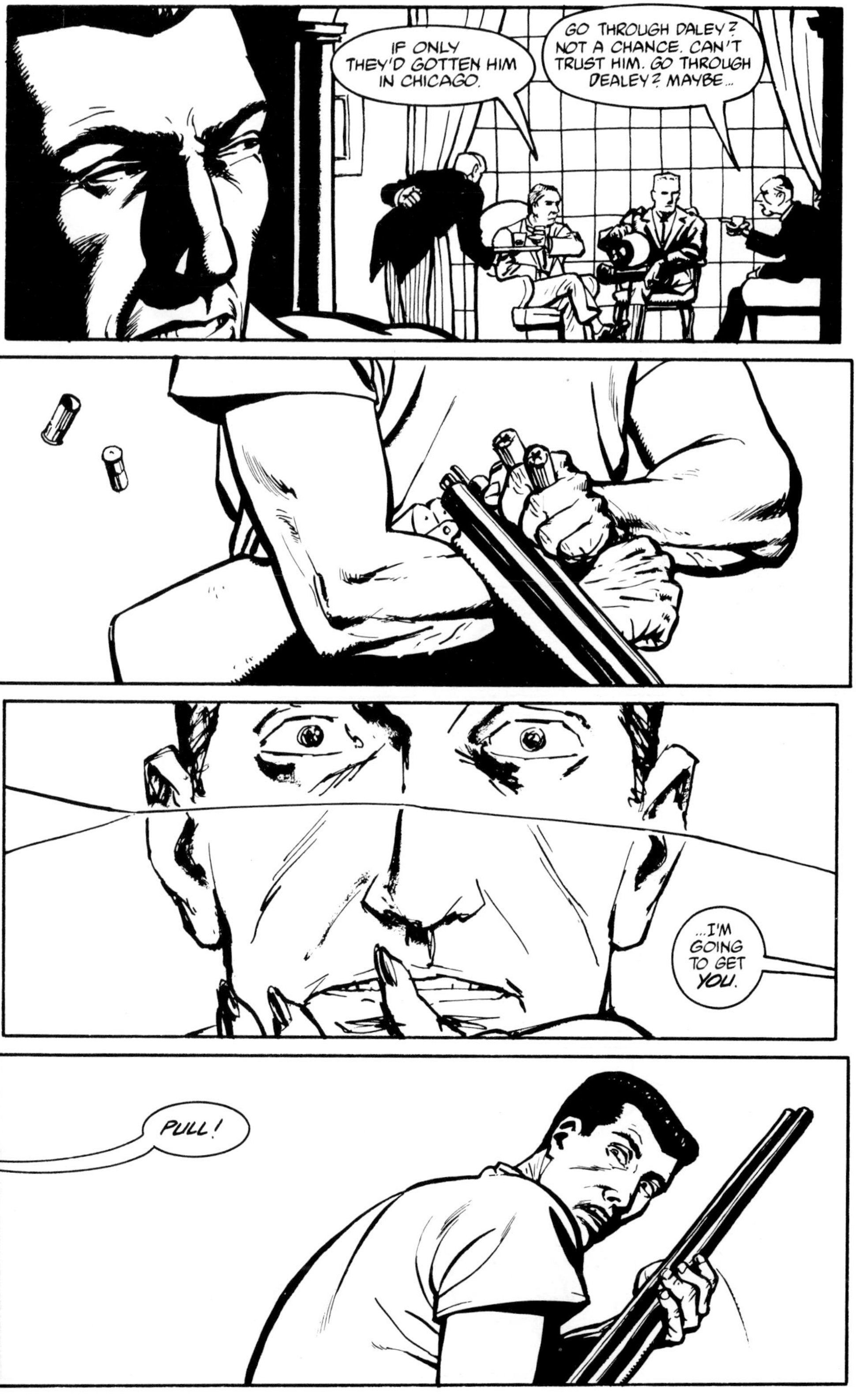
IF ONLY THEY'D GOTTEN HIM IN CHICAGO.
GO THROUGH DALEY? NOT A CHANCE. CAN'T TRUST HIM. GO THROUGH DEALEY? MAYBE...
...I'M GOING TO GET YOU.
PULL!

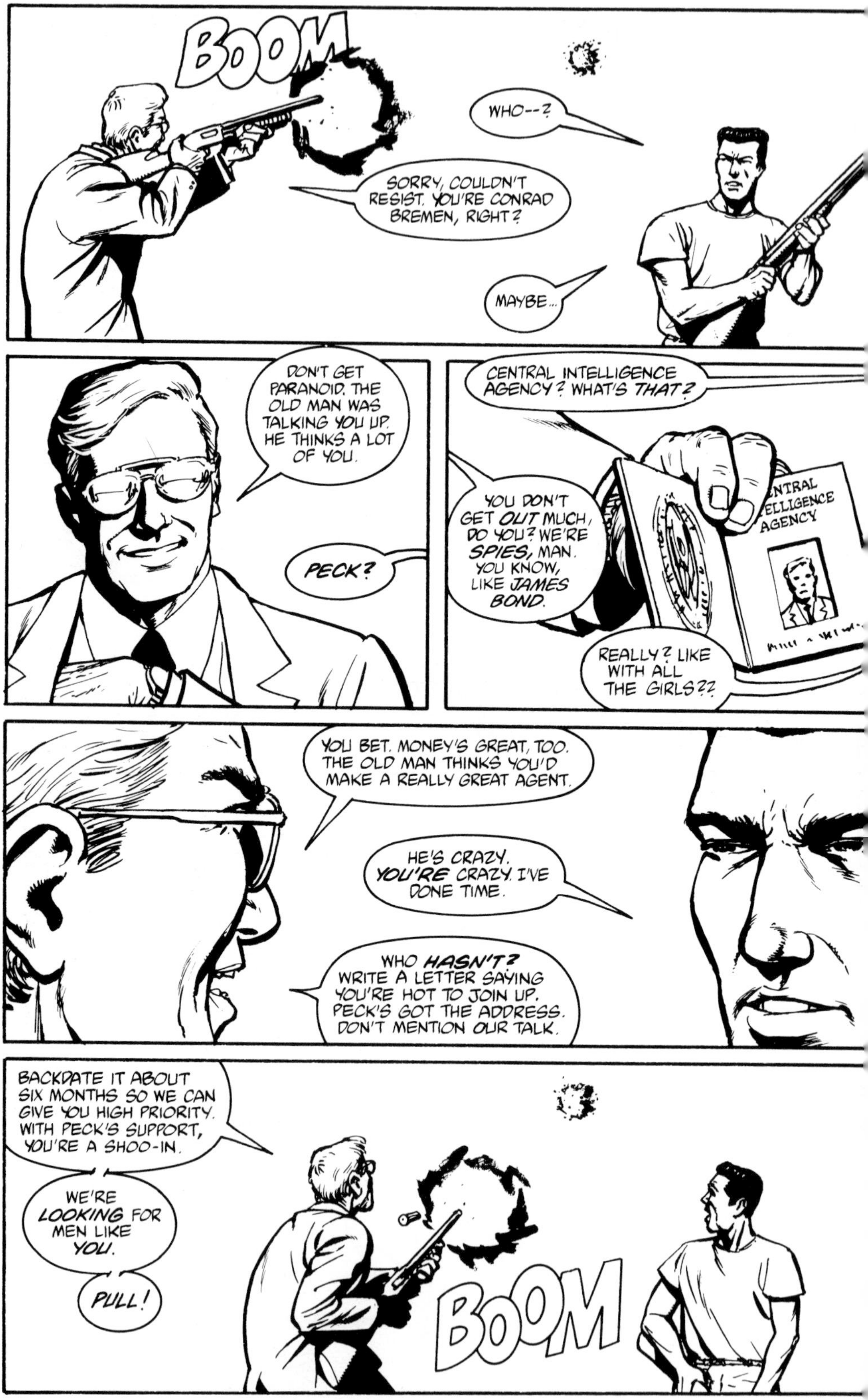
BOOM
WHO--?
SORRY, COULDN'T RESIST. YOU'RE CONRAD BREMEN, RIGHT?
MAYBE...
DON'T GET PARANOID. THE OLD MAN WAS TALKING YOU UP. HE THINKS A LOT OF YOU.
PECK?
CENTRAL INTELLIGENCE AGENCY? WHAT'S THAT?
YOU DON'T GET OUT MUCH, DO YOU? WE'RE SPIES, MAN. YOU KNOW, LIKE JAMES BOND.
AGENCY
REALLY? LIKE WITH ALL THE GIRLS??
YOU BET. MONEY'S GREAT, TOO. THE OLD MAN THINKS YOU'D MAKE A REALLY GREAT AGENT.
HE'S CRAZY. YOU'RE CRAZY. I'VE DONE TIME.
WHO HASN'T? WRITE A LETTER SAYING YOU'RE HOT TO JOIN UP. PECK'S GOT THE ADDRESS. DON'T MENTION OUR TALK.
BACKDATE IT ABOUT SIX MONTHS SO WE CAN GIVE YOU HIGH PRIORITY. WITH PECK'S SUPPORT, YOU'RE A SHOO-IN.
WE'RE LOOKING FOR MEN LIKE YOU.
PULL!
BOOM

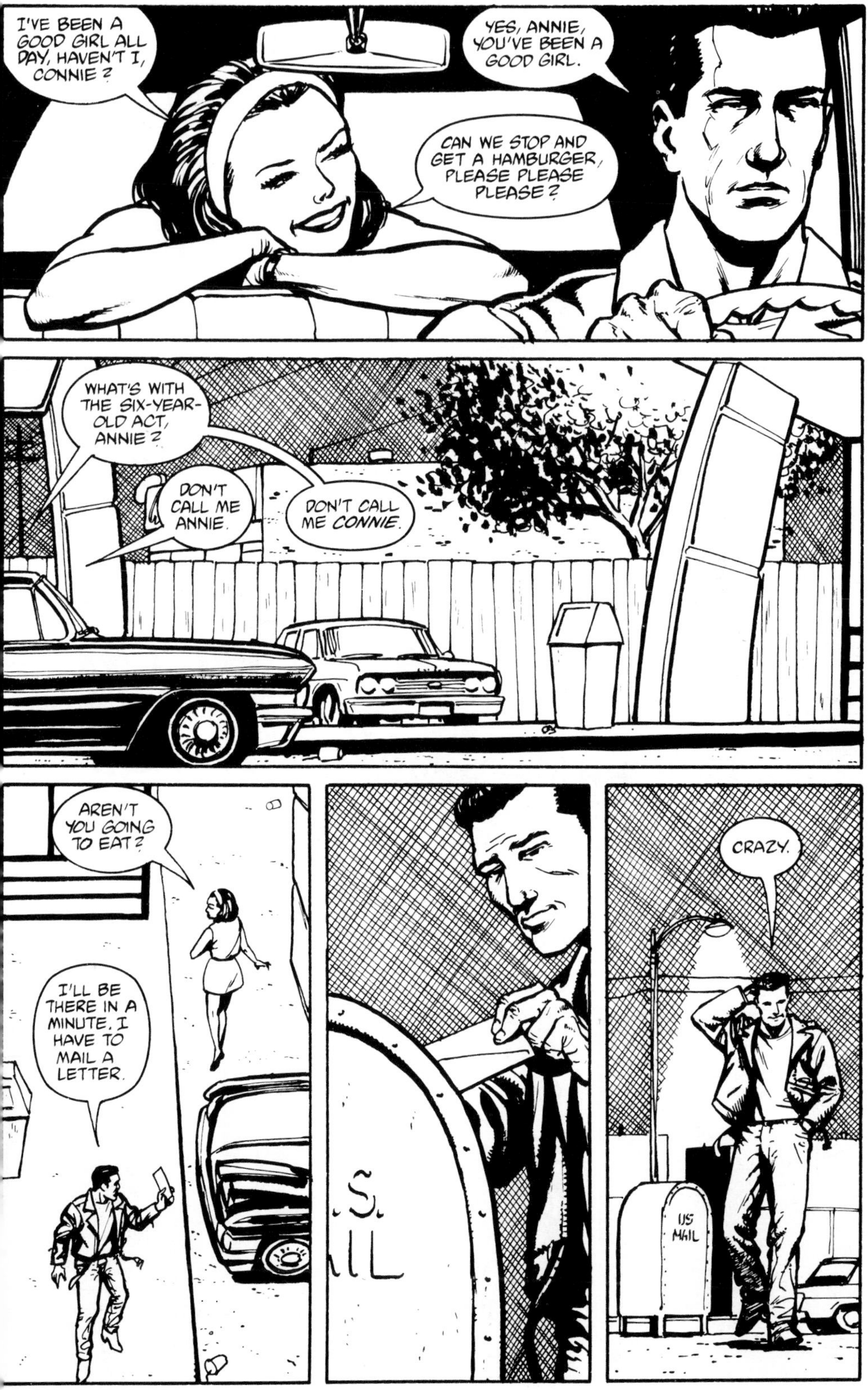

I'VE BEEN A GOOD GIRL ALL DAY, HAVEN'T I, CONNIE?
YES, ANNIE, YOU'VE BEEN A GOOD GIRL.
CAN WE STOP AND GET A HAMBURGER, PLEASE PLEASE PLEASE?
WHAT'S WITH THE SIX-YEAR-OLD ACT, ANNIE?
DON'T CALL ME ANNIE.
DON'T CALL ME *CONNIE*.
AREN'T YOU GOING TO EAT?
I'LL BE THERE IN A MINUTE. I HAVE TO MAIL A LETTER.
CRAZY.
US MAIL

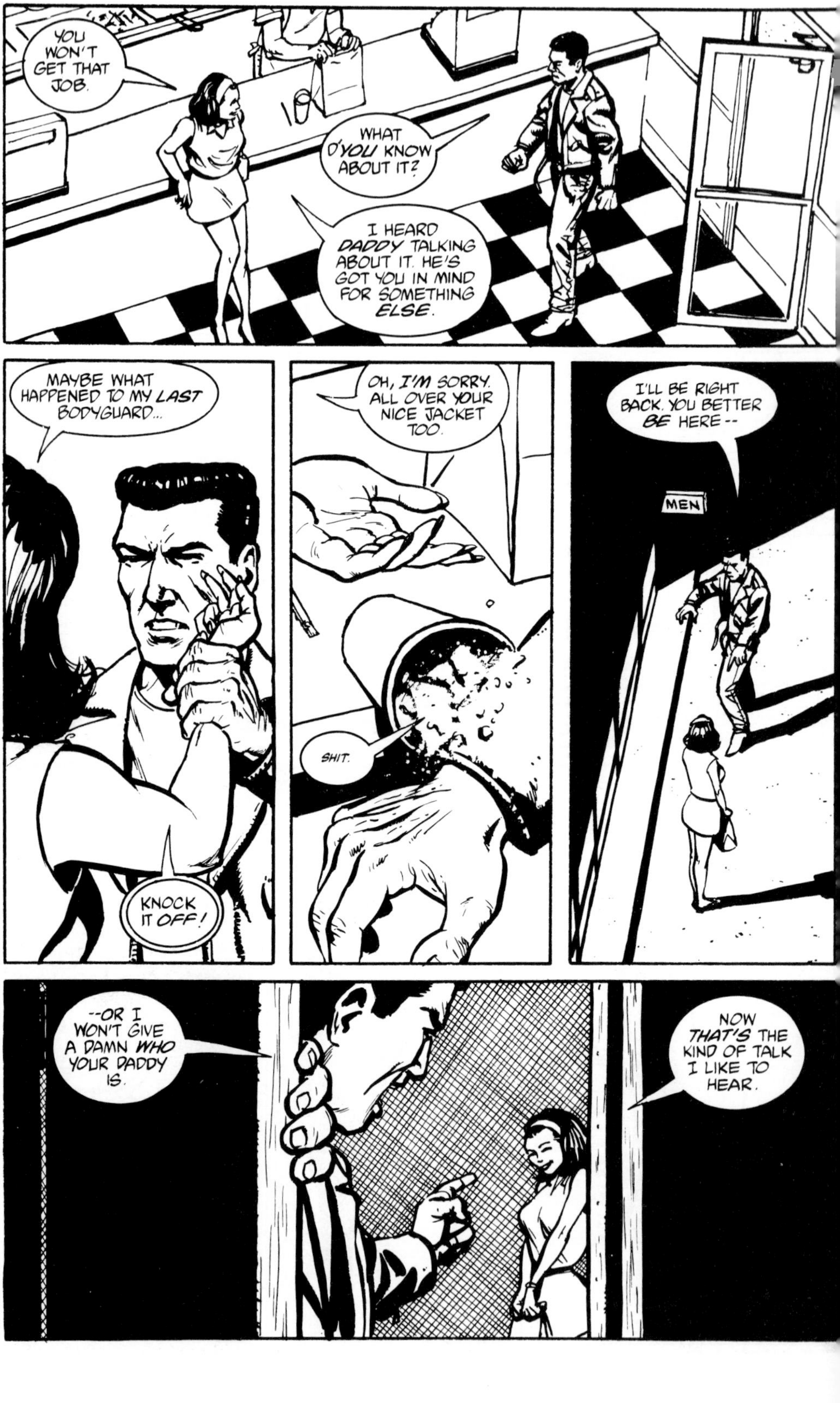
YOU WON'T GET THAT JOB.
WHAT D'YOU KNOW ABOUT IT?
I HEARD DADDY TALKING ABOUT IT. HE'S GOT YOU IN MIND FOR SOMETHING ELSE.
MAYBE WHAT HAPPENED TO MY LAST BODYGUARD...
KNOCK IT OFF!
OH, I'M SORRY. ALL OVER YOUR NICE JACKET TOO.
SHIT.
I'LL BE RIGHT BACK. YOU BETTER BE HERE --
MEN
--OR I WON'T GIVE A DAMN WHO YOUR DADDY IS.
NOW THAT'S THE KIND OF TALK I LIKE TO HEAR.

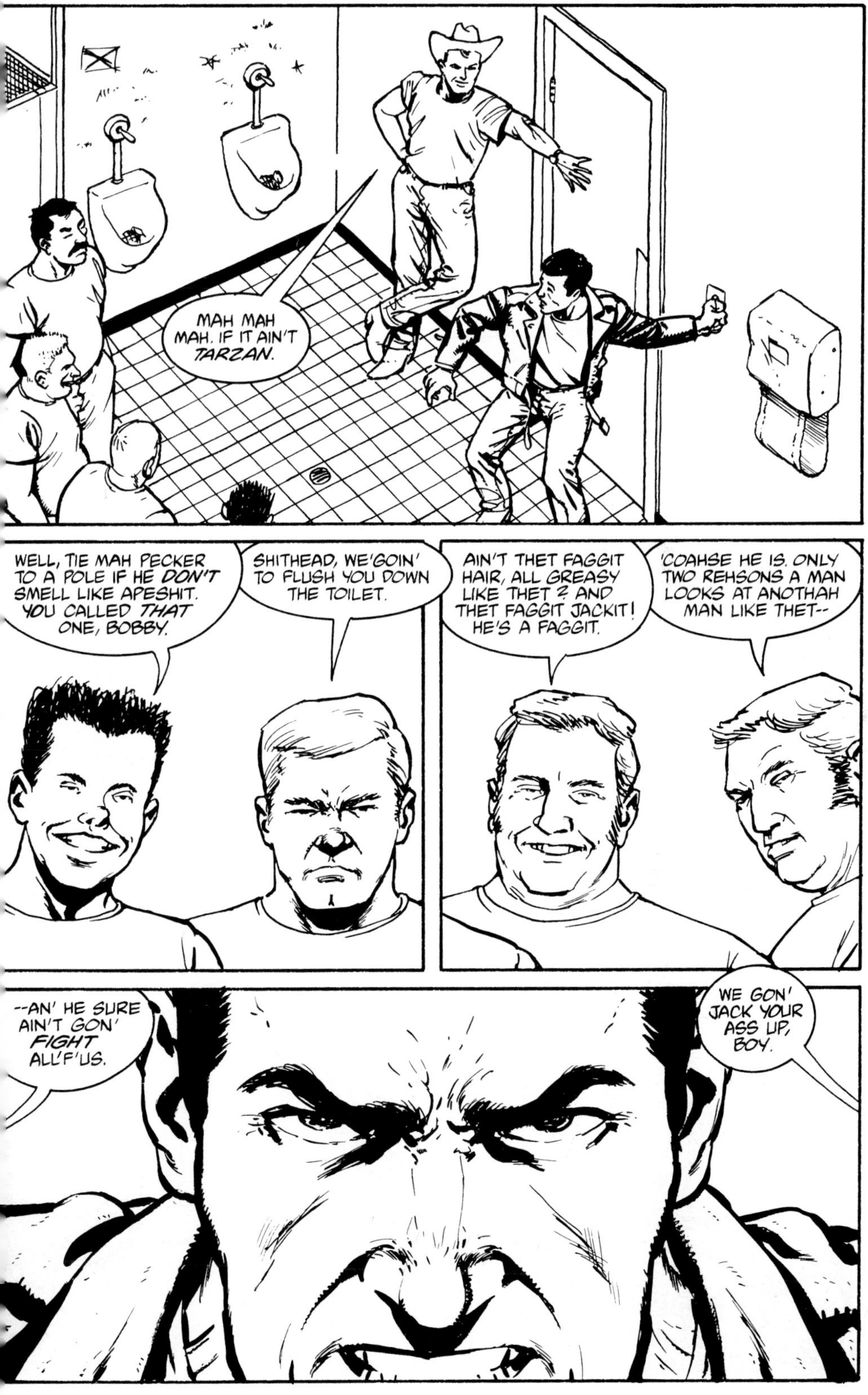
MAH MAH MAH. IF IT AIN'T *TARZAN.*
WELL, TIE MAH PECKER TO A POLE IF HE *DON'T* SMELL LIKE APESHIT. *YOU* CALLED *THAT* ONE, BOBBY.
SHITHEAD, WE'GOIN' TO FLUSH YOU DOWN THE TOILET.
AIN'T THET FAGGIT HAIR, ALL GREASY LIKE THET? AND THET FAGGIT JACKIT! HE'S A FAGGIT.
'COAHSE HE IS. ONLY TWO REHSONS A MAN LOOKS AT ANOTHAH MAN LIKE THET--
--AN' HE SURE AIN'T GON' *FIGHT* ALL'F'US.
WE GON' JACK YOUR ASS UP, BOY.

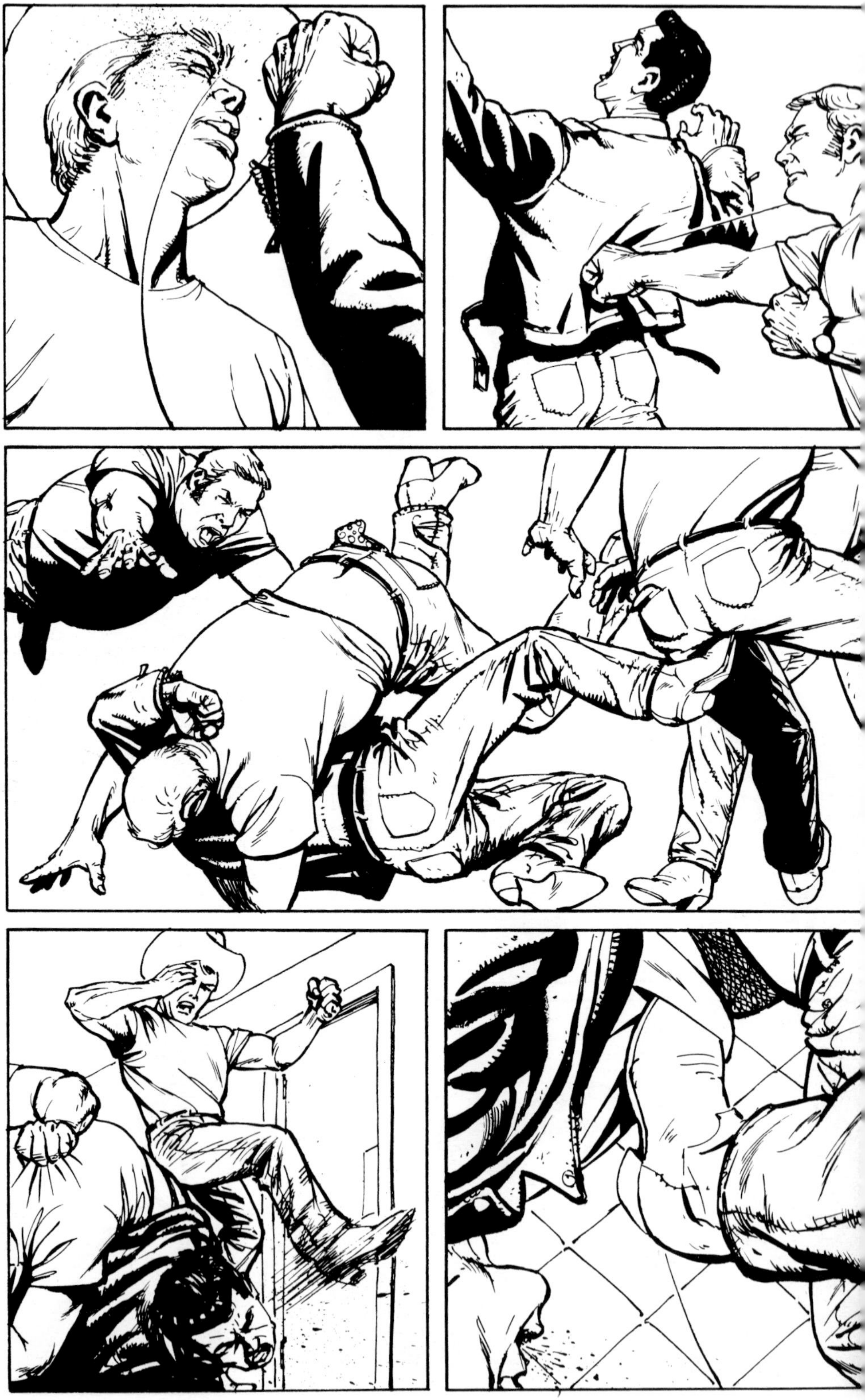

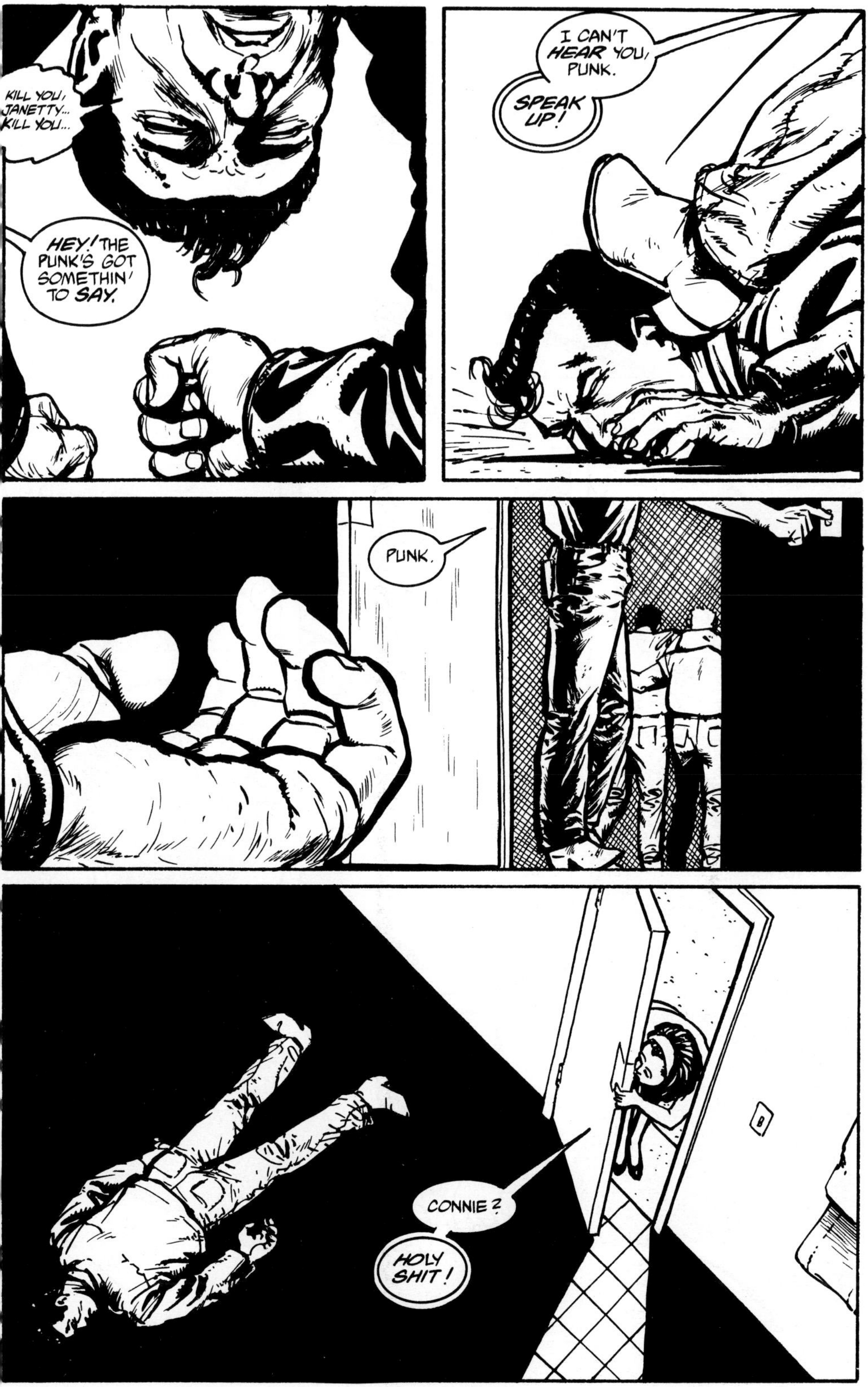

KILL YOU, JANETTY... KILL YOU...
HEY! THE PUNK'S GOT SOMETHIN' TO SAY.
I CAN'T HEAR YOU, PUNK.
SPEAK UP!
PUNK.
CONNIE?
HOLY SHIT!

CONNIE? YOU FEELING BETTER? I'VE BEEN TAKING CARE OF YOU.

DADDY DOESN'T KNOW. HE HAD TO GO TO NEW ORLEANS ON BUSINESS.

WE'VE GOT THE WHOLE PLACE TO OURSELVES.

DIDN'T YOU HEAR ME, CONNIE?

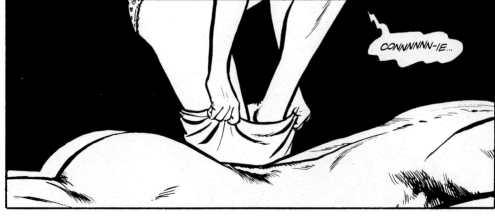

CONNNNNN-IE...

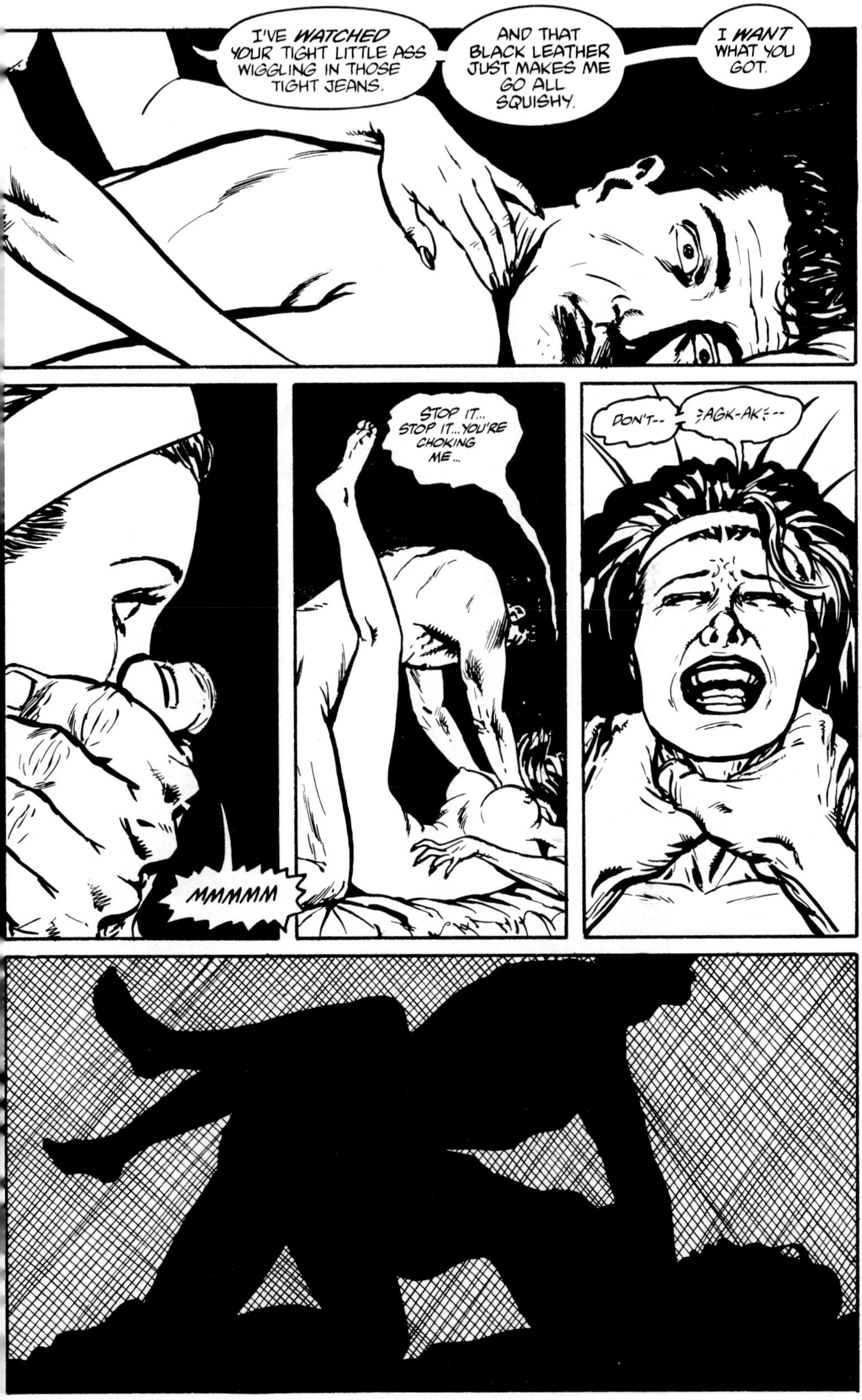
I'VE WATCHED YOUR TIGHT LITTLE ASS WIGGLING IN THOSE TIGHT JEANS.
AND THAT BLACK LEATHER JUST MAKES ME GO ALL SQUISHY.
I WANT WHAT YOU GOT.
MMMMM
STOP IT... STOP IT... YOU'RE CHOKING ME...
DON'T--
AGK-AK--

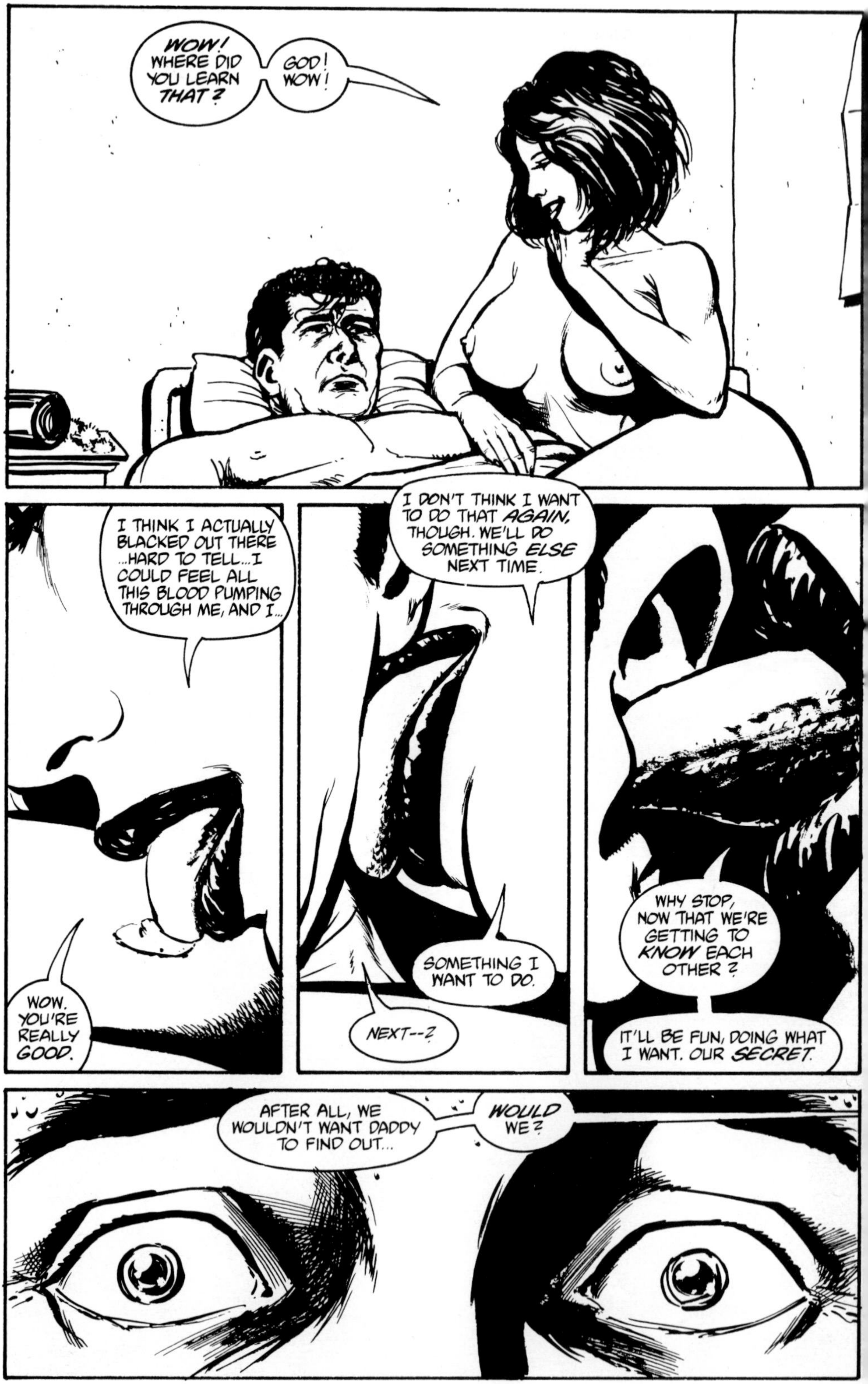
WOW! WHERE DID YOU LEARN THAT?
GOD! WOW!
I THINK I ACTUALLY BLACKED OUT THERE ...HARD TO TELL...I COULD FEEL ALL THIS BLOOD PUMPING THROUGH ME, AND I...
WOW. YOU'RE REALLY GOOD.
I DON'T THINK I WANT TO DO THAT AGAIN, THOUGH. WE'LL DO SOMETHING ELSE NEXT TIME.
SOMETHING I WANT TO DO.
NEXT--?
WHY STOP, NOW THAT WE'RE GETTING TO KNOW EACH OTHER?
IT'LL BE FUN, DOING WHAT I WANT. OUR SECRET.
AFTER ALL, WE WOULDN'T WANT DADDY TO FIND OUT...
WOULD WE?

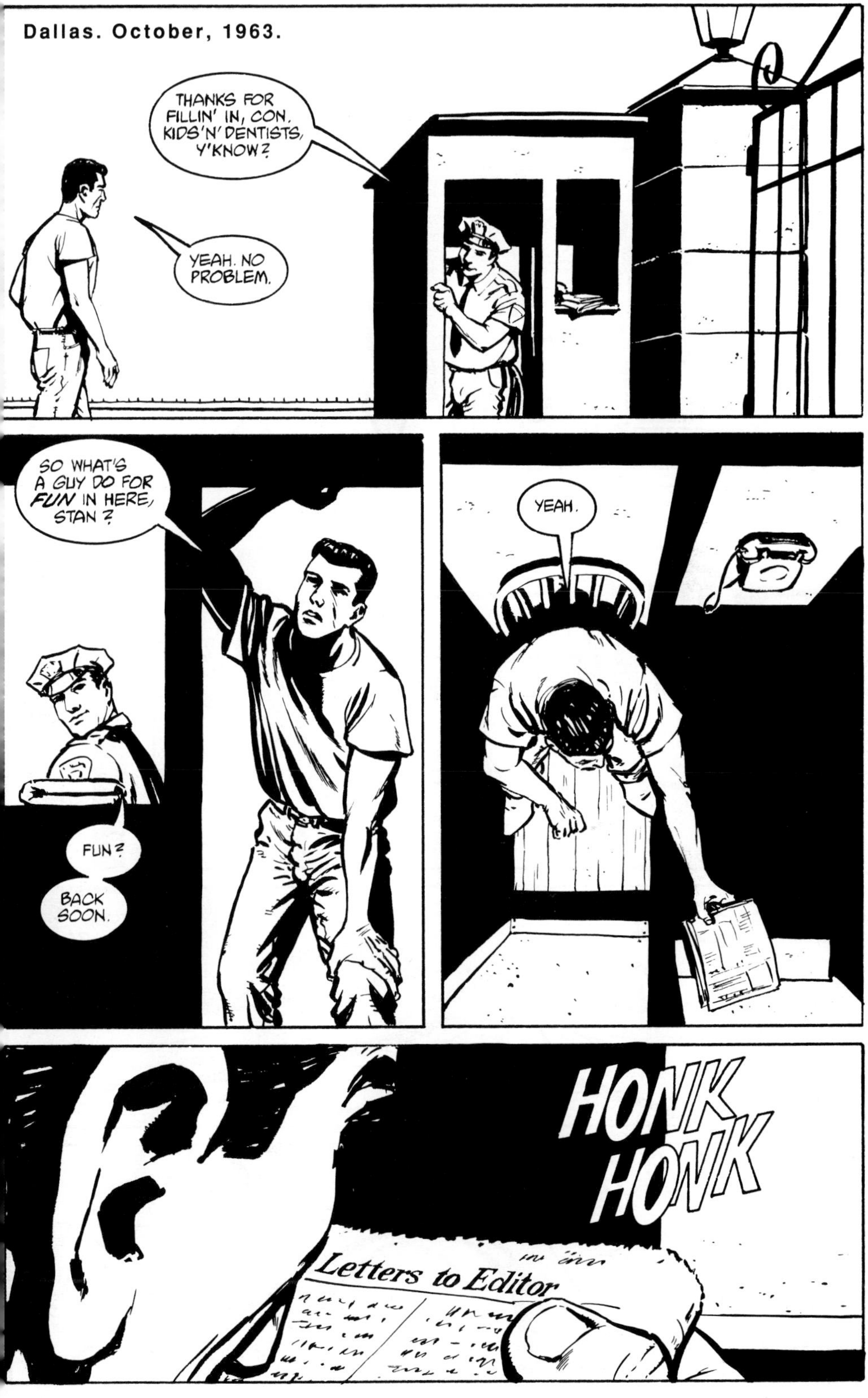
Dallas. October, 1963.
THANKS FOR FILLIN' IN, CON. KIDS'N'DENTISTS, Y'KNOW?
YEAH. NO PROBLEM.
SO WHAT'S A GUY DO FOR FUN IN HERE, STAN?
FUN?
BACK SOON.
YEAH.
HONK
HONK
Letters to Editor

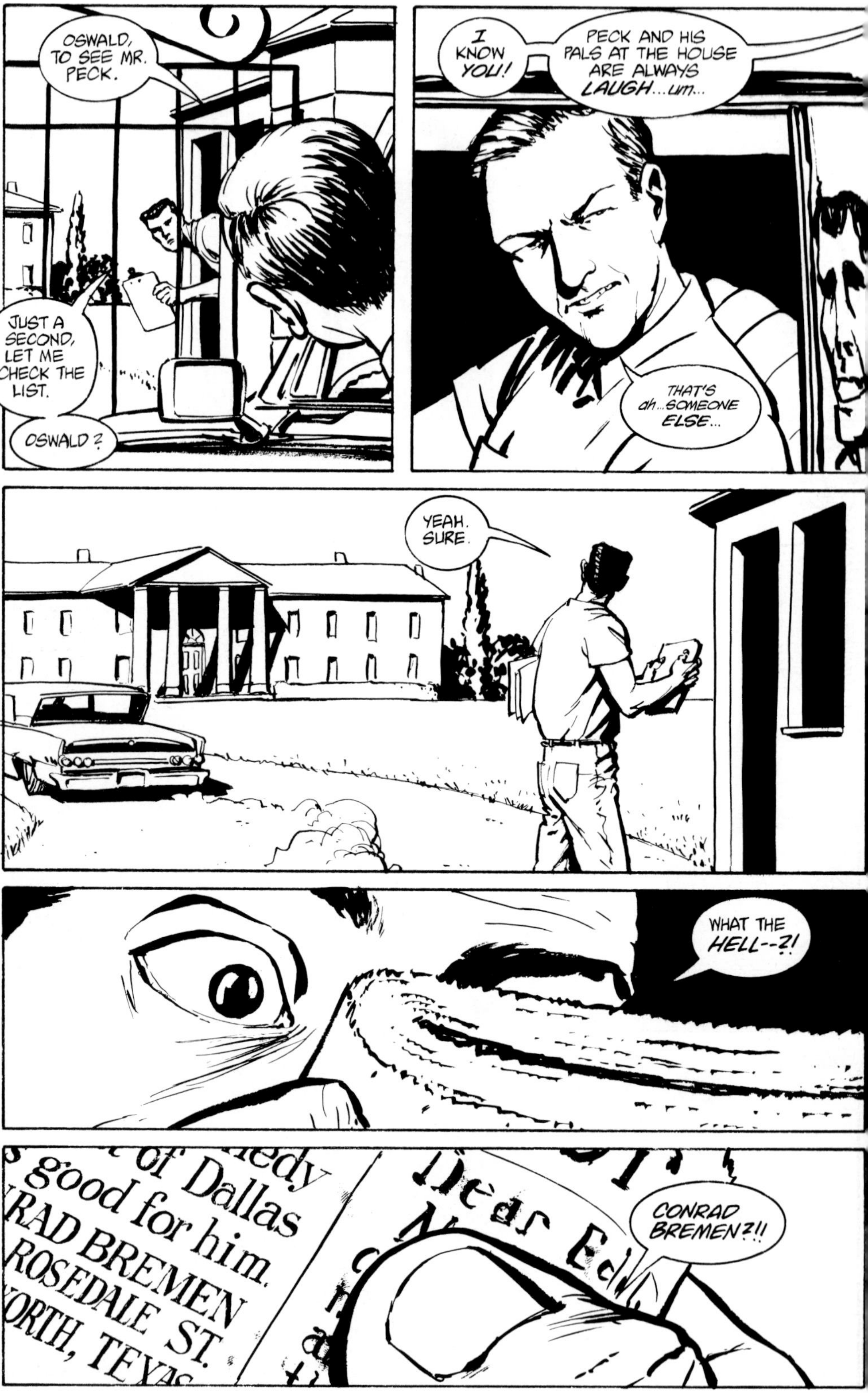
OSWALD, TO SEE MR. PECK.
JUST A SECOND, LET ME CHECK THE LIST.
OSWALD?
I KNOW YOU!
PECK AND HIS PALS AT THE HOUSE ARE ALWAYS LAUGH...um...
THAT'S ah...SOMEONE ELSE...
YEAH. SURE.
WHAT THE HELL--?!
CONRAD BREMEN?!!

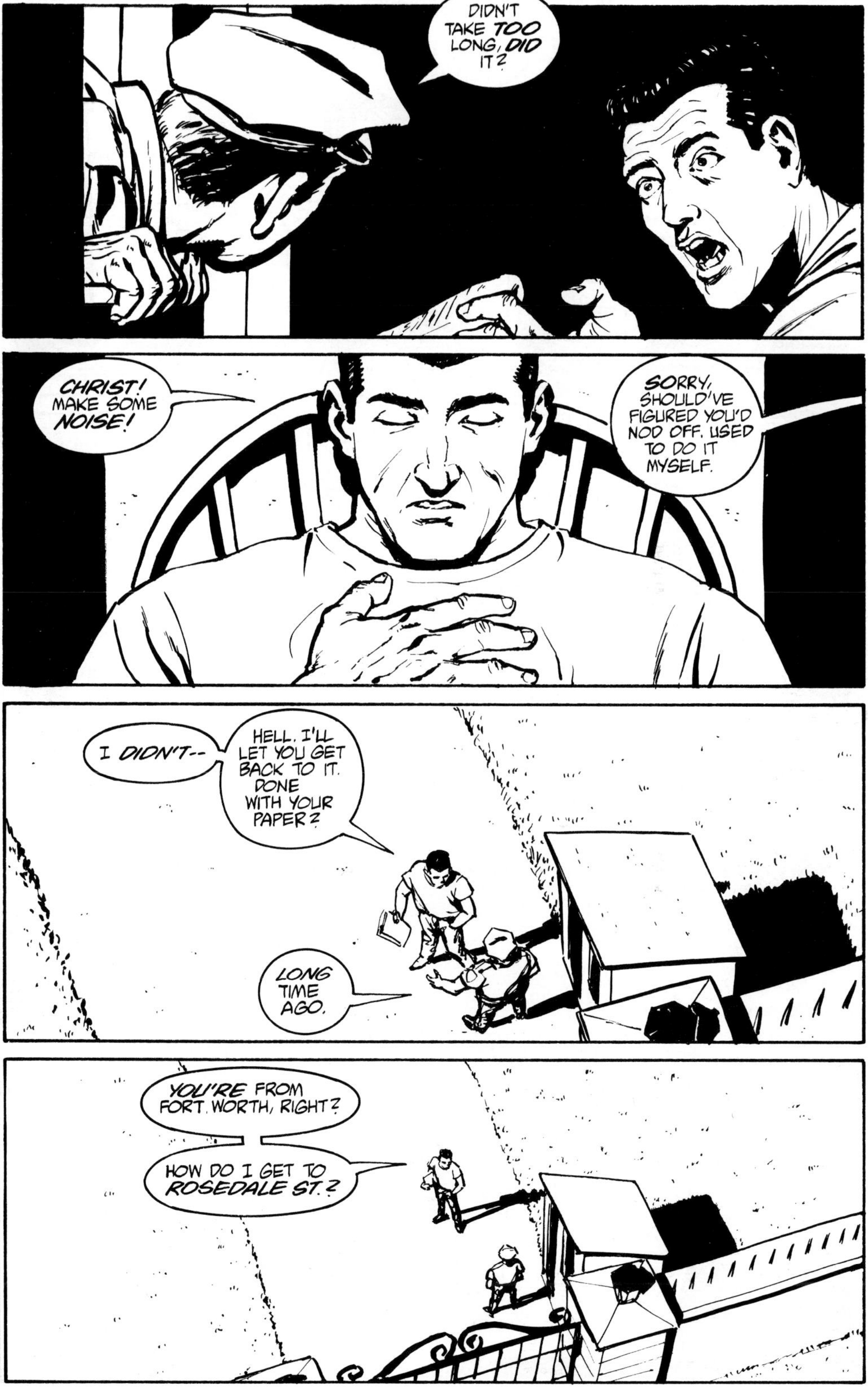
DIDN'T TAKE TOO LONG, DID IT?
CHRIST! MAKE SOME NOISE!
SORRY, SHOULD'VE FIGURED YOU'D NOD OFF. USED TO DO IT MYSELF.
I DIDN'T--
HELL, I'LL LET YOU GET BACK TO IT. DONE WITH YOUR PAPER?
LONG TIME AGO.
YOU'RE FROM FORT WORTH, RIGHT?
HOW DO I GET TO ROSEDALE ST.?

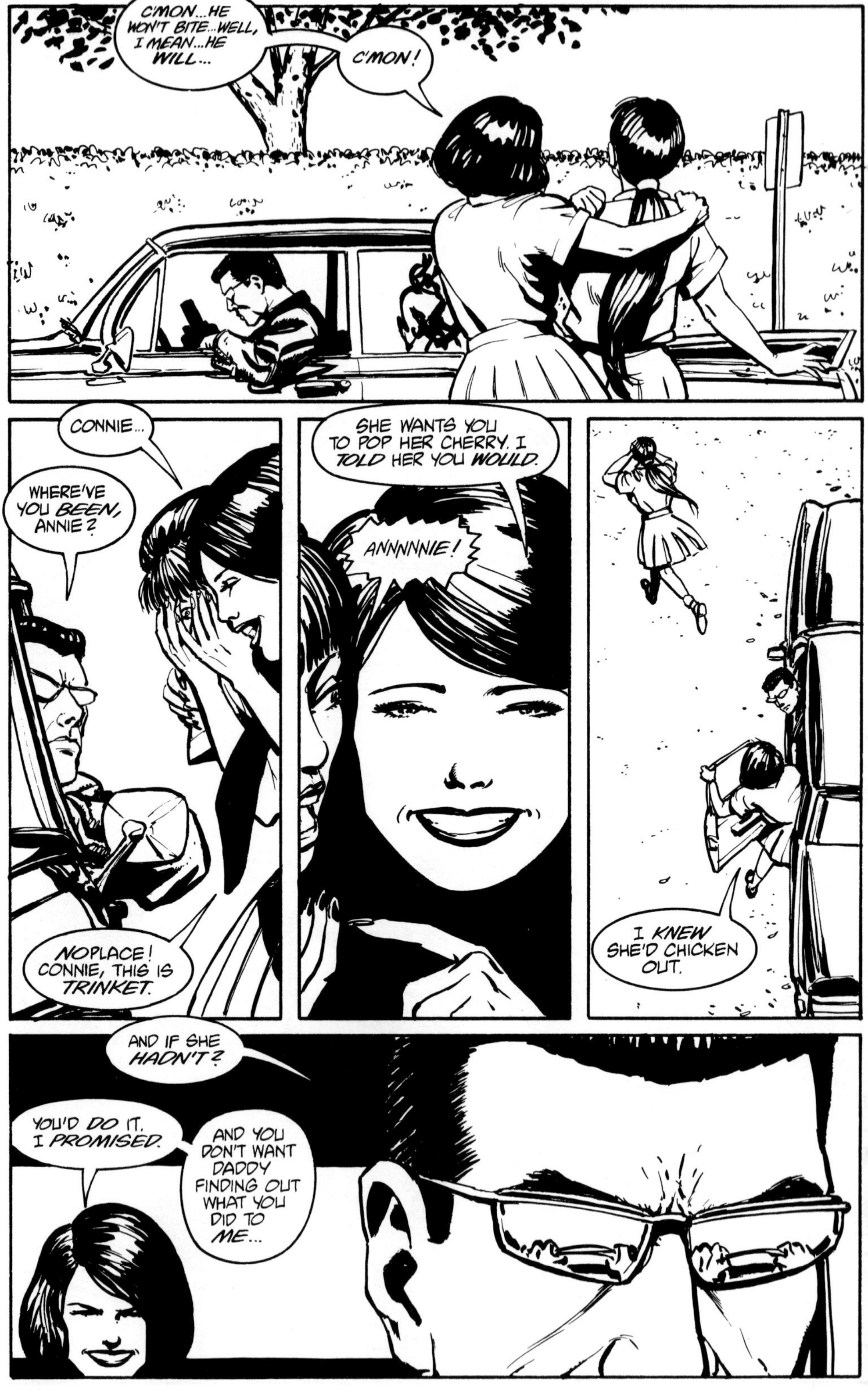
C'MON...HE WON'T BITE...WELL, I MEAN...HE WILL...
C'MON!
CONNIE...
WHERE'VE YOU BEEN, ANNIE?
NOPLACE! CONNIE, THIS IS TRINKET.
SHE WANTS YOU TO POP HER CHERRY. I TOLD HER YOU WOULD.
ANNNNNIE!
I KNEW SHE'D CHICKEN OUT.
AND IF SHE HADN'T?
YOU'D DO IT. I PROMISED.
AND YOU DON'T WANT DADDY FINDING OUT WHAT YOU DID TO ME...

PARK SOME-
WHERE. I WANT
TO DO SOME
SHOPPING.

MEAT
MARKET'S
BACK *THAT*
WAY.

THAT'S SO
FUNNY I
FORGOT TO
LAUGH.

ANY IDEA WHEN
YOU'LL BE BACK?

WHEN I'M
DONE. JUST *STAY*
HERE.

and people who pander to the
traitor who let noble Cuban
liberators go down in defeat.
The people of Texas don't lik

liberators go down in defeat.
The people of Texas don't like
traitors.
He'll stay out of Dallas

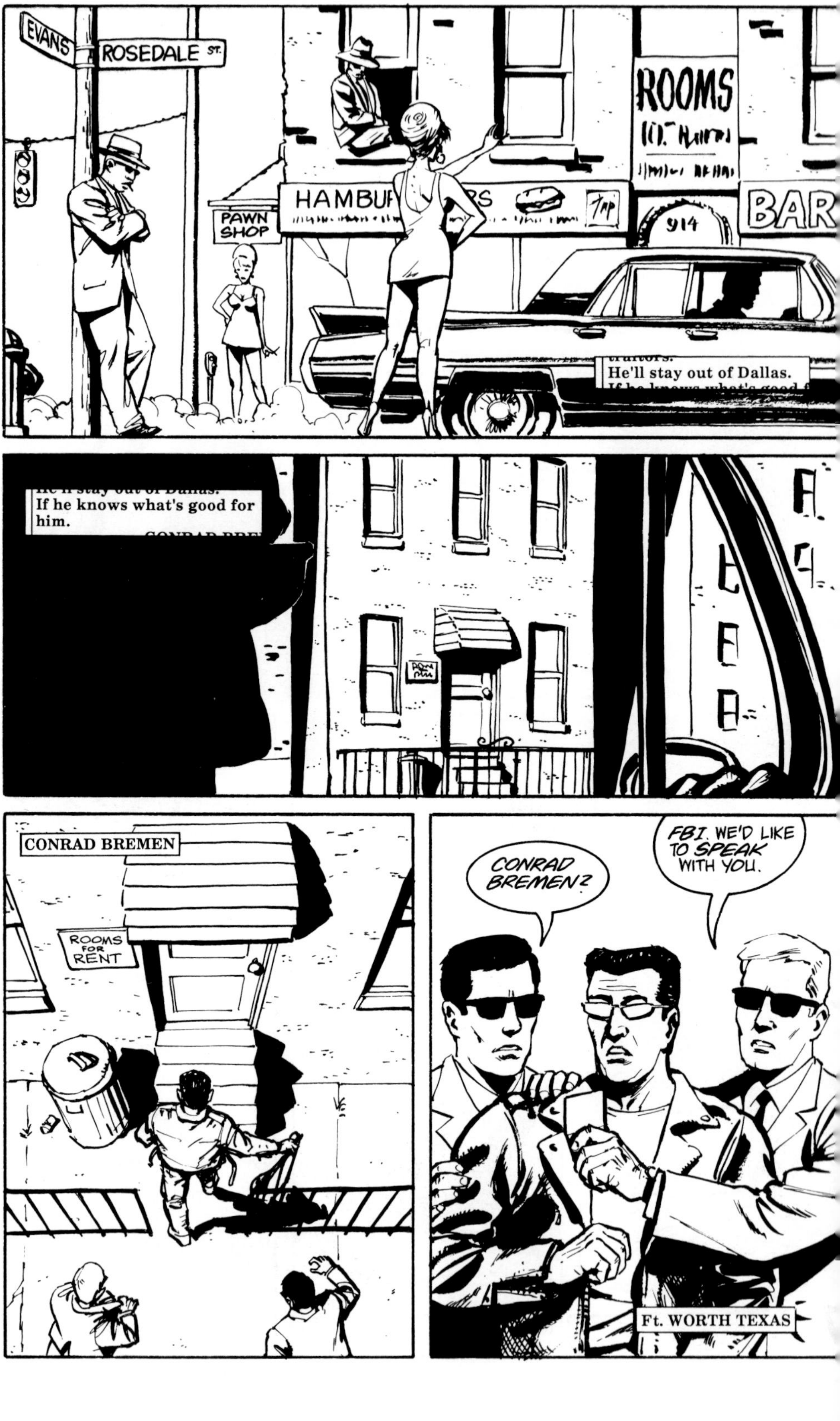
EVANS
ROSEDALE ST.
ROOMS
PAWN SHOP
914
BAR
He'll stay out of Dallas.
If he knows what's good for him.
CONRAD BREMEN
ROOMS FOR RENT
CONRAD BREMEN?
FBI. WE'D LIKE TO SPEAK WITH YOU.
Ft. WORTH TEXAS

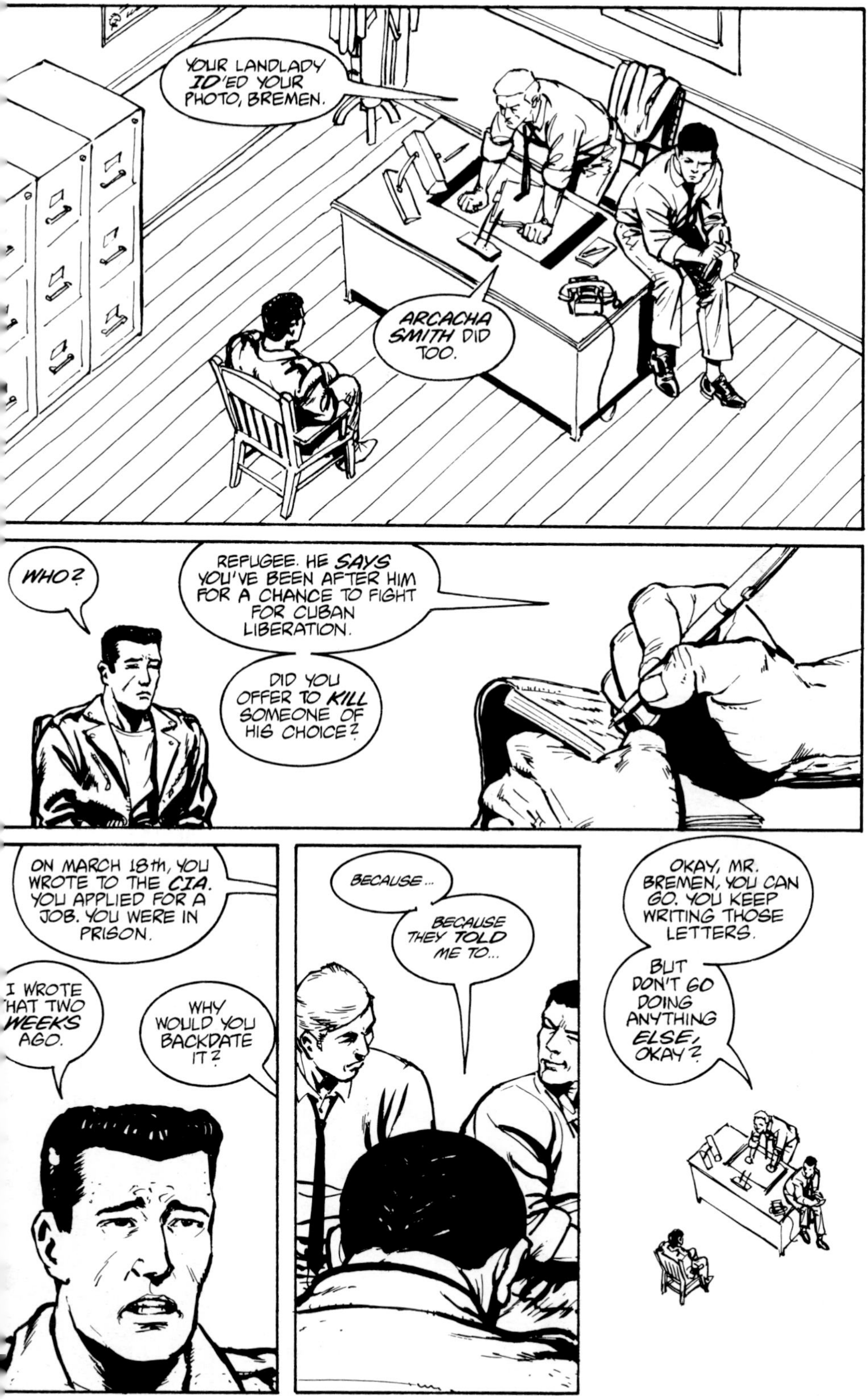
YOUR LANDLADY ID'ED YOUR PHOTO, BREMEN.
ARCACHA SMITH DID TOO.
WHO?
REFUGEE. HE SAYS YOU'VE BEEN AFTER HIM FOR A CHANCE TO FIGHT FOR CUBAN LIBERATION.
DID YOU OFFER TO KILL SOMEONE OF HIS CHOICE?
ON MARCH 18th, YOU WROTE TO THE CIA. YOU APPLIED FOR A JOB. YOU WERE IN PRISON.
I WROTE THAT TWO WEEKS AGO.
WHY WOULD YOU BACKDATE IT?
BECAUSE...
BECAUSE THEY TOLD ME TO...
OKAY, MR. BREMEN, YOU CAN GO. YOU KEEP WRITING THOSE LETTERS.
BUT DON'T GO DOING ANYTHING ELSE, OKAY?

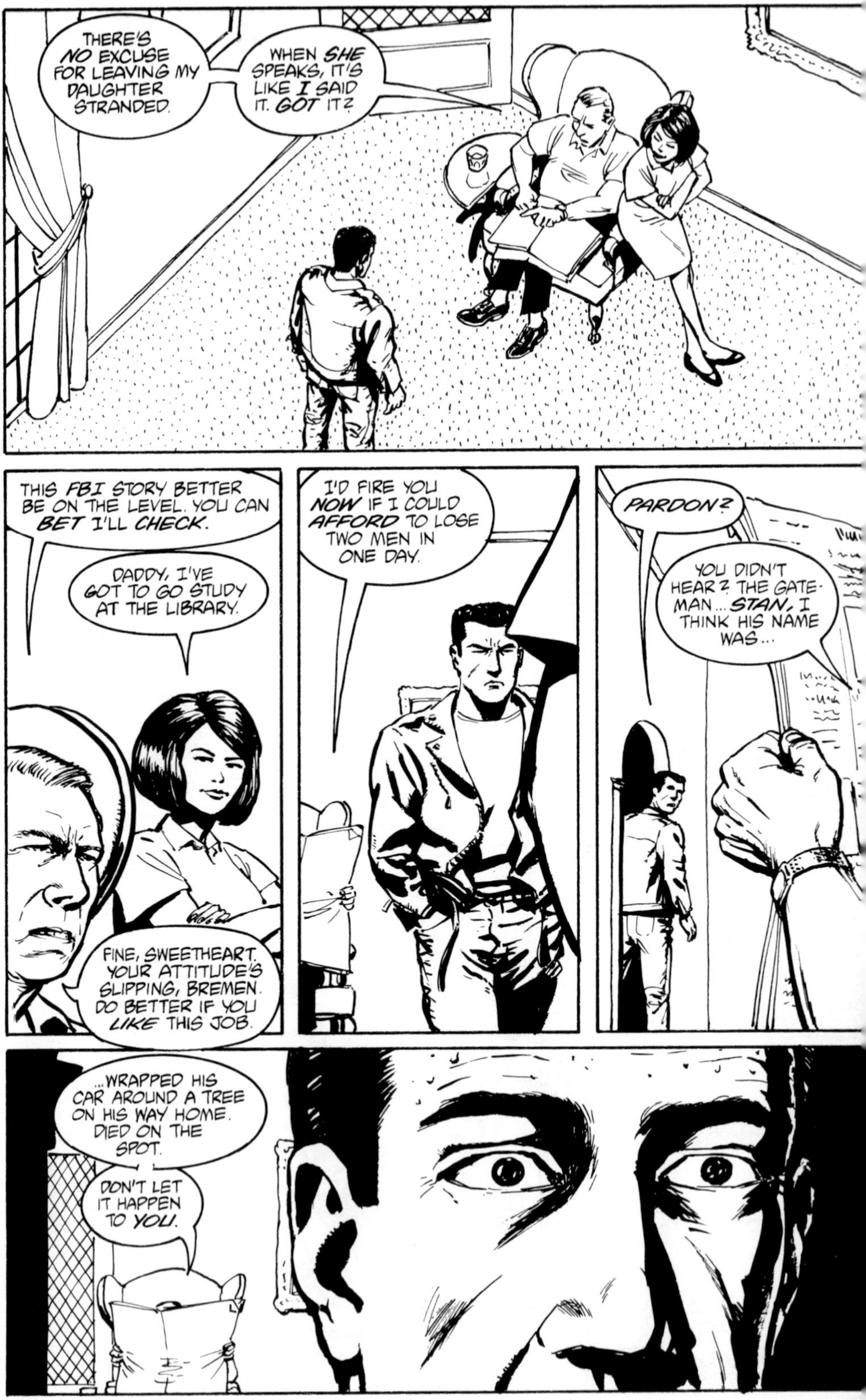
THERE'S NO EXCUSE FOR LEAVING MY DAUGHTER STRANDED.
WHEN SHE SPEAKS, IT'S LIKE I SAID IT. GOT IT?
THIS FBI STORY BETTER BE ON THE LEVEL. YOU CAN BET I'LL CHECK.
DADDY, I'VE GOT TO GO STUDY AT THE LIBRARY.
FINE, SWEETHEART. YOUR ATTITUDE'S SLIPPING, BREMEN. DO BETTER IF YOU LIKE THIS JOB.
I'D FIRE YOU NOW IF I COULD AFFORD TO LOSE TWO MEN IN ONE DAY.
PARDON?
YOU DIDN'T HEAR? THE GATE-MAN... STAN, I THINK HIS NAME WAS...
...WRAPPED HIS CAR AROUND A TREE ON HIS WAY HOME. DIED ON THE SPOT.
DON'T LET IT HAPPEN TO YOU.

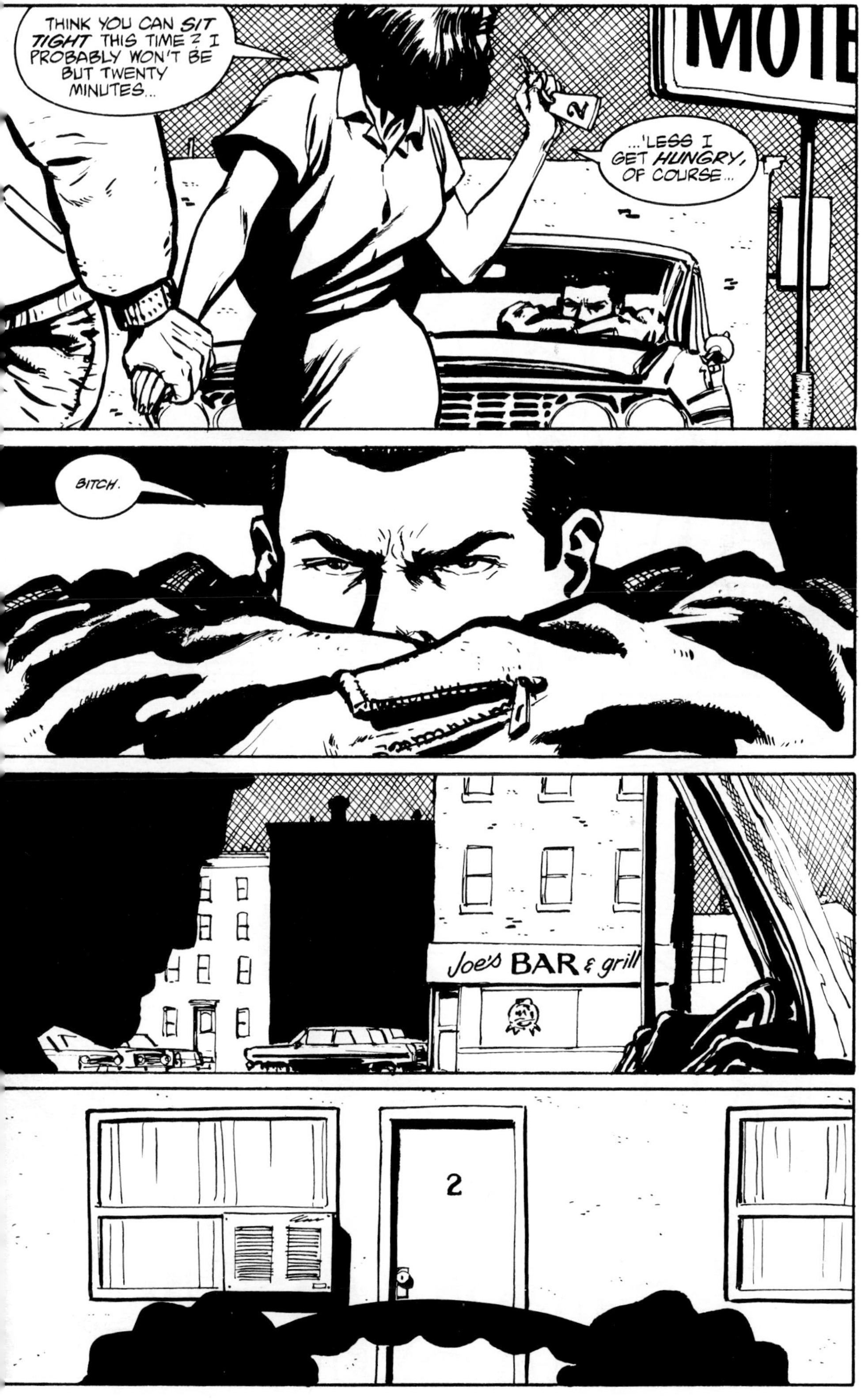
THINK YOU CAN SIT TIGHT THIS TIME? I PROBABLY WON'T BE BUT TWENTY MINUTES...
MOTE
...'LESS I GET HUNGRY, OF COURSE...
BITCH.
Joe's BAR & grill
2

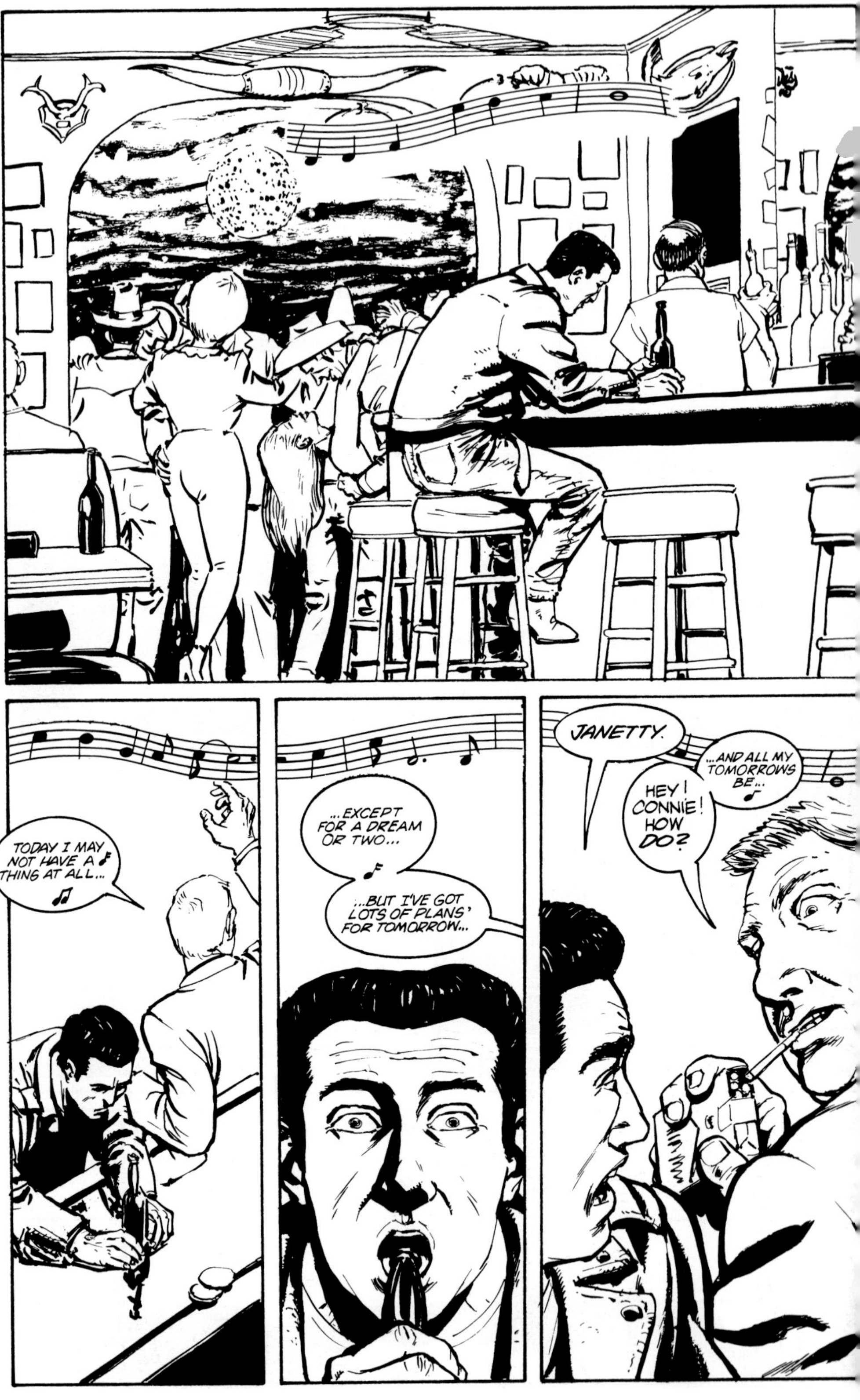
TODAY I MAY NOT HAVE A THING AT ALL...
...EXCEPT FOR A DREAM OR TWO...
...BUT I'VE GOT LOTS OF PLANS' FOR TOMORROW...
JANETTY.
...AND ALL MY TOMORROWS BE...
HEY! CONNIE! HOW DO?

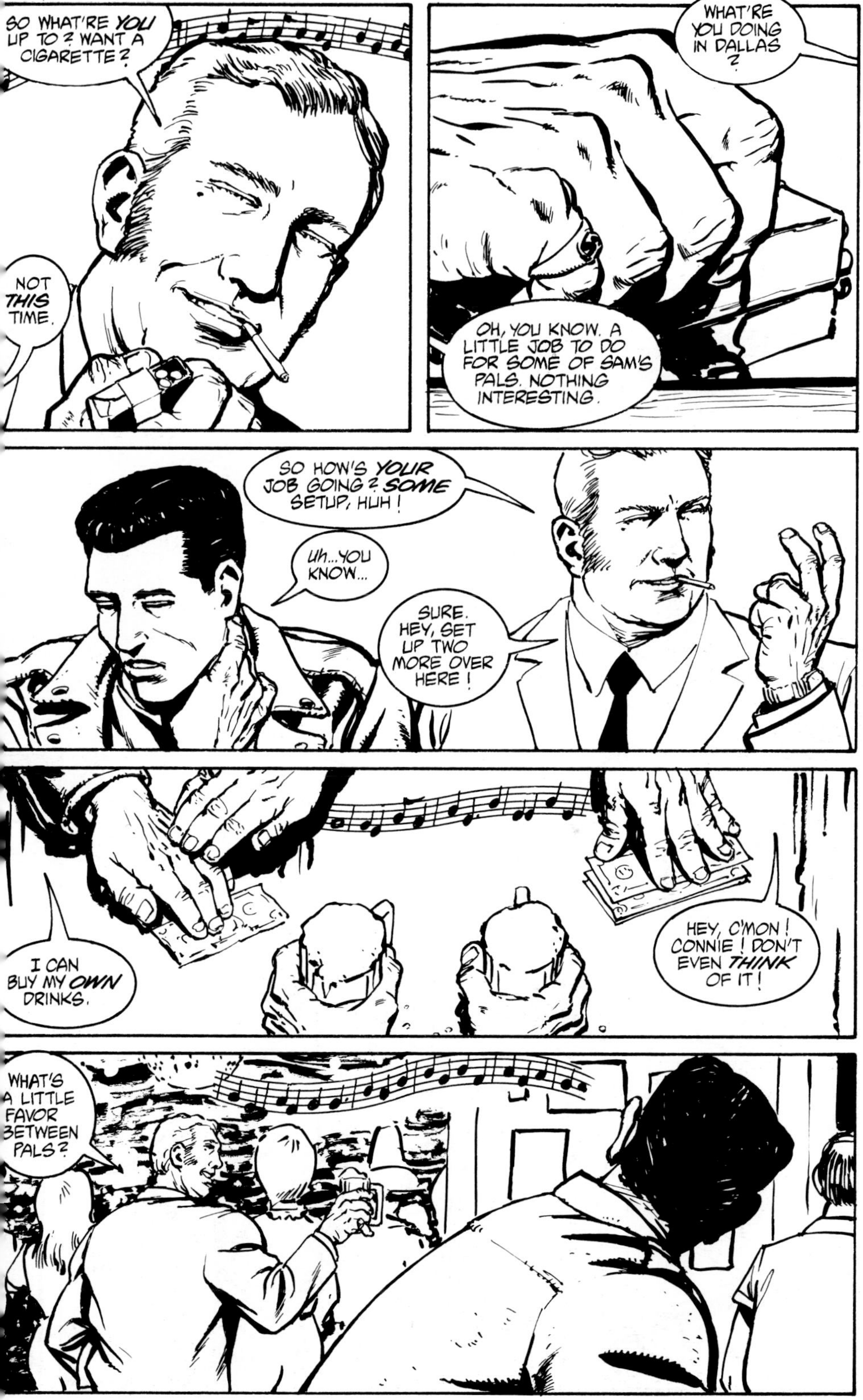
SO WHAT'RE YOU UP TO? WANT A CIGARETTE?
NOT THIS TIME.
WHAT'RE YOU DOING IN DALLAS?
OH, YOU KNOW. A LITTLE JOB TO DO FOR SOME OF SAM'S PALS. NOTHING INTERESTING.
SO HOW'S YOUR JOB GOING? SOME SETUP, HUH!
UH...YOU KNOW...
SURE. HEY, SET UP TWO MORE OVER HERE!
I CAN BUY MY OWN DRINKS.
HEY, C'MON! CONNIE! DON'T EVEN THINK OF IT!
WHAT'S A LITTLE FAVOR BETWEEN PALS?

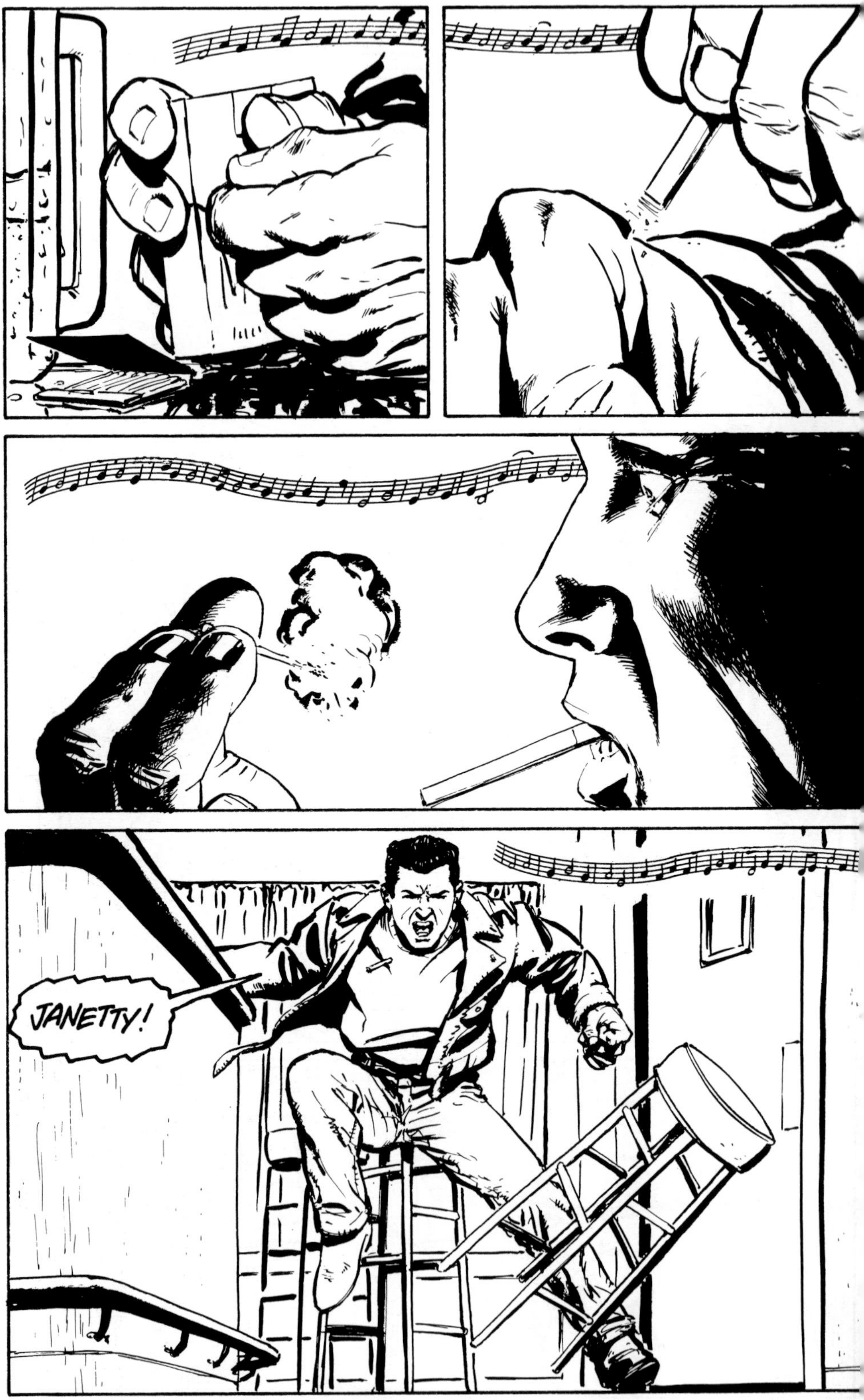
JANETTY!

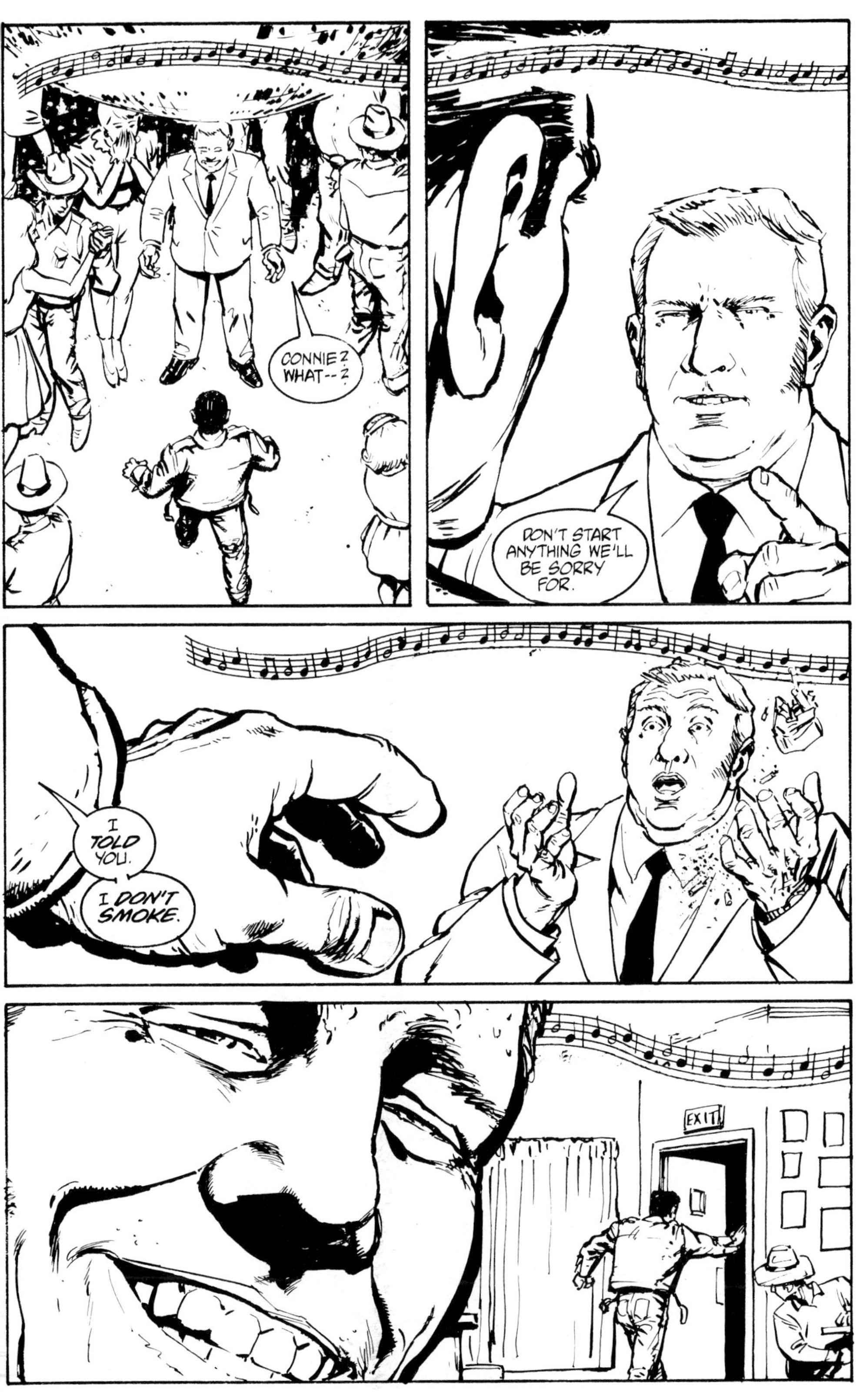
CONNIE? WHAT--?
DON'T START ANYTHING WE'LL BE SORRY FOR.
I TOLD YOU.
I DON'T SMOKE.
EXIT

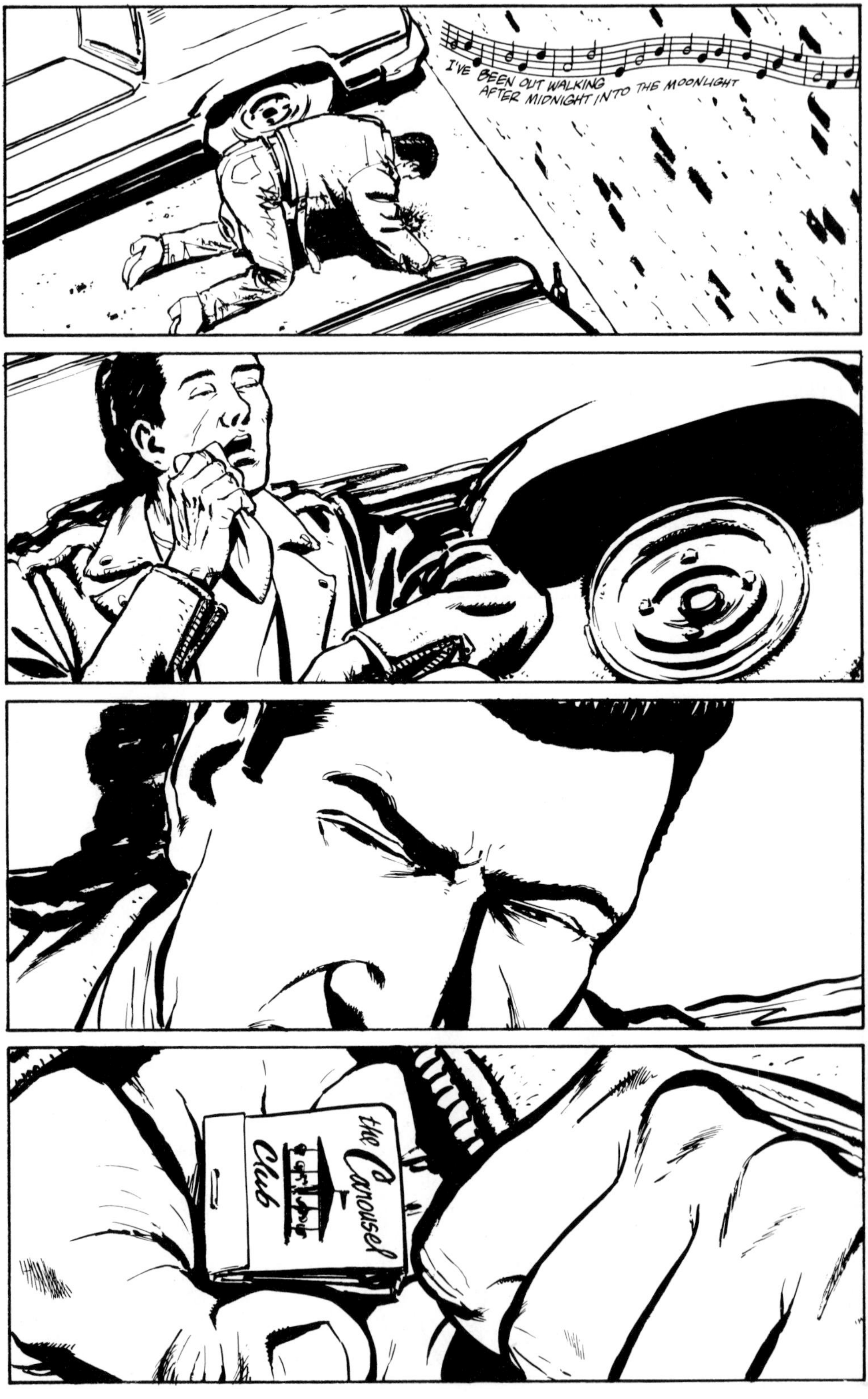
I'VE BEEN OUT WALKING
AFTER MIDNIGHT INTO THE MOONLIGHT
the Carousel Club

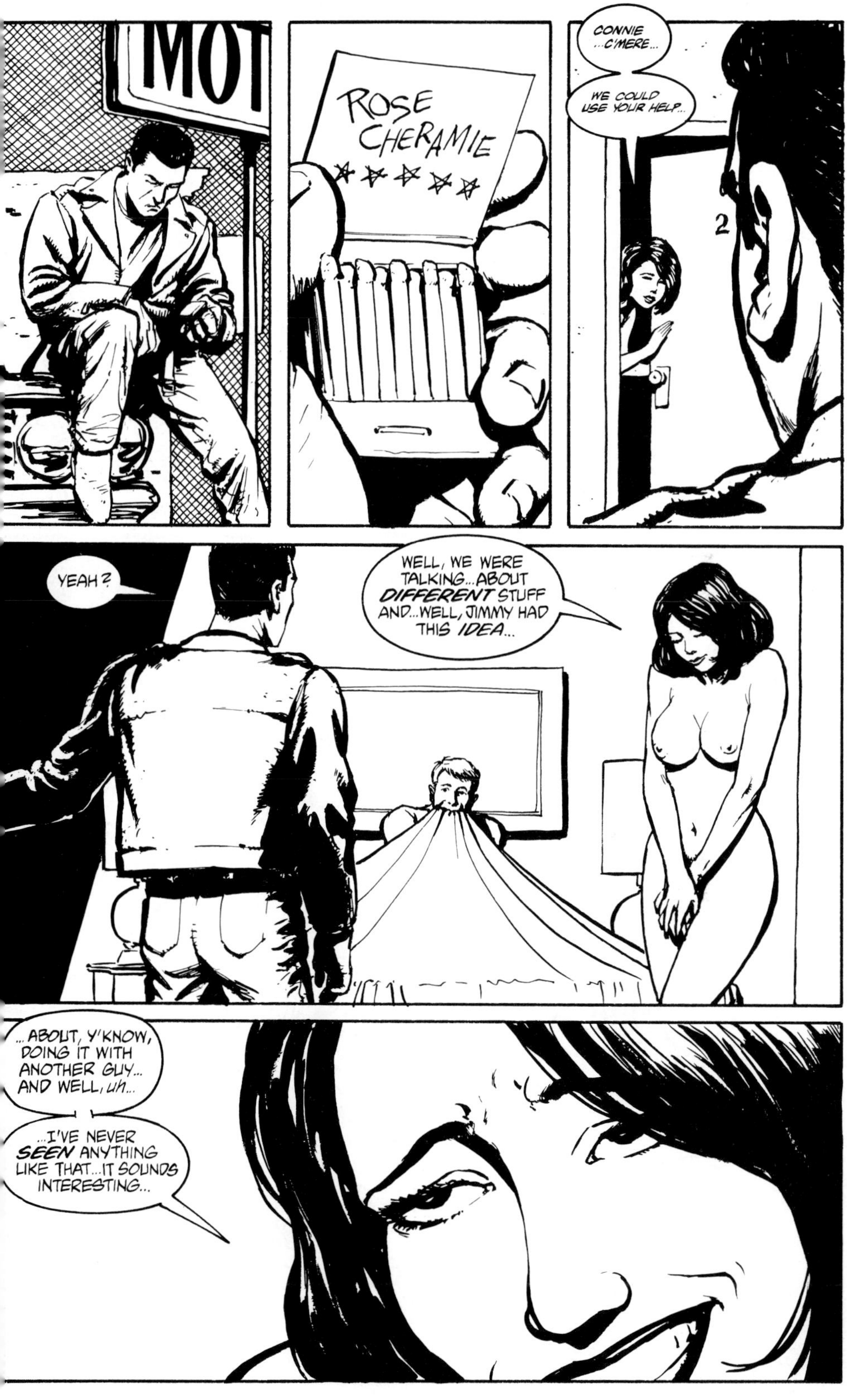
MOT
ROSE CHERAMIE
CONNIE ...C'MERE...
WE COULD USE YOUR HELP...
2
YEAH?
WELL, WE WERE TALKING...ABOUT *DIFFERENT* STUFF AND...WELL, JIMMY HAD THIS *IDEA*...
...ABOUT, Y'KNOW, DOING IT WITH ANOTHER GUY... AND WELL, *uh*...
...I'VE NEVER *SEEN* ANYTHING LIKE THAT...IT SOUNDS INTERESTING...

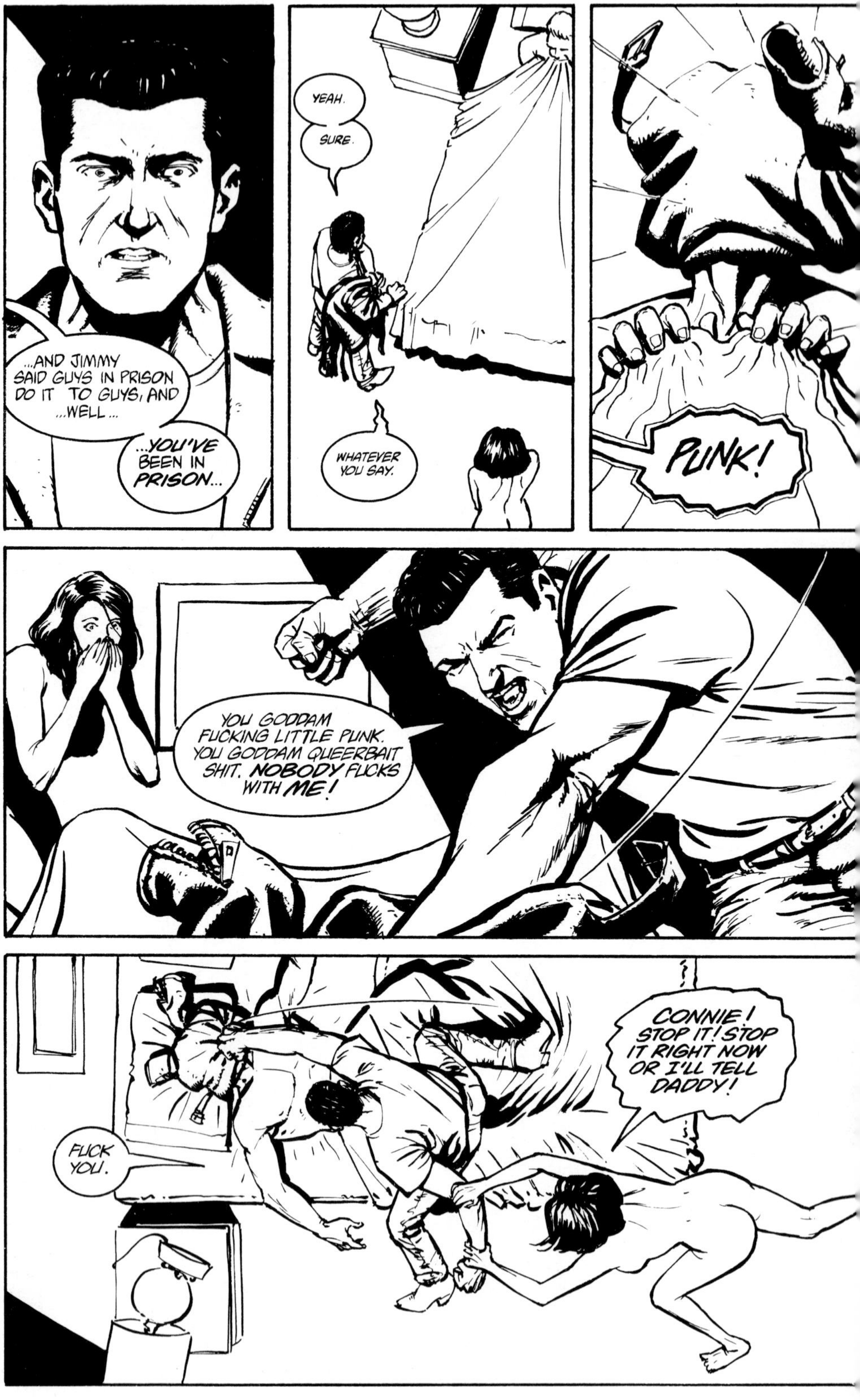
...AND JIMMY SAID GUYS IN PRISON DO IT TO GUYS, AND ...WELL ...
...YOU'VE BEEN IN PRISON...
YEAH.
SURE.
WHATEVER YOU SAY.
PUNK!
YOU GODDAM FUCKING LITTLE PUNK. YOU GODDAM QUEERBAIT SHIT. NOBODY FUCKS WITH ME!
CONNIE! STOP IT! STOP IT RIGHT NOW OR I'LL TELL DADDY!
FUCK YOU.

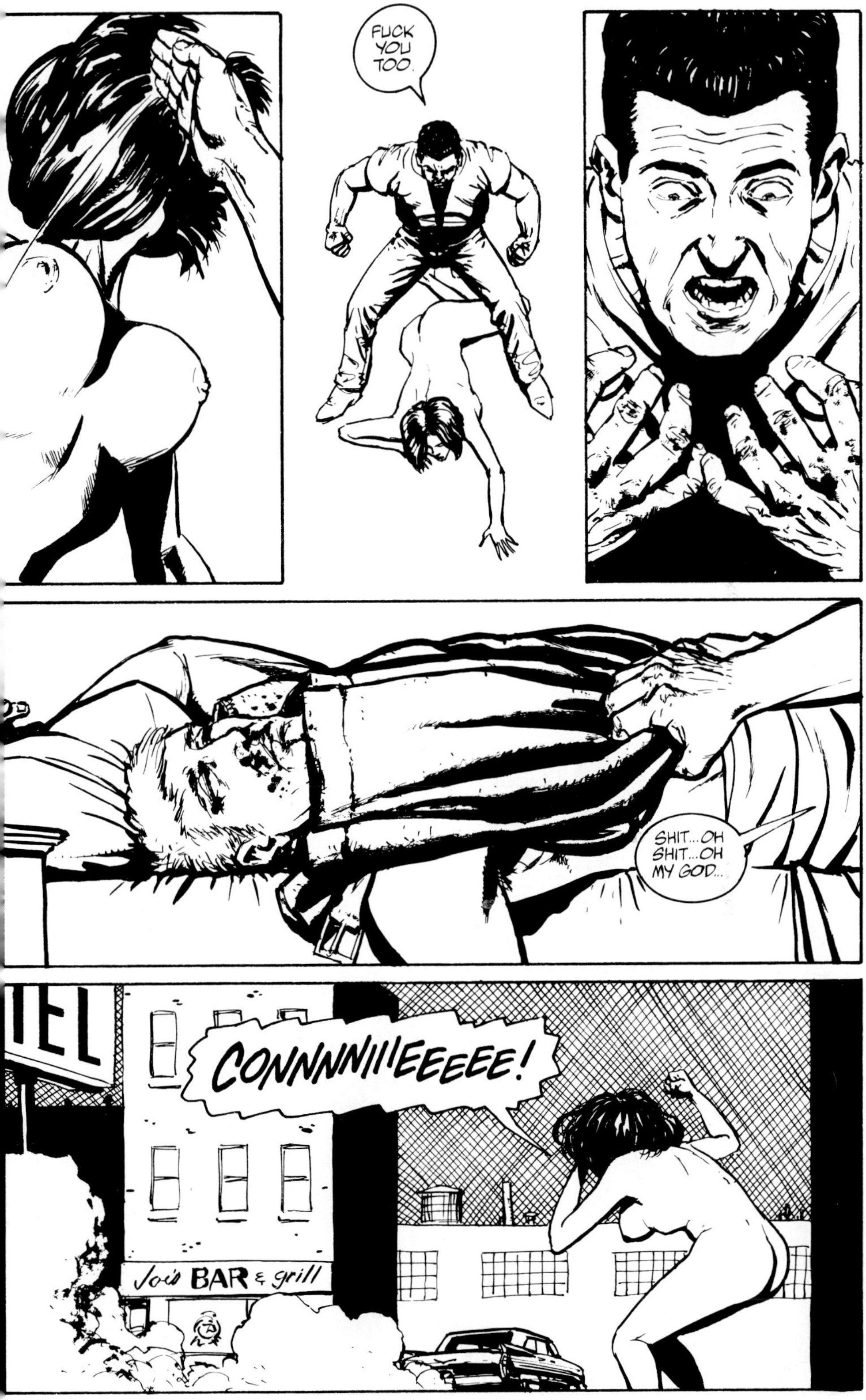
FUCK YOU TOO.
SHIT...OH SHIT...OH MY GOD...
CONNNNIIIEEEEEE!
Joe's BAR & grill

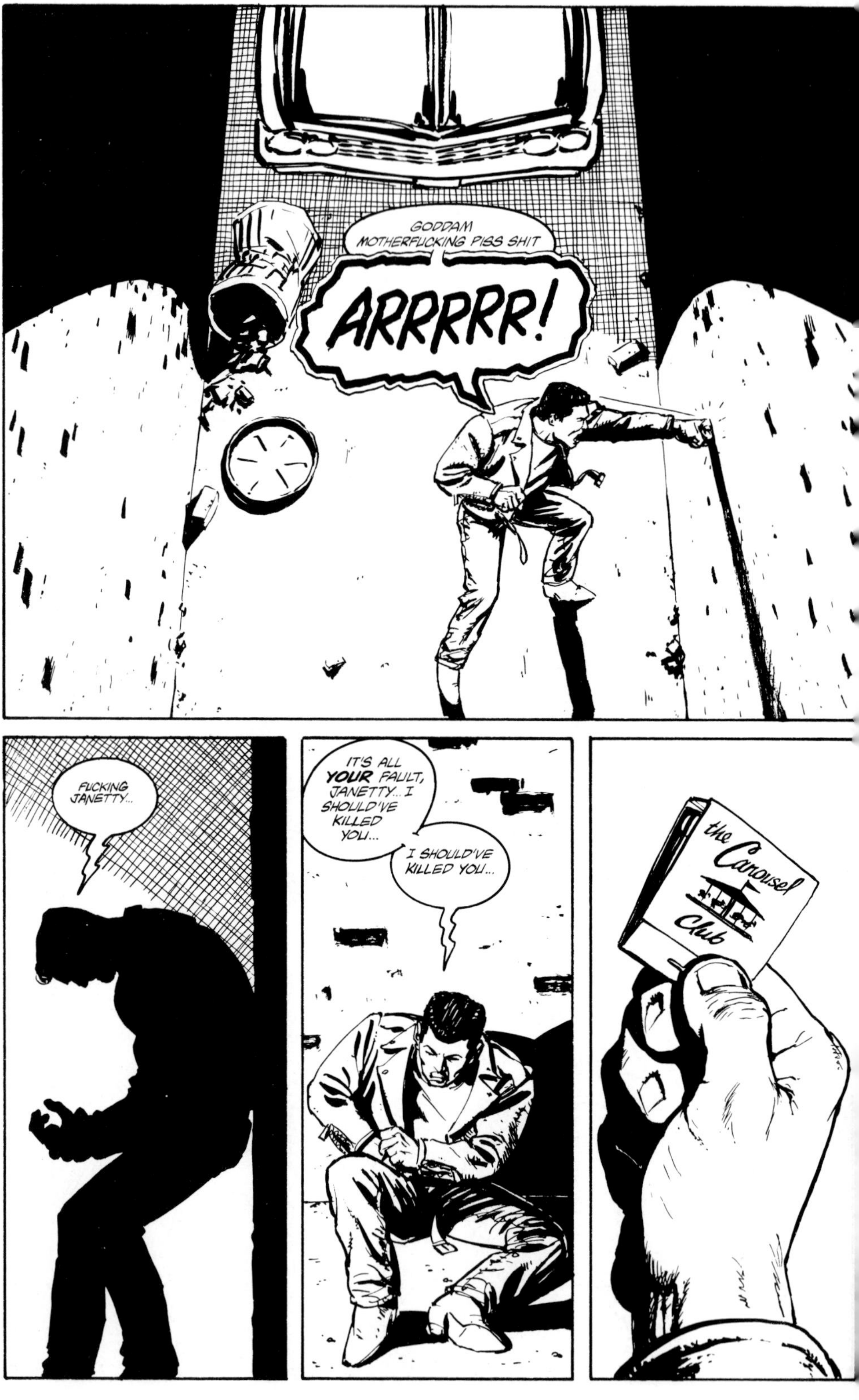
GODDAM MOTHERFUCKING PISS SHIT
ARRRRR!
FUCKING JANETTY...
IT'S ALL YOUR FAULT, JANETTY... I SHOULD'VE KILLED YOU...
I SHOULD'VE KILLED YOU...
the Carousel Club

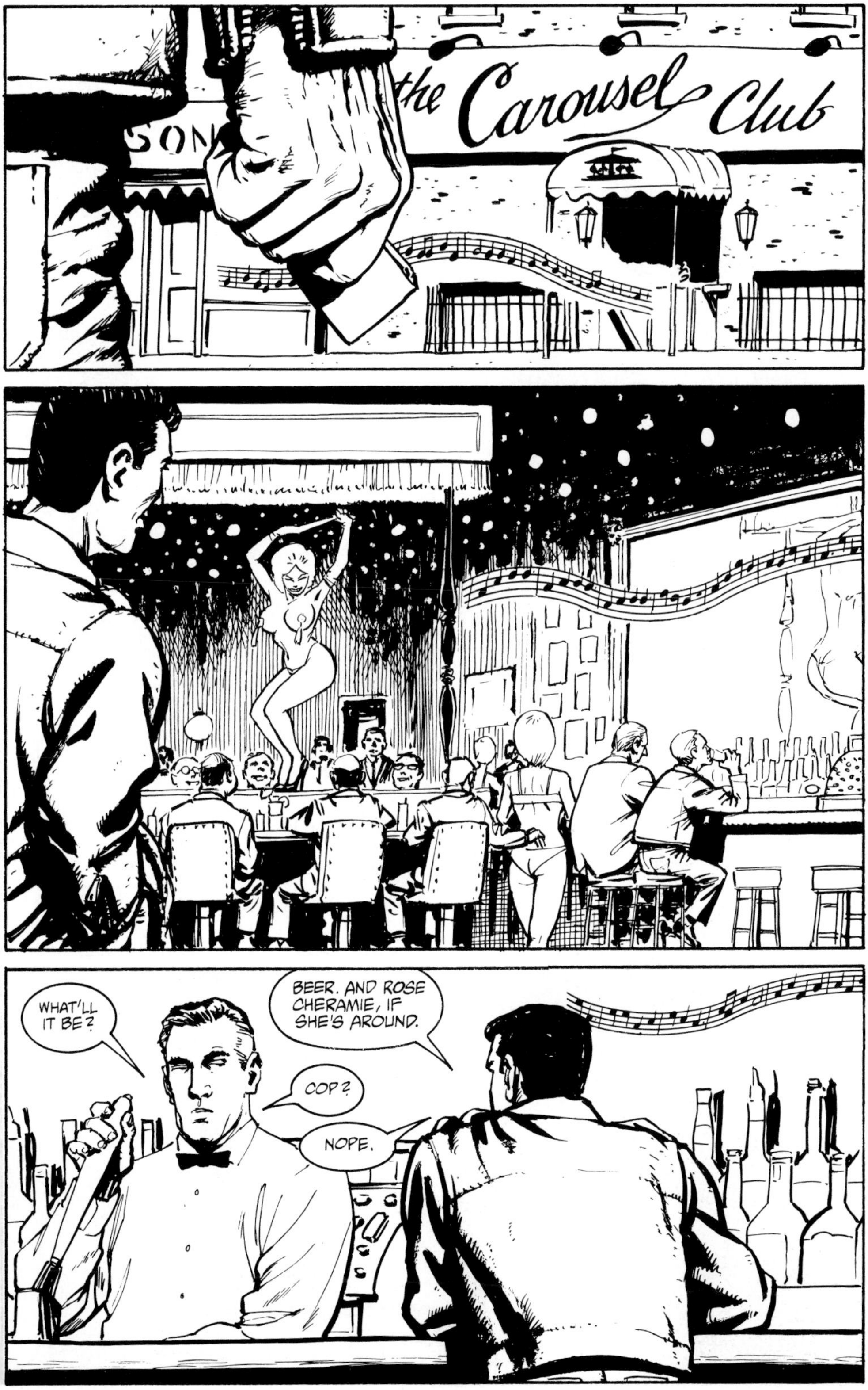
the Carousel Club
SON
WHAT'LL IT BE?
BEER. AND ROSE CHERAMIE, IF SHE'S AROUND.
COP?
NOPE.

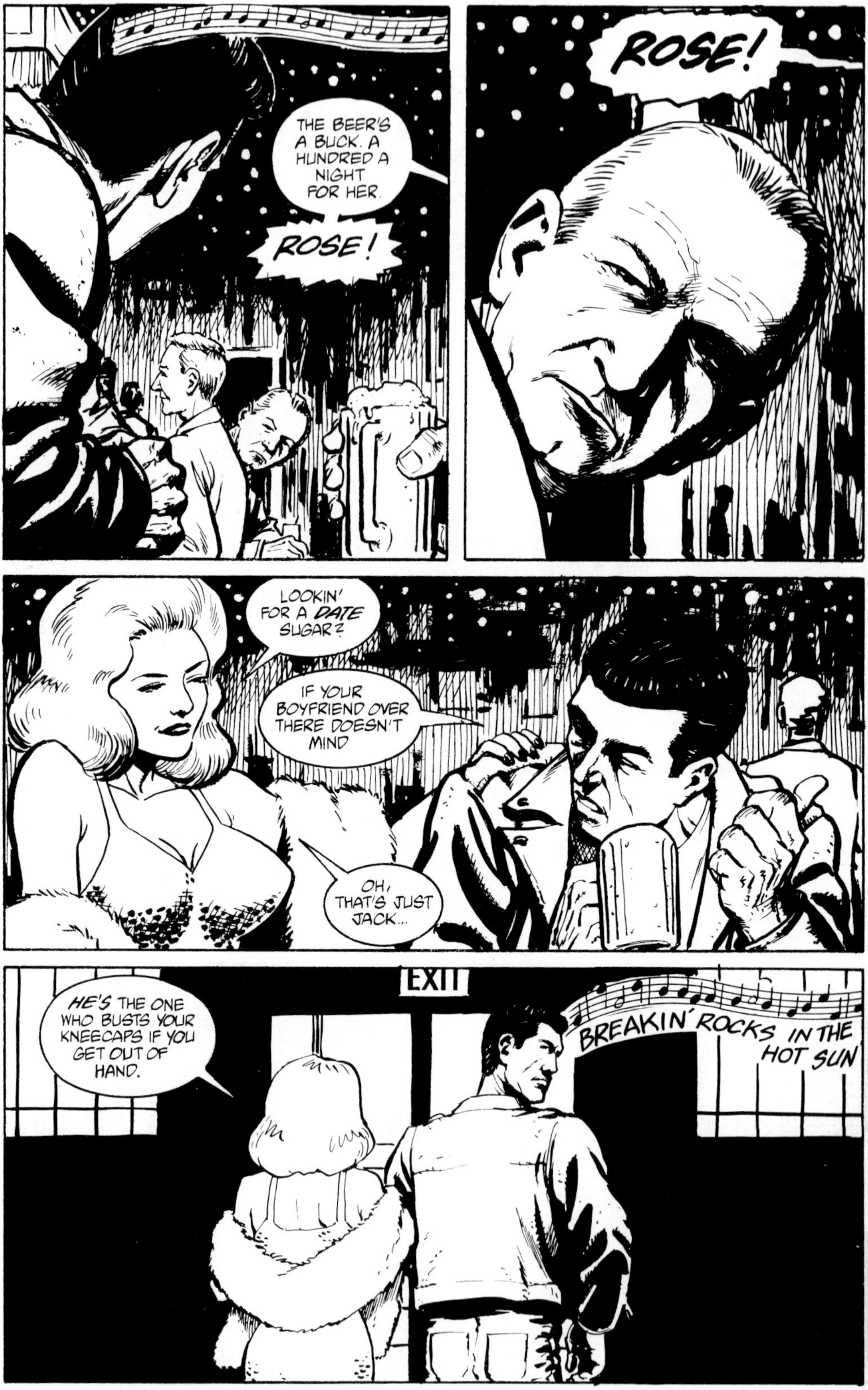
THE BEER'S A BUCK. A HUNDRED A NIGHT FOR HER.
ROSE!
ROSE!
LOOKIN' FOR A DATE SUGAR?
IF YOUR BOYFRIEND OVER THERE DOESN'T MIND
OH, THAT'S JUST JACK...
EXIT
HE'S THE ONE WHO BUSTS YOUR KNEECAPS IF YOU GET OUT OF HAND.
BREAKIN' ROCKS IN THE HOT SUN

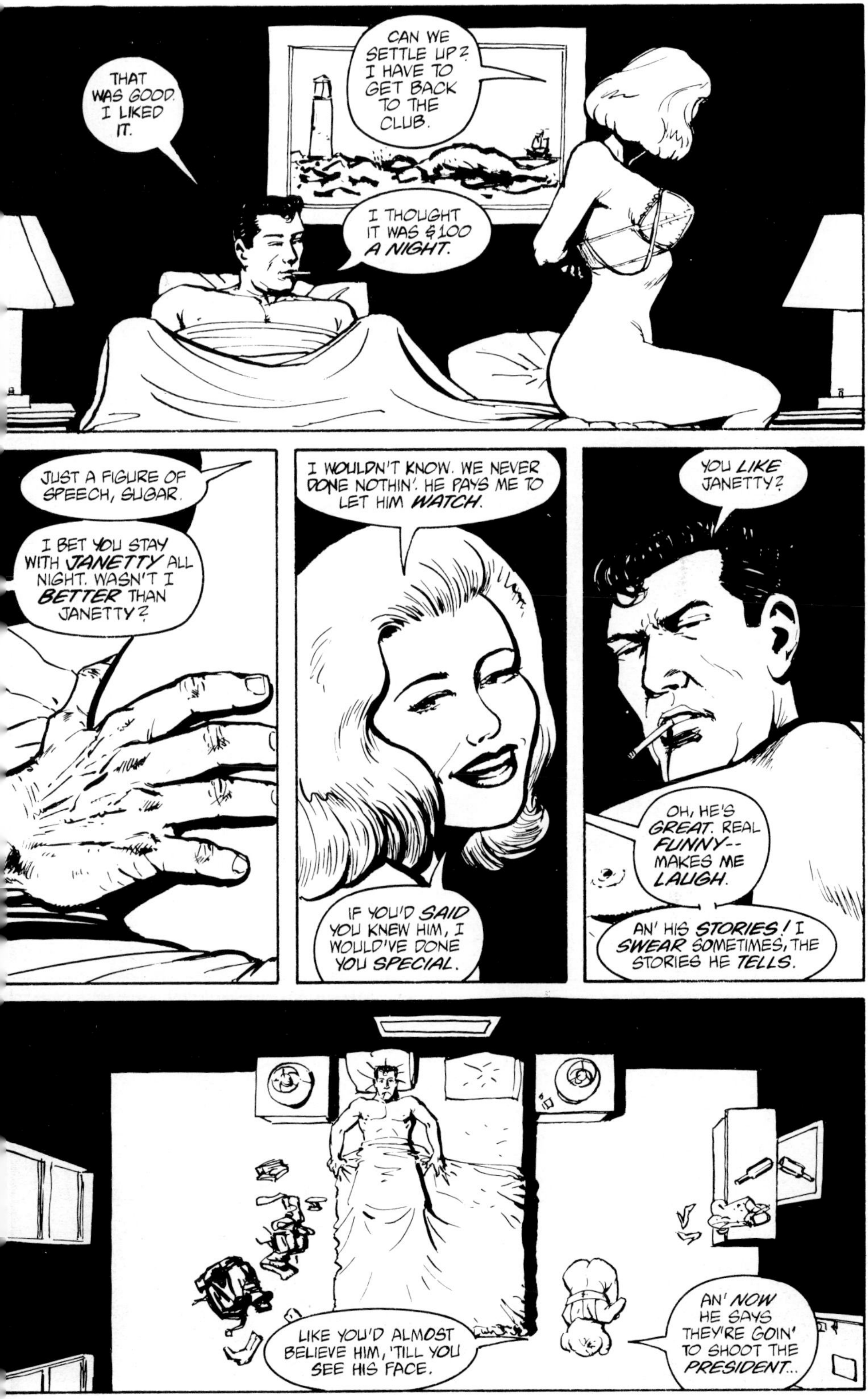
THAT WAS GOOD. I LIKED IT.
CAN WE SETTLE UP? I HAVE TO GET BACK TO THE CLUB.
I THOUGHT IT WAS $100 A NIGHT.
JUST A FIGURE OF SPEECH, SUGAR.
I BET YOU STAY WITH JANETTY ALL NIGHT. WASN'T I BETTER THAN JANETTY?
I WOULDN'T KNOW. WE NEVER DONE NOTHIN'. HE PAYS ME TO LET HIM WATCH.
IF YOU'D SAID YOU KNEW HIM, I WOULD'VE DONE YOU SPECIAL.
YOU LIKE JANETTY?
OH, HE'S GREAT. REAL FUNNY-- MAKES ME LAUGH.
AN' HIS STORIES! I SWEAR SOMETIMES, THE STORIES HE TELLS.
LIKE YOU'D ALMOST BELIEVE HIM, 'TILL YOU SEE HIS FACE.
AN' NOW HE SAYS THEY'RE GOIN' TO SHOOT THE PRESIDENT...

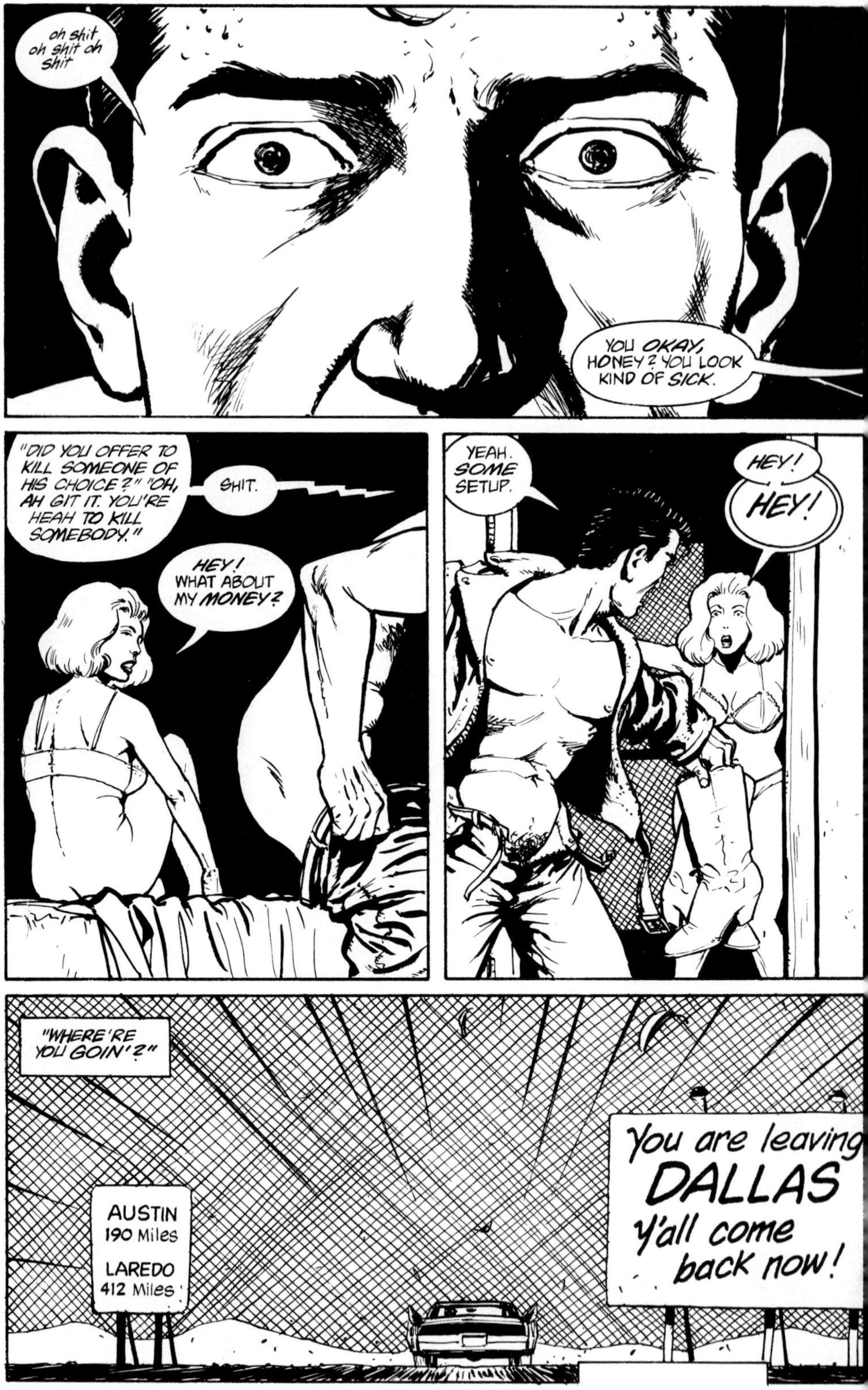
oh shit oh shit oh shit
YOU OKAY, HONEY? YOU LOOK KIND OF SICK.
"DID YOU OFFER TO KILL SOMEONE OF HIS CHOICE?" "OH, AH GIT IT. YOU'RE HEAH TO KILL SOMEBODY."
SHIT.
HEY! WHAT ABOUT MY MONEY?
YEAH. SOME SETUP.
HEY!
HEY!
"WHERE'RE YOU GOIN'?"
AUSTIN 190 Miles
LAREDO 412 Miles
You are leaving DALLAS y'all come back now!

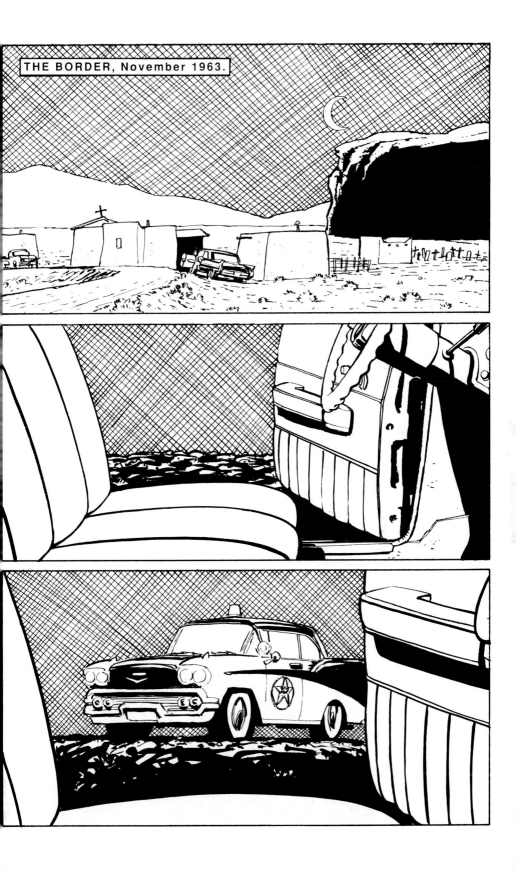

THE BORDER, November 1963.

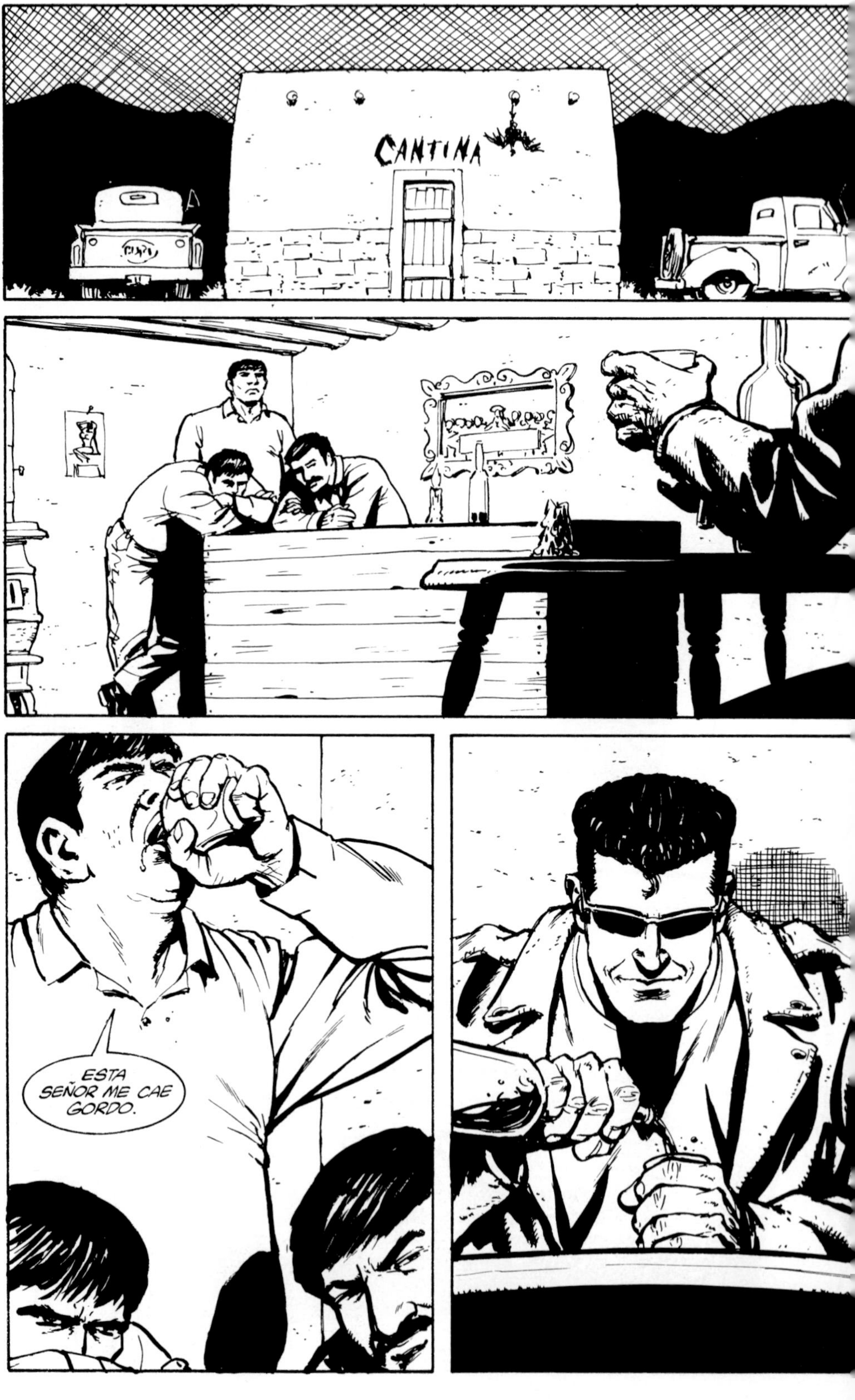
CANTINA
ESTA SEÑOR ME CAE GORDO.

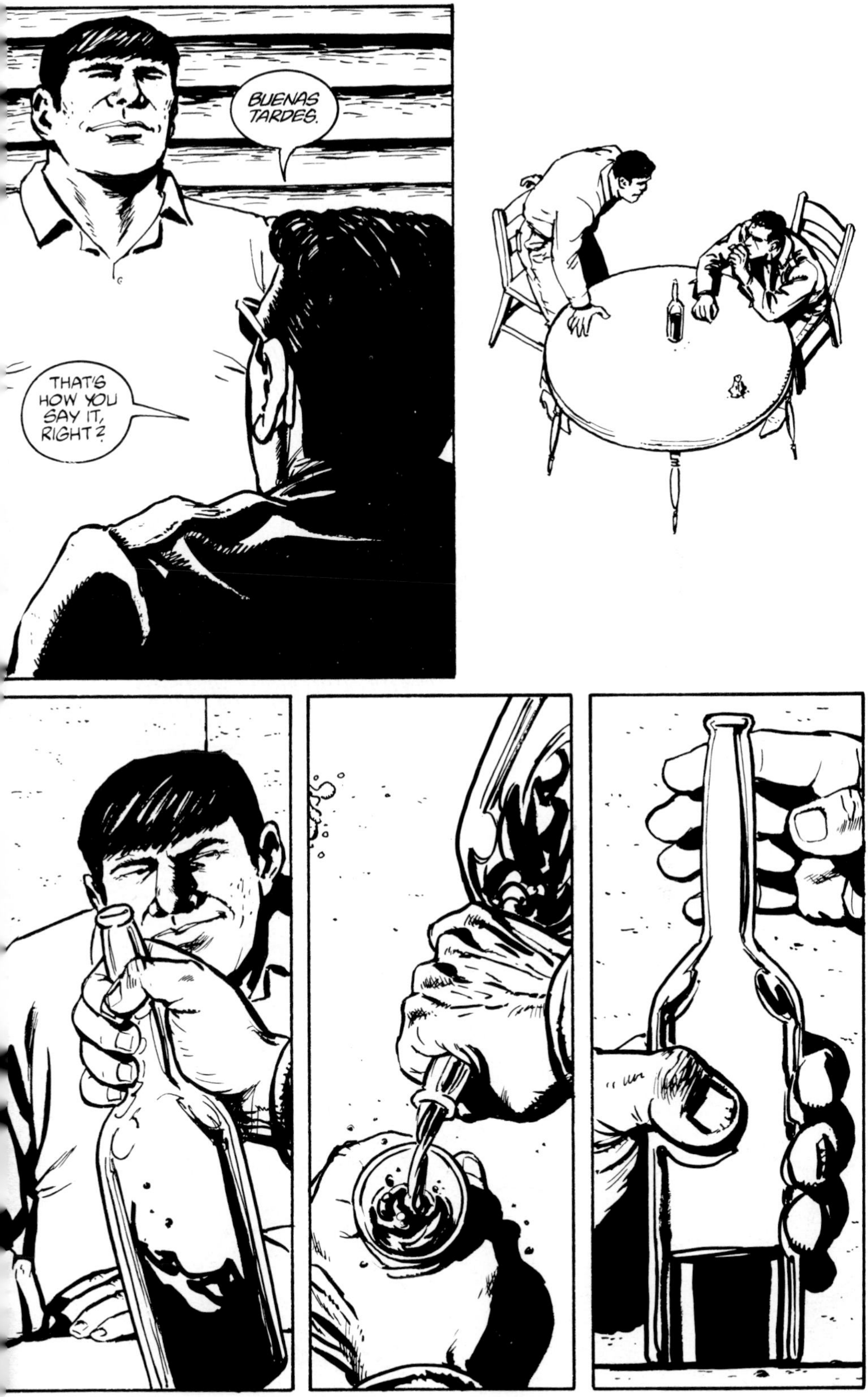
BUENAS TARDES.
THAT'S HOW YOU SAY IT, RIGHT?

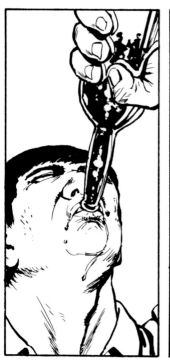

GO FUCK YOURSELF.

ESTÁ CUETE.

MARICÓN.

HAHAHAHAHAHAHAHA

HEY!

SHITHEAD!

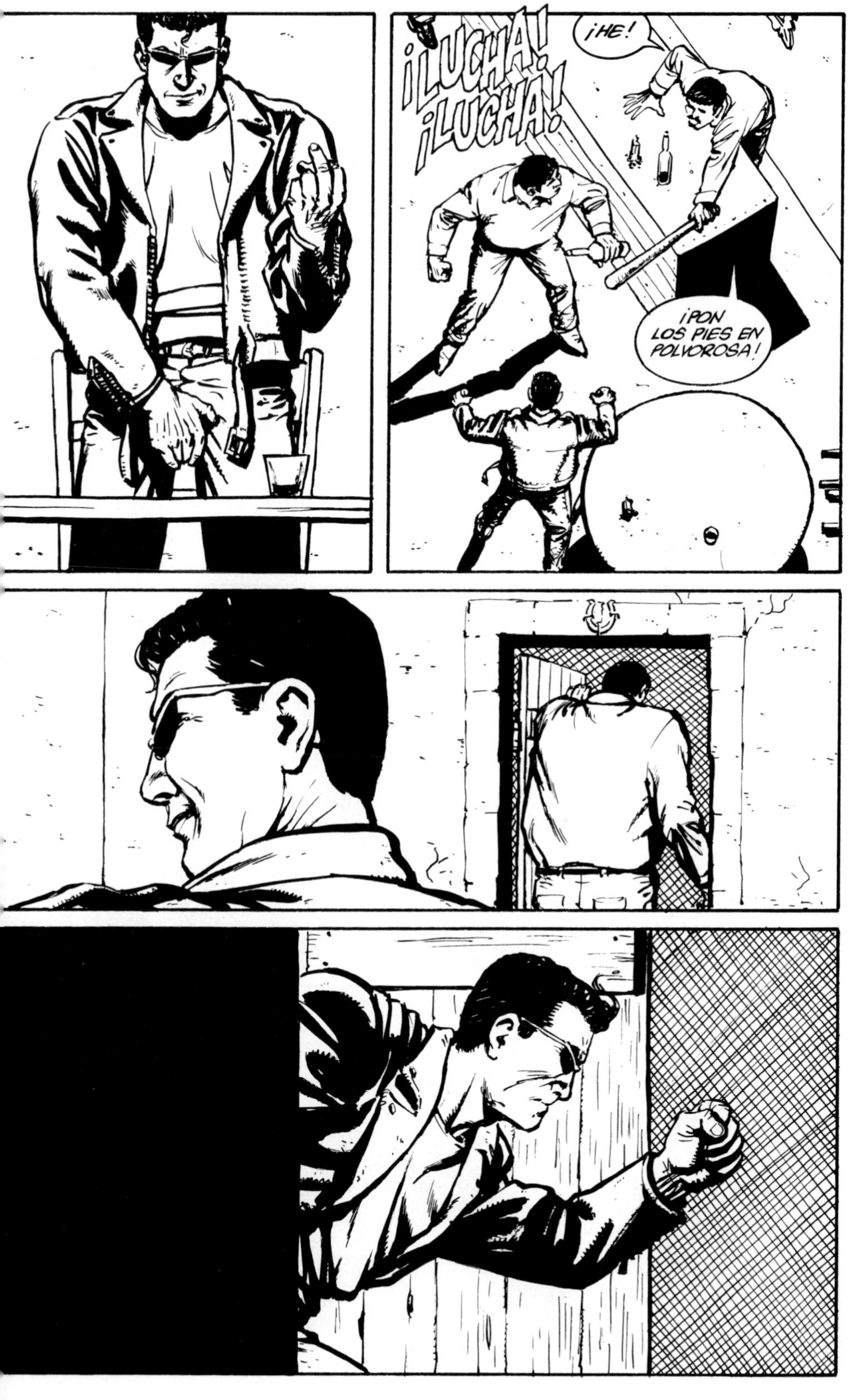
¡LUCHA! ¡LUCHA!
¡HE!
¡PON LOS PIES EN POLVOROSA!

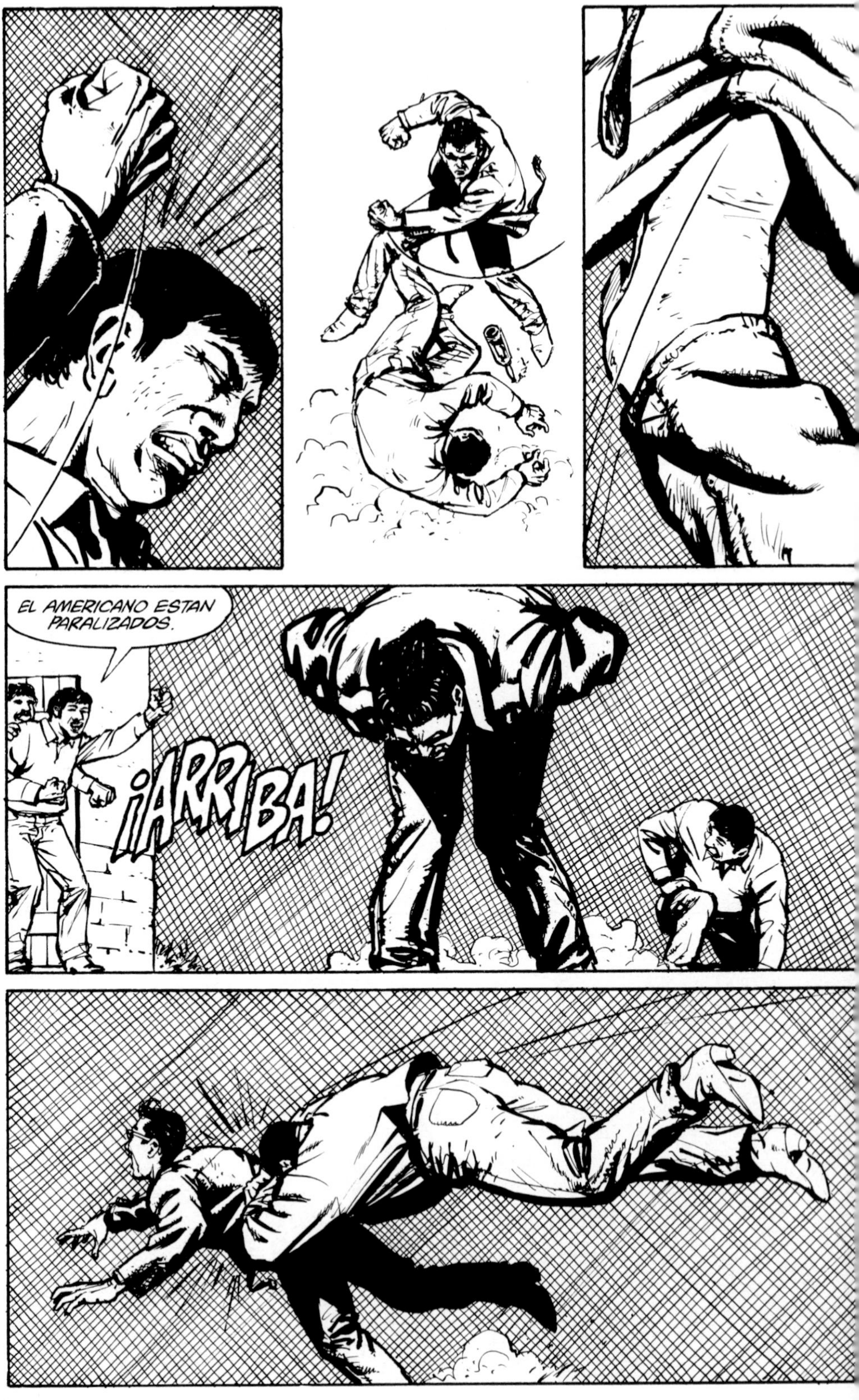
EL AMERICANO ESTAN PARALIZADOS.
¡ARRIBA!

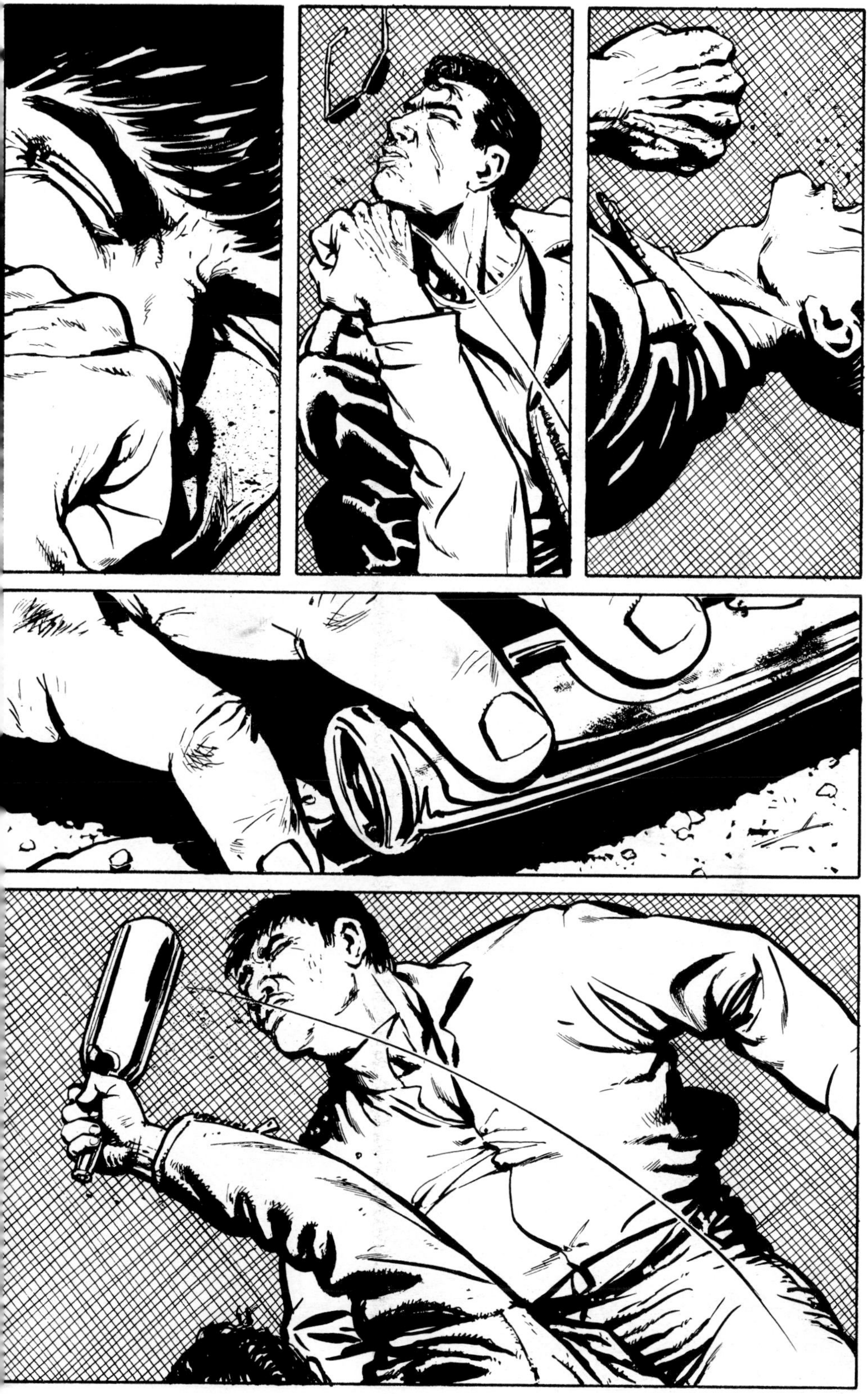

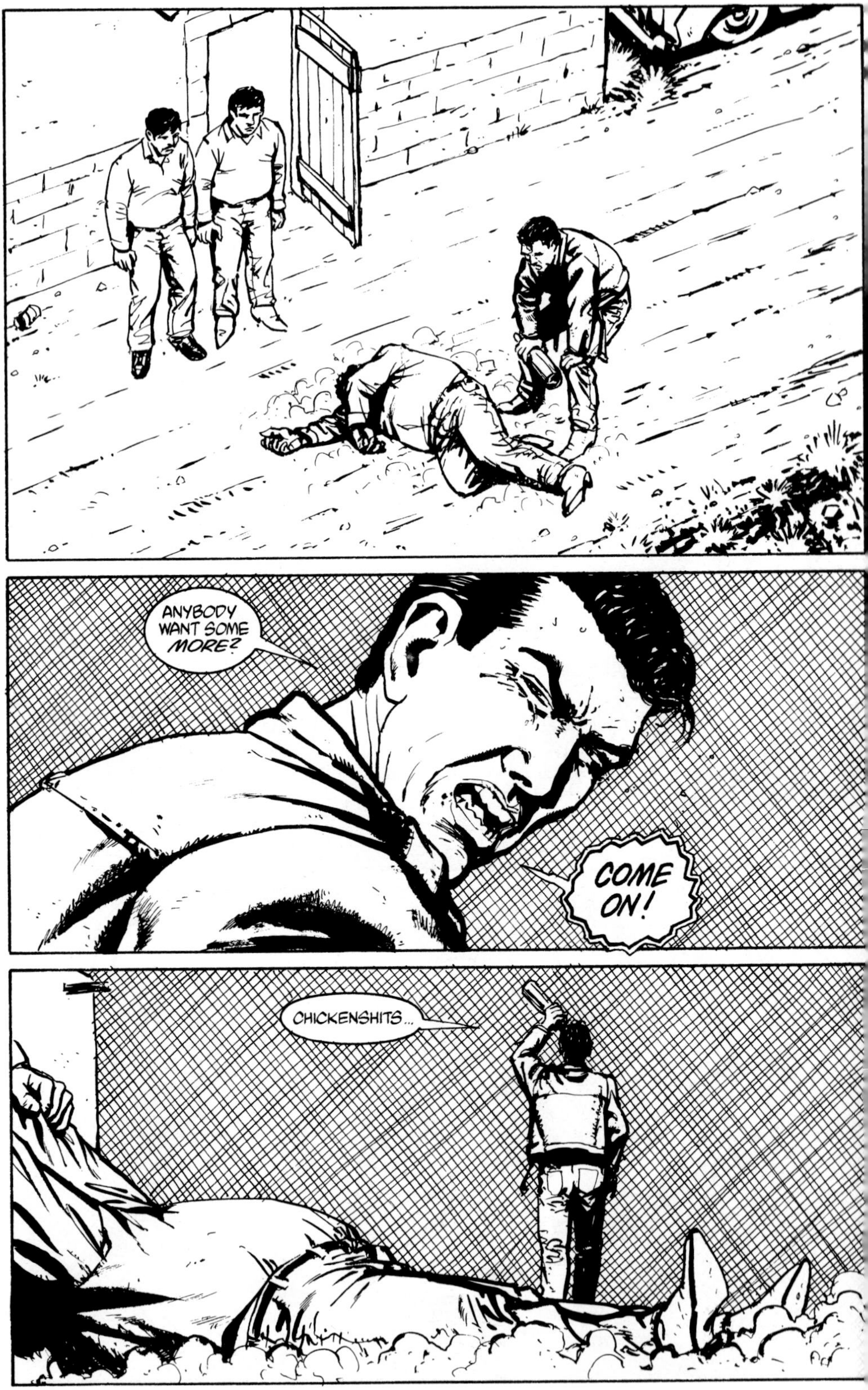
ANYBODY WANT SOME MORE?
COME ON!
CHICKENSHITS...

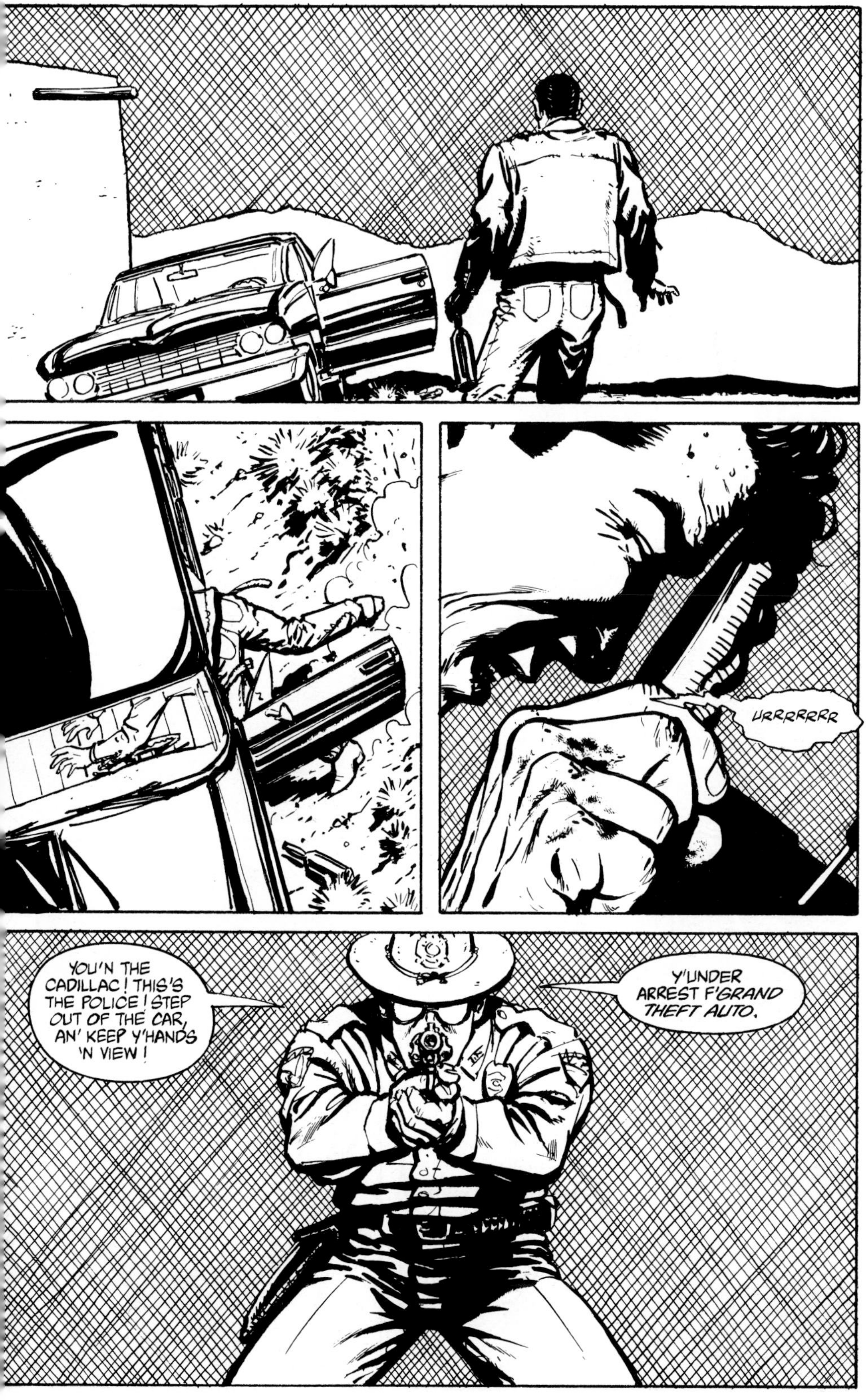
URRRRRRR
YOU'N THE CADILLAC! THIS'S THE POLICE! STEP OUT OF THE CAR, AN' KEEP Y'HANDS 'N VIEW!
Y'UNDER ARREST F'GRAND THEFT AUTO.

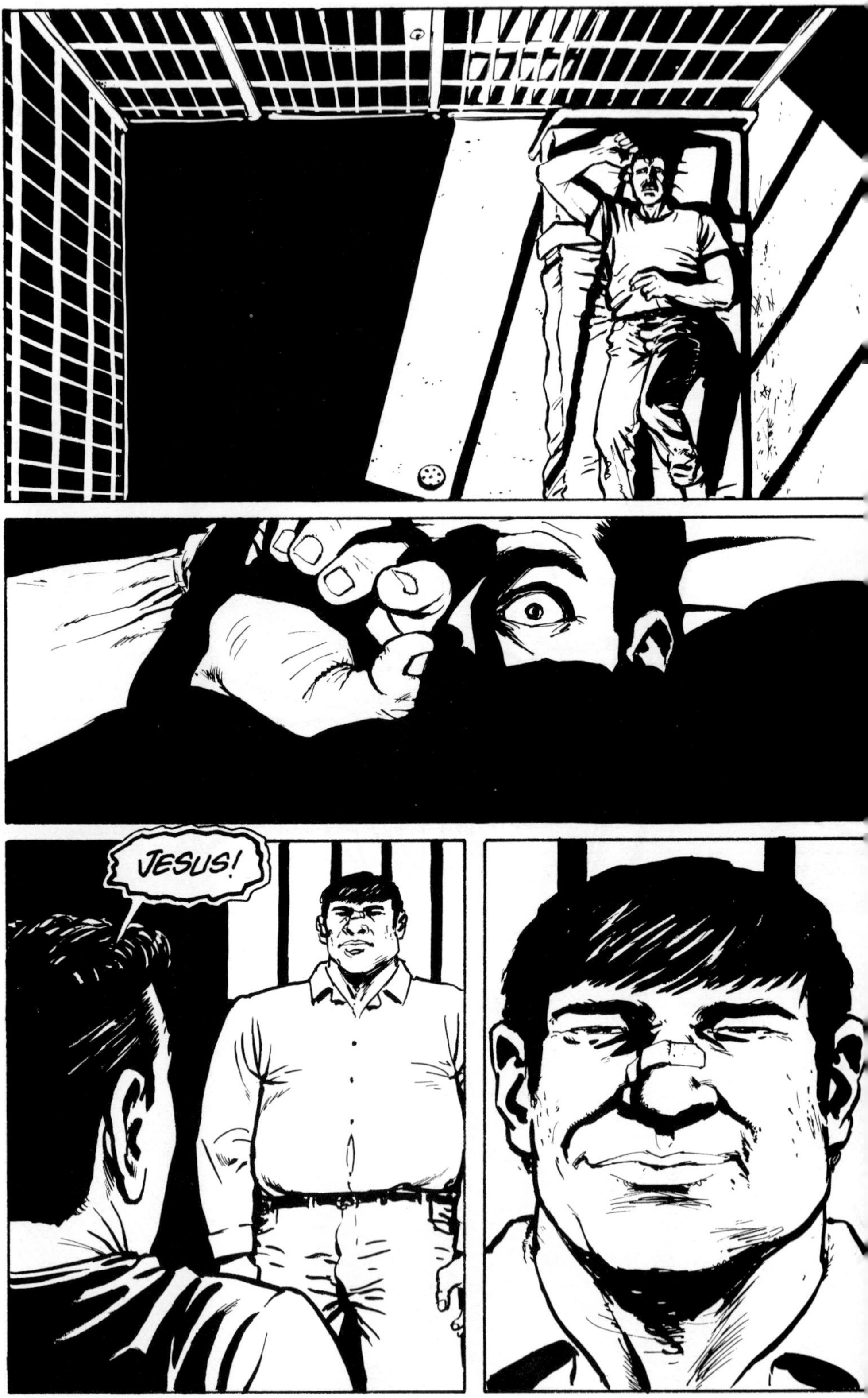

JESUS!

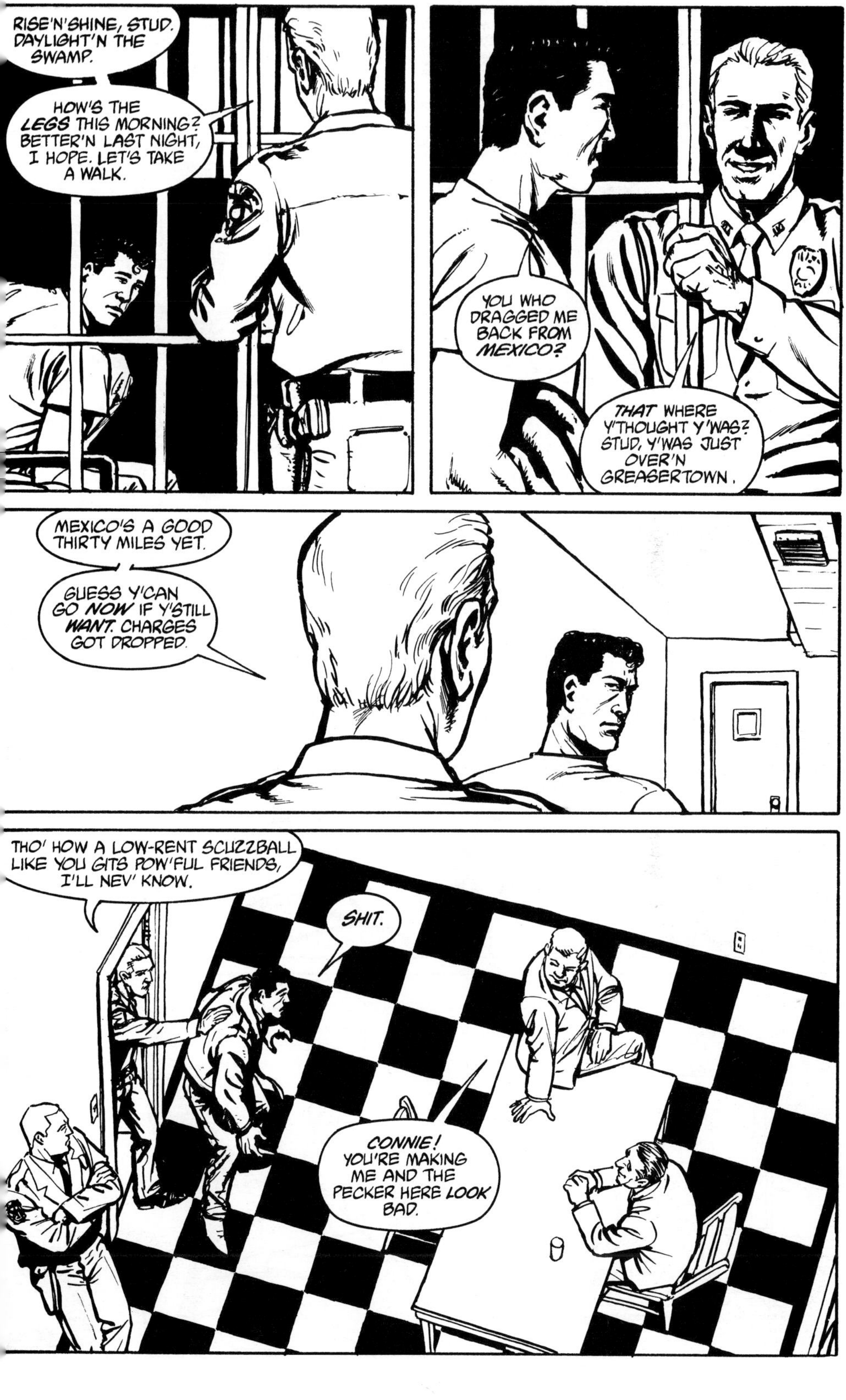
RISE'N'SHINE, STUD. DAYLIGHT'N THE SWAMP.
HOW'S THE LEGS THIS MORNING? BETTER'N LAST NIGHT, I HOPE. LET'S TAKE A WALK.
YOU WHO DRAGGED ME BACK FROM MEXICO?
THAT WHERE Y'THOUGHT Y'WAS? STUD, Y'WAS JUST OVER'N GREASERTOWN.
MEXICO'S A GOOD THIRTY MILES YET.
GUESS Y'CAN GO NOW IF Y'STILL WANT. CHARGES GOT DROPPED.
THO' HOW A LOW-RENT SCUZZBALL LIKE YOU GITS POW'FUL FRIENDS, I'LL NEV' KNOW.
SHIT.
CONNIE! YOU'RE MAKING ME AND THE PECKER HERE LOOK BAD.

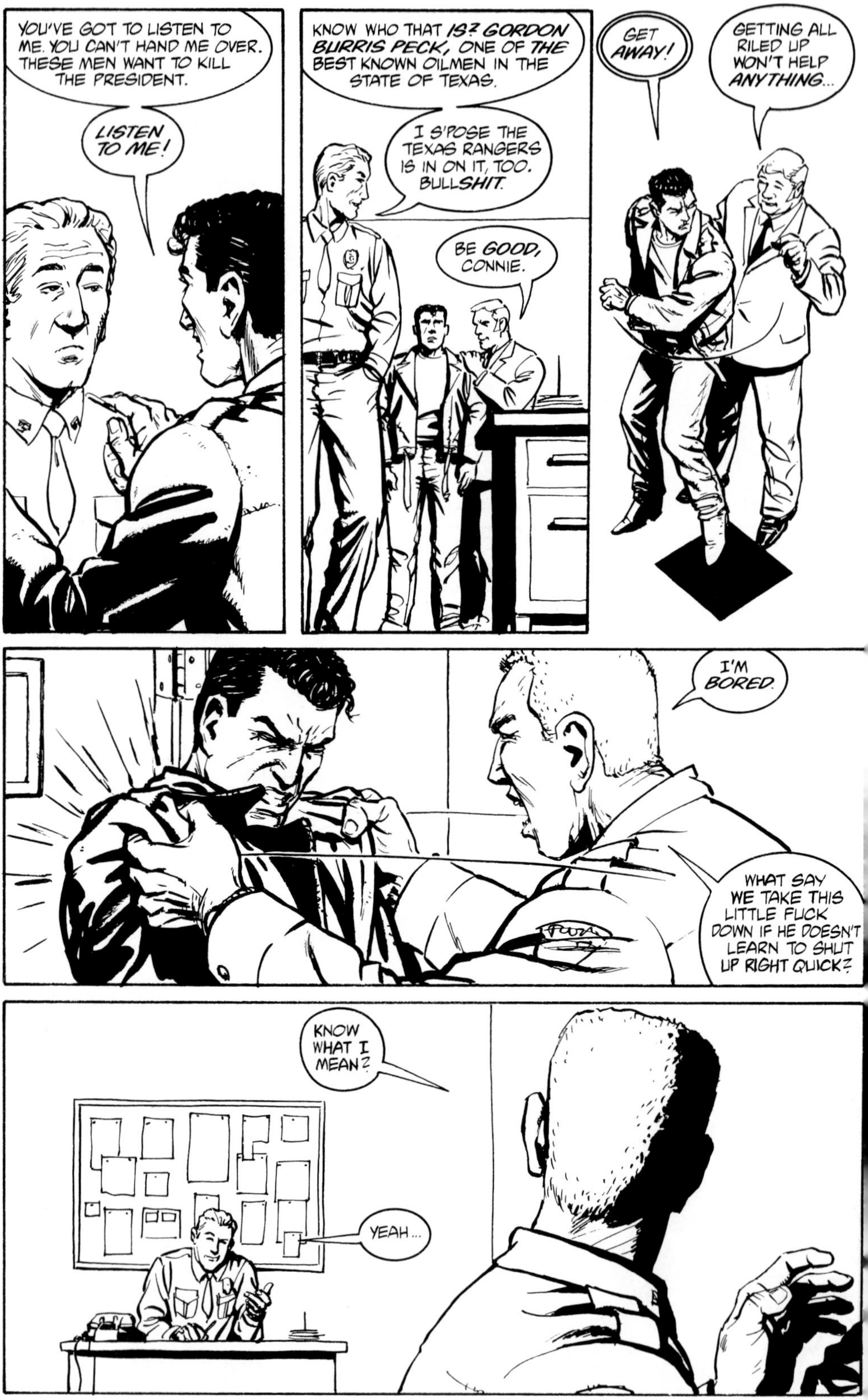
YOU'VE GOT TO LISTEN TO ME. YOU CAN'T HAND ME OVER. THESE MEN WANT TO KILL THE PRESIDENT.
LISTEN TO ME!
KNOW WHO THAT IS? GORDON BURRIS PECK, ONE OF THE BEST KNOWN OILMEN IN THE STATE OF TEXAS.
I S'POSE THE TEXAS RANGERS IS IN ON IT, TOO. BULLSHIT.
BE GOOD, CONNIE.
GET AWAY!
GETTING ALL RILED UP WON'T HELP ANYTHING...
I'M BORED.
WHAT SAY WE TAKE THIS LITTLE FUCK DOWN IF HE DOESN'T LEARN TO SHUT UP RIGHT QUICK?
KNOW WHAT I MEAN?
YEAH...

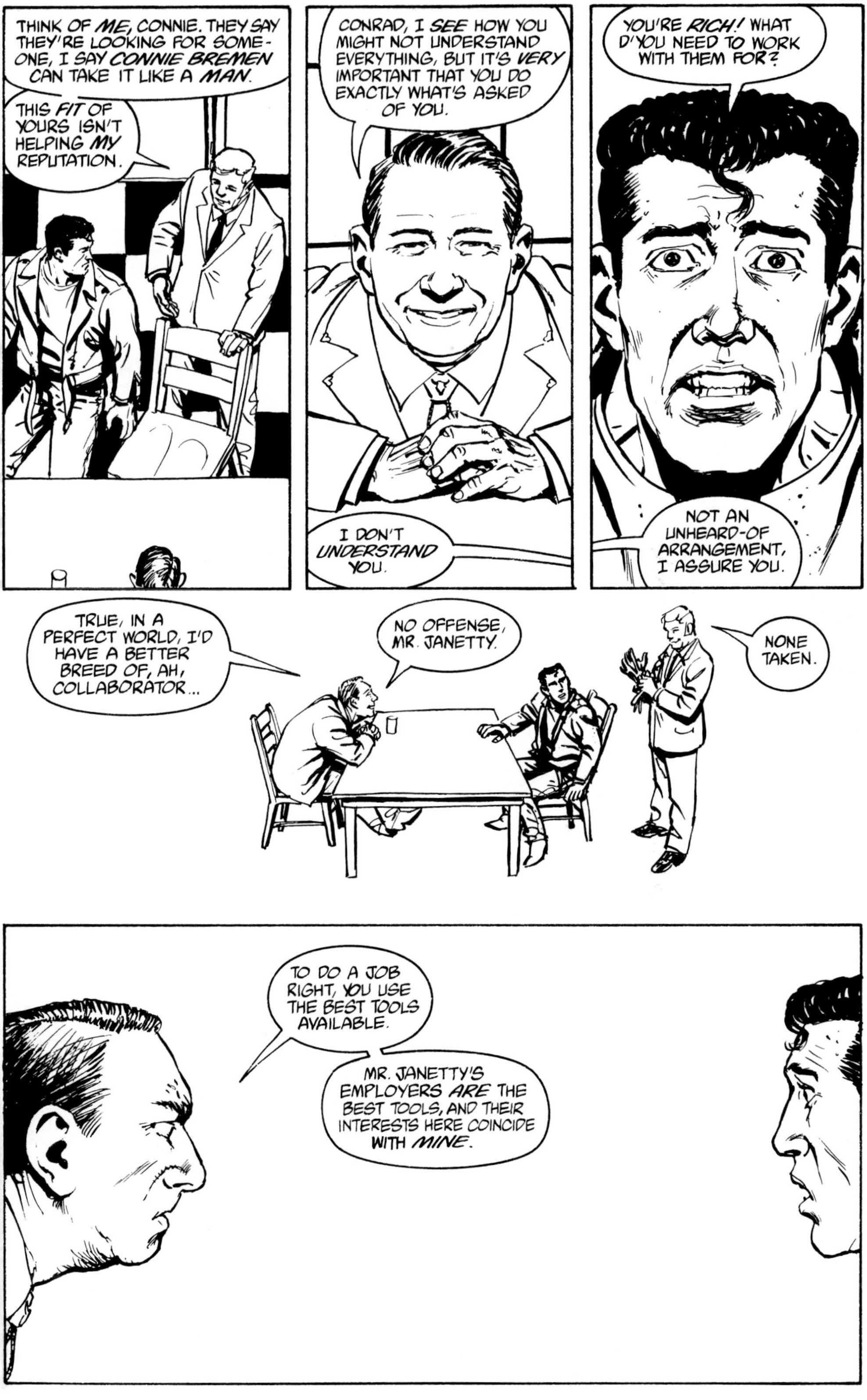
THINK OF ME, CONNIE. THEY SAY THEY'RE LOOKING FOR SOME-ONE, I SAY CONNIE BREMEN CAN TAKE IT LIKE A MAN.
THIS FIT OF YOURS ISN'T HELPING MY REPUTATION.
CONRAD, I SEE HOW YOU MIGHT NOT UNDERSTAND EVERYTHING, BUT IT'S VERY IMPORTANT THAT YOU DO EXACTLY WHAT'S ASKED OF YOU.
I DON'T UNDERSTAND YOU.
YOU'RE RICH! WHAT D'YOU NEED TO WORK WITH THEM FOR?
NOT AN UNHEARD-OF ARRANGEMENT, I ASSURE YOU.
TRUE, IN A PERFECT WORLD, I'D HAVE A BETTER BREED OF, AH, COLLABORATOR...
NO OFFENSE, MR. JANETTY.
NONE TAKEN.
TO DO A JOB RIGHT, YOU USE THE BEST TOOLS AVAILABLE.
MR. JANETTY'S EMPLOYERS ARE THE BEST TOOLS, AND THEIR INTERESTS HERE COINCIDE WITH MINE.

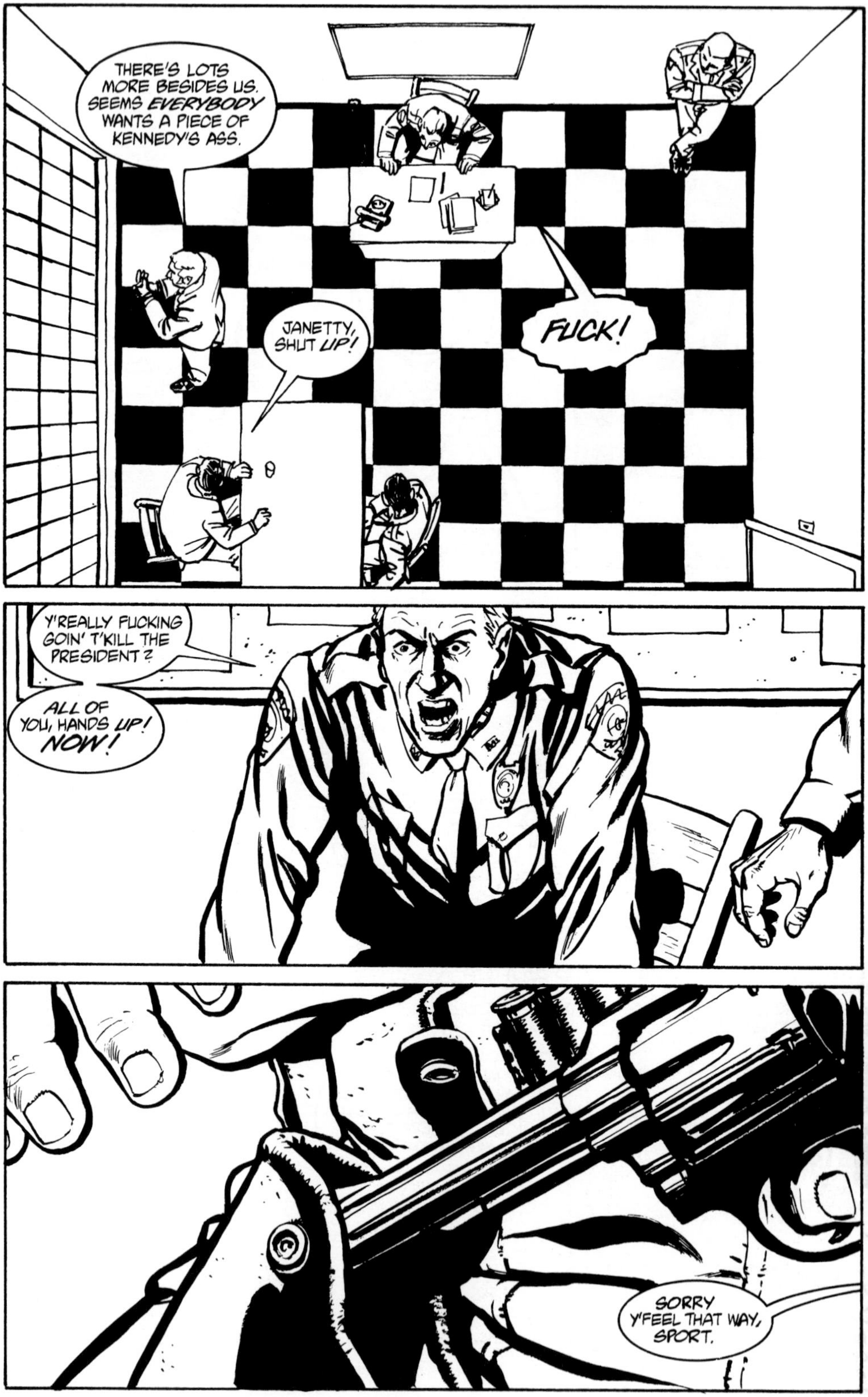
THERE'S LOTS MORE BESIDES US. SEEMS *EVERYBODY* WANTS A PIECE OF KENNEDY'S ASS.
FUCK!
JANETTY, SHUT *UP!*
Y'REALLY FUCKING GOIN' T'KILL THE PRESIDENT ?
ALL OF YOU, HANDS UP! NOW!
SORRY Y'FEEL THAT WAY, SPORT.

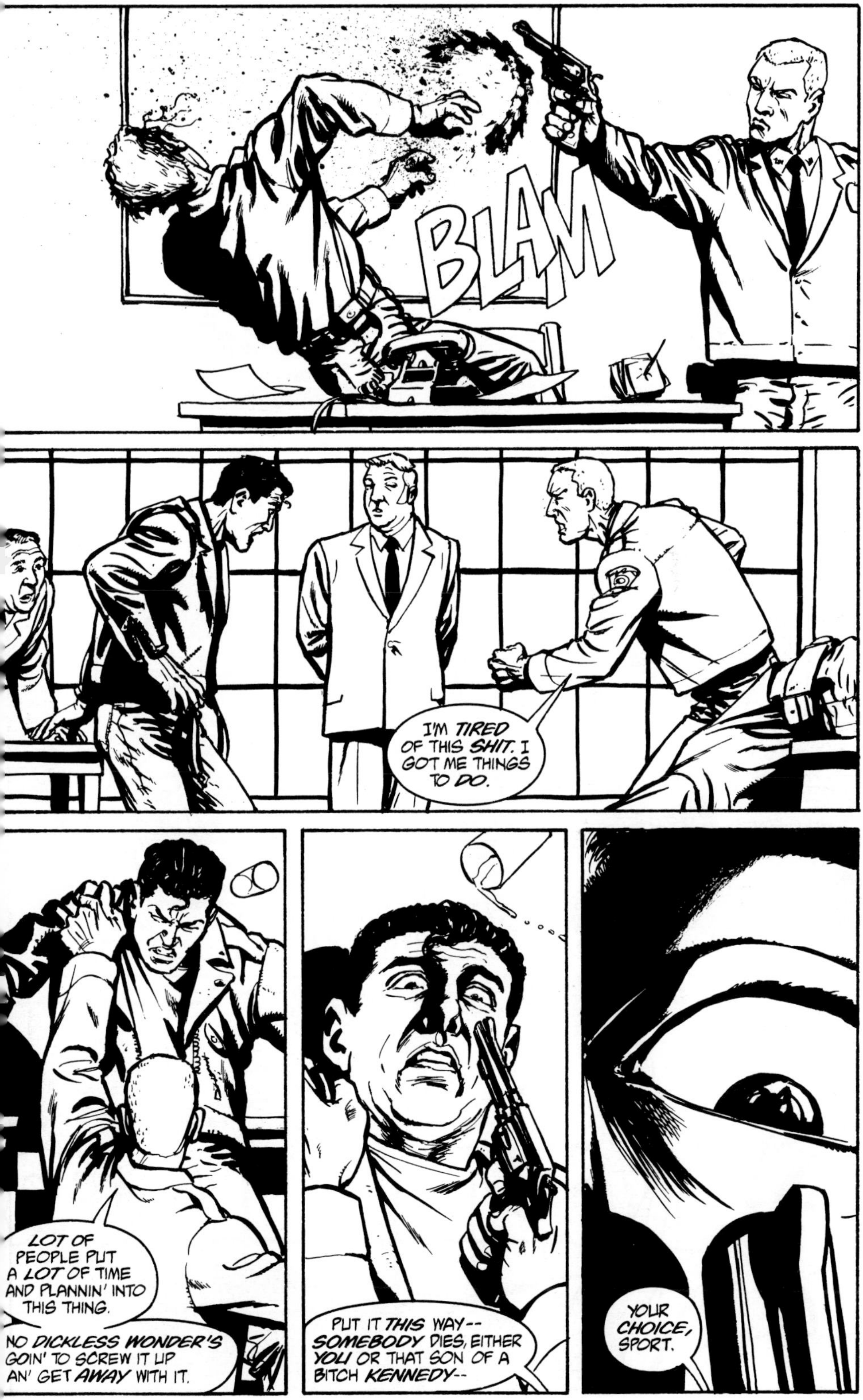
BLAM
I'M TIRED OF THIS SHIT. I GOT ME THINGS TO DO.
LOT OF PEOPLE PUT A LOT OF TIME AND PLANNIN' INTO THIS THING.
NO DICKLESS WONDER'S GOIN' TO SCREW IT UP AN' GET AWAY WITH IT.
PUT IT THIS WAY-- SOMEBODY DIES, EITHER YOU OR THAT SON OF A BITCH KENNEDY--
YOUR CHOICE, SPORT.

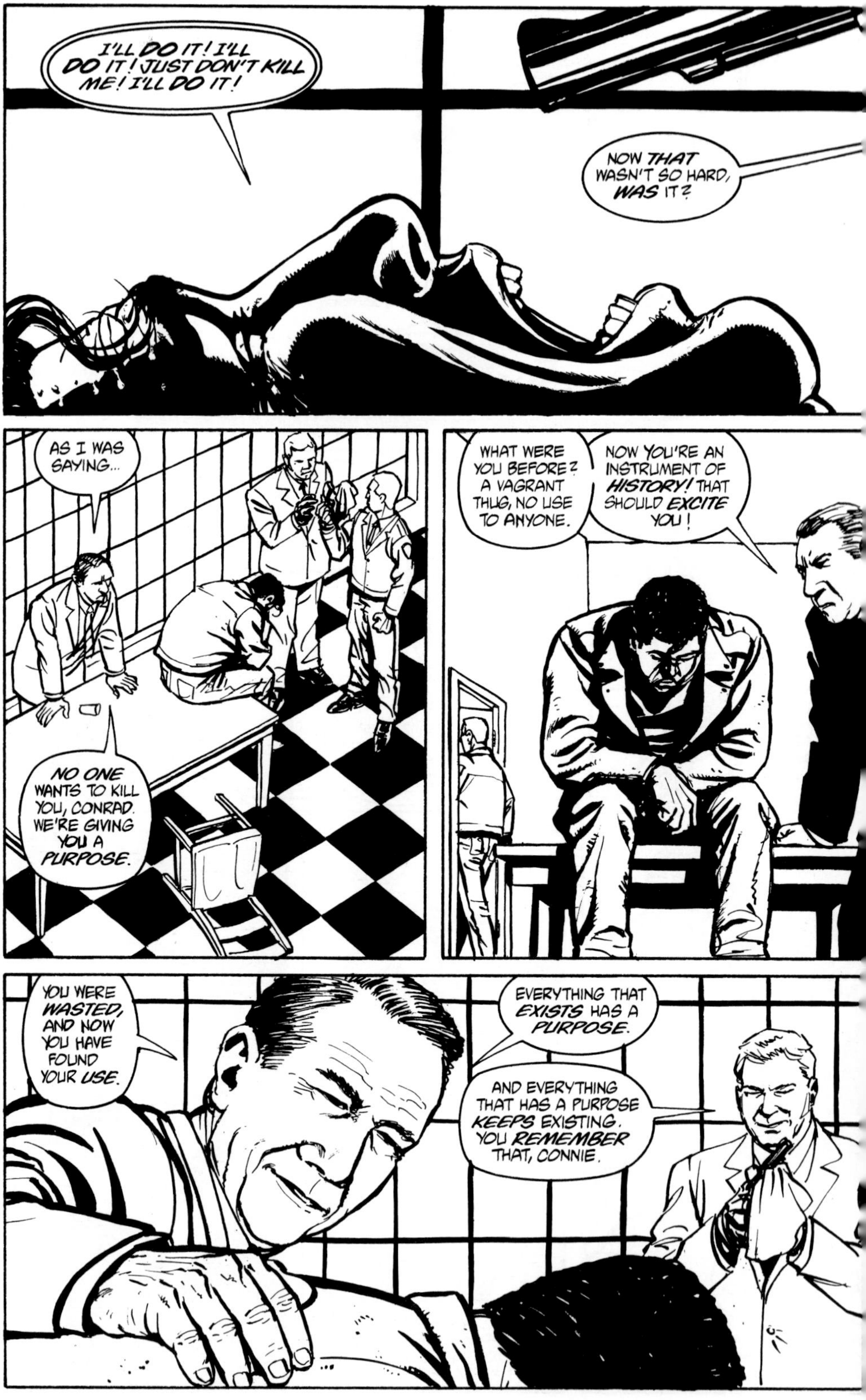
I'LL DO IT! I'LL DO IT! JUST DON'T KILL ME! I'LL DO IT!
NOW THAT WASN'T SO HARD, WAS IT?
AS I WAS SAYING...
NO ONE WANTS TO KILL YOU, CONRAD. WE'RE GIVING YOU A PURPOSE.
WHAT WERE YOU BEFORE? A VAGRANT THUG, NO USE TO ANYONE.
NOW YOU'RE AN INSTRUMENT OF HISTORY! THAT SHOULD EXCITE YOU!
YOU WERE WASTED, AND NOW YOU HAVE FOUND YOUR USE.
EVERYTHING THAT EXISTS HAS A PURPOSE.
AND EVERYTHING THAT HAS A PURPOSE KEEPS EXISTING. YOU REMEMBER THAT, CONNIE.

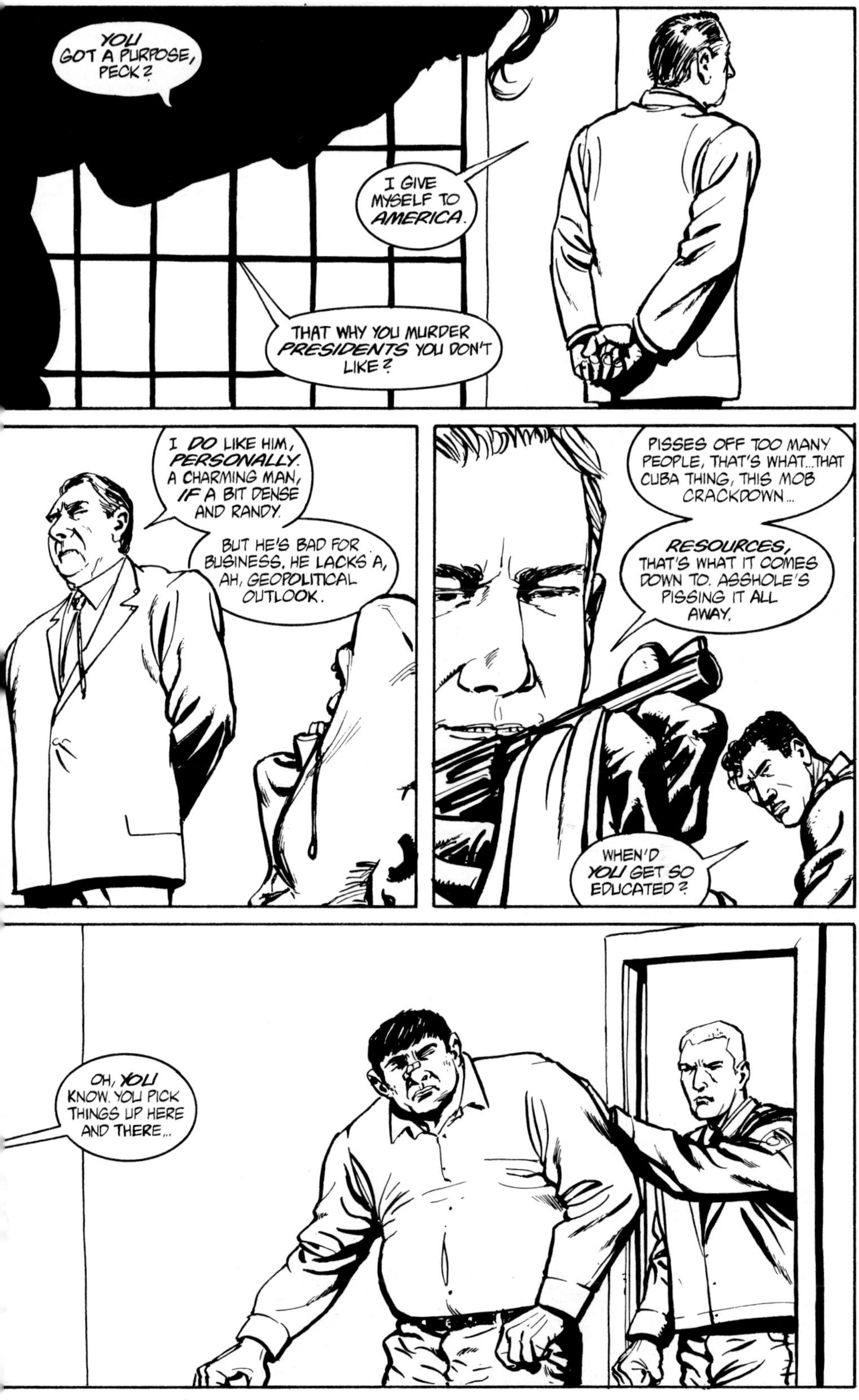
YOU GOT A PURPOSE, PECK?
I GIVE MYSELF TO AMERICA.
THAT WHY YOU MURDER PRESIDENTS YOU DON'T LIKE?
I DO LIKE HIM, PERSONALLY. A CHARMING MAN, IF A BIT DENSE AND RANDY.
BUT HE'S BAD FOR BUSINESS. HE LACKS A, AH, GEOPOLITICAL OUTLOOK.
PISSES OFF TOO MANY PEOPLE, THAT'S WHAT... THAT CUBA THING, THIS MOB CRACKDOWN...
RESOURCES, THAT'S WHAT IT COMES DOWN TO. ASSHOLE'S PISSING IT ALL AWAY.
WHEN'D YOU GET SO EDUCATED?
OH, YOU KNOW. YOU PICK THINGS UP HERE AND THERE...

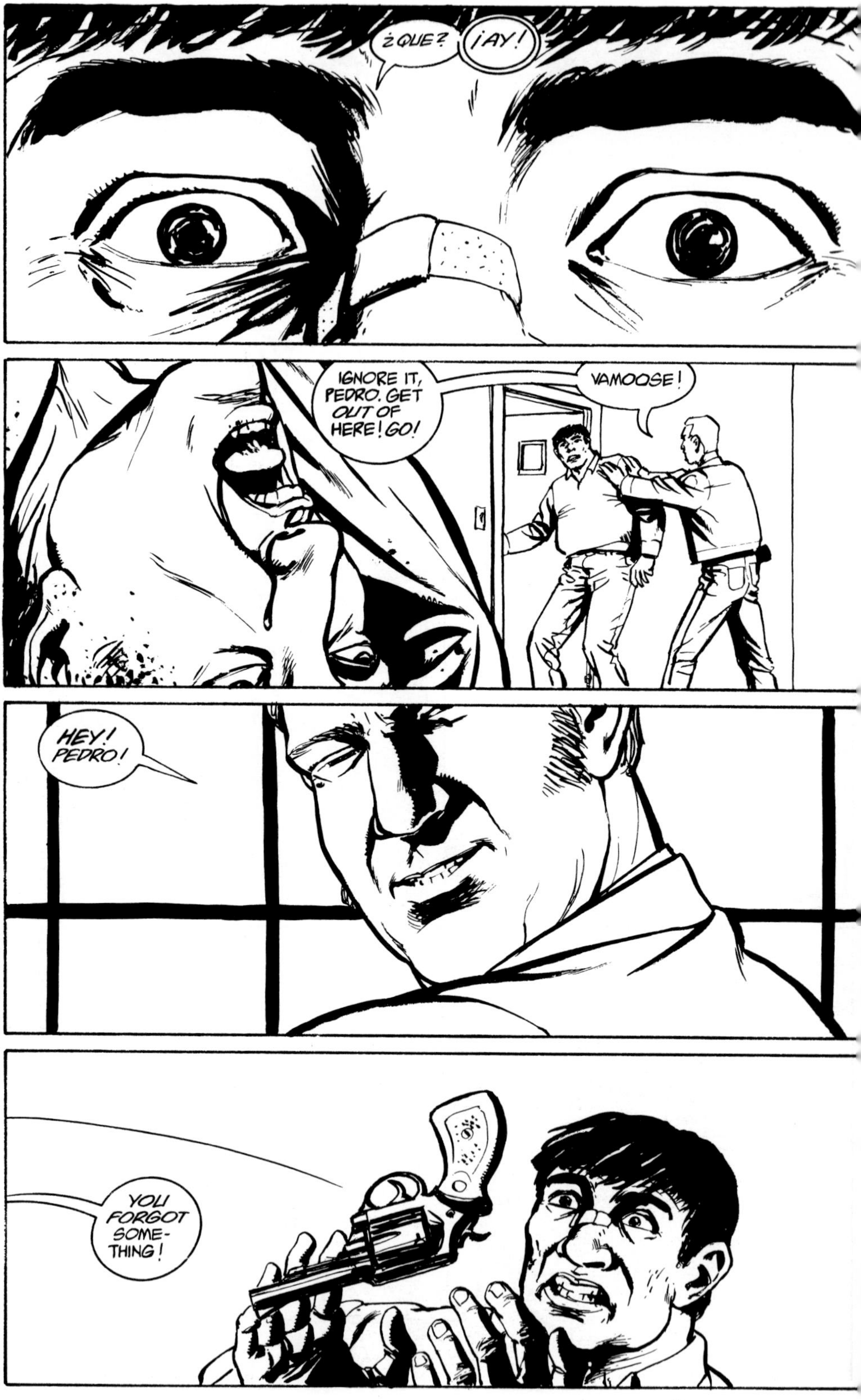
¿QUE?
¡AY!
IGNORE IT, PEDRO. GET OUT OF HERE! GO!
VAMOOSE!
HEY! PEDRO!
YOU FORGOT SOME-THING!

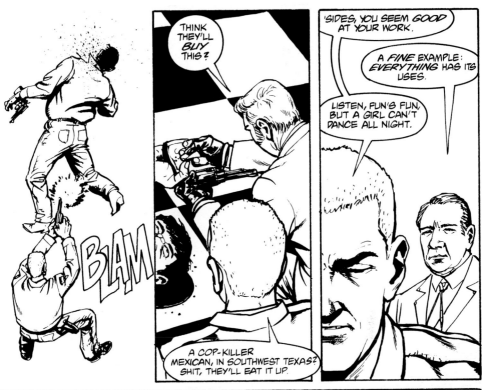

THINK THEY'LL *BUY* THIS?

A COP-KILLER MEXICAN, IN SOUTHWEST TEXAS? SHIT, THEY'LL EAT IT UP.

'SIDES, YOU SEEM *GOOD* AT YOUR WORK.

A *FINE* EXAMPLE: *EVERYTHING* HAS ITS USES.

LISTEN, FUN'S FUN, BUT A GIRL CAN'T DANCE ALL NIGHT.

LET'S *DO* IT.

POLICE

HOLD ONTO HIM THIS TIME.

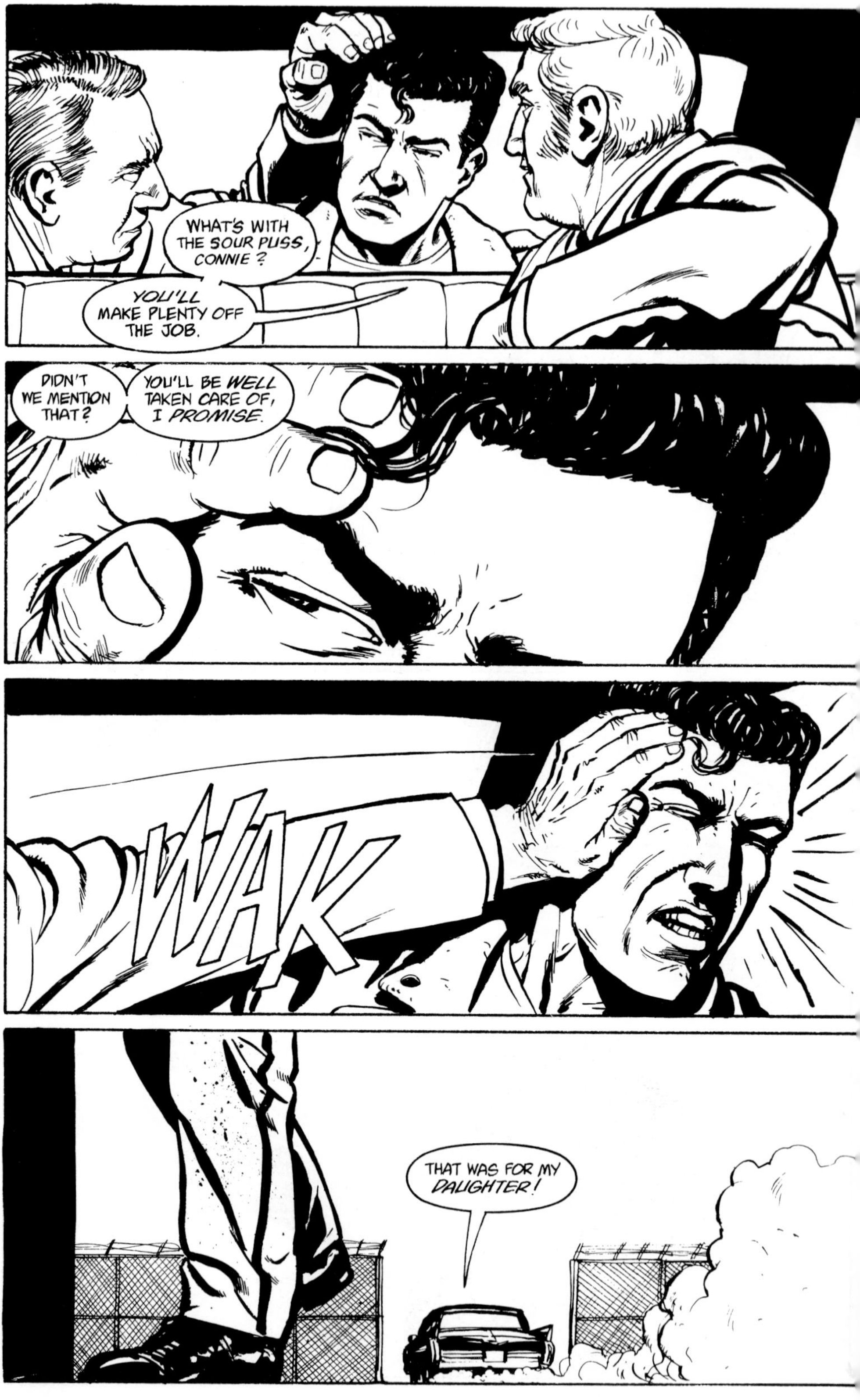
WHAT'S WITH THE SOUR PUSS, CONNIE?
YOU'LL MAKE PLENTY OFF THE JOB.
DIDN'T WE MENTION THAT?
YOU'LL BE WELL TAKEN CARE OF, I PROMISE.
WAK
THAT WAS FOR MY DAUGHTER!

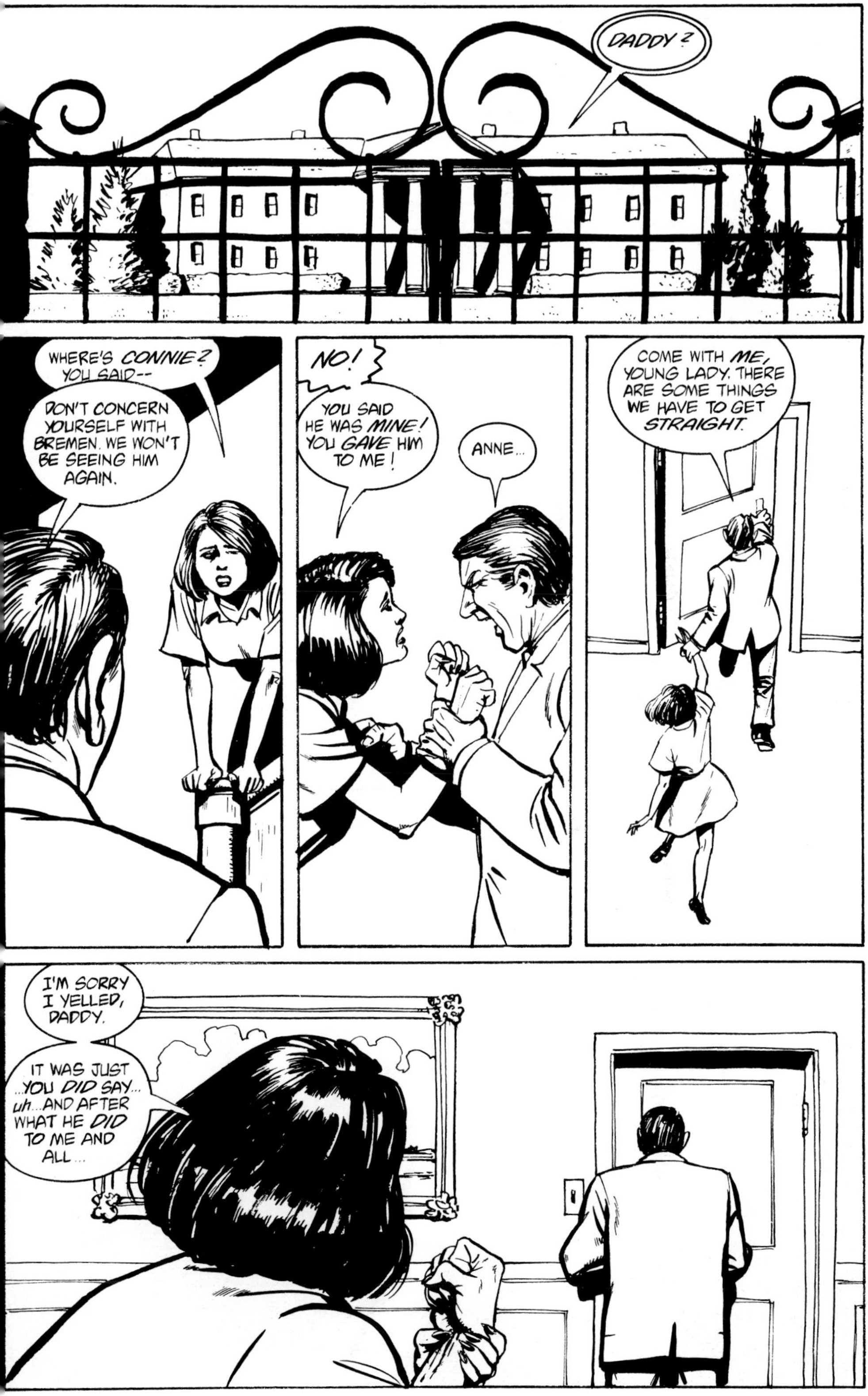

DADDY?
WHERE'S CONNIE? YOU SAID--
DON'T CONCERN YOURSELF WITH BREMEN. WE WON'T BE SEEING HIM AGAIN.
NO!
YOU SAID HE WAS MINE! YOU GAVE HIM TO ME!
ANNE...
COME WITH ME, YOUNG LADY. THERE ARE SOME THINGS WE HAVE TO GET STRAIGHT.
I'M SORRY I YELLED, DADDY.
IT WAS JUST ...YOU DID SAY... uh...AND AFTER WHAT HE DID TO ME AND ALL...

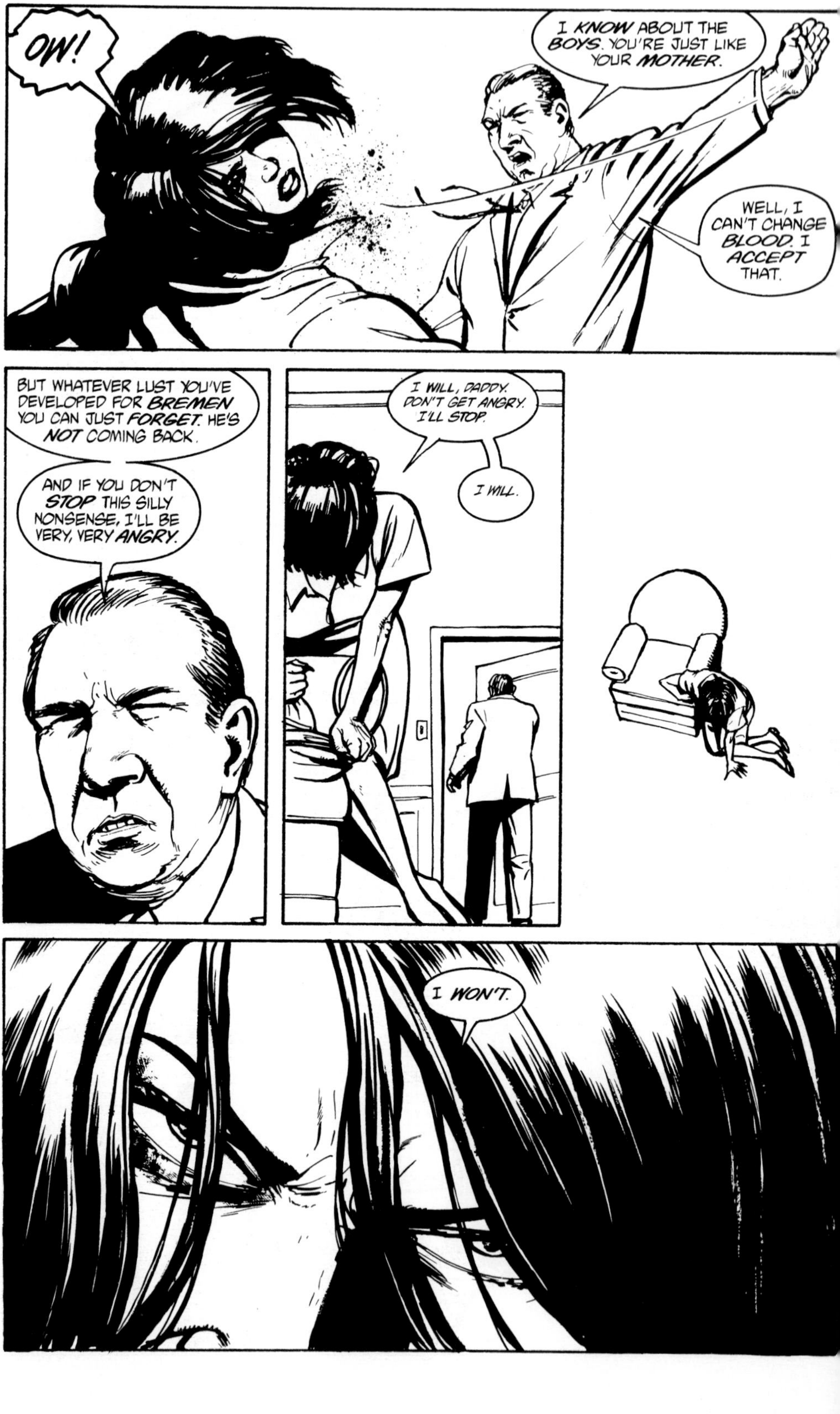
OW!
I KNOW ABOUT THE BOYS. YOU'RE JUST LIKE YOUR MOTHER.
WELL, I CAN'T CHANGE BLOOD. I ACCEPT THAT.
BUT WHATEVER LUST YOU'VE DEVELOPED FOR BREMEN YOU CAN JUST FORGET. HE'S NOT COMING BACK.
AND IF YOU DON'T STOP THIS SILLY NONSENSE, I'LL BE VERY, VERY ANGRY.
I WILL, DADDY. DON'T GET ANGRY. I'LL STOP.
I WILL.
I WON'T.

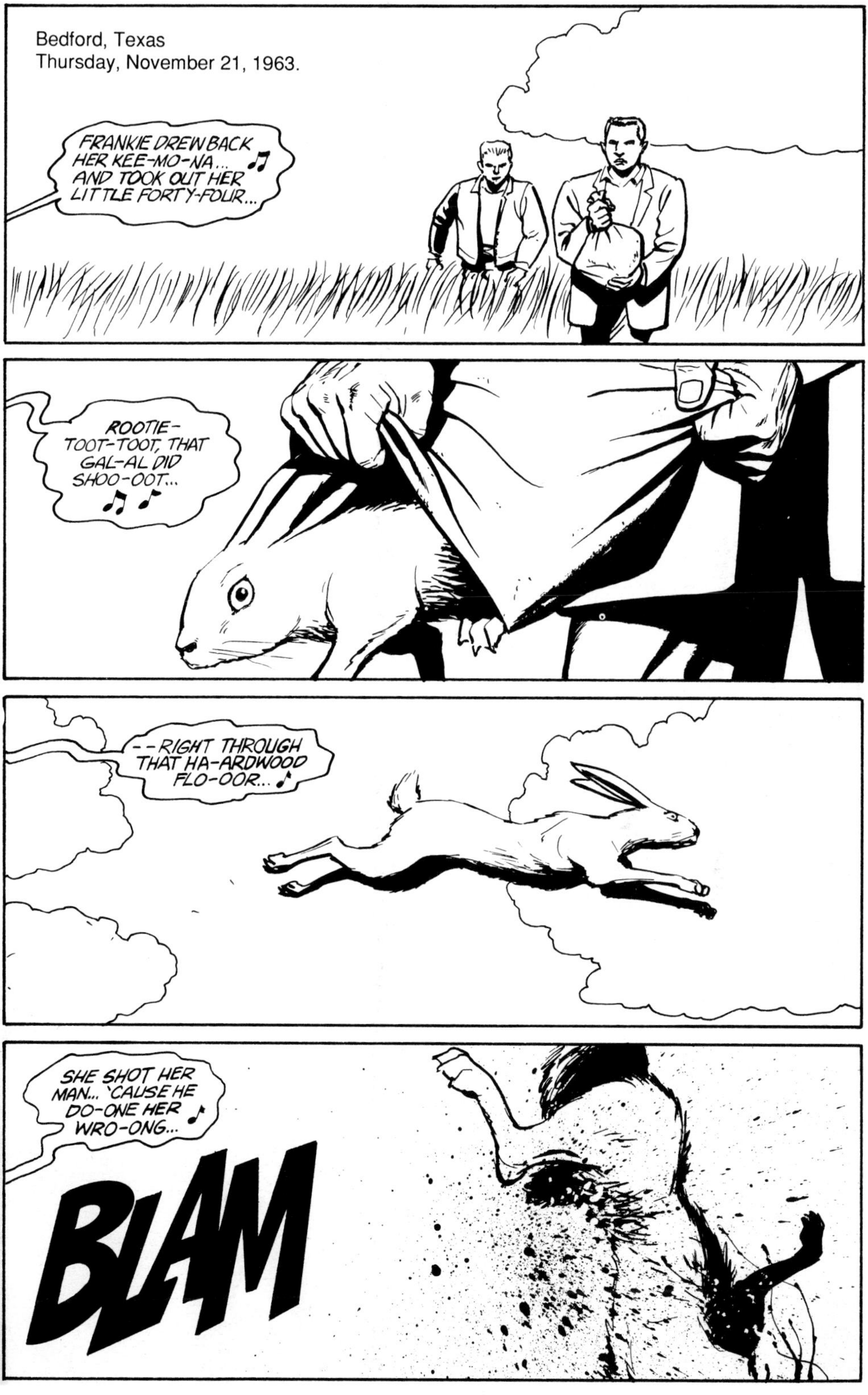
Bedford, Texas
Thursday, November 21, 1963.
FRANKIE DREW BACK HER KEE-MO-NA... AND TOOK OUT HER LITTLE FORTY-FOUR...
ROOTIE-TOOT-TOOT, THAT GAL-AL DID SHOO-OOT...
--RIGHT THROUGH THAT HA-ARDWOOD FLO-OOR...
SHE SHOT HER MAN... 'CAUSE HE DO-ONE HER WRO-ONG...
BLAM

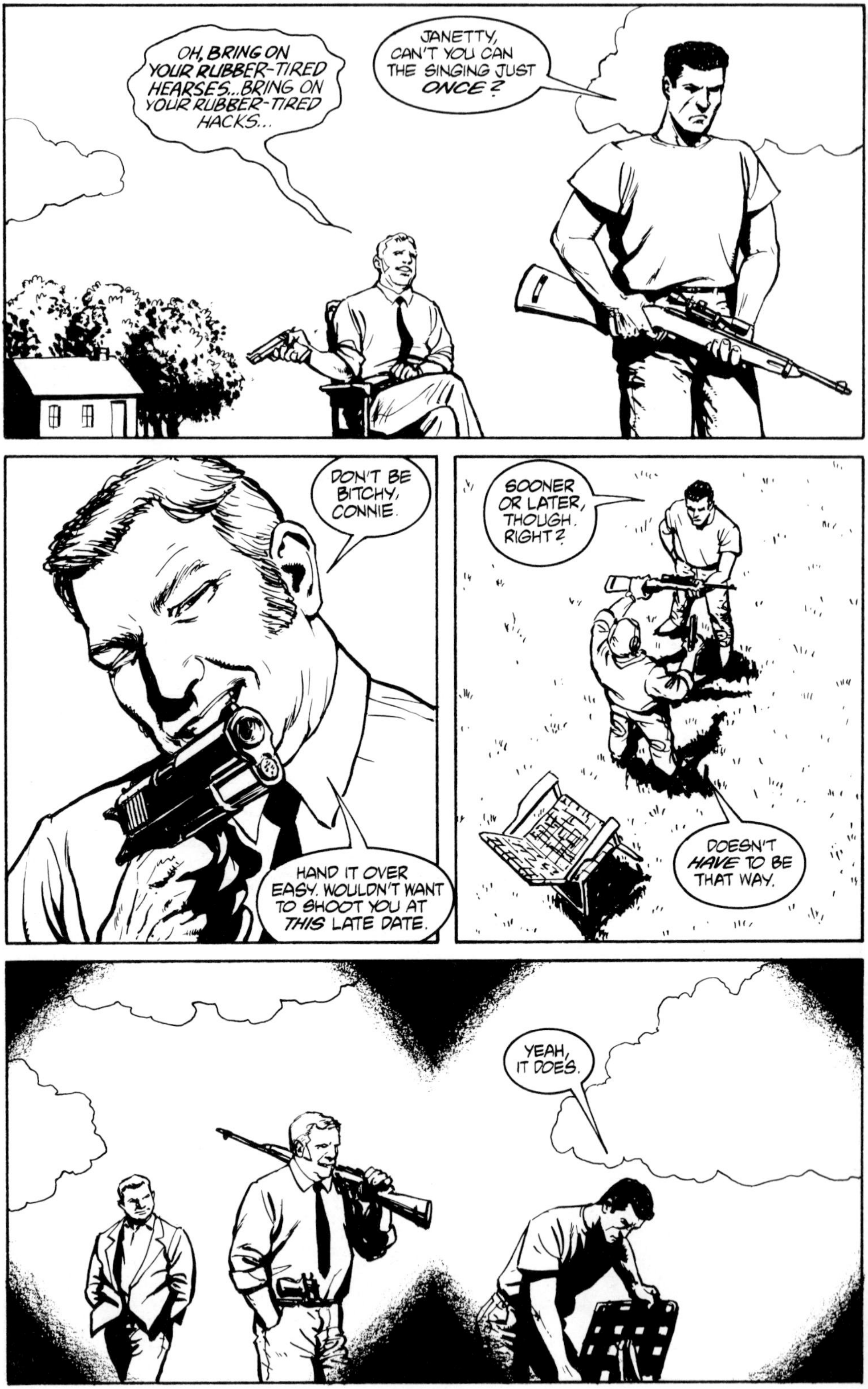

OH, BRING ON YOUR RUBBER-TIRED HEARSES...BRING ON YOUR RUBBER-TIRED HACKS...
JANETTY, CAN'T YOU CAN THE SINGING JUST ONCE?
DON'T BE BITCHY, CONNIE.
HAND IT OVER EASY. WOULDN'T WANT TO SHOOT YOU AT THIS LATE DATE.
SOONER OR LATER, THOUGH, RIGHT?
DOESN'T HAVE TO BE THAT WAY.
YEAH, IT DOES.

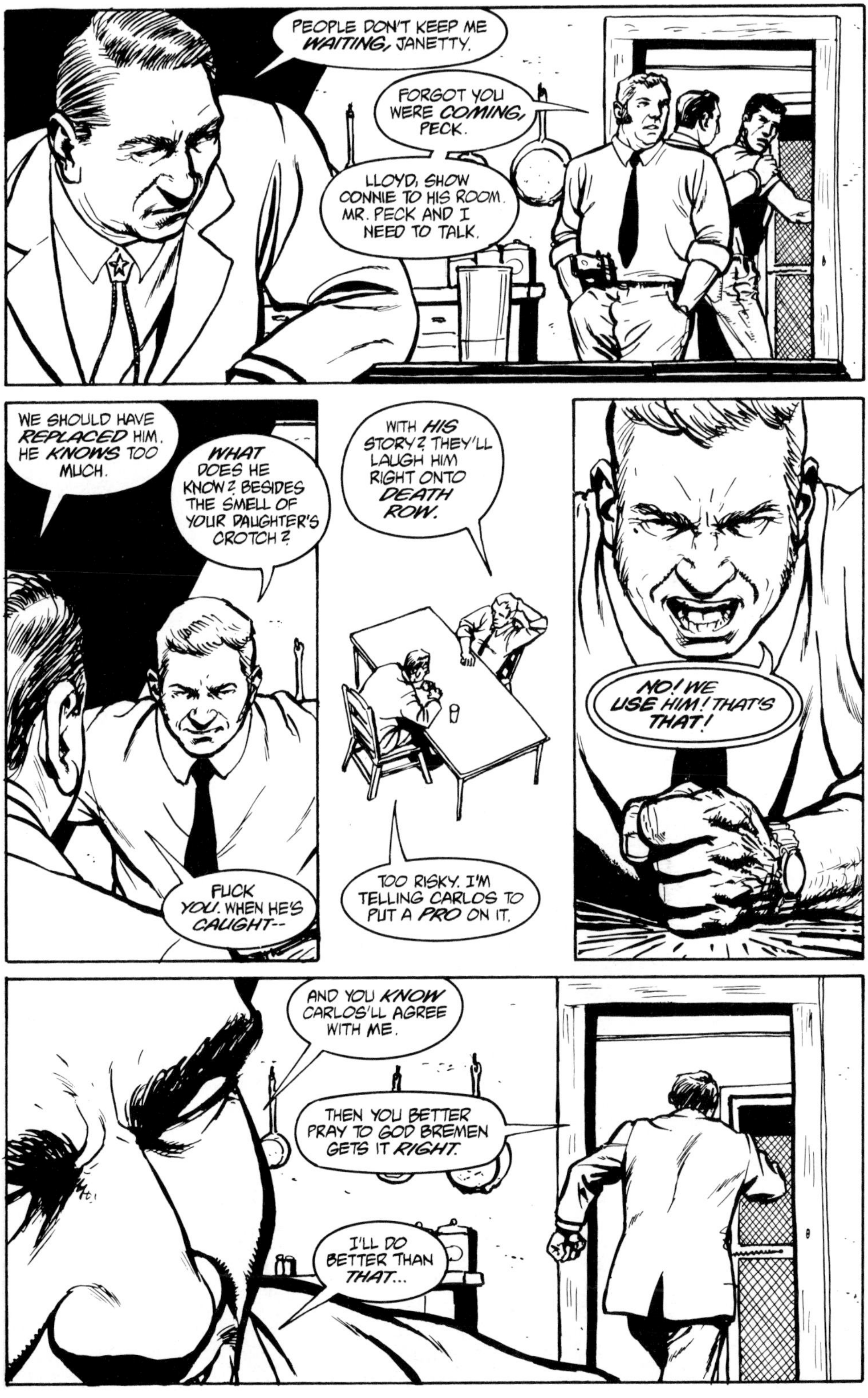
PEOPLE DON'T KEEP ME WAITING, JANETTY.
FORGOT YOU WERE COMING, PECK.
LLOYD, SHOW CONNIE TO HIS ROOM. MR. PECK AND I NEED TO TALK.
WE SHOULD HAVE REPLACED HIM. HE KNOWS TOO MUCH.
WHAT DOES HE KNOW? BESIDES THE SMELL OF YOUR DAUGHTER'S CROTCH?
FUCK YOU. WHEN HE'S CAUGHT--
WITH HIS STORY? THEY'LL LAUGH HIM RIGHT ONTO DEATH ROW.
TOO RISKY. I'M TELLING CARLOS TO PUT A PRO ON IT.
NO! WE USE HIM! THAT'S THAT!
AND YOU KNOW CARLOS'LL AGREE WITH ME.
THEN YOU BETTER PRAY TO GOD BREMEN GETS IT RIGHT.
I'LL DO BETTER THAN THAT...

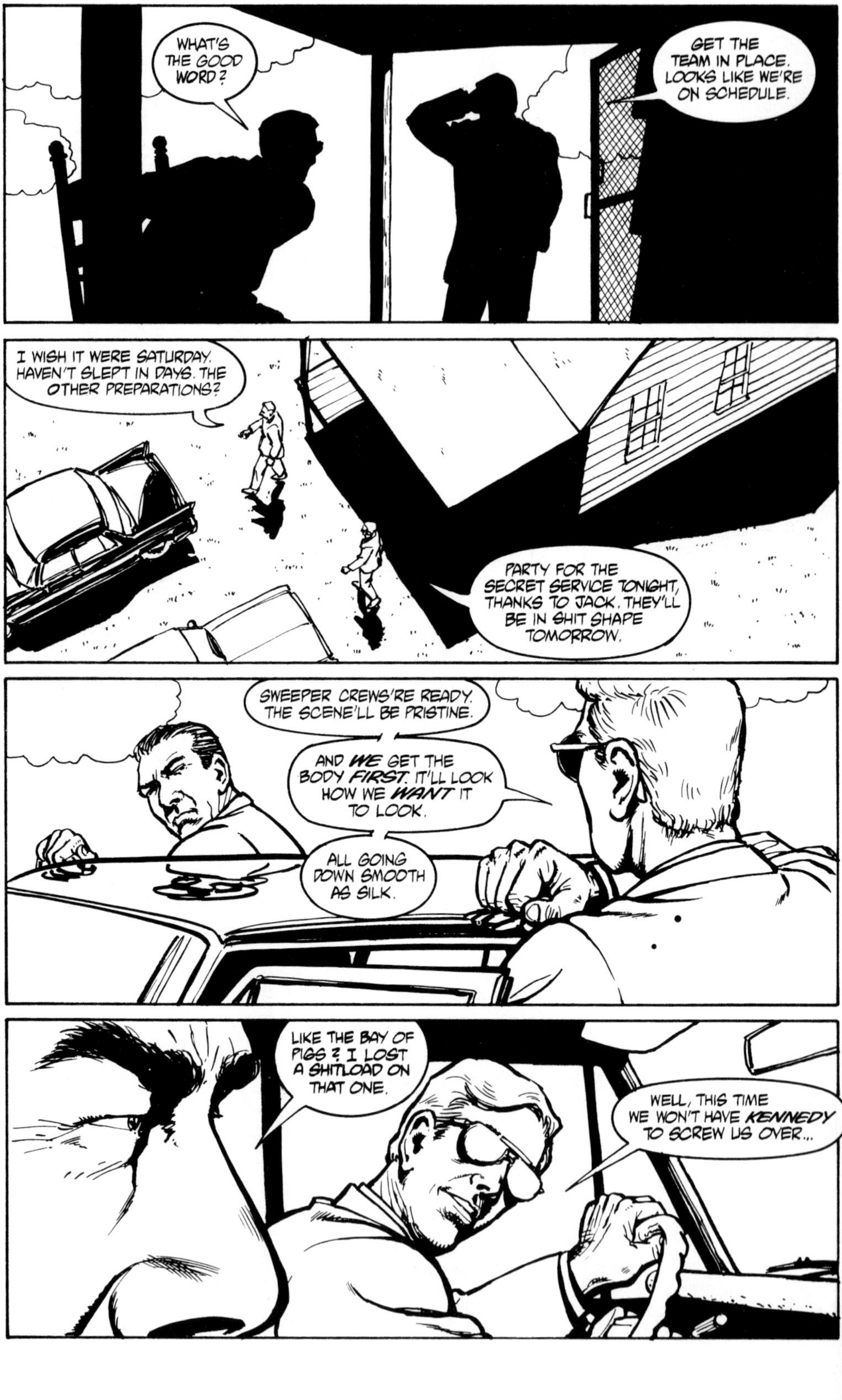
WHAT'S THE GOOD WORD?
GET THE TEAM IN PLACE. LOOKS LIKE WE'RE ON SCHEDULE.
I WISH IT WERE SATURDAY. HAVEN'T SLEPT IN DAYS. THE OTHER PREPARATIONS?
PARTY FOR THE SECRET SERVICE TONIGHT, THANKS TO JACK. THEY'LL BE IN SHIT SHAPE TOMORROW.
SWEEPER CREWS'RE READY. THE SCENE'LL BE PRISTINE.
AND WE GET THE BODY FIRST. IT'LL LOOK HOW WE WANT IT TO LOOK.
ALL GOING DOWN SMOOTH AS SILK.
LIKE THE BAY OF PIGS? I LOST A SHITLOAD ON THAT ONE.
WELL, THIS TIME WE WON'T HAVE KENNEDY TO SCREW US OVER...

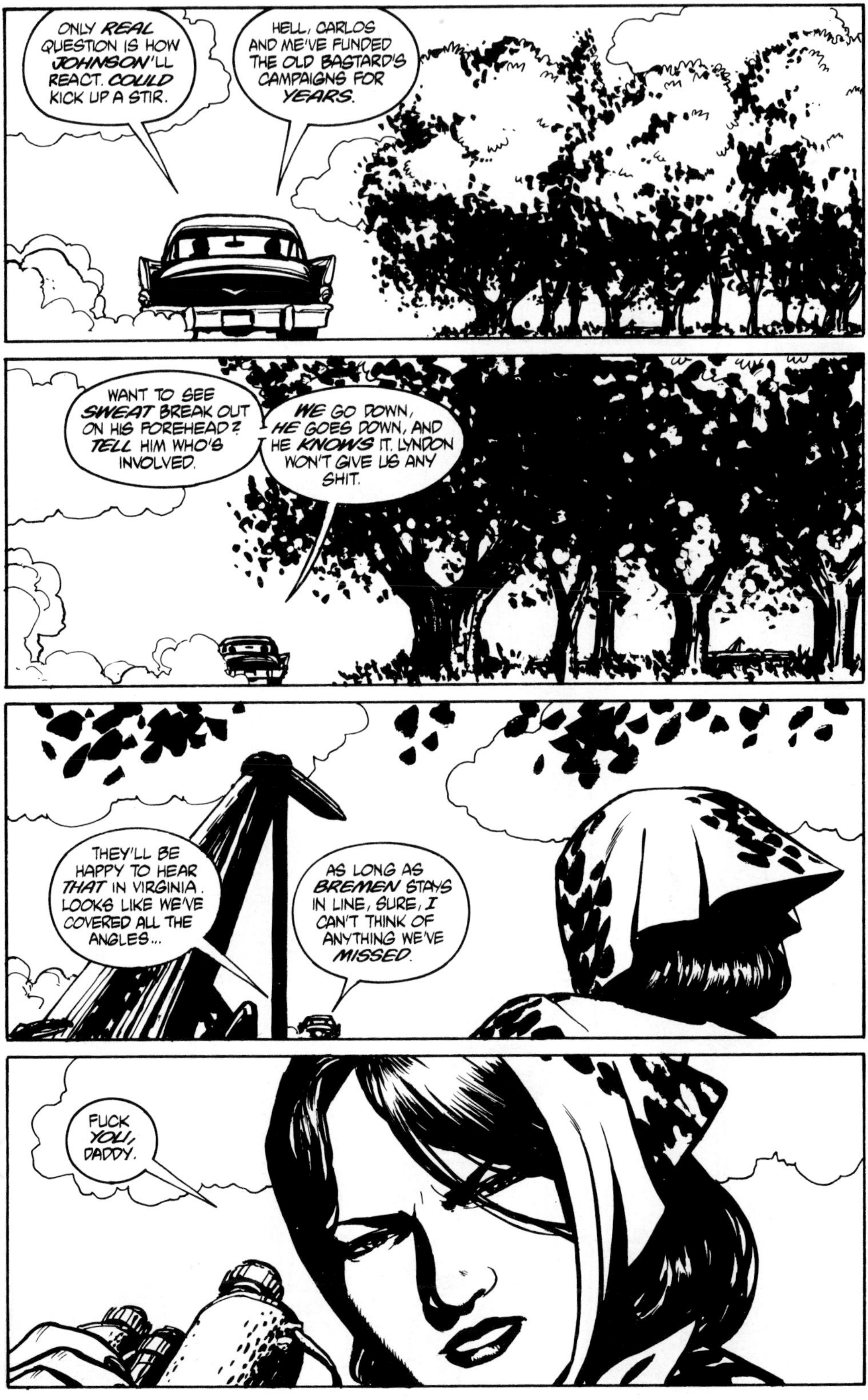
ONLY REAL QUESTION IS HOW JOHNSON'LL REACT. COULD KICK UP A STIR.
HELL, CARLOS AND ME'VE FUNDED THE OLD BASTARD'S CAMPAIGNS FOR YEARS.
WANT TO SEE SWEAT BREAK OUT ON HIS FOREHEAD? TELL HIM WHO'S INVOLVED.
WE GO DOWN, HE GOES DOWN, AND HE KNOWS IT. LYNDON WON'T GIVE US ANY SHIT.
THEY'LL BE HAPPY TO HEAR THAT IN VIRGINIA. LOOKS LIKE WE'VE COVERED ALL THE ANGLES...
AS LONG AS BREMEN STAYS IN LINE, SURE, I CAN'T THINK OF ANYTHING WE'VE MISSED.
FUCK YOU, DADDY.

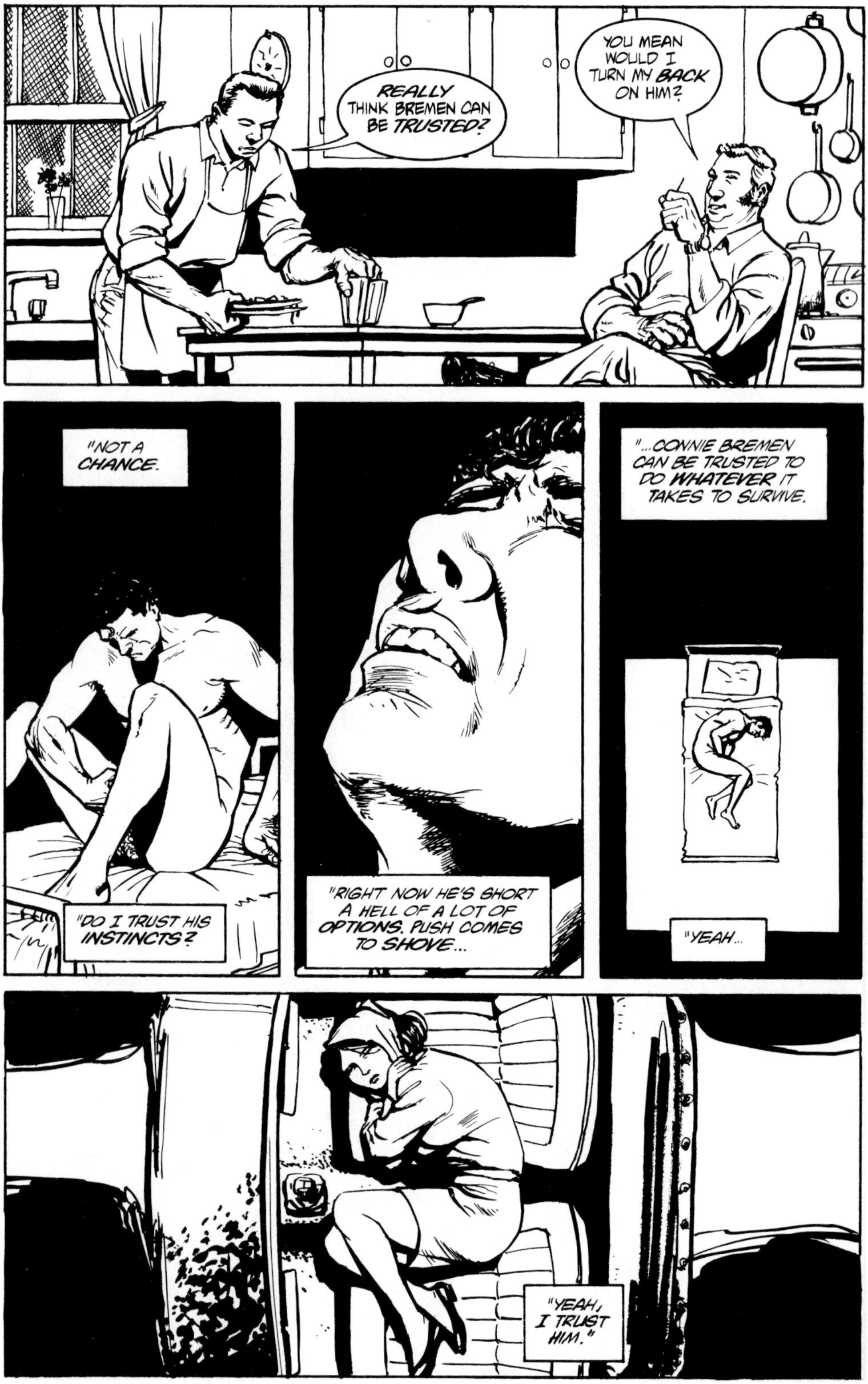
REALLY THINK BREMEN CAN BE TRUSTED?
YOU MEAN WOULD I TURN MY BACK ON HIM?
"NOT A CHANCE.
"DO I TRUST HIS INSTINCTS?
"RIGHT NOW HE'S SHORT A HELL OF A LOT OF OPTIONS. PUSH COMES TO SHOVE...
"...CONNIE BREMEN CAN BE TRUSTED TO DO WHATEVER IT TAKES TO SURVIVE.
"YEAH...
"YEAH, I TRUST HIM."

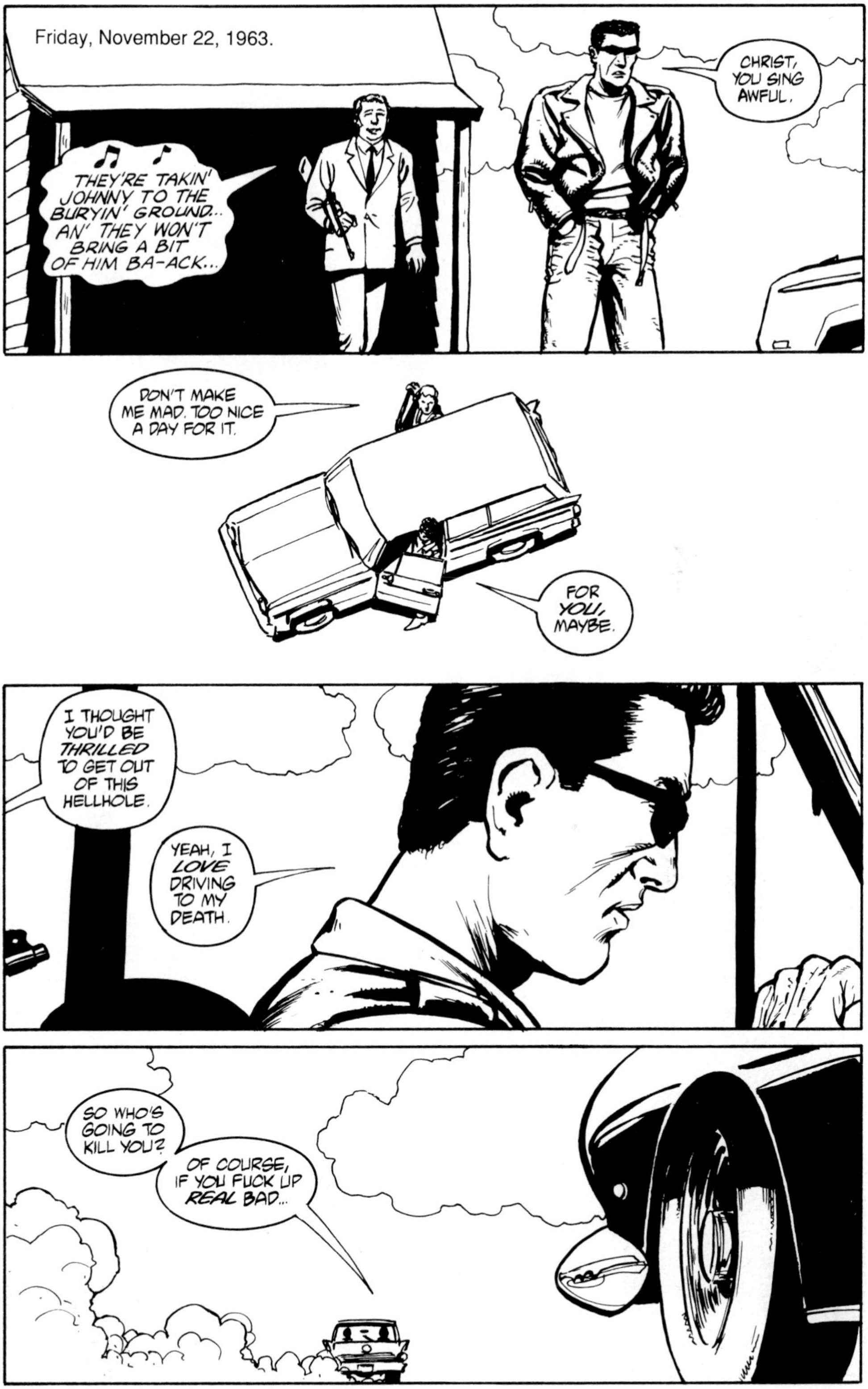
Friday, November 22, 1963.
THEY'RE TAKIN' JOHNNY TO THE BURYIN' GROUND... AN' THEY WON'T BRING A BIT OF HIM BA-ACK...
CHRIST, YOU SING AWFUL.
DON'T MAKE ME MAD. TOO NICE A DAY FOR IT.
FOR YOU, MAYBE.
I THOUGHT YOU'D BE THRILLED TO GET OUT OF THIS HELLHOLE.
YEAH, I LOVE DRIVING TO MY DEATH.
SO WHO'S GOING TO KILL YOU?
OF COURSE, IF YOU FUCK UP REAL BAD...

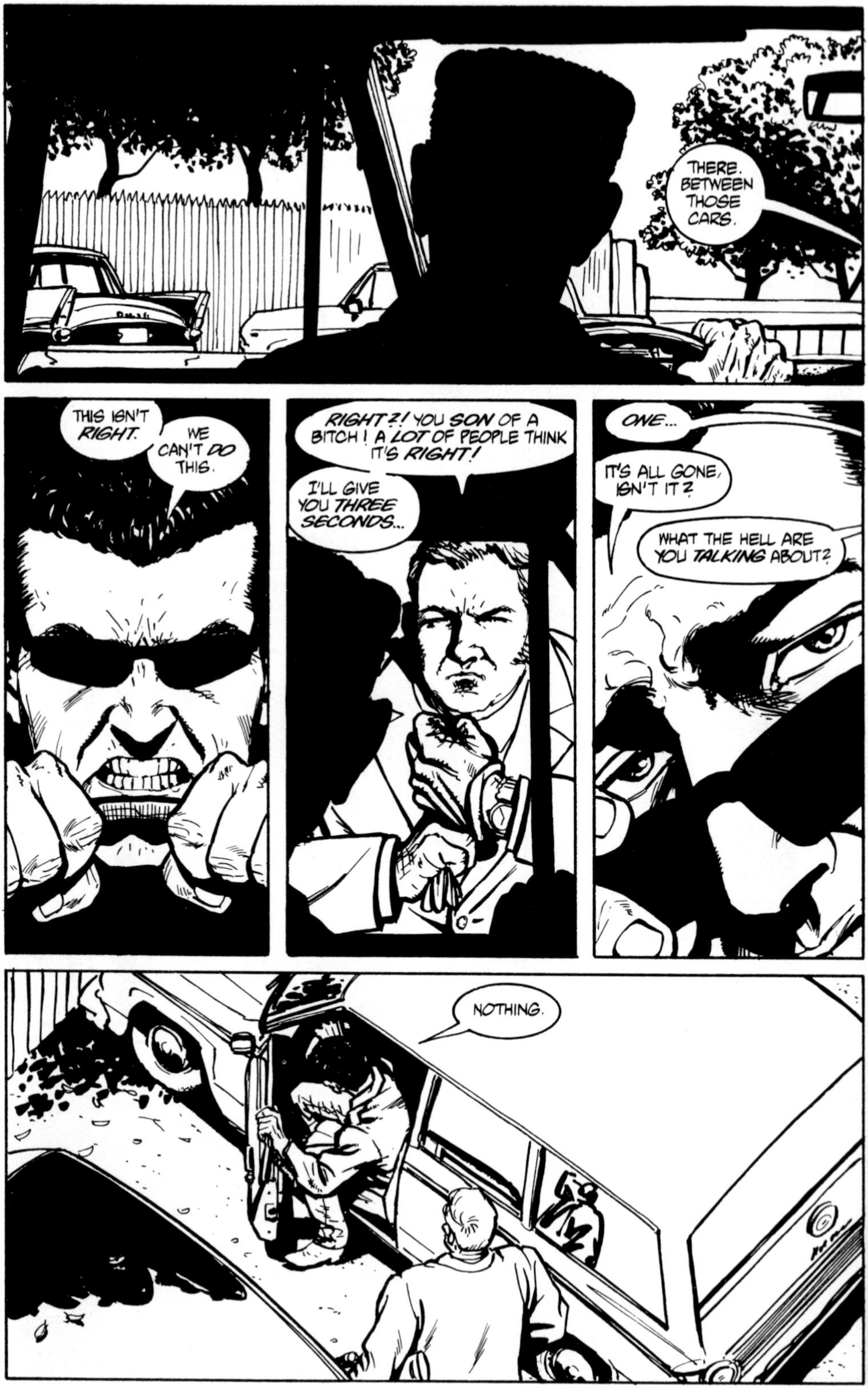
THERE. BETWEEN THOSE CARS.
THIS ISN'T RIGHT.
WE CAN'T DO THIS.
RIGHT?! YOU SON OF A BITCH! A LOT OF PEOPLE THINK IT'S RIGHT!
I'LL GIVE YOU THREE SECONDS...
ONE...
IT'S ALL GONE, ISN'T IT?
WHAT THE HELL ARE YOU TALKING ABOUT?
NOTHING.

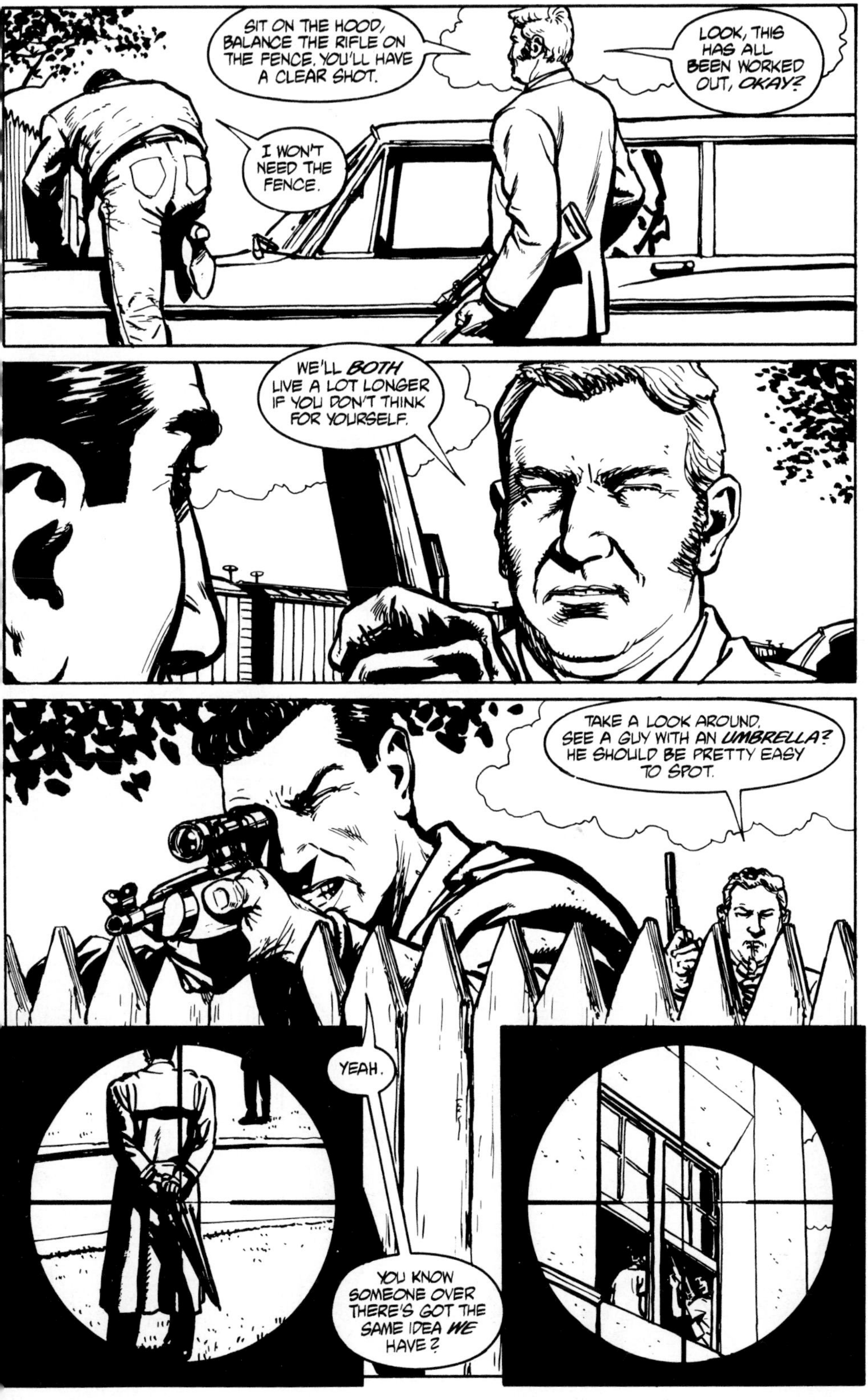
SIT ON THE HOOD, BALANCE THE RIFLE ON THE FENCE. YOU'LL HAVE A CLEAR SHOT.
LOOK, THIS HAS ALL BEEN WORKED OUT, OKAY?
I WON'T NEED THE FENCE.
WE'LL BOTH LIVE A LOT LONGER IF YOU DON'T THINK FOR YOURSELF.
TAKE A LOOK AROUND. SEE A GUY WITH AN UMBRELLA? HE SHOULD BE PRETTY EASY TO SPOT.
YEAH.
YOU KNOW SOMEONE OVER THERE'S GOT THE SAME IDEA WE HAVE?

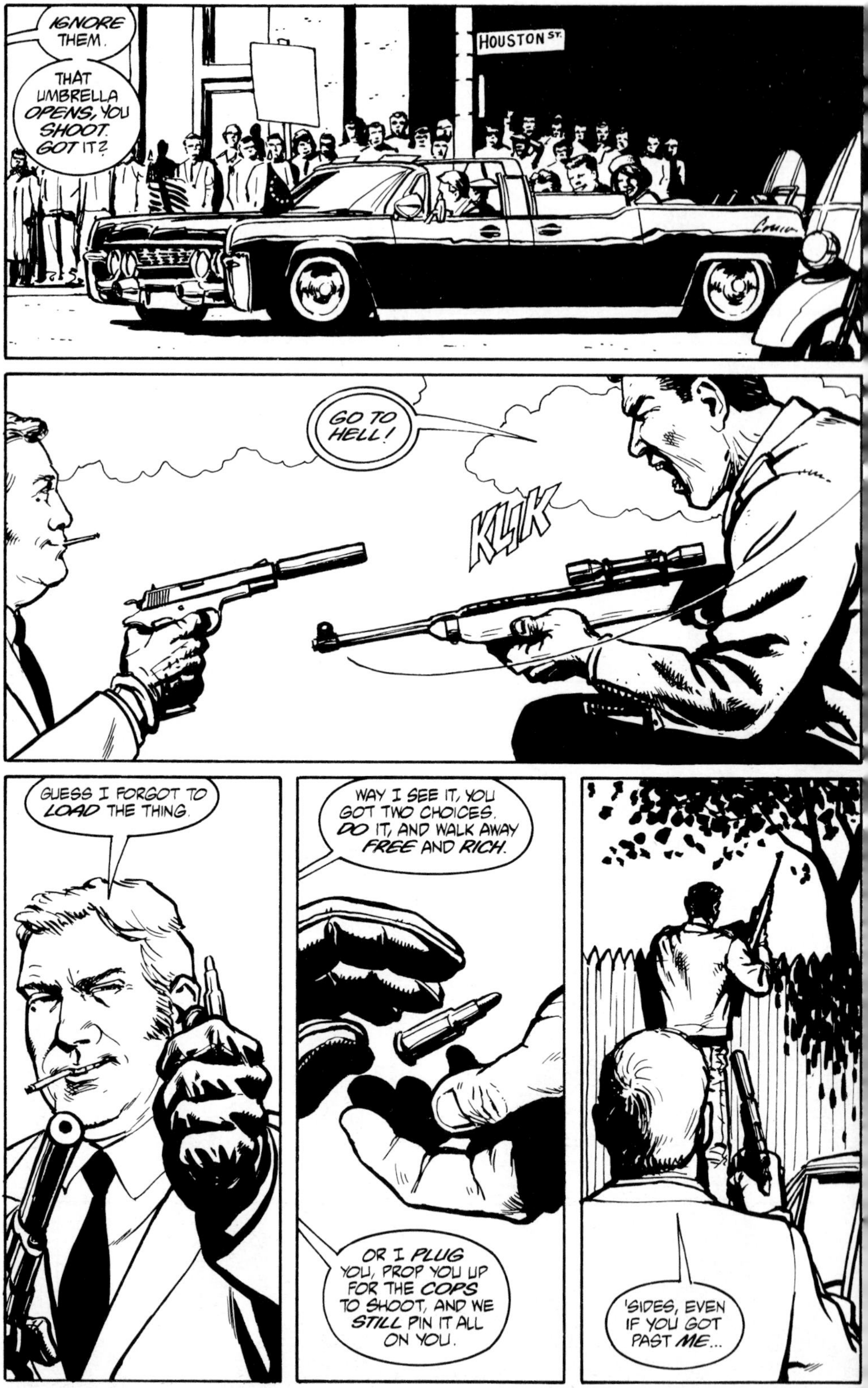
IGNORE THEM.
THAT UMBRELLA OPENS, YOU SHOOT. GOT IT?
HOUSTON ST.
GO TO HELL!
KLIK
GUESS I FORGOT TO LOAD THE THING.
WAY I SEE IT, YOU GOT TWO CHOICES. DO IT, AND WALK AWAY FREE AND RICH.
OR I PLUG YOU, PROP YOU UP FOR THE COPS TO SHOOT, AND WE STILL PIN IT ALL ON YOU.
'SIDES, EVEN IF YOU GOT PAST ME...

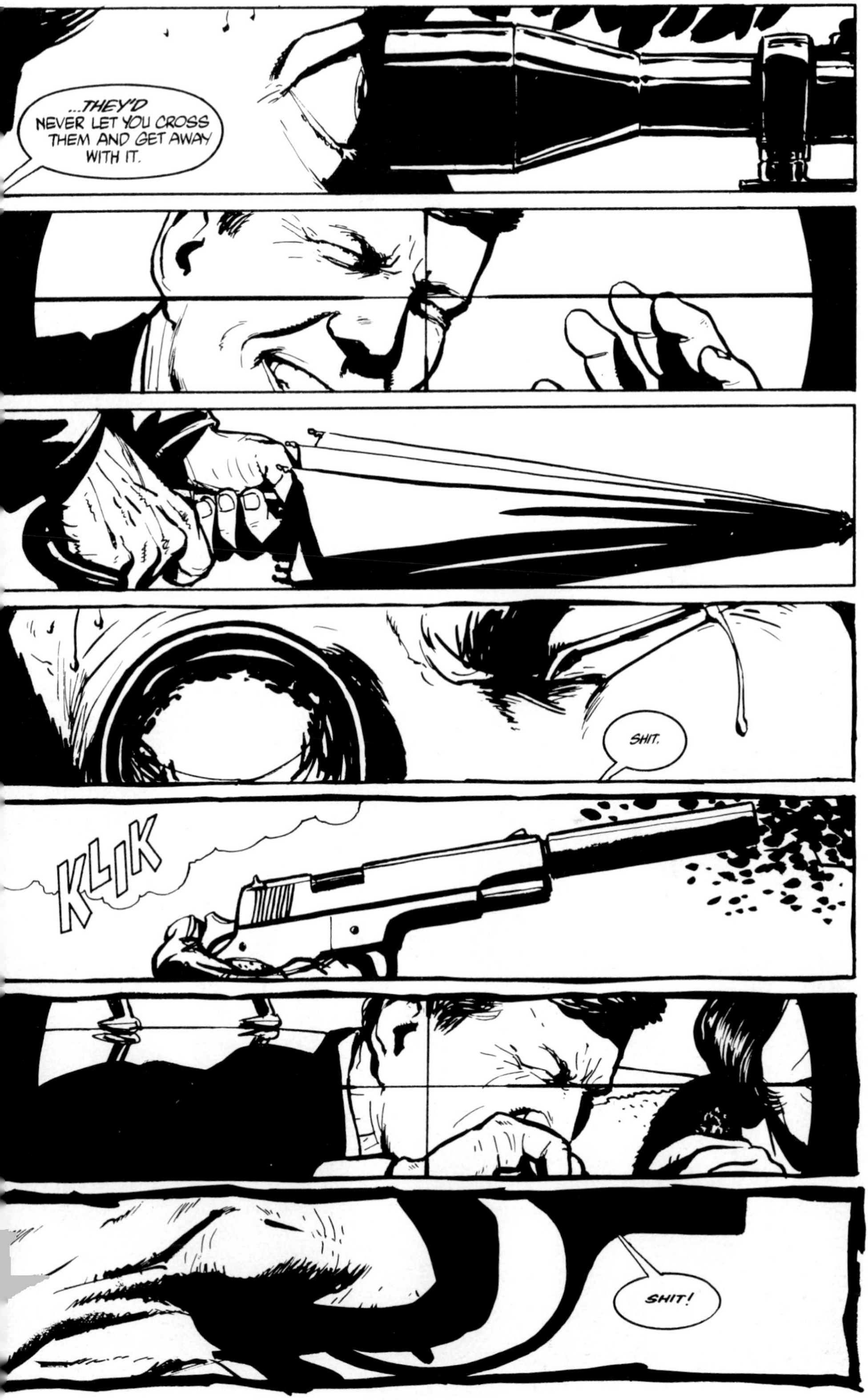
...THEY'D NEVER LET YOU CROSS THEM AND GET AWAY WITH IT.
SHIT.
KLIK
SHIT!

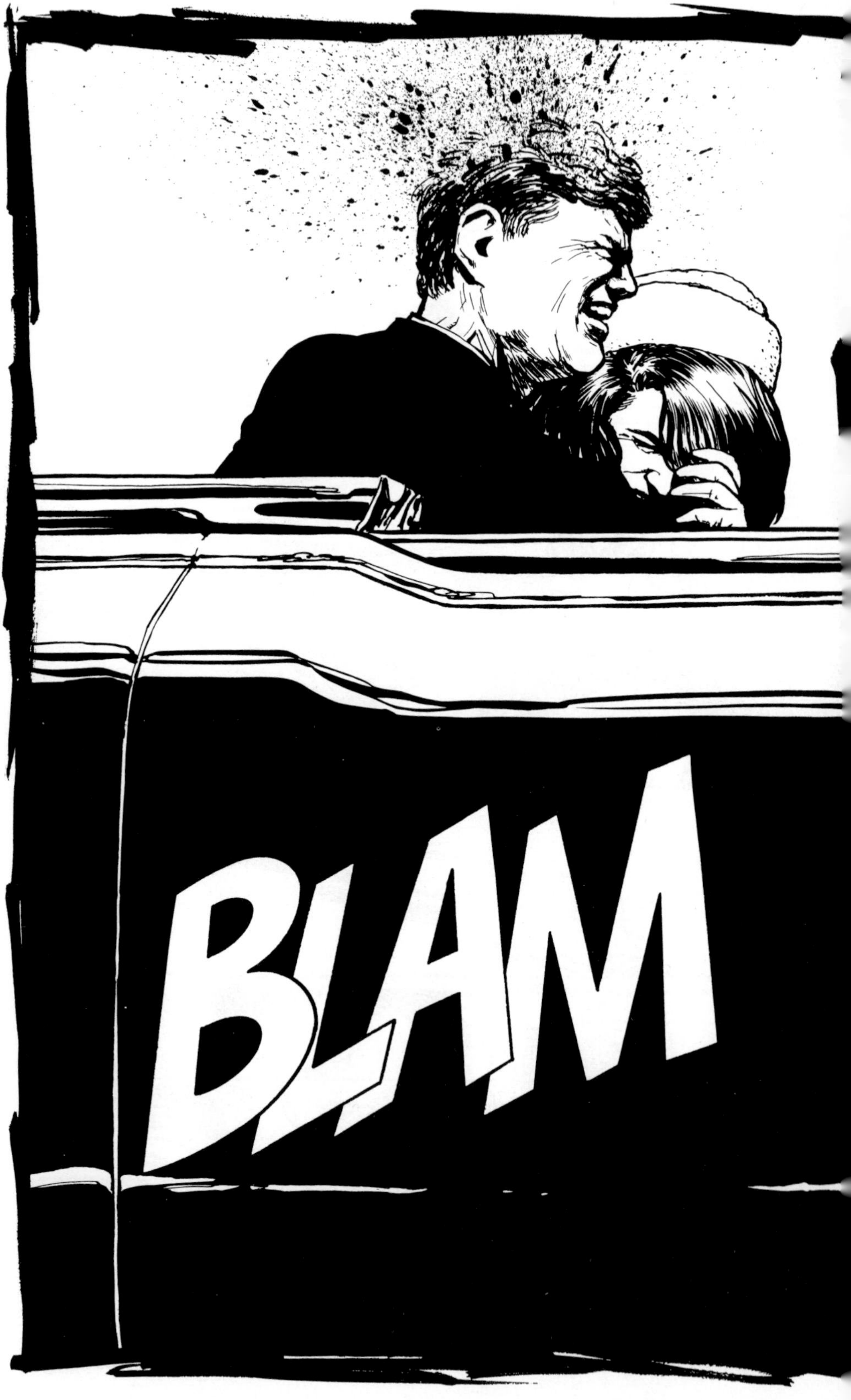
BLAM

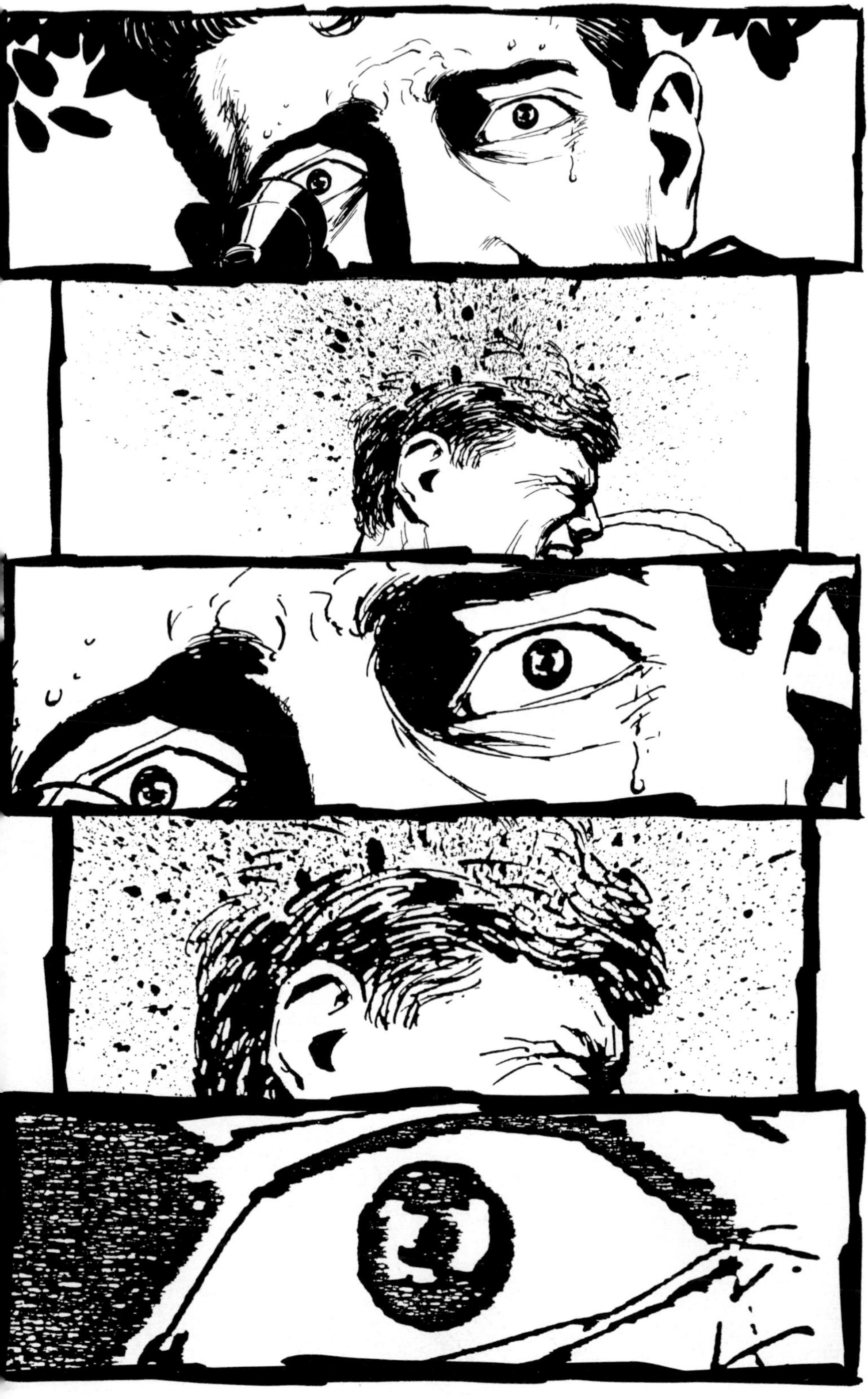

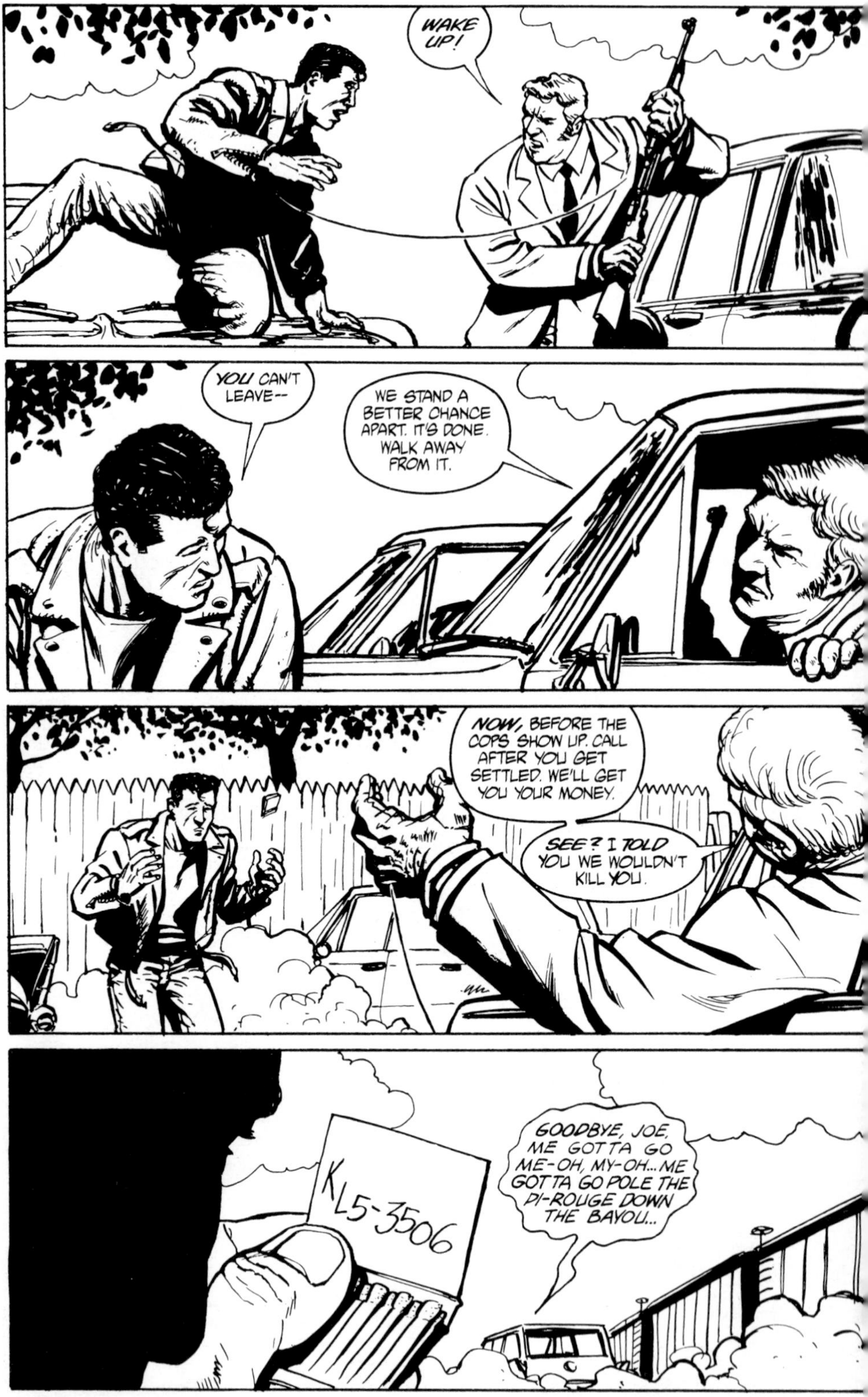
WAKE UP!
YOU CAN'T LEAVE--
WE STAND A BETTER CHANCE APART. IT'S DONE. WALK AWAY FROM IT.
NOW, BEFORE THE COPS SHOW UP. CALL AFTER YOU GET SETTLED. WE'LL GET YOU YOUR MONEY.
SEE? I TOLD YOU WE WOULDN'T KILL YOU.
KL5-3506
GOODBYE, JOE, ME GOTTA GO ME-OH, MY-OH... ME GOTTA GO POLE THE PI-ROUGE DOWN THE BAYOU...

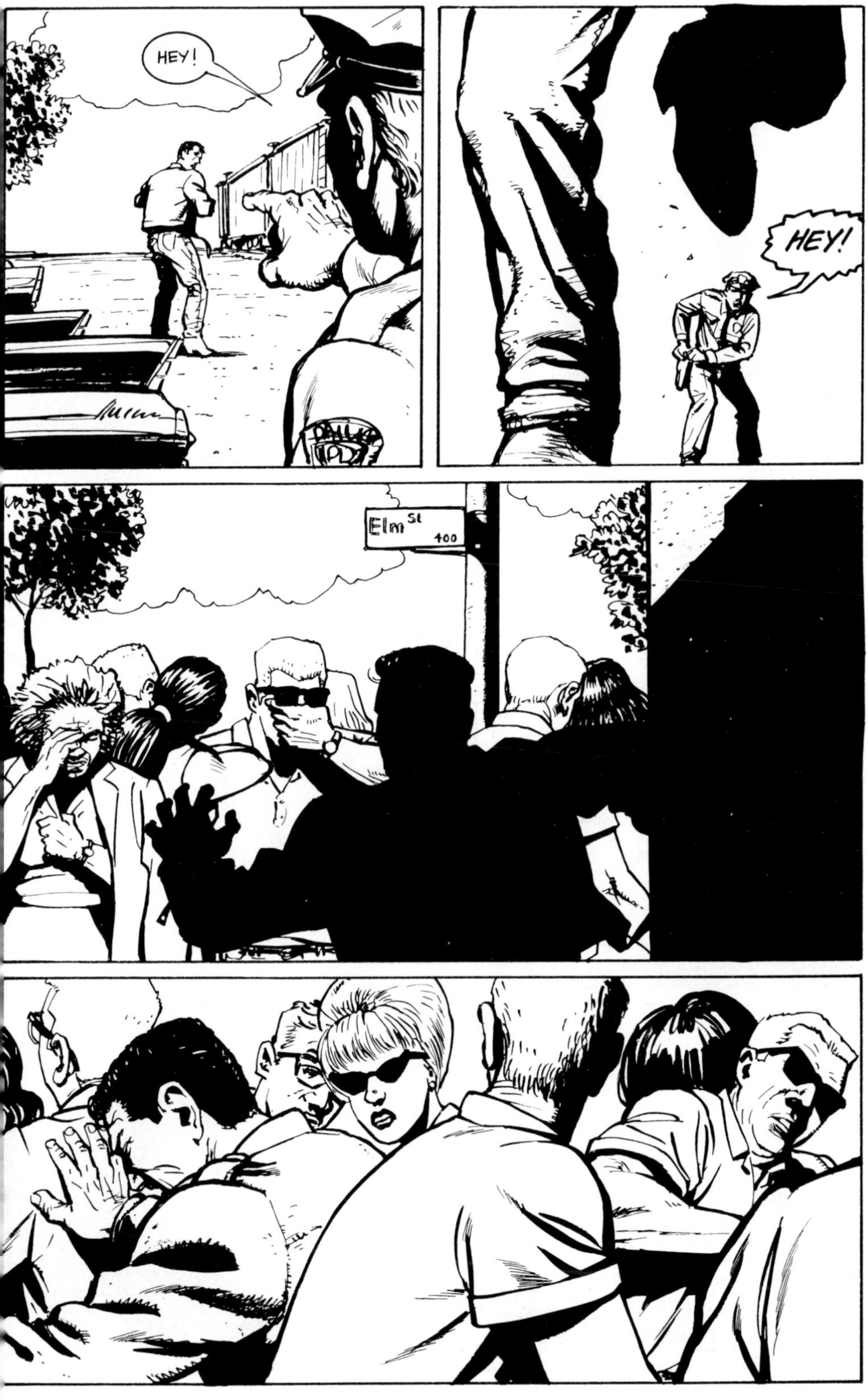
HEY!
HEY!
Elm St
400

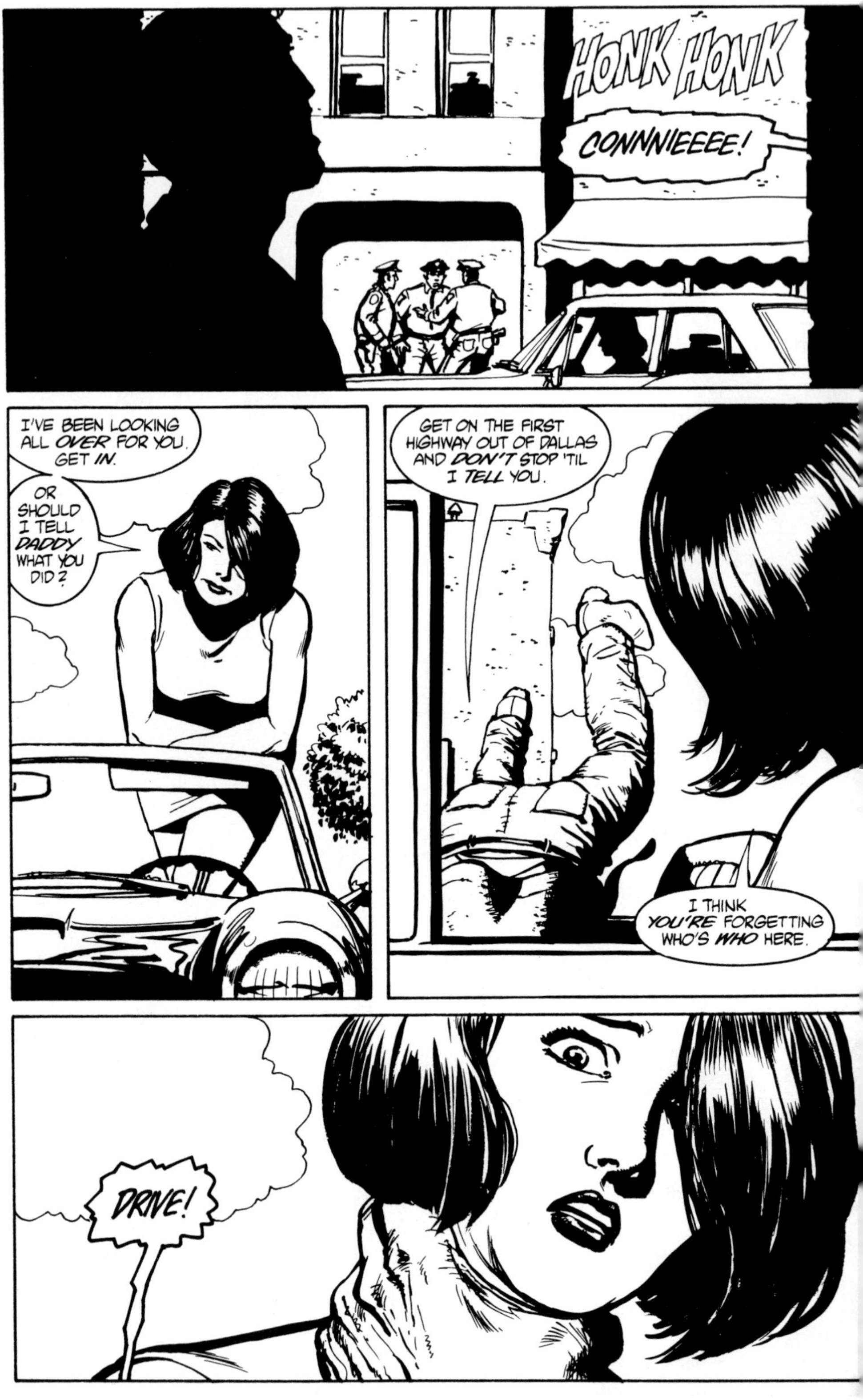
HONK HONK
CONNIEEEE!
I'VE BEEN LOOKING ALL OVER FOR YOU. GET IN.
OR SHOULD I TELL DADDY WHAT YOU DID?
GET ON THE FIRST HIGHWAY OUT OF DALLAS AND DON'T STOP 'TIL I TELL YOU.
I THINK YOU'RE FORGETTING WHO'S WHO HERE.
DRIVE!

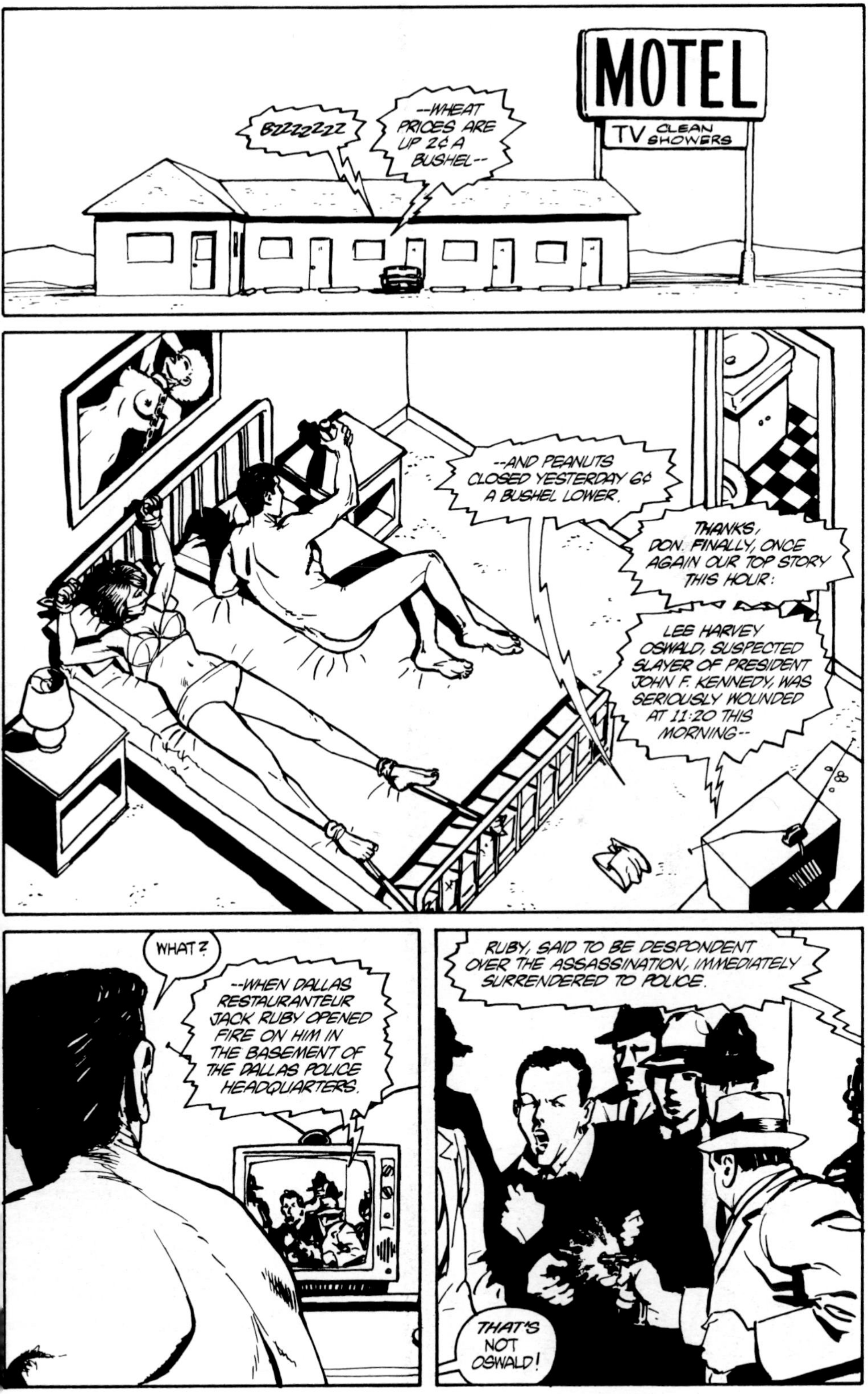
MOTEL
TV CLEAN SHOWERS
BZZZZZZZ
--WHEAT PRICES ARE UP 2¢ A BUSHEL--
--AND PEANUTS CLOSED YESTERDAY 6¢ A BUSHEL LOWER.
THANKS, DON. FINALLY, ONCE AGAIN OUR TOP STORY THIS HOUR:
LEE HARVEY OSWALD, SUSPECTED SLAYER OF PRESIDENT JOHN F. KENNEDY, WAS SERIOUSLY WOUNDED AT 11:20 THIS MORNING--
WHAT?
--WHEN DALLAS RESTAURANTEUR JACK RUBY OPENED FIRE ON HIM IN THE BASEMENT OF THE DALLAS POLICE HEADQUARTERS.
RUBY, SAID TO BE DESPONDENT OVER THE ASSASSINATION, IMMEDIATELY SURRENDERED TO POLICE.
THAT'S NOT OSWALD!

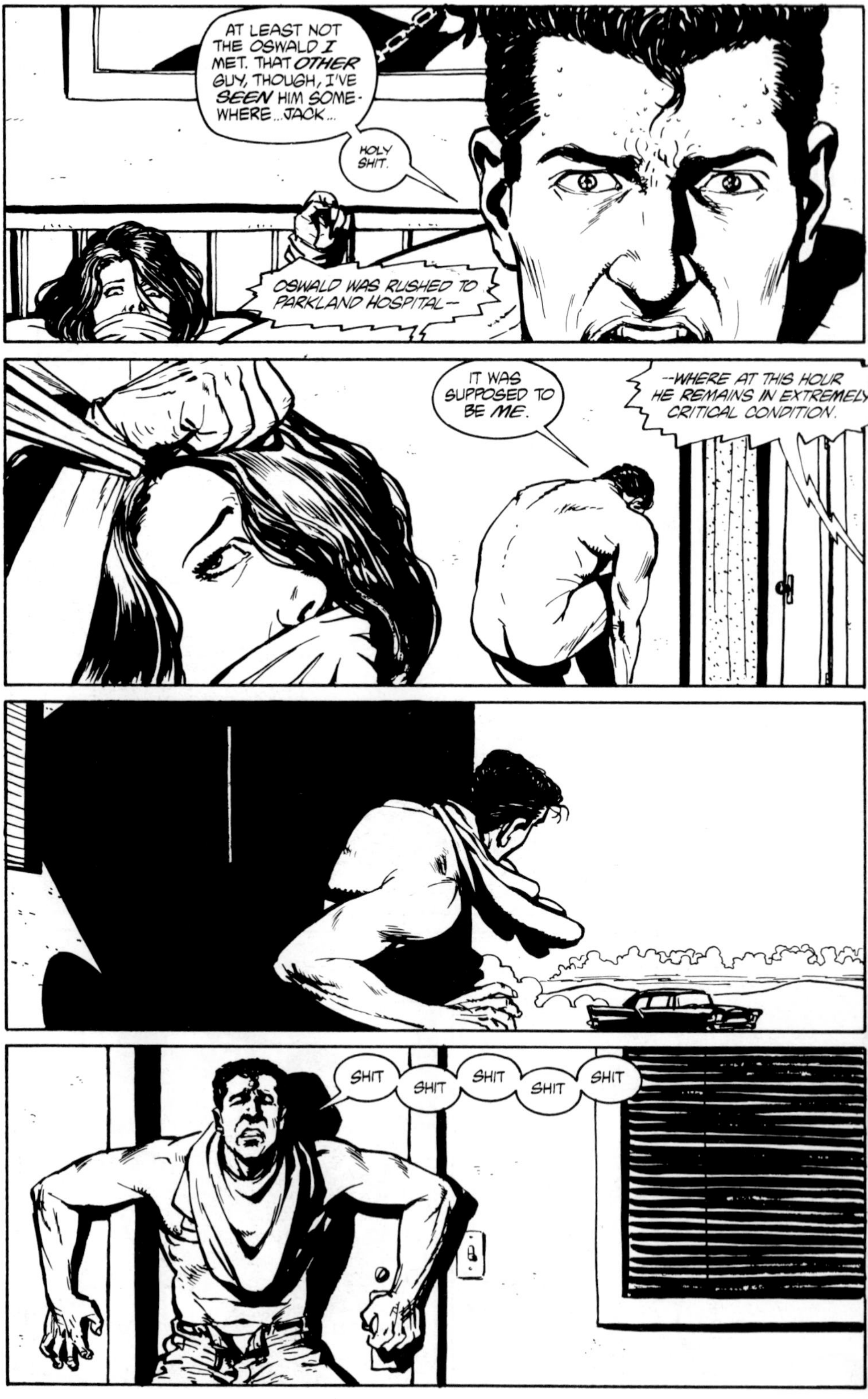
AT LEAST NOT THE OSWALD *I* MET. THAT *OTHER* GUY, THOUGH, I'VE *SEEN* HIM SOME-WHERE... JACK...
HOLY SHIT.
OSWALD WAS RUSHED TO PARKLAND HOSPITAL--
IT WAS SUPPOSED TO BE *ME*.
--WHERE AT THIS HOUR HE REMAINS IN EXTREMELY CRITICAL CONDITION.
SHIT
SHIT
SHIT
SHIT
SHIT

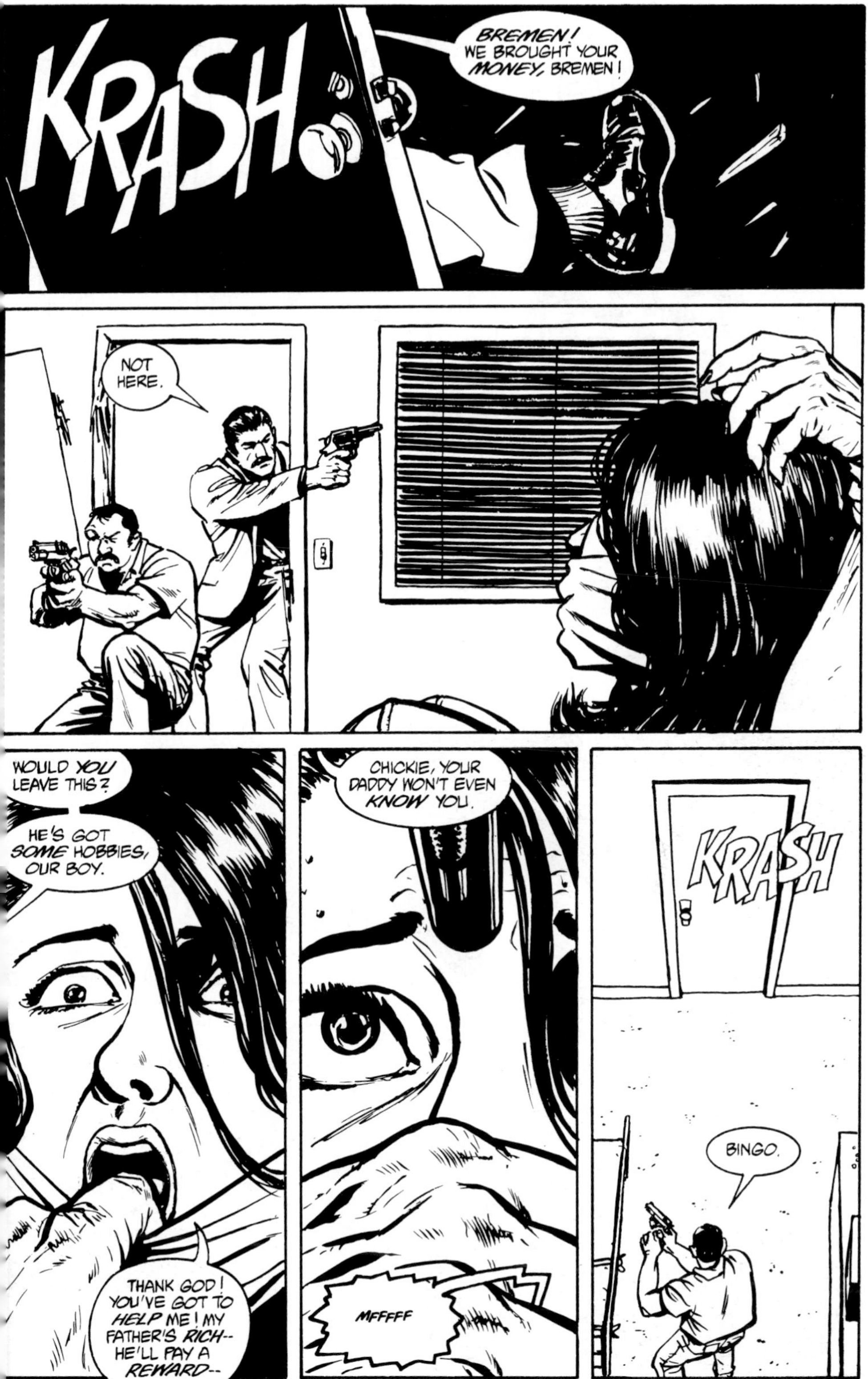
KRASH
BREMEN! WE BROUGHT YOUR MONEY, BREMEN!
NOT HERE.
WOULD YOU LEAVE THIS?
HE'S GOT SOME HOBBIES, OUR BOY.
THANK GOD! YOU'VE GOT TO HELP ME! MY FATHER'S RICH-- HE'LL PAY A REWARD--
CHICKIE, YOUR DADDY WON'T EVEN KNOW YOU.
MFFFFF
KRASH
BINGO.

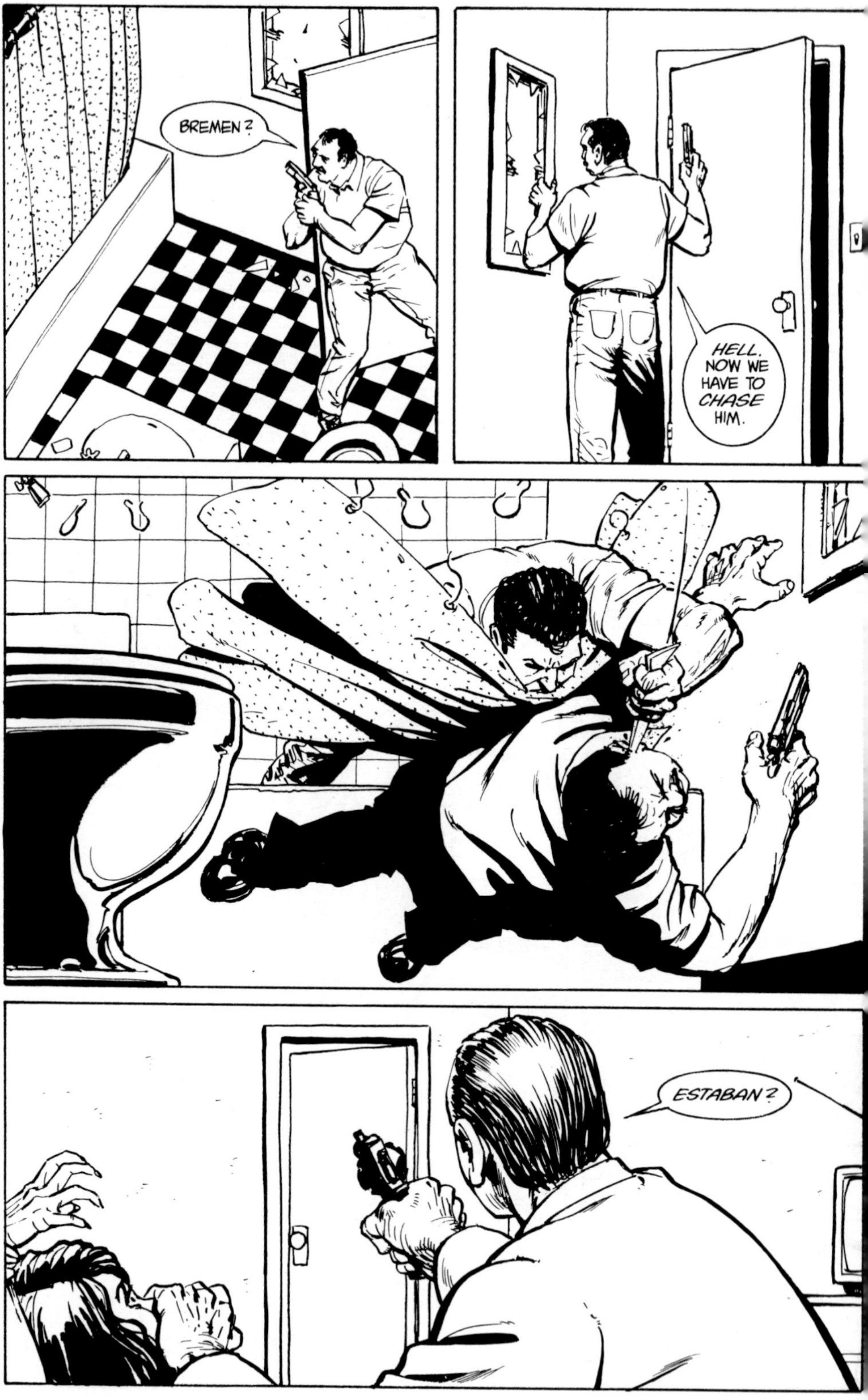
BREMEN?
HELL. NOW WE HAVE TO CHASE HIM.
ESTABAN?

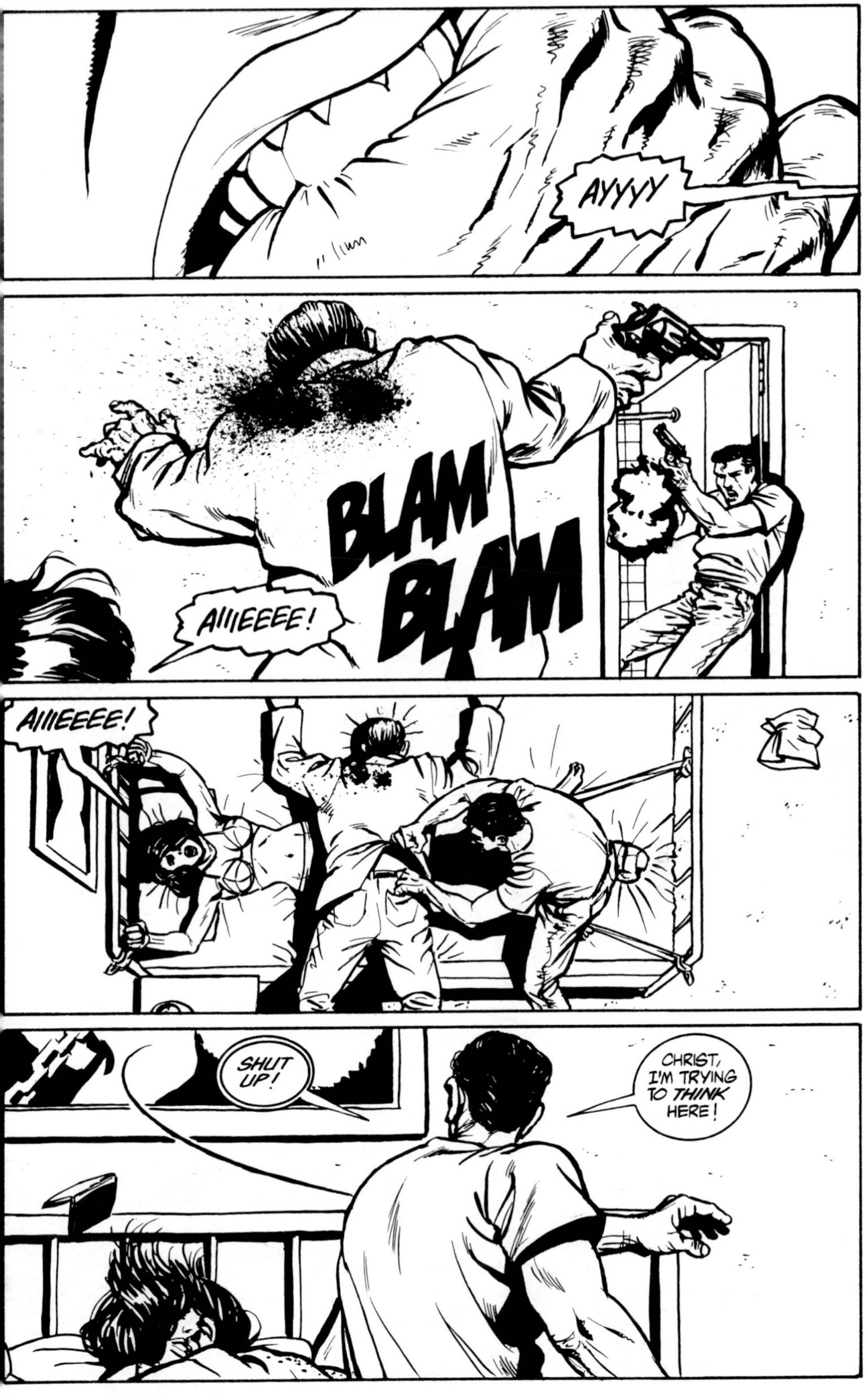
AYYYY
BLAM
BLAM
AIIIEEEE!
AIIIEEEE!
SHUT UP!
CHRIST, I'M TRYING TO *THINK* HERE!

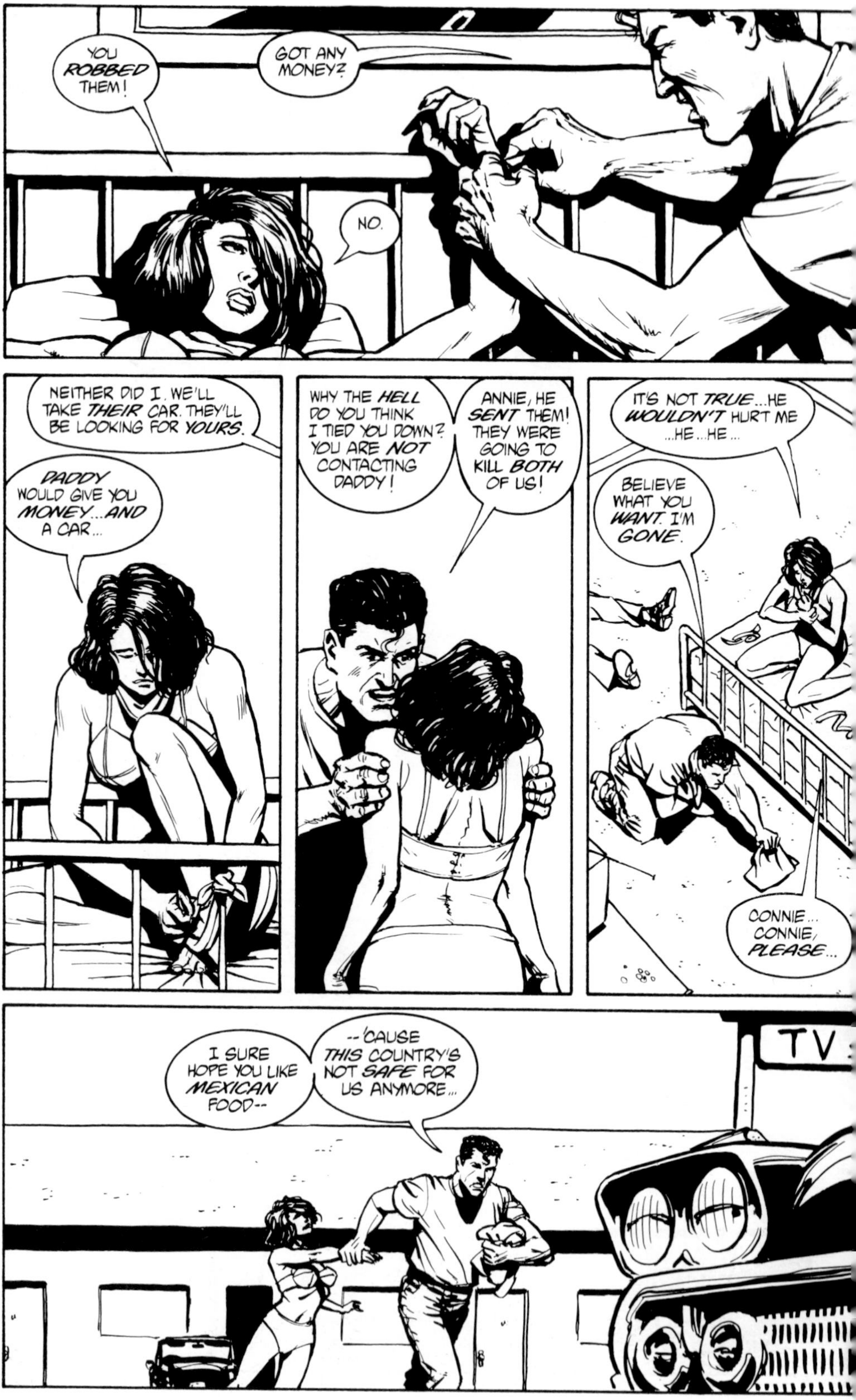
YOU ROBBED THEM!
GOT ANY MONEY?
NO.
NEITHER DID I. WE'LL TAKE THEIR CAR. THEY'LL BE LOOKING FOR YOURS.
DADDY WOULD GIVE YOU MONEY...AND A CAR...
WHY THE HELL DO YOU THINK I TIED YOU DOWN? YOU ARE NOT CONTACTING DADDY!
ANNIE, HE SENT THEM! THEY WERE GOING TO KILL BOTH OF US!
IT'S NOT TRUE...HE WOULDN'T HURT ME ...HE...HE...
BELIEVE WHAT YOU WANT. I'M GONE.
CONNIE... CONNIE, PLEASE...
I SURE HOPE YOU LIKE MEXICAN FOOD--
--'CAUSE THIS COUNTRY'S NOT SAFE FOR US ANYMORE...
TV

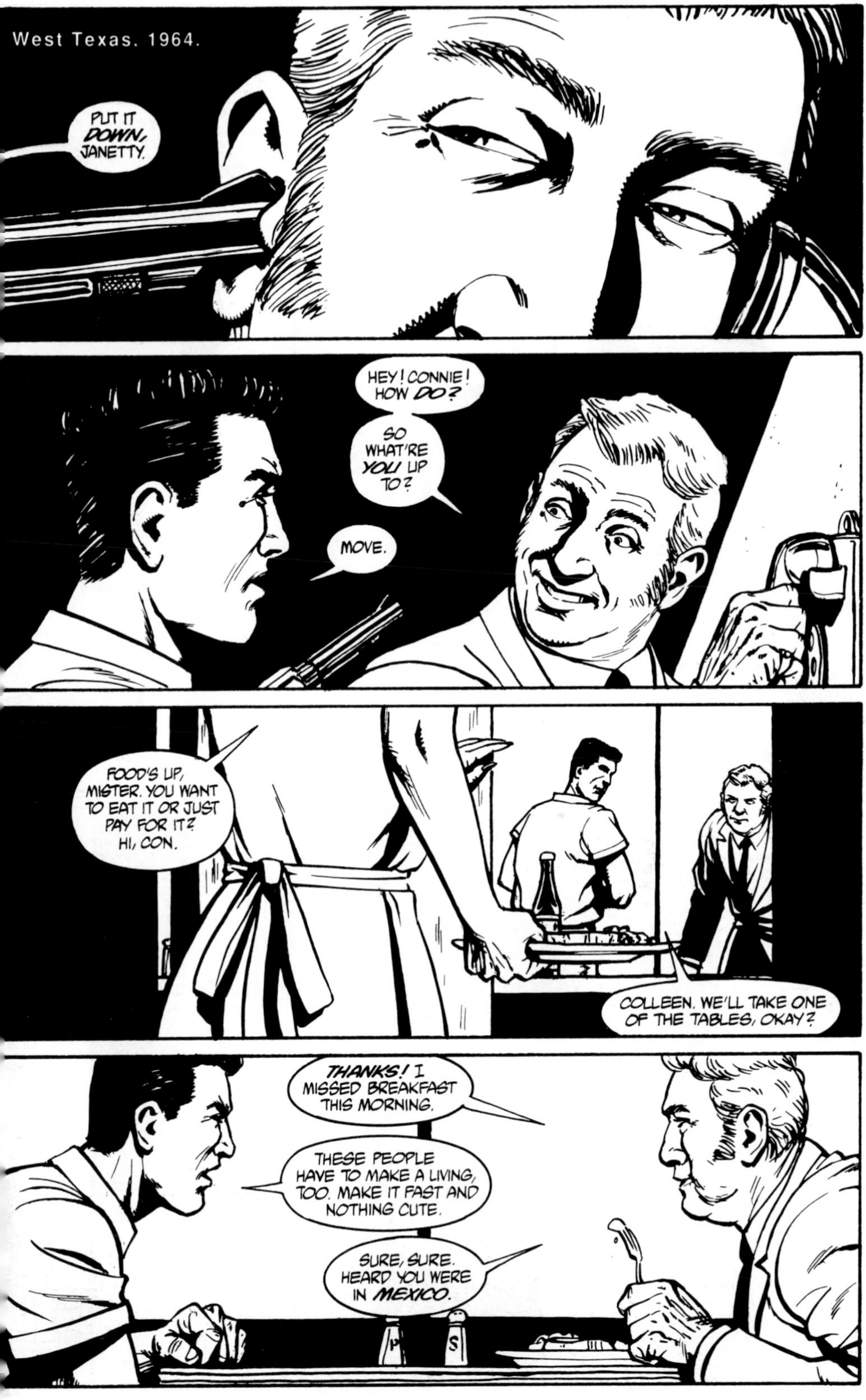
West Texas. 1964.
PUT IT DOWN, JANETTY.
HEY! CONNIE! HOW DO?
SO WHAT'RE YOU UP TO?
MOVE.
FOOD'S UP, MISTER. YOU WANT TO EAT IT OR JUST PAY FOR IT? HI, CON.
COLLEEN. WE'LL TAKE ONE OF THE TABLES, OKAY?
THANKS! I MISSED BREAKFAST THIS MORNING.
THESE PEOPLE HAVE TO MAKE A LIVING, TOO. MAKE IT FAST AND NOTHING CUTE.
SURE, SURE. HEARD YOU WERE IN MEXICO.

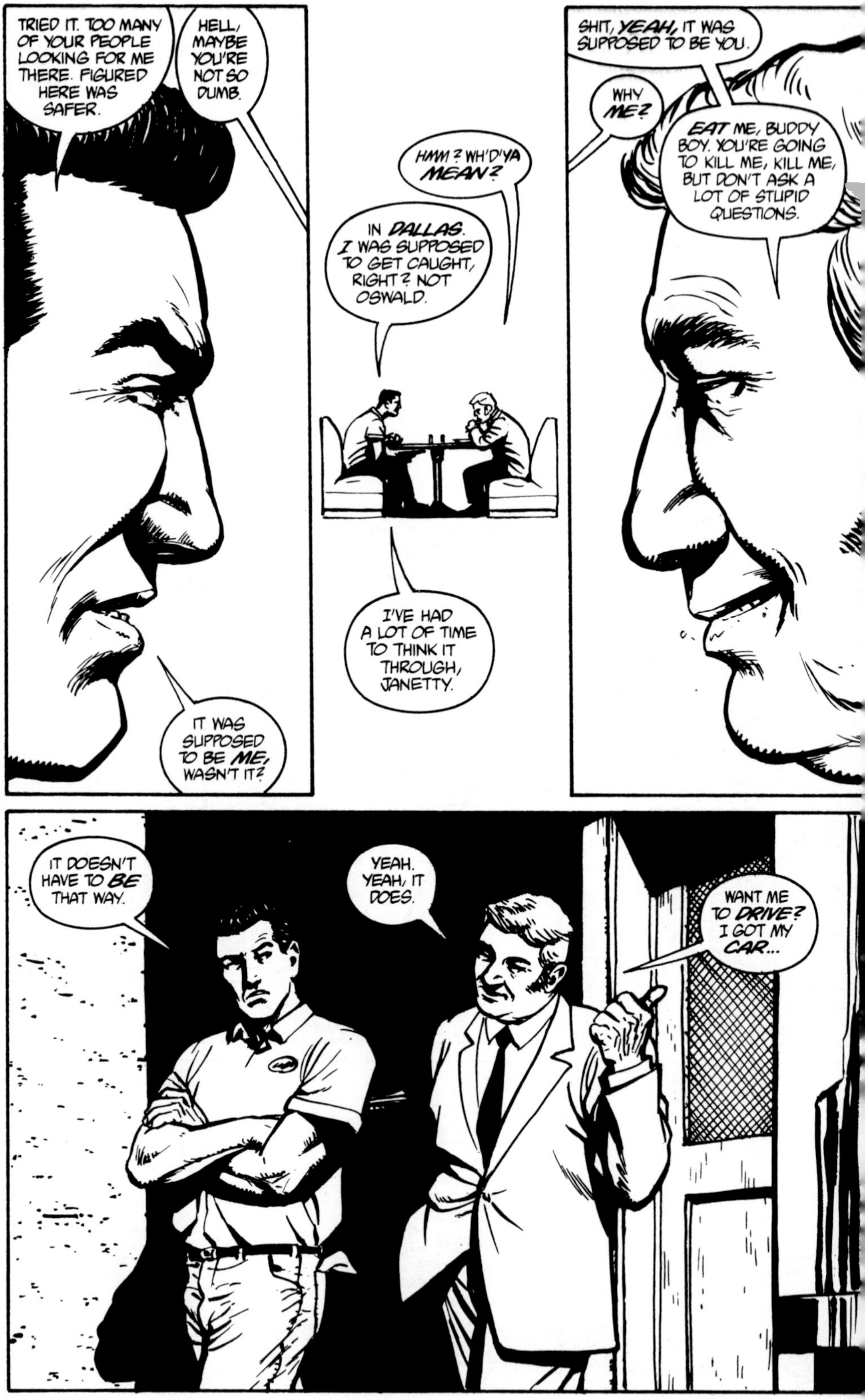
TRIED IT. TOO MANY OF YOUR PEOPLE LOOKING FOR ME THERE. FIGURED HERE WAS SAFER.
HELL, MAYBE YOU'RE NOT SO DUMB.
IT WAS SUPPOSED TO BE ME, WASN'T IT?
HMM? WH'D'YA MEAN?
IN DALLAS. I WAS SUPPOSED TO GET CAUGHT, RIGHT? NOT OSWALD.
I'VE HAD A LOT OF TIME TO THINK IT THROUGH, JANETTY.
SHIT, YEAH, IT WAS SUPPOSED TO BE YOU.
WHY ME?
EAT ME, BUDDY BOY. YOU'RE GOING TO KILL ME, KILL ME, BUT DON'T ASK A LOT OF STUPID QUESTIONS.
IT DOESN'T HAVE TO BE THAT WAY.
YEAH. YEAH, IT DOES.
WANT ME TO DRIVE? I GOT MY CAR...

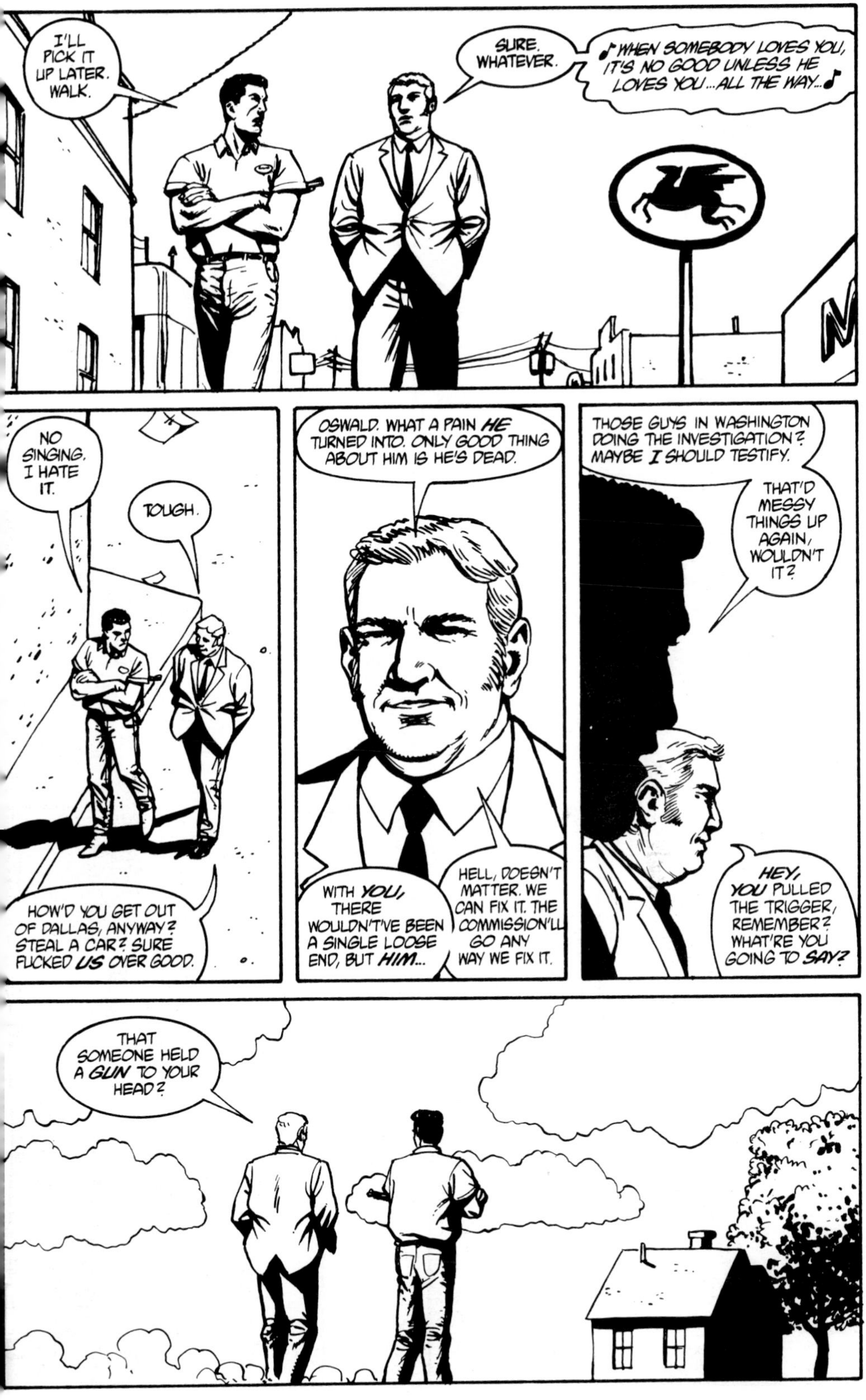

I'LL PICK IT UP LATER. WALK.
SURE. WHATEVER.
♪ WHEN SOMEBODY LOVES YOU, IT'S NO GOOD UNLESS HE LOVES YOU... ALL THE WAY... ♪
NO SINGING. I HATE IT.
TOUGH.
HOW'D YOU GET OUT OF DALLAS, ANYWAY? STEAL A CAR? SURE FUCKED US OVER GOOD.
OSWALD. WHAT A PAIN HE TURNED INTO. ONLY GOOD THING ABOUT HIM IS HE'S DEAD.
WITH YOU, THERE WOULDN'T'VE BEEN A SINGLE LOOSE END, BUT HIM...
HELL, DOESN'T MATTER. WE CAN FIX IT. THE COMMISSION'LL GO ANY WAY WE FIX IT.
THOSE GUYS IN WASHINGTON DOING THE INVESTIGATION? MAYBE I SHOULD TESTIFY.
THAT'D MESSY THINGS UP AGAIN, WOULDN'T IT?
HEY, YOU PULLED THE TRIGGER, REMEMBER? WHAT'RE YOU GOING TO SAY?
THAT SOMEONE HELD A GUN TO YOUR HEAD?

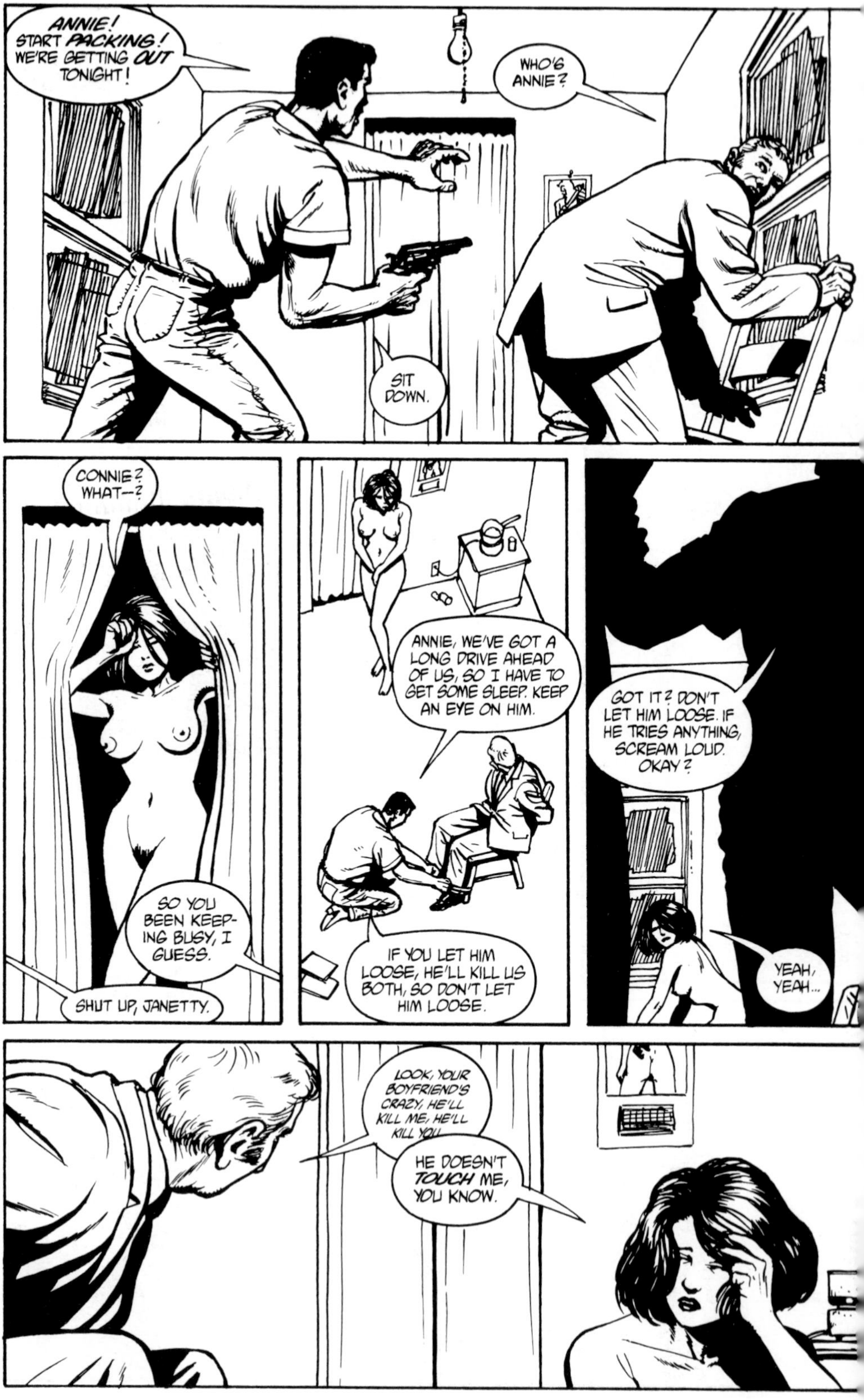
ANNIE! START PACKING! WE'RE GETTING OUT TONIGHT!
WHO'S ANNIE?
SIT DOWN.
CONNIE? WHAT--?
SO YOU BEEN KEEPING BUSY, I GUESS.
SHUT UP, JANETTY.
ANNIE, WE'VE GOT A LONG DRIVE AHEAD OF US, SO I HAVE TO GET SOME SLEEP. KEEP AN EYE ON HIM.
IF YOU LET HIM LOOSE, HE'LL KILL US BOTH, SO DON'T LET HIM LOOSE.
GOT IT? DON'T LET HIM LOOSE. IF HE TRIES ANYTHING, SCREAM LOUD. OKAY?
YEAH, YEAH...
LOOK, YOUR BOYFRIEND'S CRAZY, HE'LL KILL ME; HE'LL KILL YOU.
HE DOESN'T TOUCH ME, YOU KNOW.

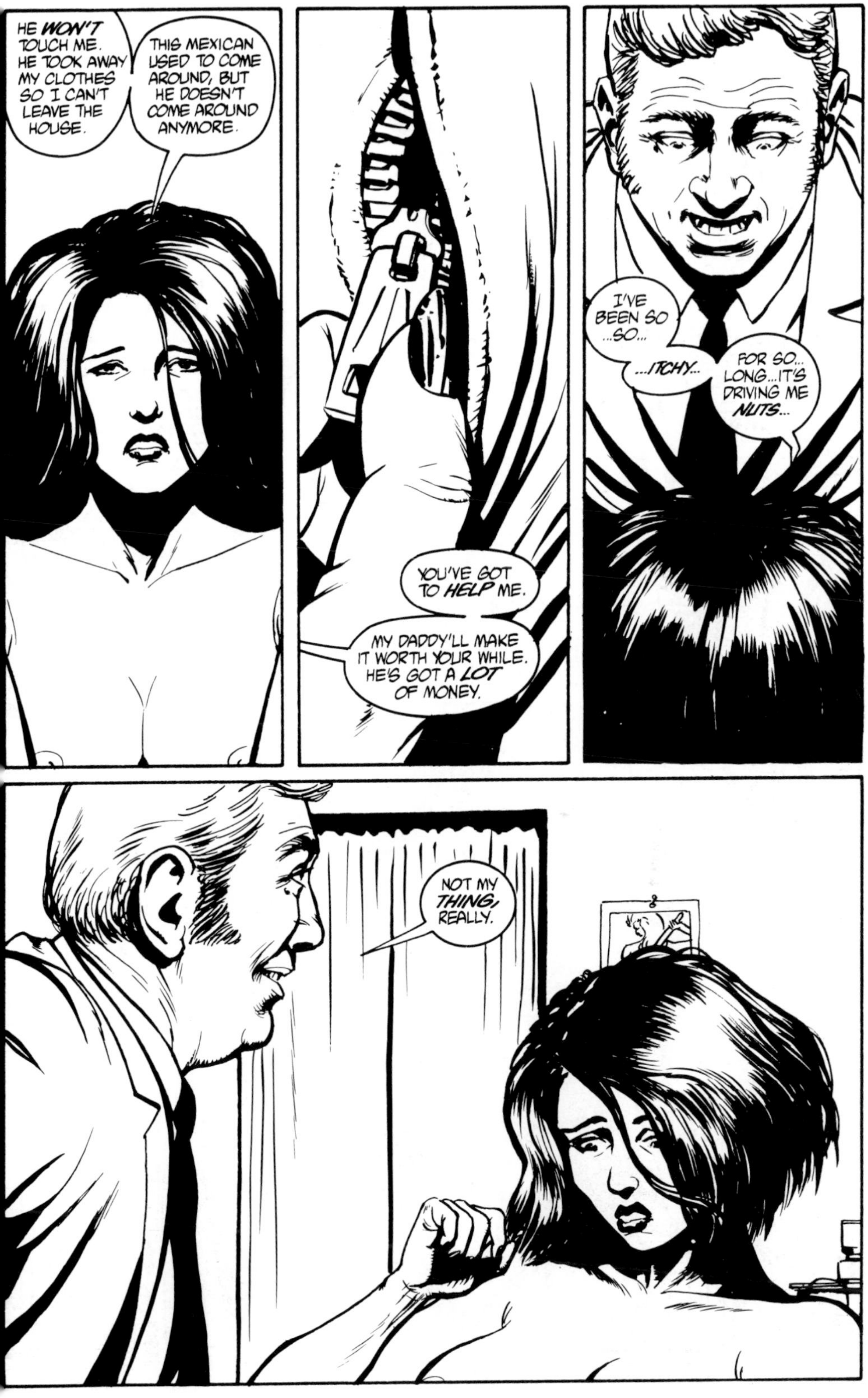
HE *WON'T* TOUCH ME. HE TOOK AWAY MY CLOTHES SO I CAN'T LEAVE THE HOUSE.
THIS MEXICAN USED TO COME AROUND, BUT HE DOESN'T COME AROUND ANYMORE.
YOU'VE GOT TO *HELP* ME.
MY DADDY'LL MAKE IT WORTH YOUR WHILE. HE'S GOT A *LOT* OF MONEY.
I'VE BEEN SO ...SO...
...*ITCHY*...
FOR SO... LONG...IT'S DRIVING ME *NUTS*...
NOT MY *THING,* REALLY.

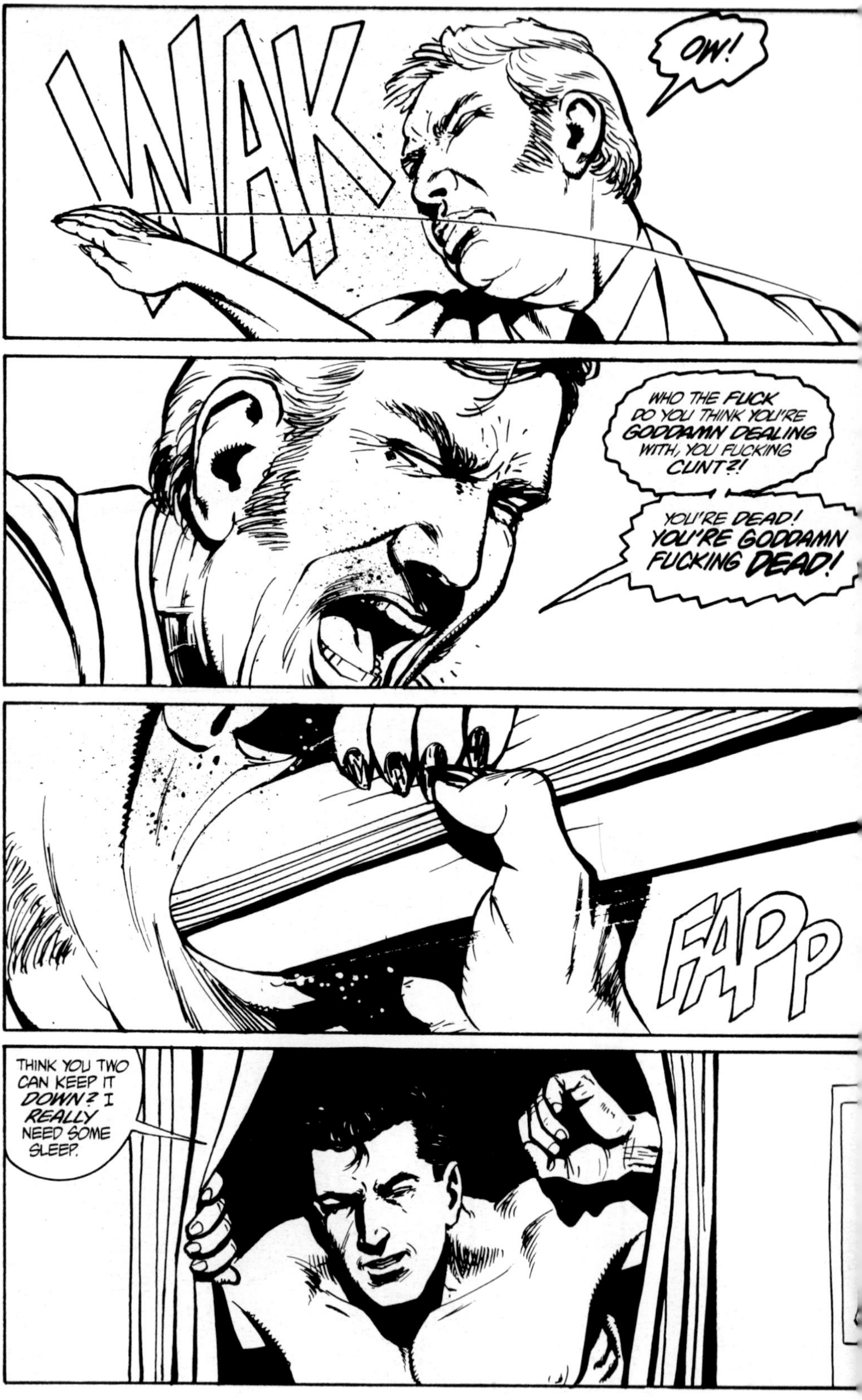
WAK
OW!
WHO THE FUCK DO YOU THINK YOU'RE GODDAMN DEALING WITH, YOU FUCKING CUNT?!
YOU'RE DEAD! YOU'RE GODDAMN FUCKING DEAD!
FAPP
THINK YOU TWO CAN KEEP IT DOWN? I REALLY NEED SOME SLEEP.

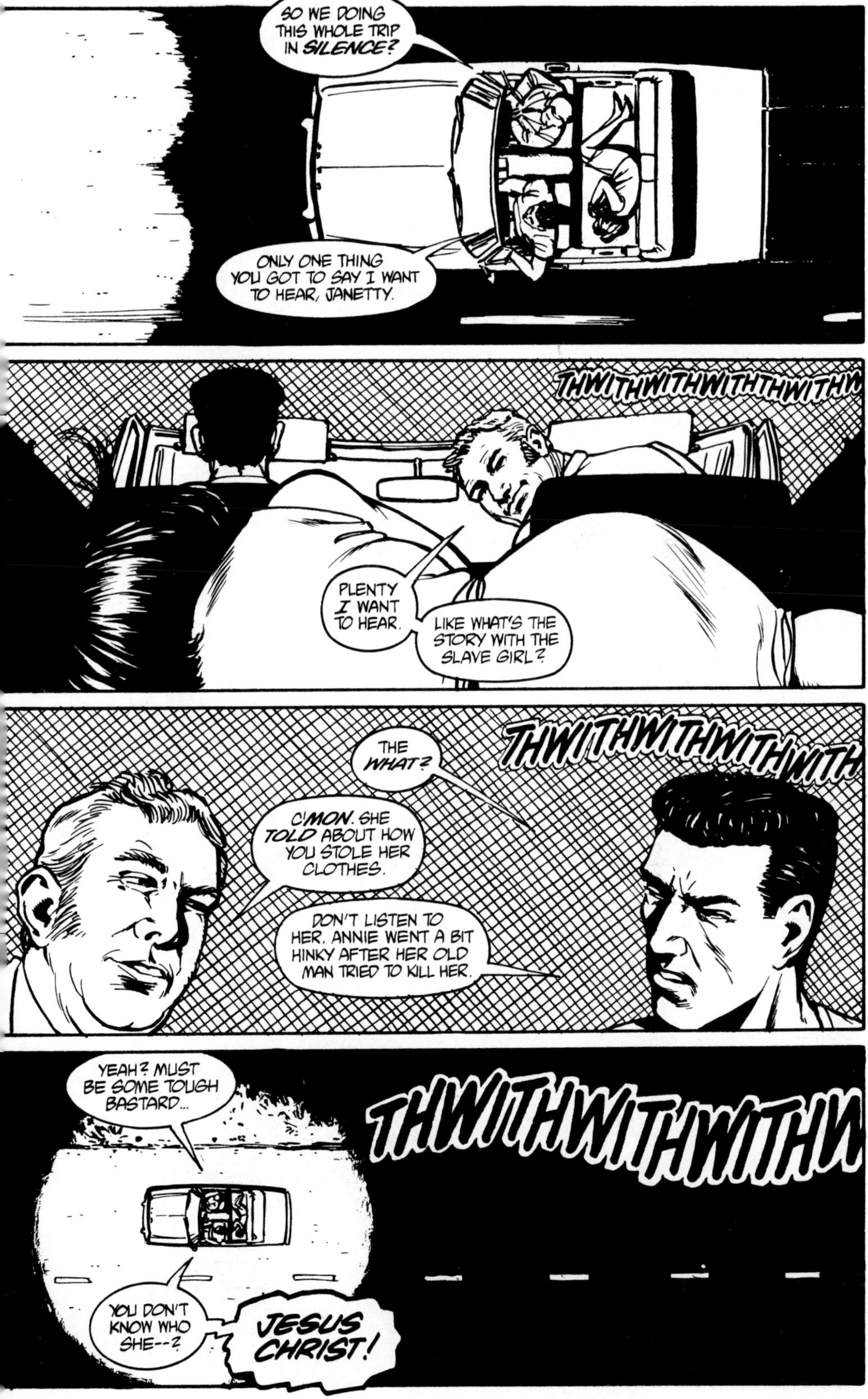
SO WE DOING THIS WHOLE TRIP IN SILENCE?
ONLY ONE THING YOU GOT TO SAY I WANT TO HEAR, JANETTY.
THWITHWITHWITHTHWITHW
PLENTY I WANT TO HEAR.
LIKE WHAT'S THE STORY WITH THE SLAVE GIRL?
THWITHWITHWITHWITH
THE WHAT?
C'MON. SHE TOLD ABOUT HOW YOU STOLE HER CLOTHES.
DON'T LISTEN TO HER. ANNIE WENT A BIT HINKY AFTER HER OLD MAN TRIED TO KILL HER.
YEAH? MUST BE SOME TOUGH BASTARD...
THWITHWITHWITHW
YOU DON'T KNOW WHO SHE--?
JESUS CHRIST!

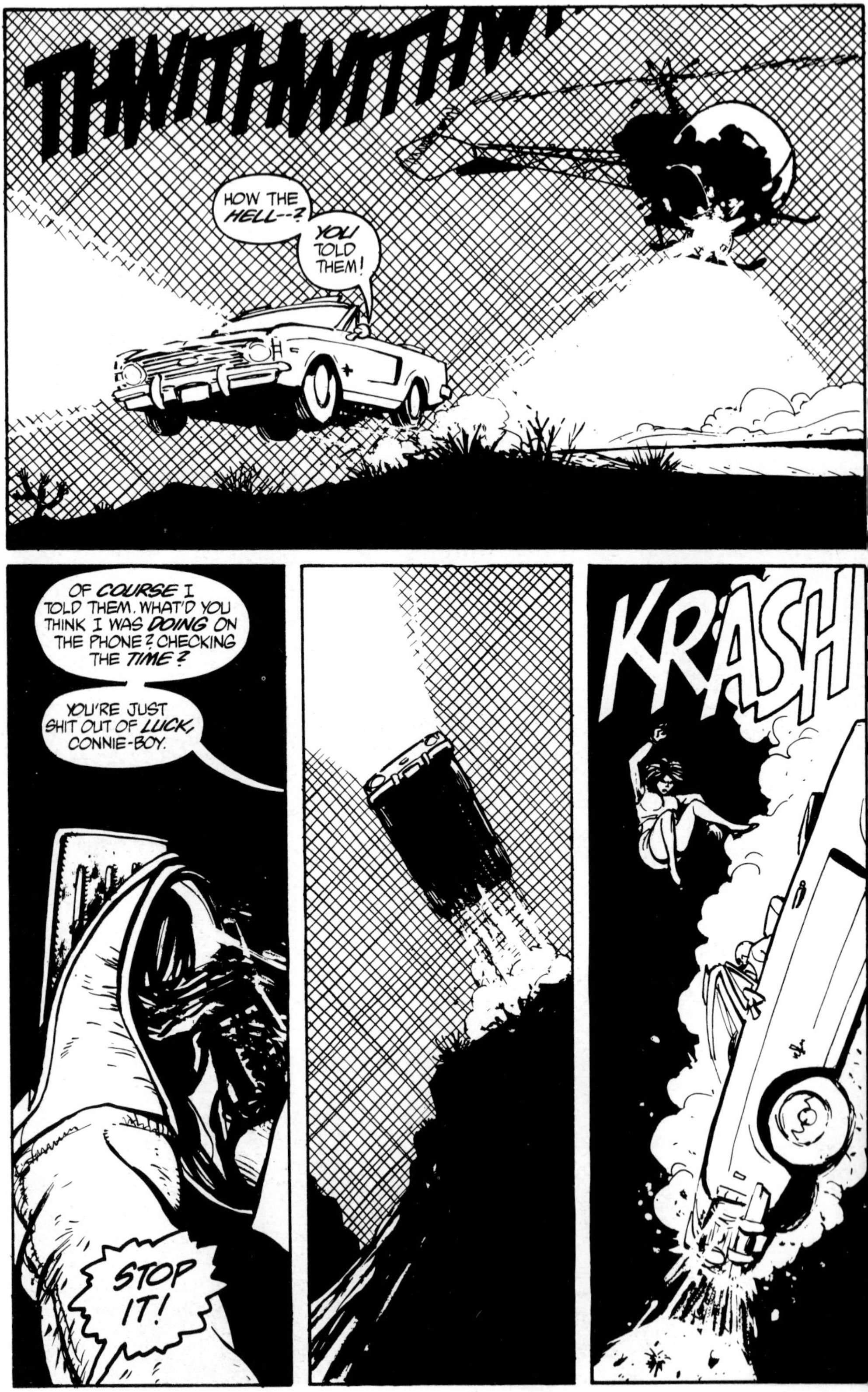
THWITHWITHW
HOW THE HELL--?
YOU! TOLD THEM!
OF COURSE I TOLD THEM. WHAT'D YOU THINK I WAS DOING ON THE PHONE? CHECKING THE TIME?
YOU'RE JUST SHIT OUT OF LUCK, CONNIE-BOY.
STOP IT!
KRASH

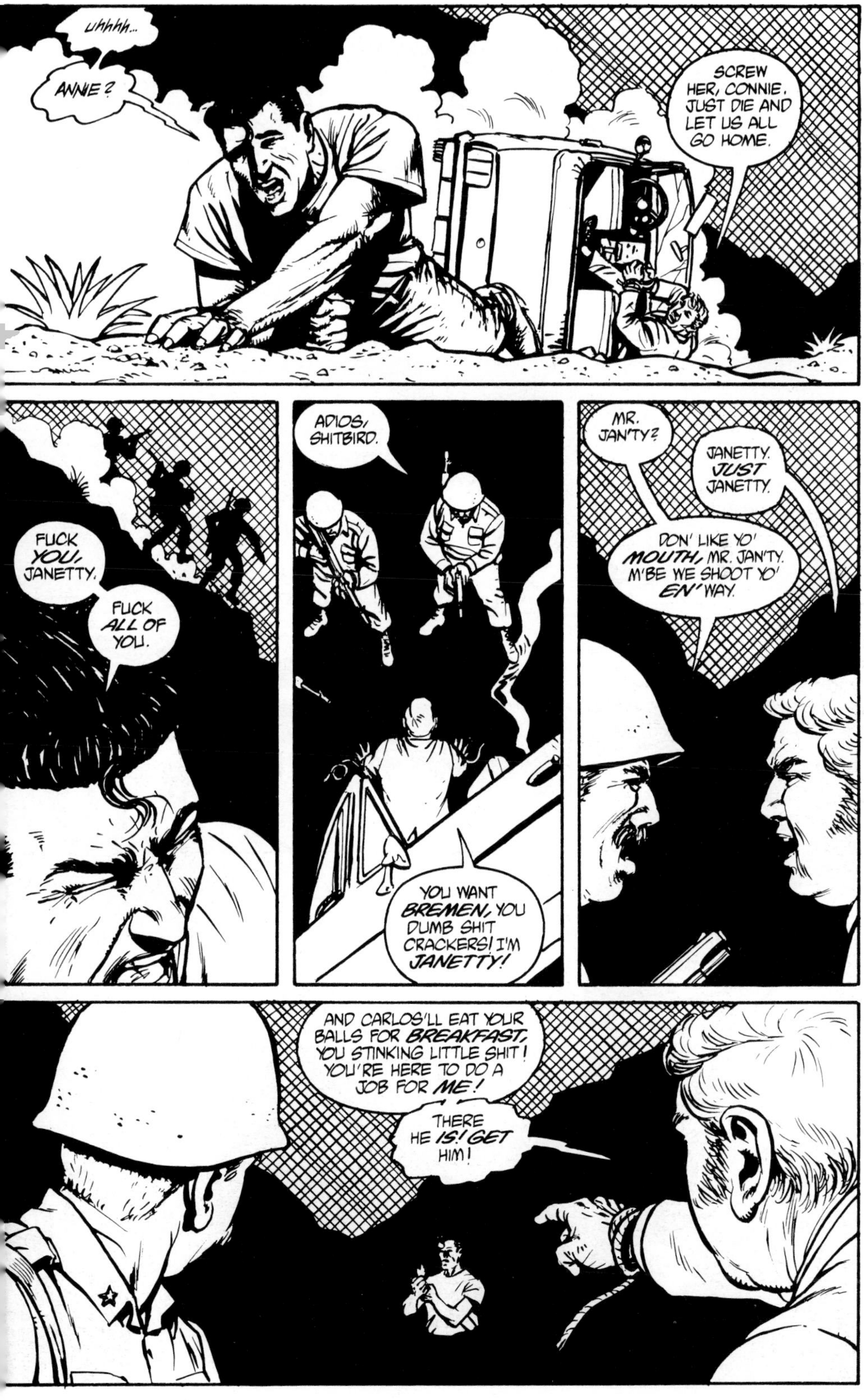
uhhhh...
ANNIE?
SCREW HER, CONNIE. JUST DIE AND LET US ALL GO HOME.
FUCK YOU, JANETTY.
FUCK ALL OF YOU.
ADIOS, SHITBIRD.
YOU WANT BREMEN, YOU DUMB SHIT CRACKERS! I'M JANETTY!
MR. JAN'TY?
JANETTY. JUST JANETTY.
DON' LIKE YO' MOUTH, MR. JAN'TY. M'BE WE SHOOT YO' EN' WAY.
AND CARLOS'LL EAT YOUR BALLS FOR BREAKFAST, YOU STINKING LITTLE SHIT! YOU'RE HERE TO DO A JOB FOR ME!
THERE HE IS! GET HIM!

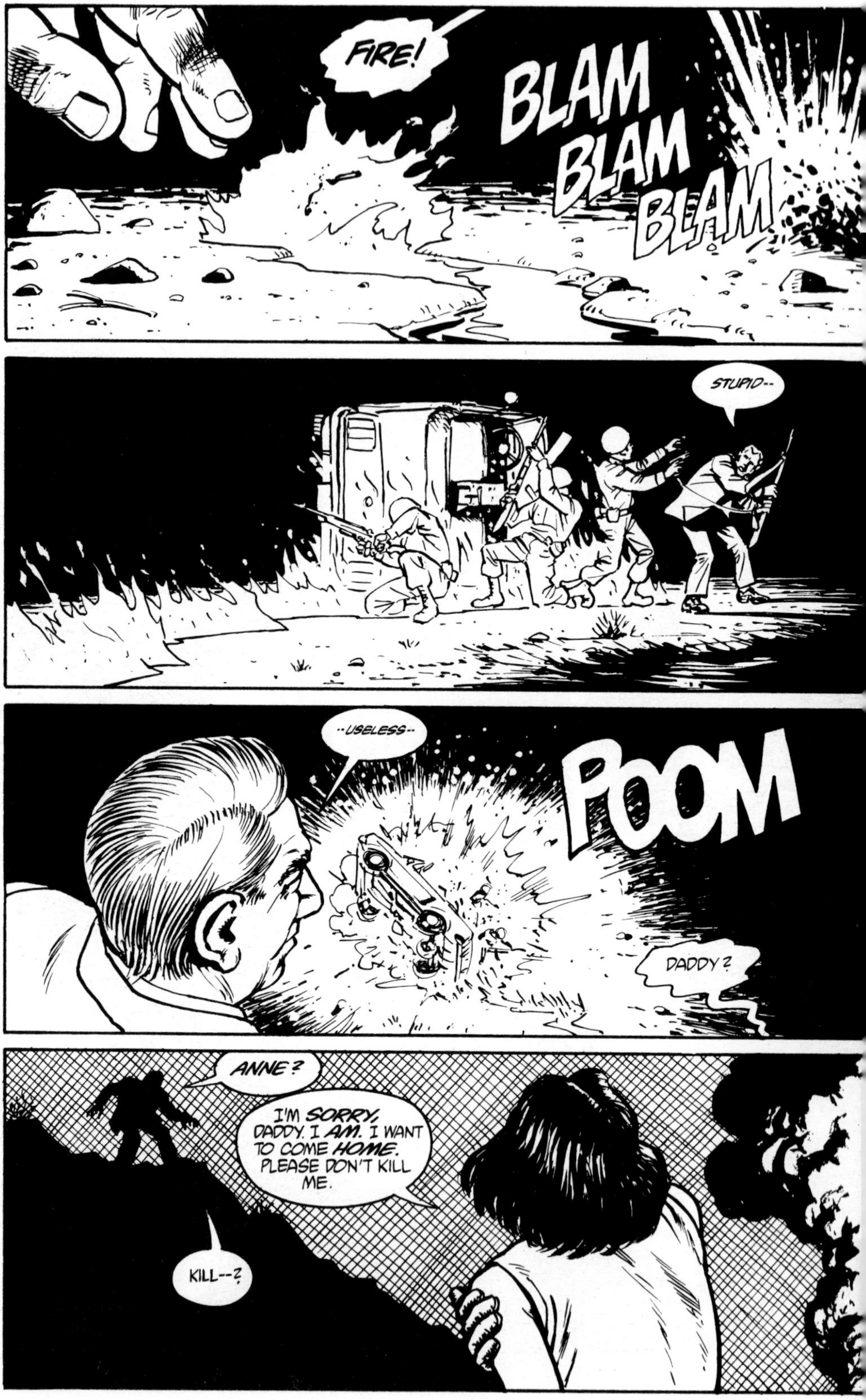
FIRE!
BLAM BLAM BLAM
STUPID--
--USELESS--
POOM
DADDY?
ANNE?
I'M SORRY, DADDY. I AM. I WANT TO COME HOME. PLEASE DON'T KILL ME.
KILL--?

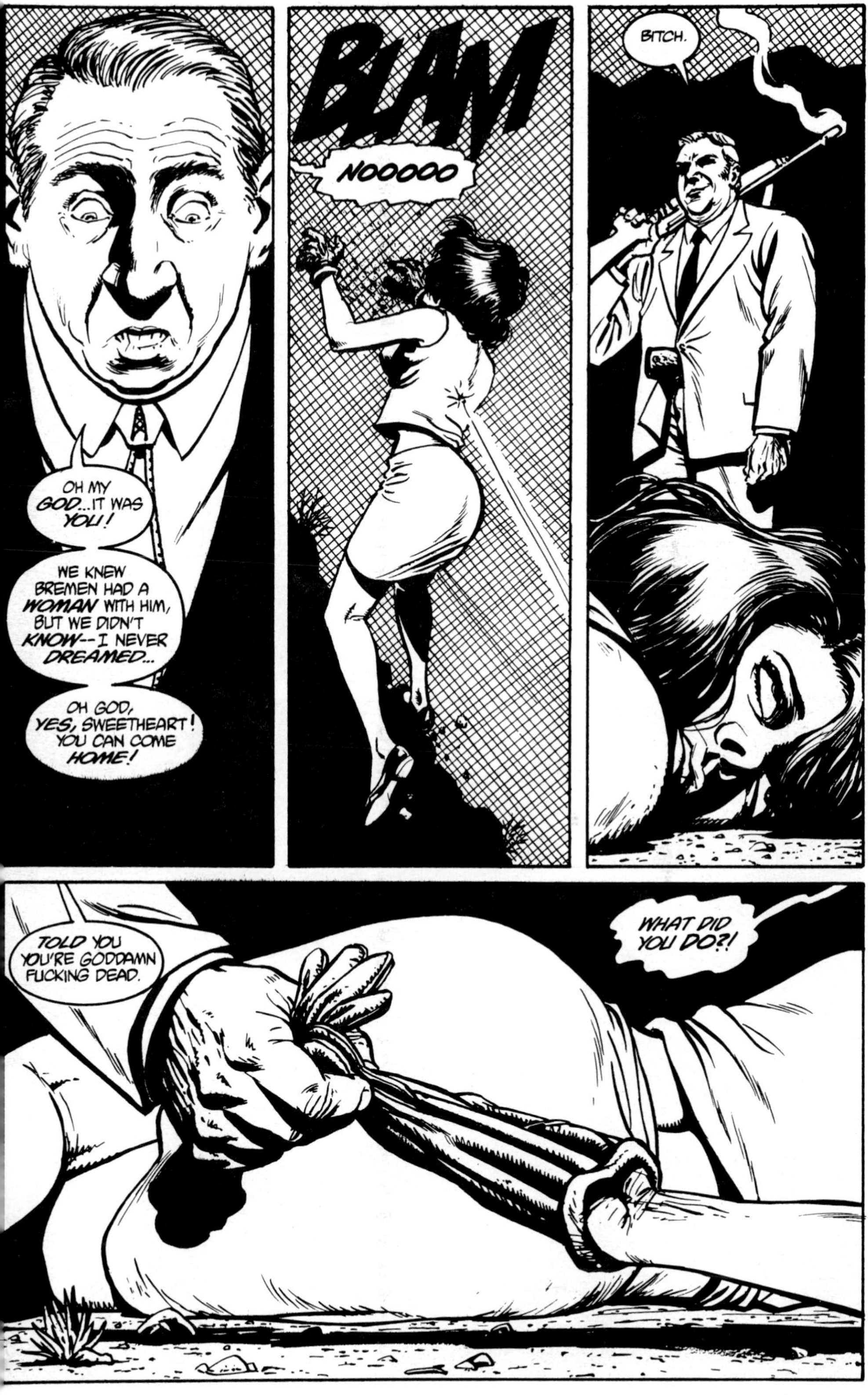

OH MY GOD...IT WAS YOU!
WE KNEW BREMEN HAD A WOMAN WITH HIM, BUT WE DIDN'T KNOW--I NEVER DREAMED...
OH GOD, YES, SWEETHEART! YOU CAN COME HOME!
BLAM
NOOOOO
BITCH.
TOLD YOU YOU'RE GODDAMN FUCKING DEAD.
WHAT DID YOU DO?!

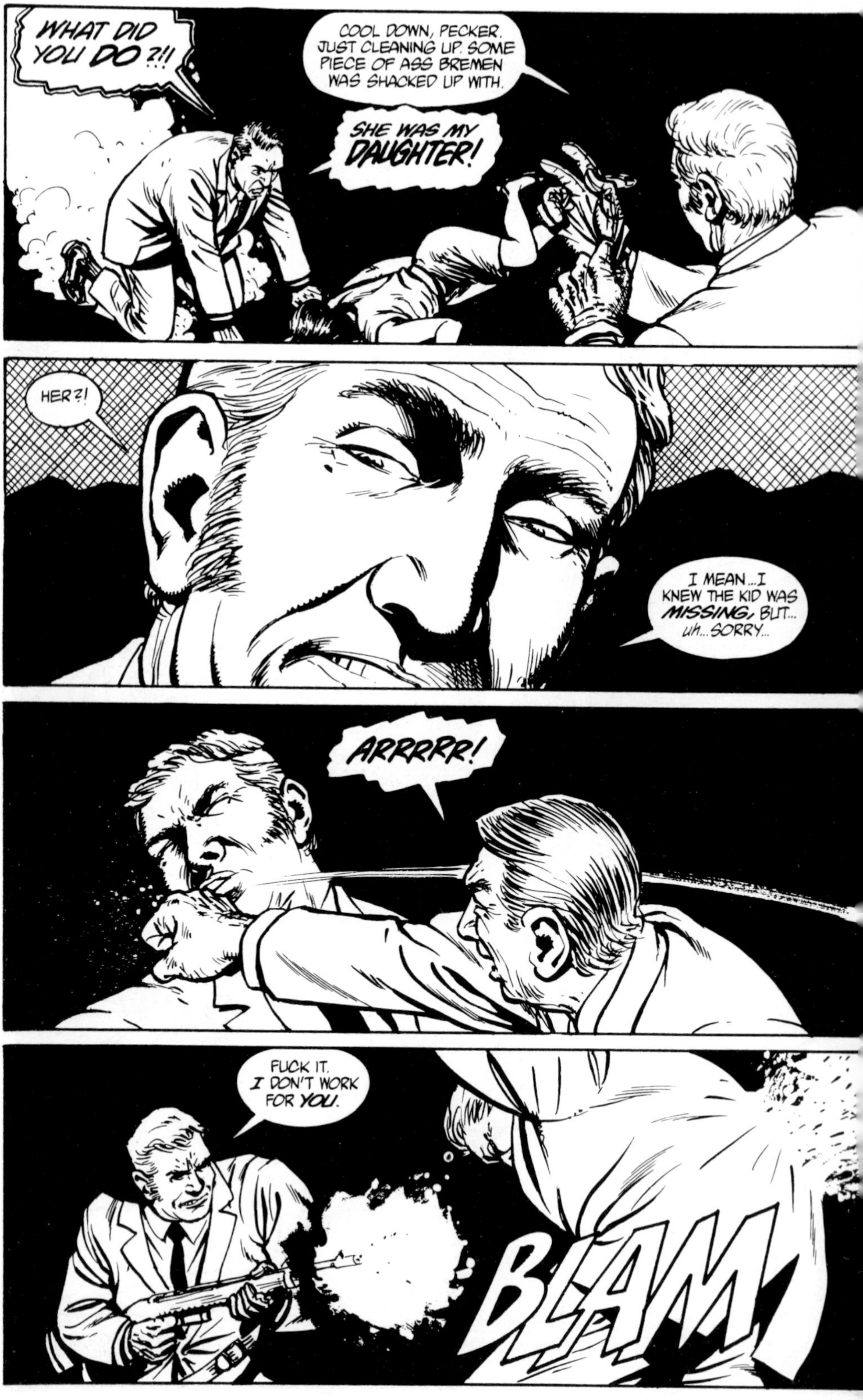
WHAT DID YOU DO ?!!
COOL DOWN, PECKER. JUST CLEANING UP. SOME PIECE OF ASS BREMEN WAS SHACKED UP WITH.
SHE WAS MY DAUGHTER!
HER?!
I MEAN...I KNEW THE KID WAS MISSING, BUT... uh...SORRY...
ARRRRR!
FUCK IT. I DON'T WORK FOR YOU.
BLAM

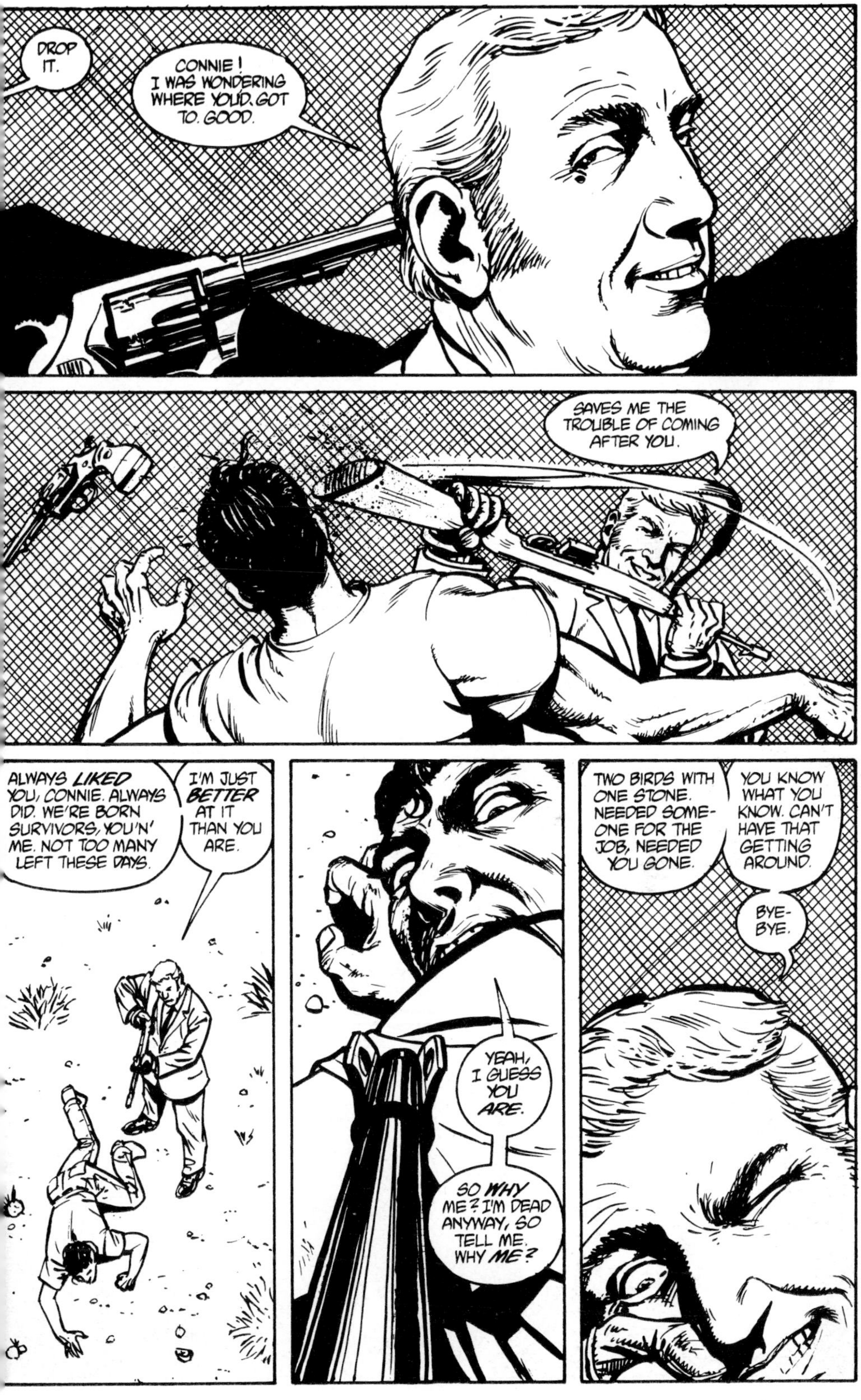
DROP IT.
CONNIE! I WAS WONDERING WHERE YOU'D GOT TO. GOOD.
SAVES ME THE TROUBLE OF COMING AFTER YOU.
ALWAYS LIKED YOU, CONNIE. ALWAYS DID. WE'RE BORN SURVIVORS, YOU'N' ME. NOT TOO MANY LEFT THESE DAYS.
I'M JUST BETTER AT IT THAN YOU ARE.
YEAH, I GUESS YOU ARE.
SO WHY ME? I'M DEAD ANYWAY, SO TELL ME. WHY ME?
TWO BIRDS WITH ONE STONE. NEEDED SOMEONE FOR THE JOB, NEEDED YOU GONE.
YOU KNOW WHAT YOU KNOW. CAN'T HAVE THAT GETTING AROUND.
BYE-BYE.

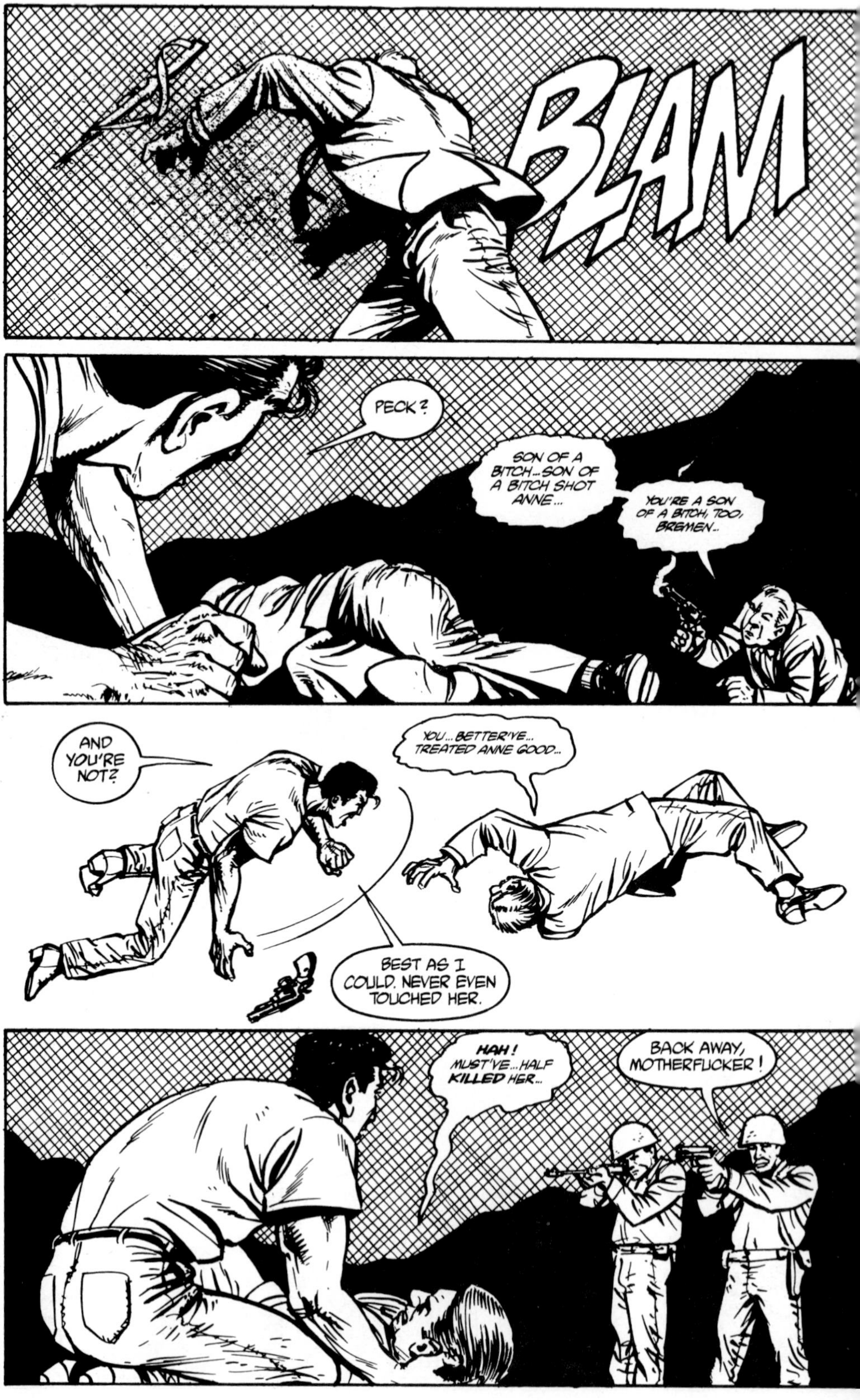
BLAM
PECK?
SON OF A BITCH...SON OF A BITCH SHOT ANNE...
YOU'RE A SON OF A BITCH, TOO, BREMEN...
AND YOU'RE NOT?
YOU...BETTER'VE... TREATED ANNE GOOD...
BEST AS I COULD. NEVER EVEN TOUCHED HER.
HAH! MUST'VE...HALF KILLED HER...
BACK AWAY, MOTHERFUCKER!

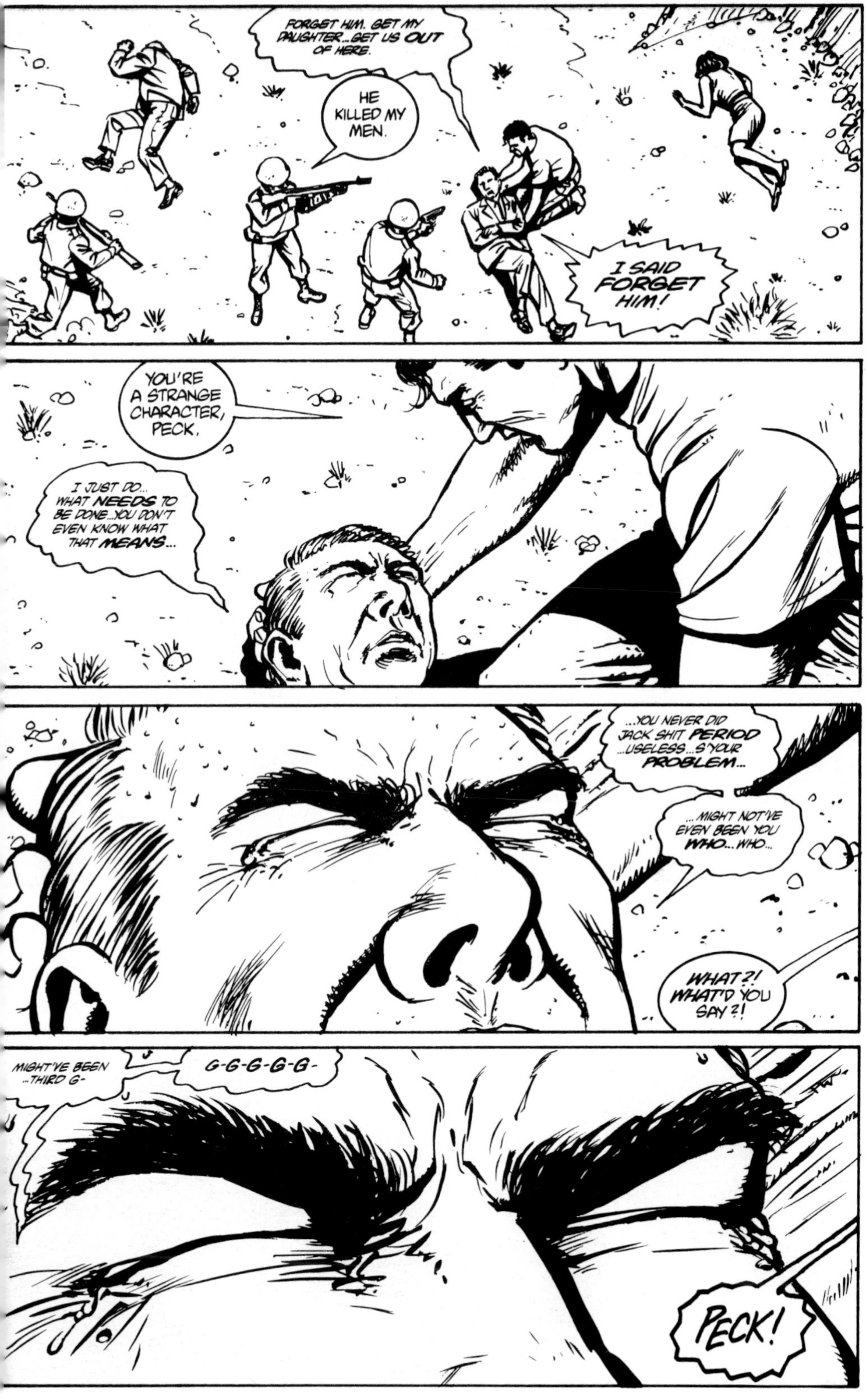
FORGET HIM. GET MY DAUGHTER...GET US OUT OF HERE.
HE KILLED MY MEN.
I SAID FORGET HIM!
YOU'RE A STRANGE CHARACTER, PECK.
I JUST DO... WHAT NEEDS TO BE DONE...YOU DON'T EVEN KNOW WHAT THAT MEANS...
...YOU NEVER DID JACK SHIT PERIOD ...USELESS...S'YOUR PROBLEM...
...MIGHT NOT'VE EVEN BEEN YOU WHO...WHO...
WHAT?! WHAT'D YOU SAY?!
MIGHT'VE BEEN ...THIRD G-
G-G-G-G-G-
PECK!

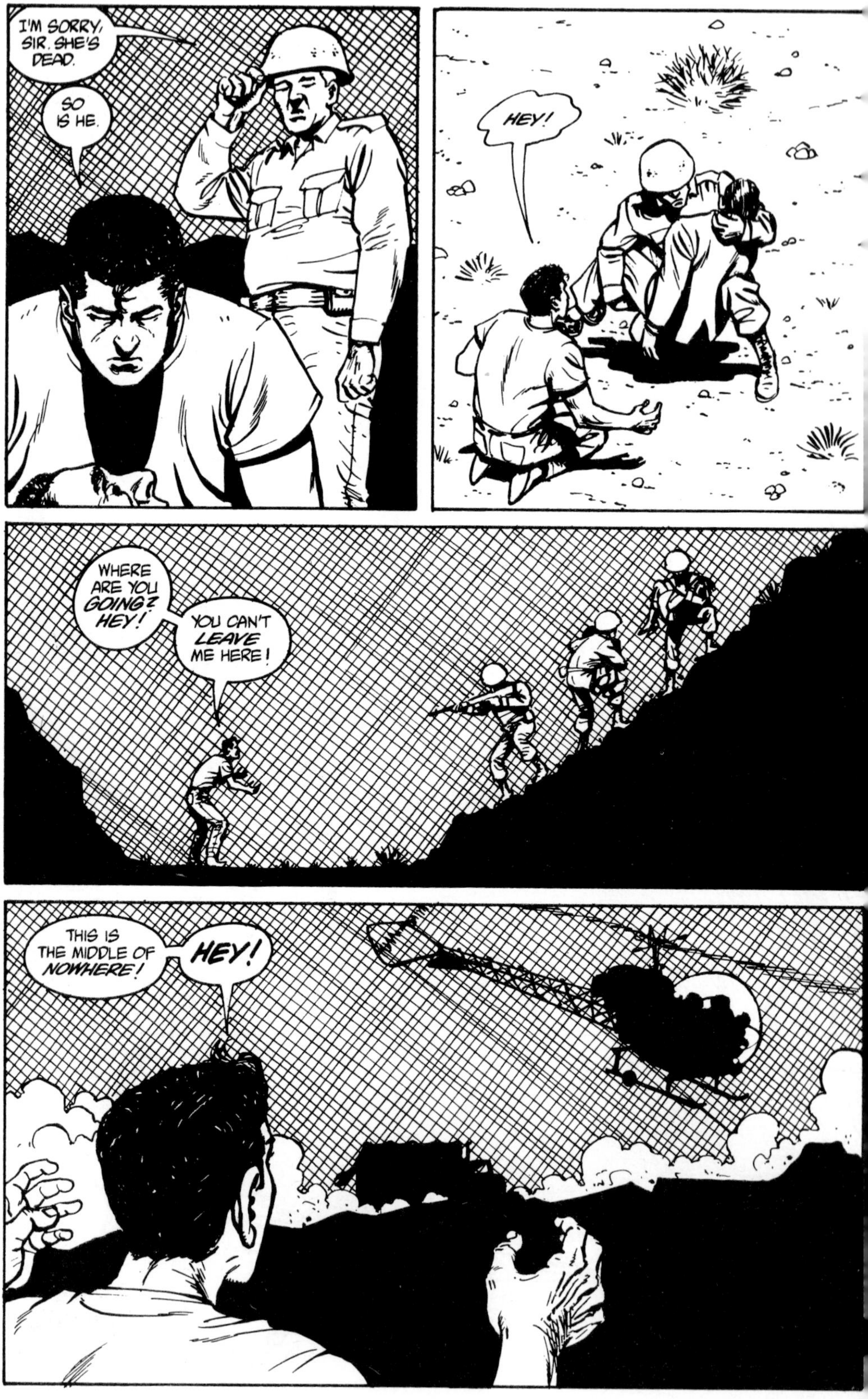
I'M SORRY, SIR. SHE'S DEAD.
SO IS HE.
HEY!
WHERE ARE YOU GOING? HEY!
YOU CAN'T LEAVE ME HERE!
THIS IS THE MIDDLE OF NOWHERE!
HEY!

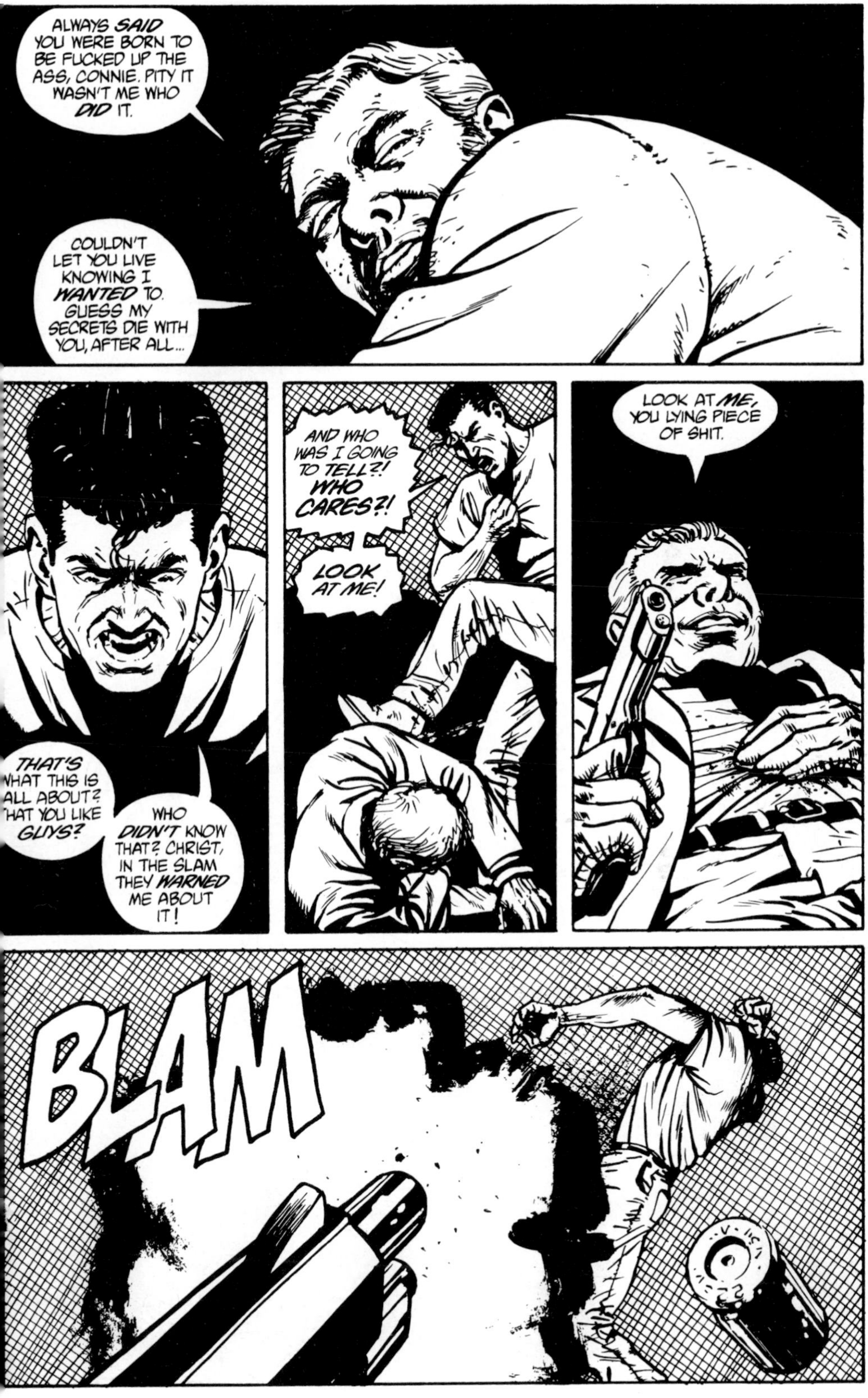
ALWAYS SAID YOU WERE BORN TO BE FUCKED UP THE ASS, CONNIE. PITY IT WASN'T ME WHO DID IT.
COULDN'T LET YOU LIVE KNOWING I WANTED TO. GUESS MY SECRETS DIE WITH YOU, AFTER ALL...
THAT'S WHAT THIS IS ALL ABOUT? THAT YOU LIKE GUYS?
WHO DIDN'T KNOW THAT? CHRIST, IN THE SLAM THEY WARNED ME ABOUT IT!
AND WHO WAS I GOING TO TELL?! WHO CARES?!
LOOK AT ME!
LOOK AT ME, YOU LYING PIECE OF SHIT.
BLAM

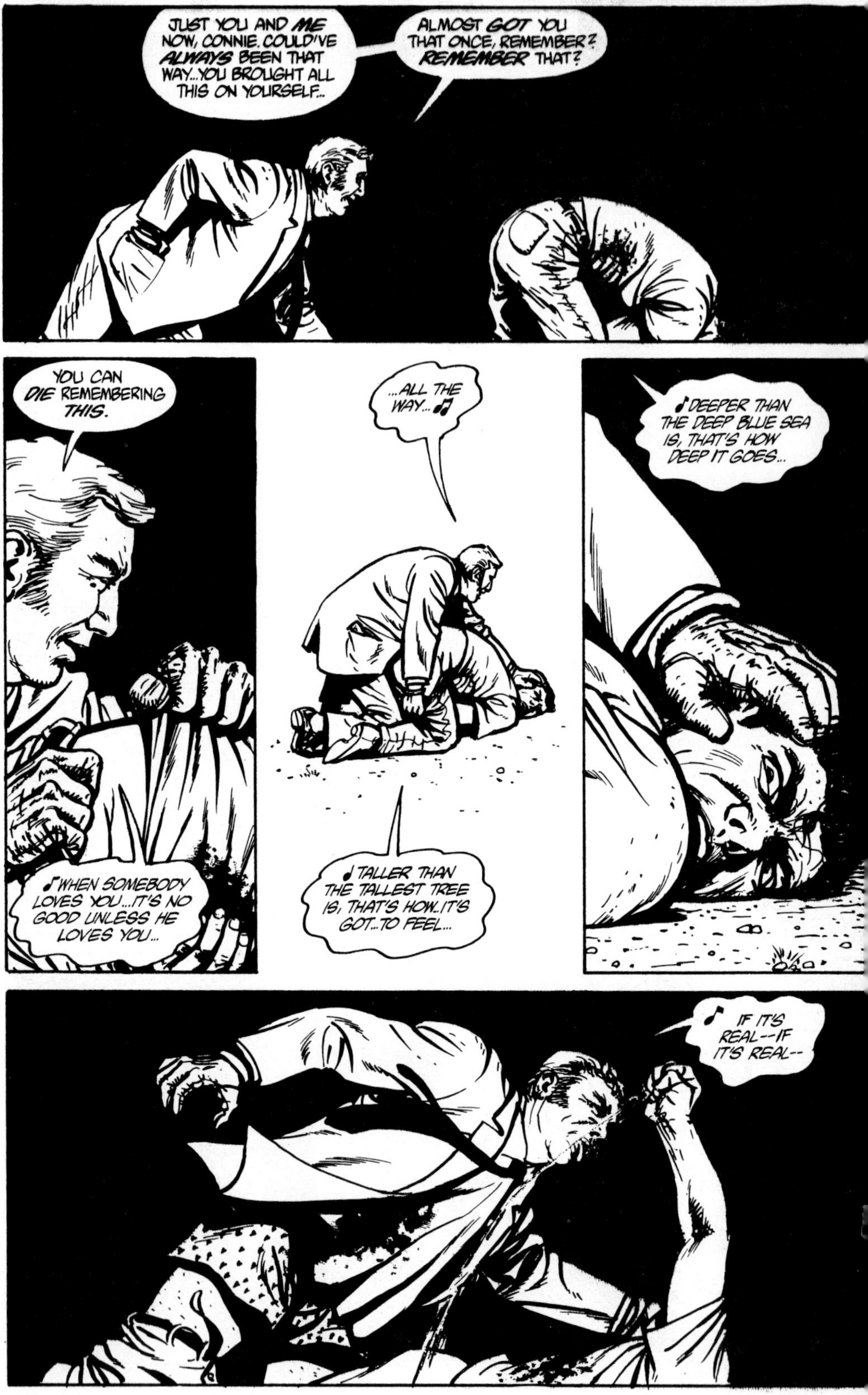
JUST YOU AND ME NOW, CONNIE. COULD'VE ALWAYS BEEN THAT WAY... YOU BROUGHT ALL THIS ON YOURSELF...
ALMOST GOT YOU THAT ONCE, REMEMBER? REMEMBER THAT?
YOU CAN DIE REMEMBERING THIS.
♪ WHEN SOMEBODY LOVES YOU... IT'S NO GOOD UNLESS HE LOVES YOU...
...ALL THE WAY... ♪
♪ TALLER THAN THE TALLEST TREE IS, THAT'S HOW.. IT'S GOT... TO FEEL...
♪ DEEPER THAN THE DEEP BLUE SEA IS, THAT'S HOW DEEP IT GOES...
♪ IF IT'S REAL--IF IT'S REAL--

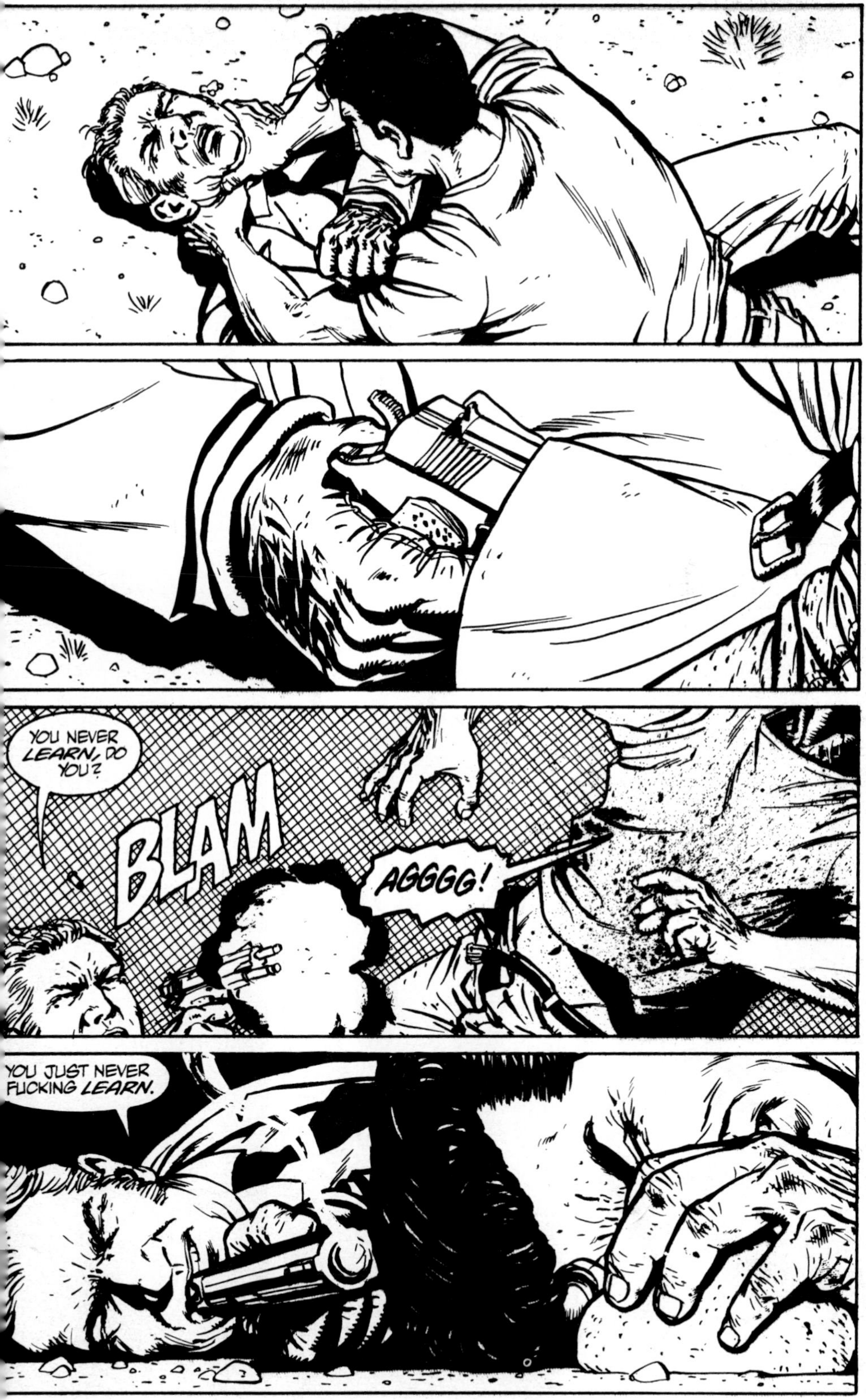
YOU NEVER LEARN, DO YOU?
BLAM
AGGGG!
YOU JUST NEVER FUCKING LEARN.

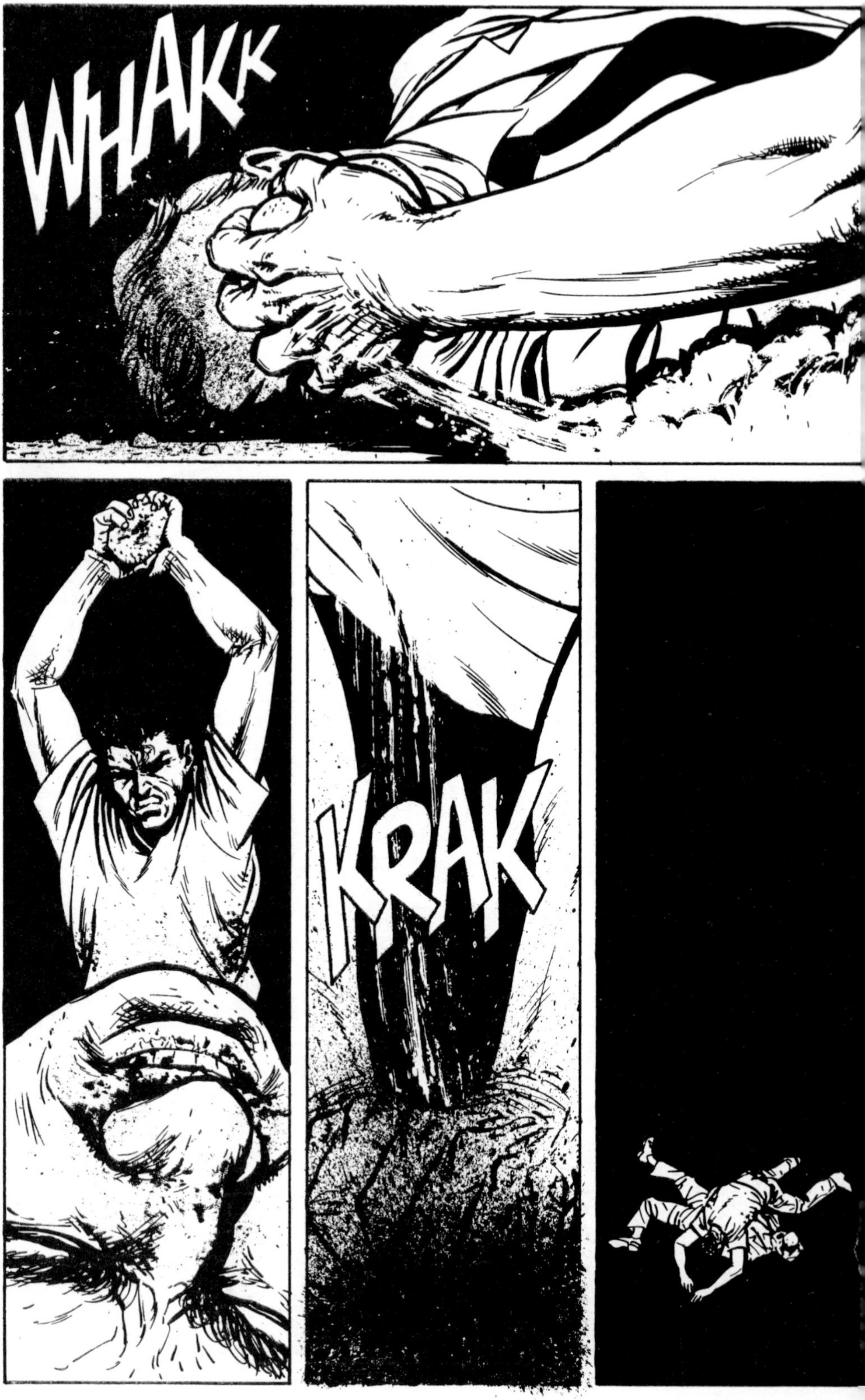
WHAKK
KRAK

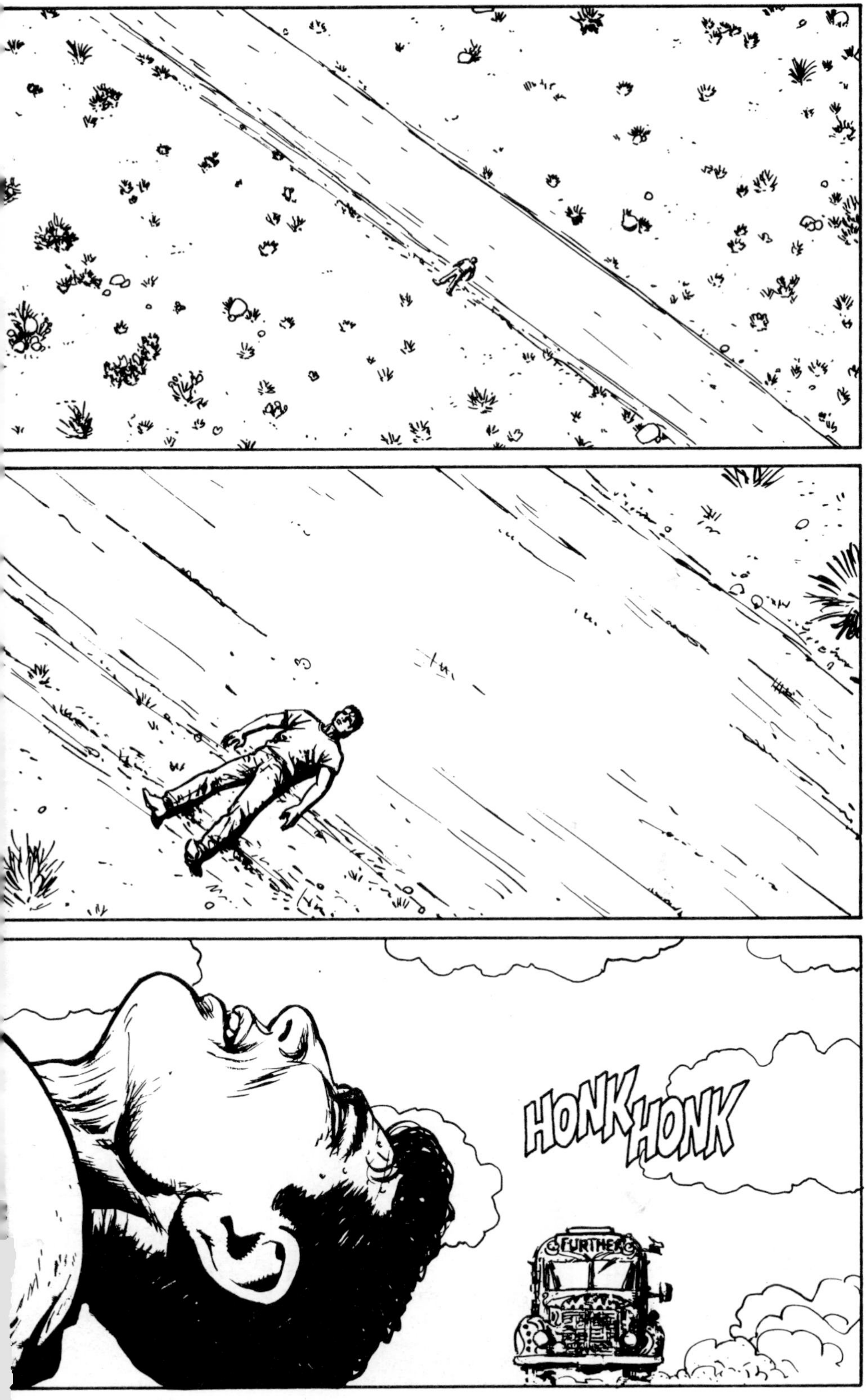
HONK HONK
FURTHER

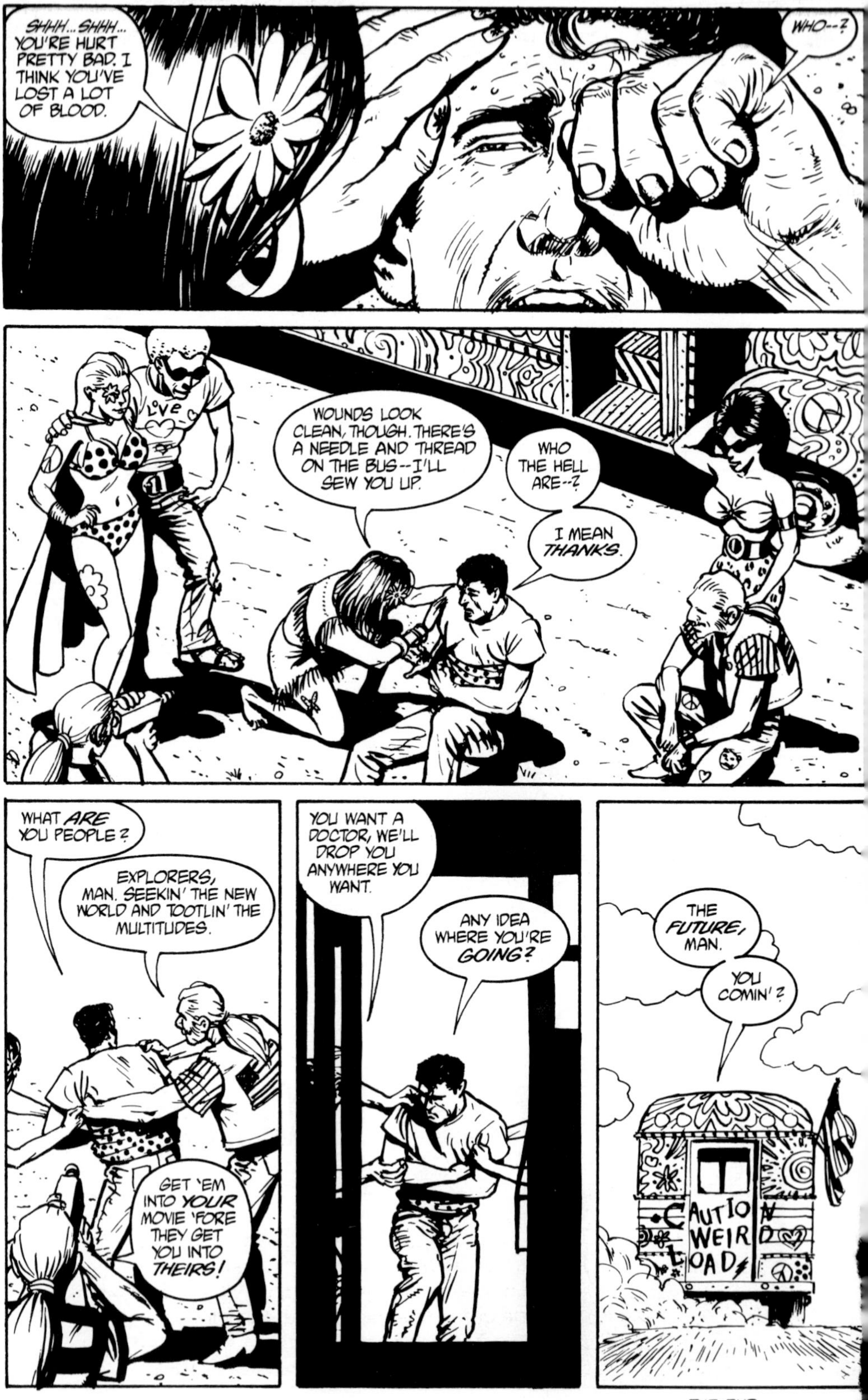
SHHH... SHHH... YOU'RE HURT PRETTY BAD. I THINK YOU'VE LOST A LOT OF BLOOD.
WHO--?
WOUNDS LOOK CLEAN, THOUGH. THERE'S A NEEDLE AND THREAD ON THE BUS--I'LL SEW YOU UP.
WHO THE HELL ARE--?
I MEAN *THANKS*.
WHAT *ARE* YOU PEOPLE?
EXPLORERS, MAN. SEEKIN' THE NEW WORLD AND TOOTLIN' THE MULTITUDES.
GET 'EM INTO *YOUR* MOVIE 'FORE THEY GET YOU INTO *THEIRS!*
YOU WANT A DOCTOR, WE'LL DROP YOU ANYWHERE YOU WANT.
ANY IDEA WHERE YOU'RE *GOING?*
THE *FUTURE,* MAN.
YOU COMIN'?
CAUTION WEIRD LOAD

THE END.

AFTERWORD
BY STEVEN GRANT

I was ten years and one month old when John Kennedy was assassinated. He meant nothing to me then, as, really, he means nothing to me now. As president, he impinged on my consciousness just once, when he named John Gronowski, the father of my classmate Stacy, as postmaster general and she vanished from our midst forever.

Then he was murdered. With his death he changed the world, as he had not done in life.

It was a gray Friday in Madison, Wisconsin, with thick sheet clouds coating the sky. On Friday afternoons in my grade school, all the classes gathered for sing-along in the gym, led by our principal. On that afternoon, however, the principal appeared at our classroom door, whispered gravely to the teacher, and then our teacher announced without elaboration that assembly was cancelled and buses would be there in ten minutes to take us all home.

Our house seemed as dark as the sky, and, puzzlingly, my mother wasn't home. I didn't think to turn on a television or radio, but she called a short time later, having heard on TV that schools were closed. She was at a friend's house a few blocks away. She had been there when the news first came over the radio that Kennedy had been shot, and, at 1 p.m., when it was announced that he was dead.

It was the first I had heard about it. On that gray Friday I sat in terror in my living room, waiting for my family to get home, keeping the curtains tightly drawn so that no one could see me through the windows and kill me too. Talking to my mother, reacting to the horror in her voice, I was gripped by the paranoia that someone was out to kill the entire country, one by one, starting at the top and working his way down. To me.

It was my first burst of political consciousness.

By Monday morning, when the funeral was televised, my attitude had brightened (partly due to increased sunshine and partly due to the suspension of school in the face of the national grief) to the point where I infuriated my mother by drawing glasses and beards on the photos of Linden and Lady Bird Johnson in the newspaper even as the funeral procession was drawing into Arlington Cemetery. My mother felt it showed grave disrespect of Our Leader, but she did forgive me, because I was just a kid. My attitude toward politicians remains unchanged to this day.

American history is an hourglass, the center of which is the first Kennedy assassination. Not that things, including political murder, only went on afterwards that did not go on before — any good student of American history can uncover and chart the non-democratic molding of our country over its first two centuries — but the immediacy of information transfer in 1963 shattered the taboo against rubbing the public's face in it. The public's face was rubbed, and rubbed hard. This was complicated by the idealism that Kennedy spoke to, whether that was a sincere gesture or, as some have charged, a cynical political ploy. The murder of Kennedy was a rabbit punch at idealism, a mocking of the naïveté of those who thought they could effect a change. So idealism, in the face of political reality, went underground, flipping the bird at the powers that be as it dropped out, put on gaudy clothes, and grew its hair.

Prior to the first Kennedy assassination, we had as our public image Ozzie and Harriet, good wars, the Marshall Plan, potato sack races. Afterward? Riots, protest marches, more assassinations, the Phoenix Program, ousted Presidents, love-ins, bad wars. In other words, the Sixties, in the shadow of which the remainder of the century still stands.

The man who killed President Kennedy midwifed the Sixties. Decades don't begin and end with zeroes and predetermined calendar dates, but with pain and change. The Forties began with Hitler's invasion of Czechoslovakia; the Fifties, that first great flowering of the Cold War, with Russia's testing of a nuclear weapon. The Sixties began with a gunshot, and ended in 1974, with the expulsion of Richard Nixon. And in between, everything changed. To that extent, the killer of John Kennedy is the hero of the age, the sire of unexpected possibilities.

Badlands sprang from a question: if Lee Harvey Oswald was not the gunman — and the most cursory examination of the evidence strongly suggests he wasn't — why Lee Harvey Oswald? Certainly a worse patsy is hard to imagine, a man linked to the CIA, the FBI, organized crime, a man who trailed questions in his wake like slime, a man whose credibility as a lone nut killer could only be established via the physically ridiculous "single bullet theory." I had pitched *Badlands* as "a crime novel set in 1963, starring the man who really killed Kennedy." I had the ending long before I had anything else, or any character besides Conrad Bremen, created for a college writing course almost two decades earlier. What I didn't have was an answer to that question — why Lee Harvey Oswald? — and once I had my answer —Oswald was sloppy seconds because the man who was supposed to take the heat got away — I had my story.

Conrad Bremen is not real, nor Janetty, nor Gordon Burris Peck and the precocious Anne. I didn't intend to write a tract on the Kennedy assassination; it has spawned its own industry of paperback revelations, and adding to it struck me as unnecessary. Kennedy, having been de-mythologized (or, I should say, re-mythologized; a fully rounded and objective assessment of the man and his career has yet to appear), is now largely irrelevant. Even the true identity of his assassin, whether it be Charles Harrelson or Jean Souetre or any number of other suspects, is irrelevant. The Kennedy assassinations, their web of circumstance and connection trading back to bootlegging in the Twenties and forward to Jonestown and Iran-Contra, did not occur in a vacuum; they are part of a continuum. We are complicit in them, if only by our ignorance, because we still shy away from the real question surrounding the assassinations, and the many people who figure in both and in others: why? "Why" can only be answered by examining context, and Americans are notoriously shy on context. *Badlands*, which, fate willing, will continue with other graphic novels, is my attempt to develop a context for the events that have shaken us in the last half of this century. It's said that fiction is a lie that tells the truth. My characters are fictitious, but I have tried to tell the truth as best as I understand it.

One lesson came of the Reagan years: there is no truth in American politics, only convenient mythologies. El Salvador is an oppressed democracy, Nicaragua a totalitarian hell worse than Nazi Germany (Henry Kissinger actually said that). One of our ships was attacked in the Gulf of Tonkin. American students were endangered in Grenada. There is no recession. We were fighting to return democracy to Kuwait, not fighting for oil. Surrounded by the lies of government, our faces regularly rubbed in them (as with all taboos, once the taboo is broken, breaking it becomes obsessive behavior), is it any wonder that Americans have felt increasingly powerless?

Conspiracy is the great myth of the powerless, which perhaps explains why 85% of Americans believe that President Kennedy was murdered by conspiracy. (One wag suggested that about the only people left who don't believe this are the Federal government and *The New York Times*.) My feeling — you may have figured this out if you've already read the book — is that it's also true, which may explain the enduring strength of the Kennedy assassination conspiracy even after thirty years of being force-fed the lone nut single bullet story; true myths are harder to shake. Or I may just be suckering out for the myth, but what some call conspiracy, others call politics as usual.

The "logical" argument against political conspiracies, especially those such as the coup that cost Kennedy his life and fundamentally altered the texture of American life, is that so many people would necessarily be involved that they couldn't possibly remain secret. But conspiracies are not kept quiet. No one even bothers to try any more. Kennedy assassination information has been steadily accumulating for three decades. Watergate, Iran-Contra, and the S&L scandals and cover-ups, like most other acknowledged conspiracies of recent times, were played out in scattered newspaper clippings long before they coalesced into something the TV networks and government officials were unable to ignore or brush under the rug.

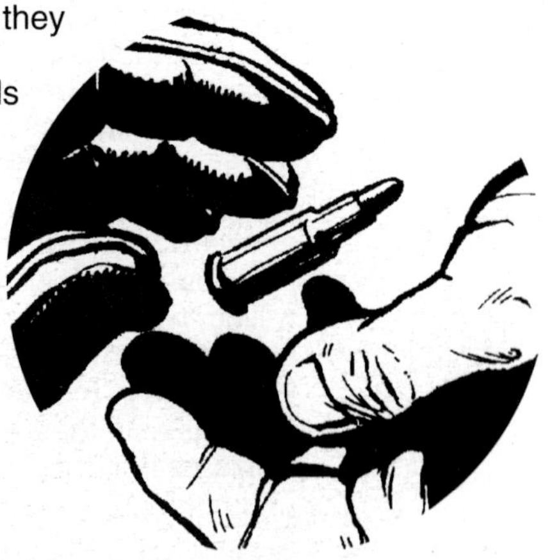

Keith Reid, lyricist for the '60s rock group Procol Harum, once wrote, "There's nothing hidden anywhere; it's all there to be sought." Truer words were never spoken. Maybe it's time we, as a society, started.